# THE C
# TALES FROM THE CON™

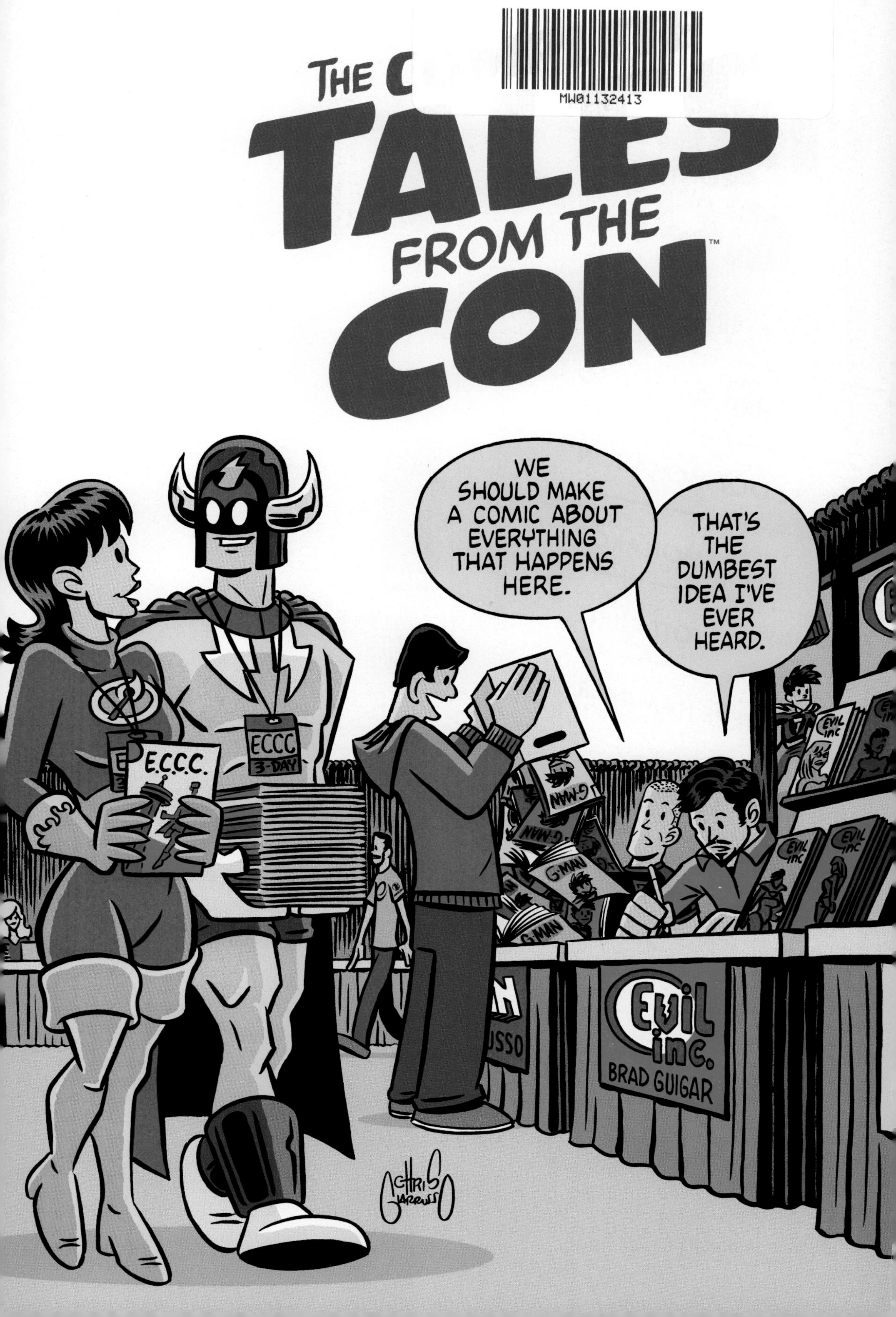
WE SHOULD MAKE A COMIC ABOUT EVERYTHING THAT HAPPENS HERE.
THAT'S THE DUMBEST IDEA I'VE EVER HEARD.
ECCC 3-DAY
E.C.C.C.
G-MAN
G-MAN
G-MAN
G-MAN
USSO
EVIL inc.
BRAD GUIGAR
EVIL inc
EVIL inc
EVIL inc

## THE COMPLETE TALES FROM THE CON™

WRITER
**BRAD GUIGAR**
guigar.com · evil-inc.com · webcomics.com

ARTIST - PART 1 & COVER
**CHRIS GIARRUSSO**
chrisgiarrusso.com

ARTIST - PART 2
**SCOOT McMAHON**
scootcomics.com

EDITOR
**JIM DEMONAKOS**
sofos.com

VARIANT COVER ILLUSTRATED BY
**SKOTT KURTZ**
pvponline.com

VARIANT COVER COLORS BY
**STEVE HAMAKER**
steve-hamaker.com

www.emeraldcitycomicon.com

www.reedpop.com

*image*

THE COMPLETE TALES FROM THE CON TP. First printing. March 2017. Published by Image Comics, Inc. Office of publication: 2701 NW Vaughn St., Suite 780, Portland, OR 97210. TM & Copyright © 2017 Reed Exhibitions. All rights reserved. Licensed characters that appear in this book are intended as parody. Image Comics makes no claim to the characters' copyrights, trademarks or proprietary rights. "Image" and the Image Comics logos are registered trademarks of Image Comics, Inc. No part of this publication may be reproduced or transmitted, in any form or by any means (except for short excerpts for journalistic or review purposes), without the express written permission of Reed Exhibitions, or Image Comics, Inc. All names, characters, events, and locales in this publication are entirely fictional. Any resemblance to actual persons (living or dead), events, or places, without satiric intent, is coincidental. Printed in the USA. For information regarding the CPSIA on this printed material call: 203-595-3636 and provide reference #RICH–726081. For international rights, contact: foreignlicensing@imagecomics.com. ISBN: 978-1-5343-0100-9. ECCC variant ISBN: 978-1-5343-0290-7.

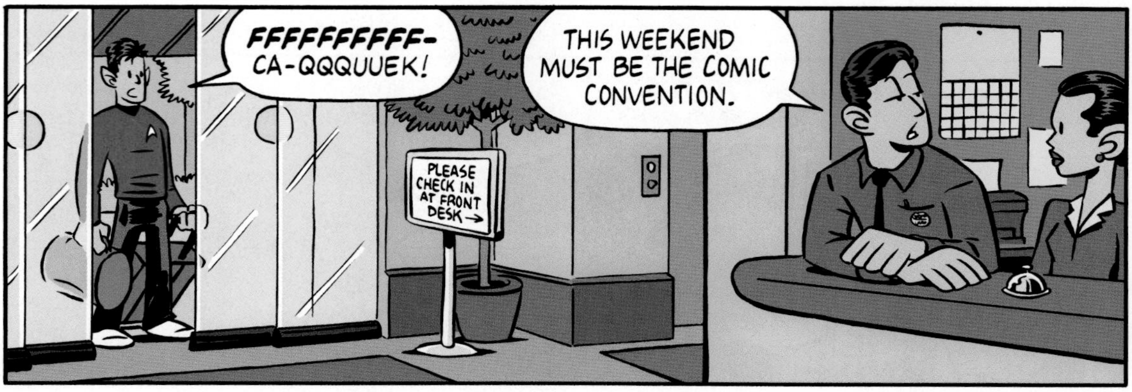
FFFFFFFFFF-
CA-QQQUUEK!
PLEASE CHECK IN AT FRONT DESK →
THIS WEEKEND MUST BE THE COMIC CONVENTION.

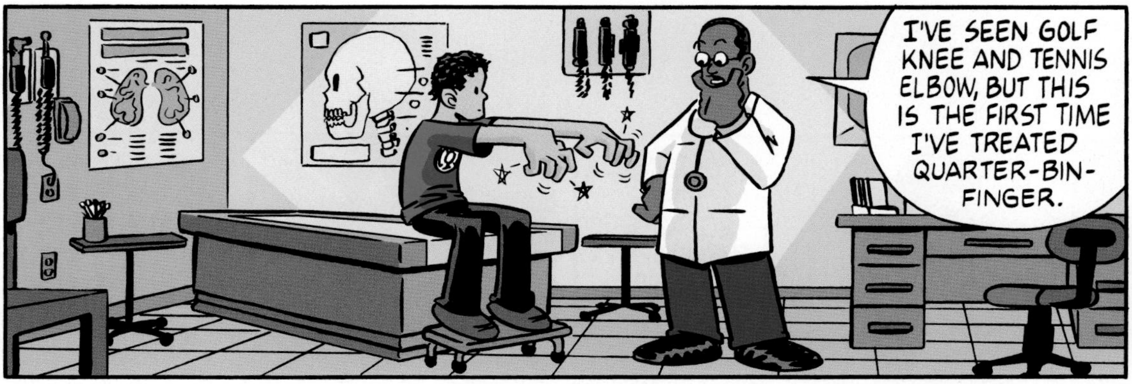
I'VE SEEN GOLF KNEE AND TENNIS ELBOW, BUT THIS IS THE FIRST TIME I'VE TREATED QUARTER-BIN-FINGER.

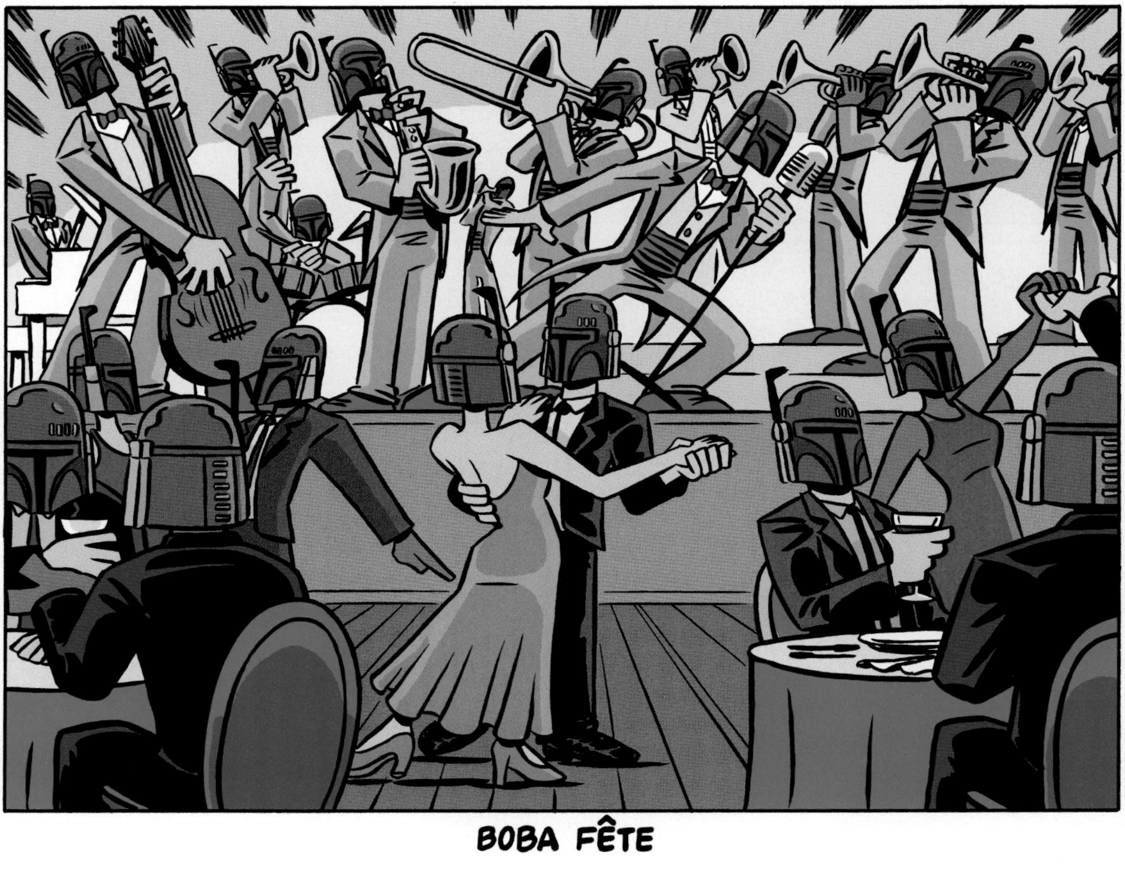

**BOBA FÊTE**

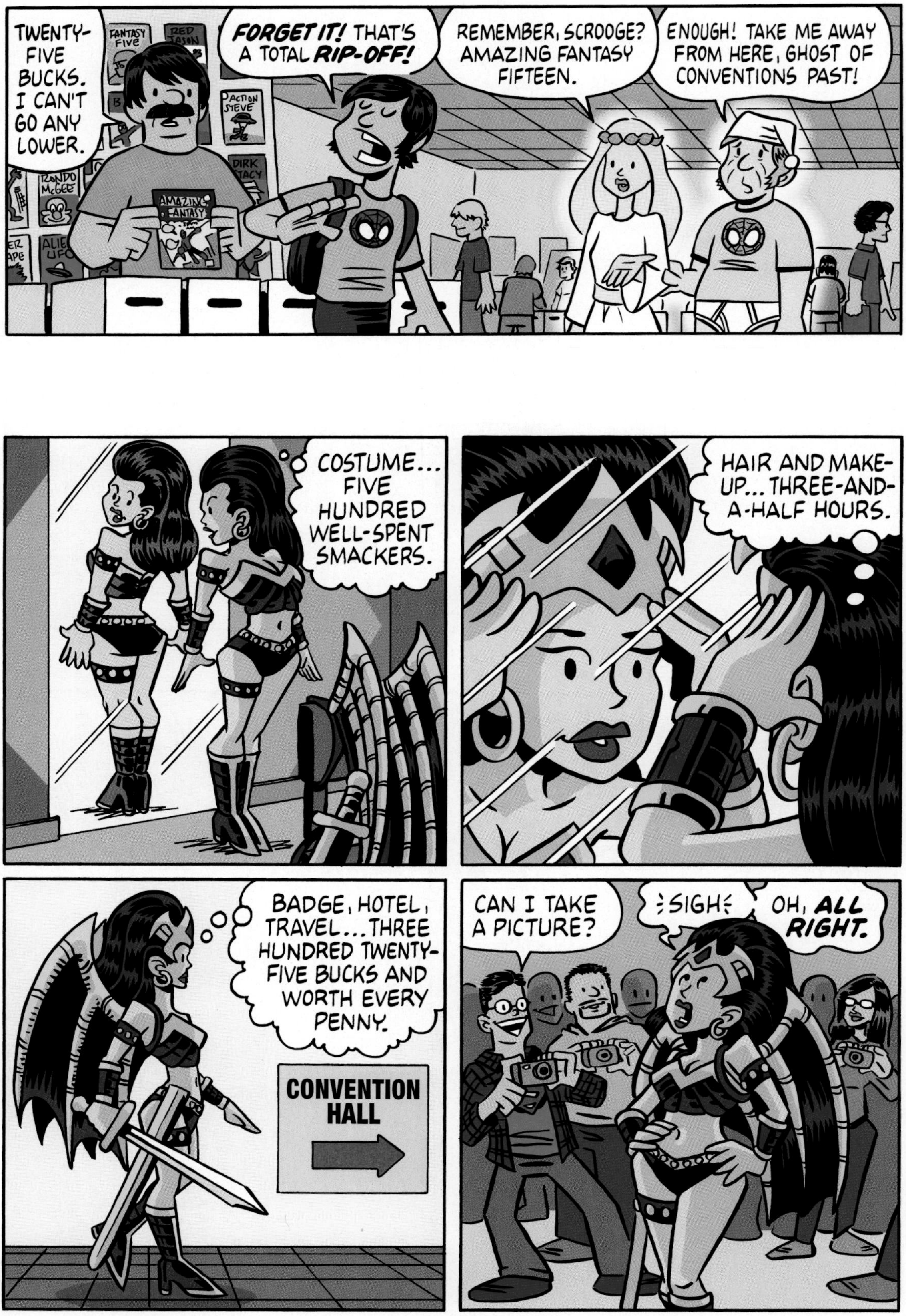
TWENTY-FIVE BUCKS. I CAN'T GO ANY LOWER.
FANTASY FIVE
RED JASON
ACTION STEVE
DIRK STACY
RONDO McGEE
AMAZING FANTASY
**FORGET IT!** THAT'S A TOTAL **RIP-OFF!**
REMEMBER, SCROOGE? AMAZING FANTASY FIFTEEN.
ENOUGH! TAKE ME AWAY FROM HERE, GHOST OF CONVENTIONS PAST!
COSTUME... FIVE HUNDRED WELL-SPENT SMACKERS.
HAIR AND MAKE-UP... THREE-AND-A-HALF HOURS.
BADGE, HOTEL, TRAVEL... THREE HUNDRED TWENTY-FIVE BUCKS AND WORTH EVERY PENNY.
CONVENTION HALL
CAN I TAKE A PICTURE?
SIGH
OH, **ALL RIGHT.**

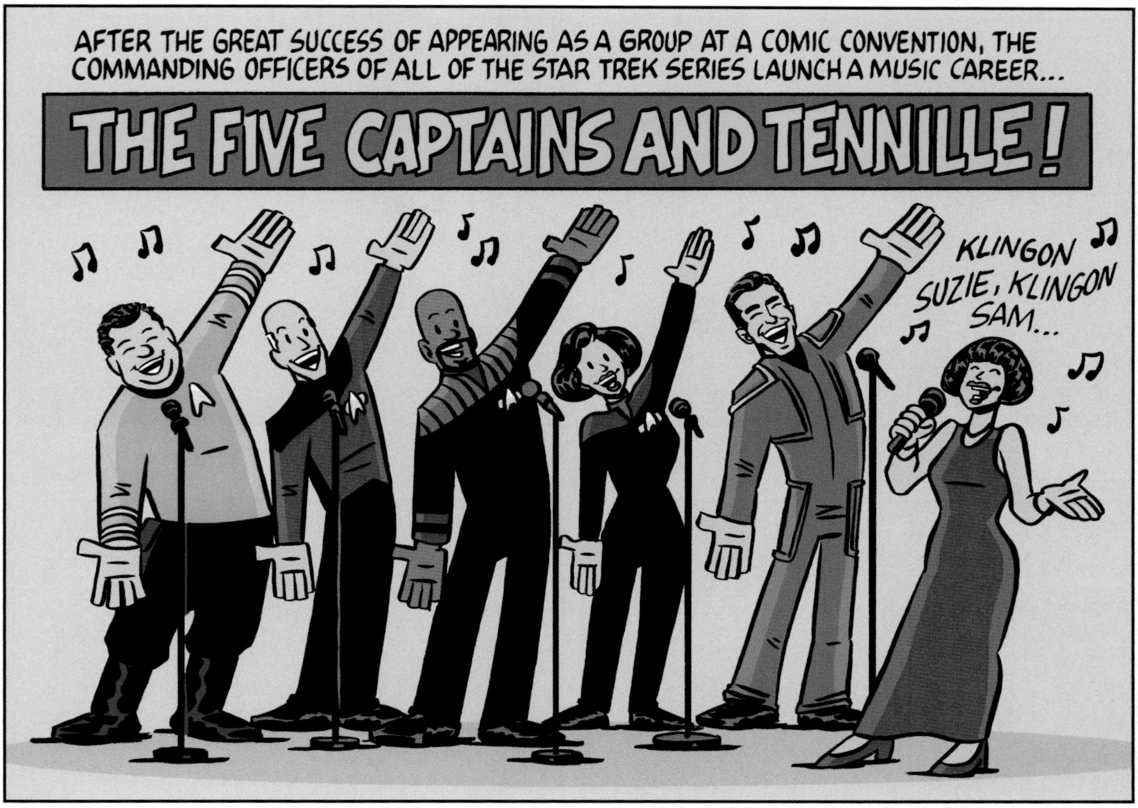
AFTER THE GREAT SUCCESS OF APPEARING AS A GROUP AT A COMIC CONVENTION, THE COMMANDING OFFICERS OF ALL OF THE STAR TREK SERIES LAUNCH A MUSIC CAREER...
THE FIVE CAPTAINS AND TENNILLE!
KLINGON SUZIE, KLINGON SAM...

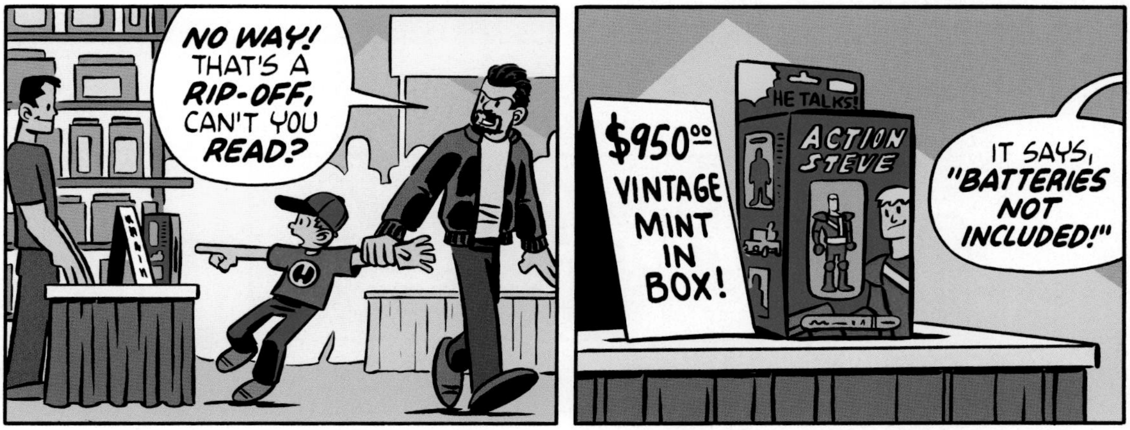
NO WAY! THAT'S A RIP-OFF, CAN'T YOU READ?
$950.00 VINTAGE MINT IN BOX!
HE TALKS!
ACTION STEVE
IT SAYS, "BATTERIES NOT INCLUDED!"

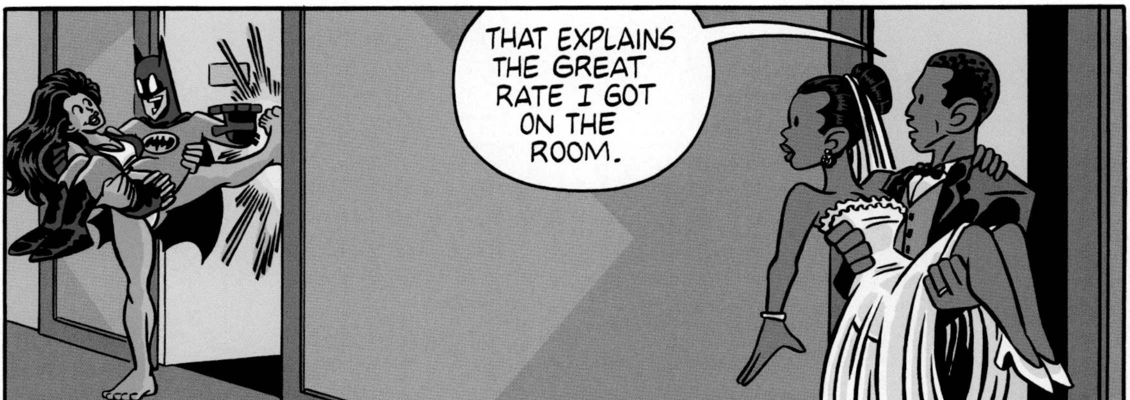
THAT EXPLAINS THE GREAT RATE I GOT ON THE ROOM.

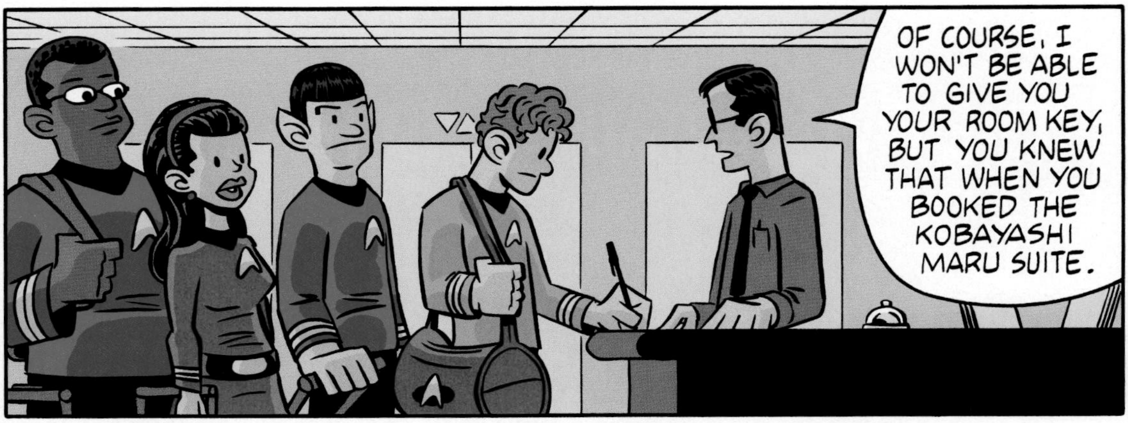
OF COURSE, I WON'T BE ABLE TO GIVE YOU YOUR ROOM KEY, BUT YOU KNEW THAT WHEN YOU BOOKED THE KOBAYASHI MARU SUITE.

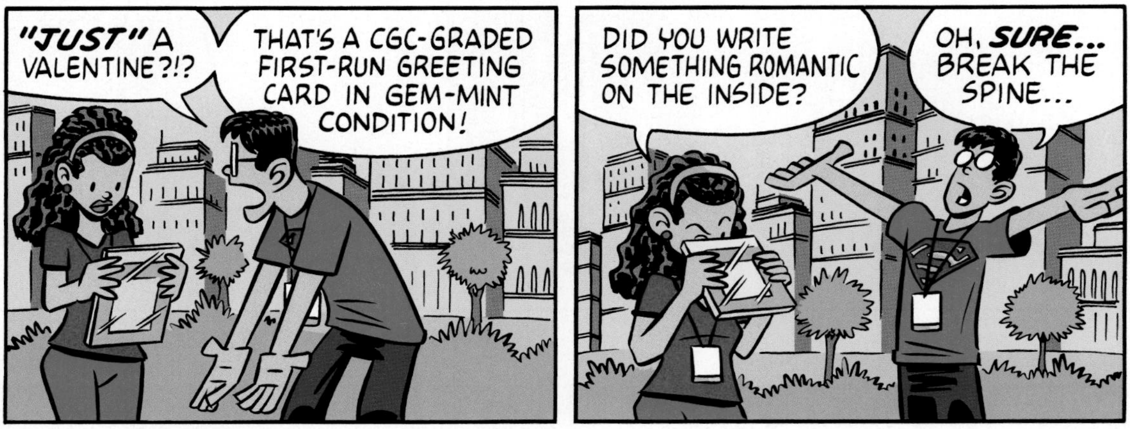
"JUST" A VALENTINE?!?
THAT'S A CGC-GRADED FIRST-RUN GREETING CARD IN GEM-MINT CONDITION!
DID YOU WRITE SOMETHING ROMANTIC ON THE INSIDE?
OH, SURE... BREAK THE SPINE...

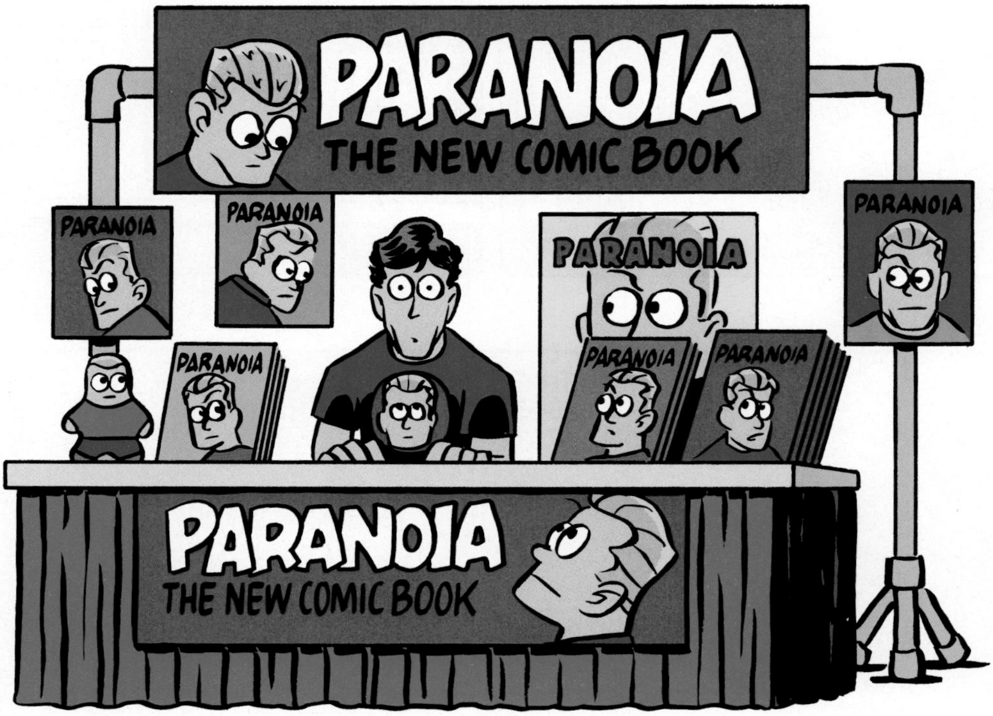
PARANOIA
THE NEW COMIC BOOK
PARANOIA
PARANOIA
PARANOIA
PARANOIA
PARANOIA
PARANOIA
PARANOIA
PARANOIA
THE NEW COMIC BOOK

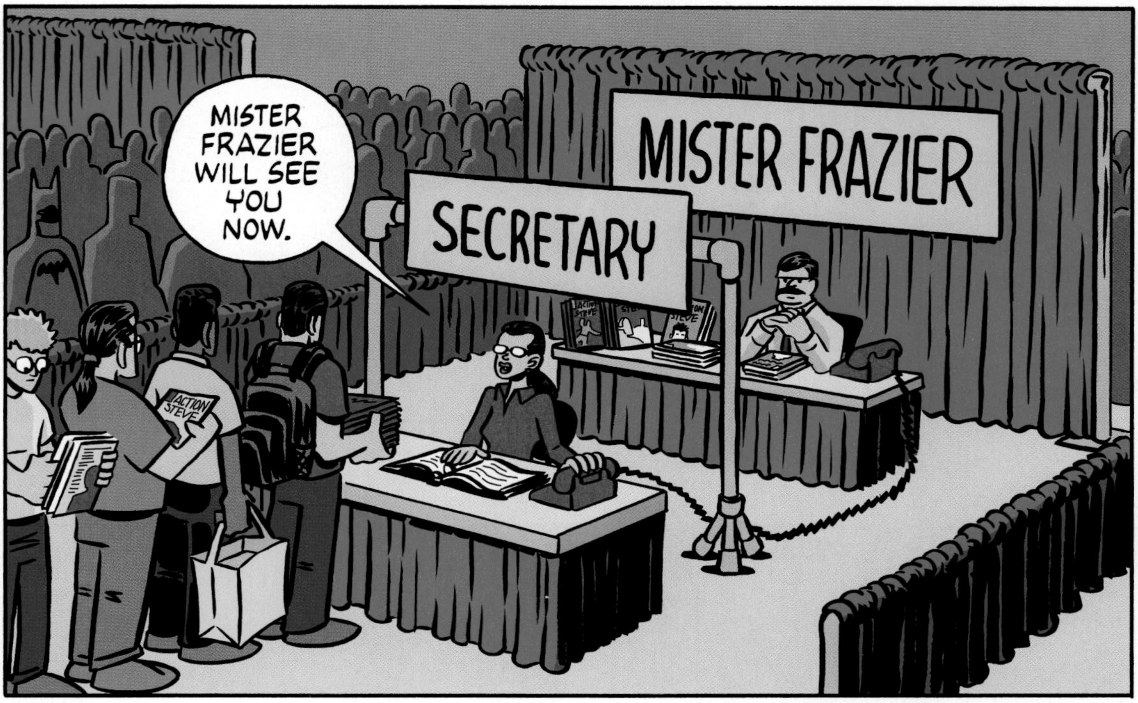
MISTER FRAZIER
SECRETARY
MISTER FRAZIER WILL SEE YOU NOW.
ACTION STEVE

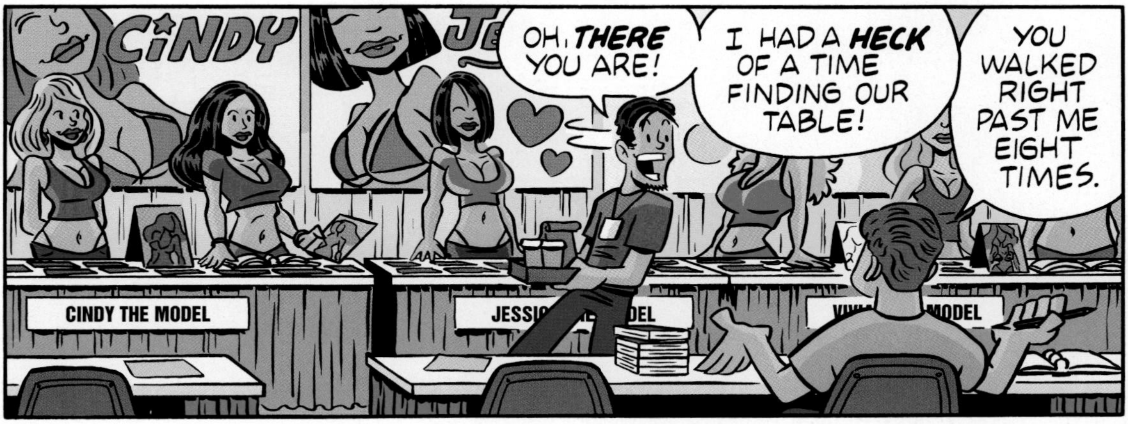
CINDY
CINDY THE MODEL
OH, THERE YOU ARE!
I HAD A HECK OF A TIME FINDING OUR TABLE!
YOU WALKED RIGHT PAST ME EIGHT TIMES.

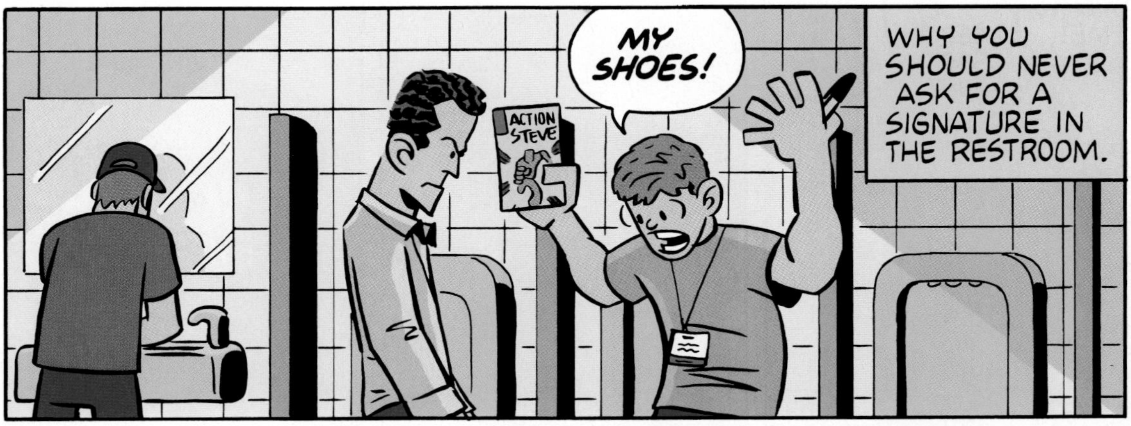
WHY YOU SHOULD NEVER ASK FOR A SIGNATURE IN THE RESTROOM.
ACTION STEVE
MY SHOES!

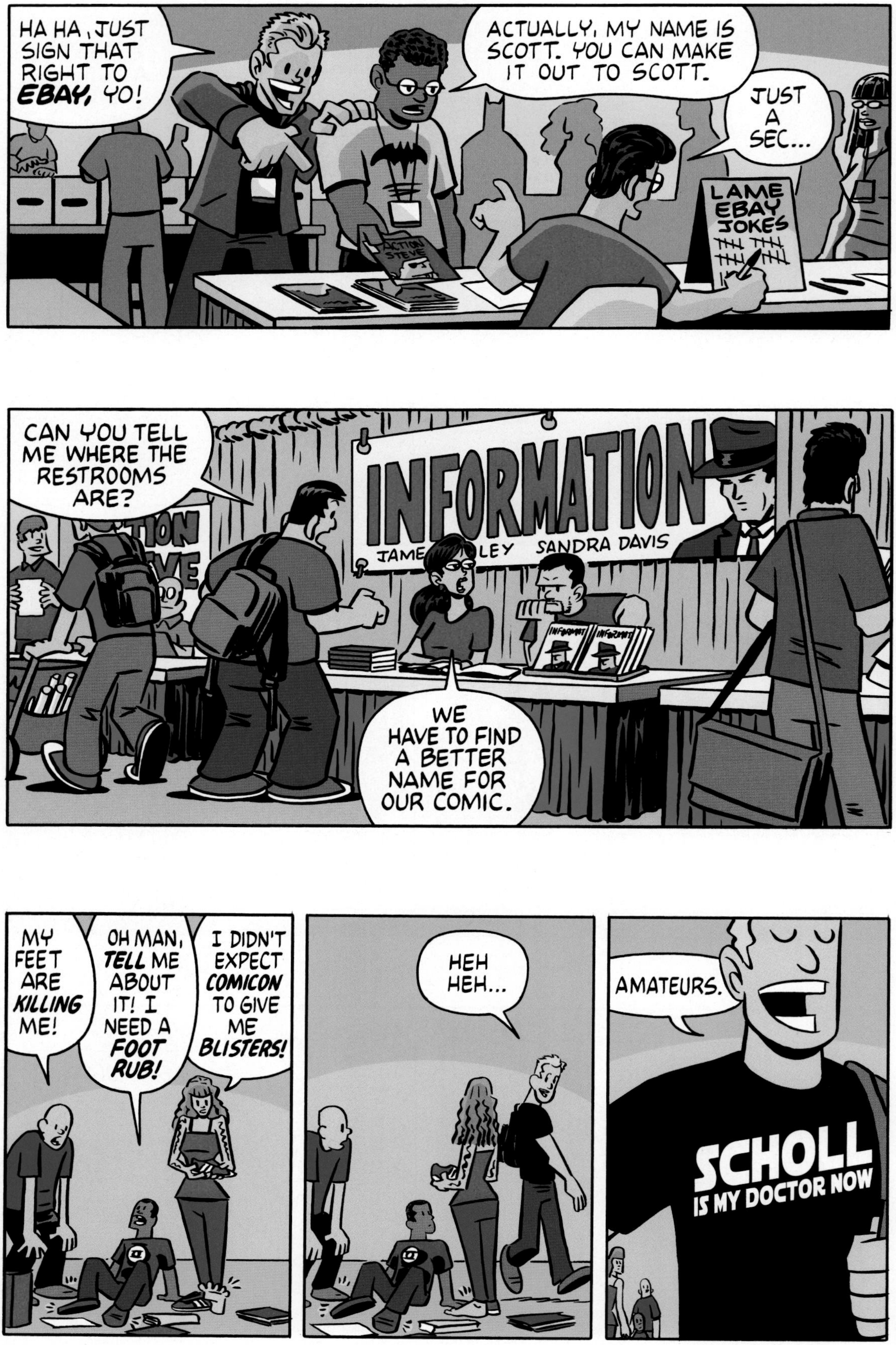
HA HA, JUST SIGN THAT RIGHT TO **EBAY,** YO!
ACTUALLY, MY NAME IS SCOTT. YOU CAN MAKE IT OUT TO SCOTT.
JUST A SEC...
LAME EBAY JOKES
CAN YOU TELL ME WHERE THE RESTROOMS ARE?
INFORMATION
SANDRA DAVIS
WE HAVE TO FIND A BETTER NAME FOR OUR COMIC.
MY FEET ARE ***KILLING*** ME!
OH MAN, ***TELL*** ME ABOUT IT! I NEED A ***FOOT RUB!***
I DIDN'T EXPECT ***COMICON*** TO GIVE ME ***BLISTERS!***
HEH HEH...
AMATEURS.
SCHOLL IS MY DOCTOR NOW

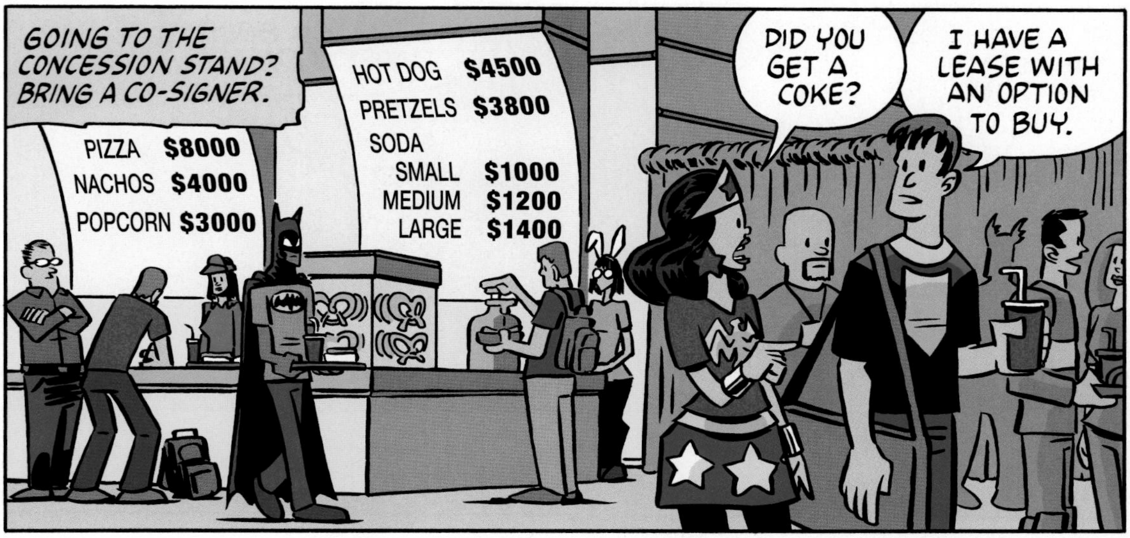
GOING TO THE CONCESSION STAND? BRING A CO-SIGNER.
PIZZA $8000
NACHOS $4000
POPCORN $3000
HOT DOG $4500
PRETZELS $3800
SODA
SMALL $1000
MEDIUM $1200
LARGE $1400
DID YOU GET A COKE?
I HAVE A LEASE WITH AN OPTION TO BUY.

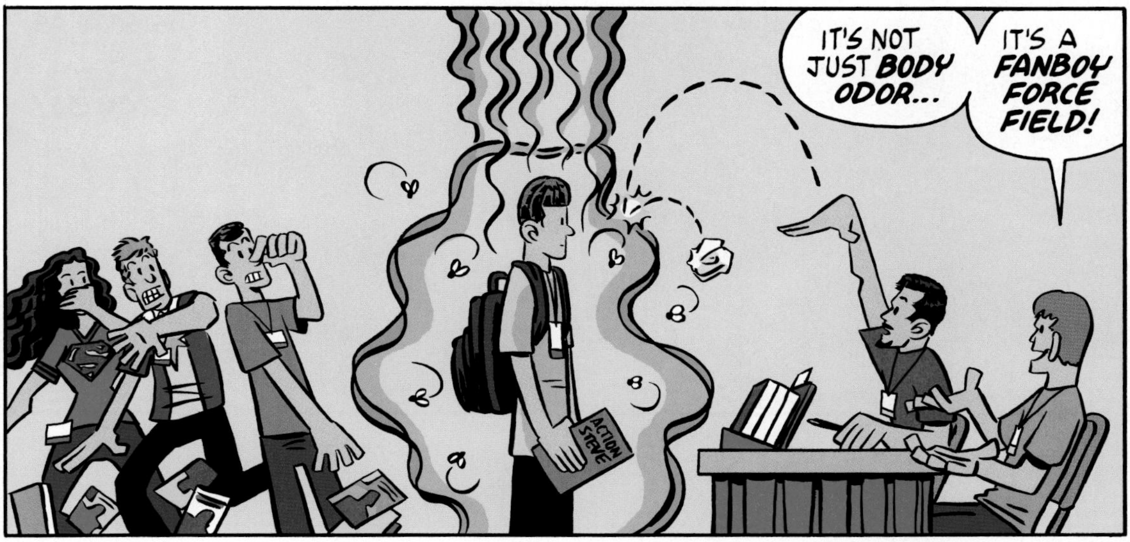
IT'S NOT JUST BODY ODOR...
IT'S A FANBOY FORCE FIELD!
ACTION STEVE

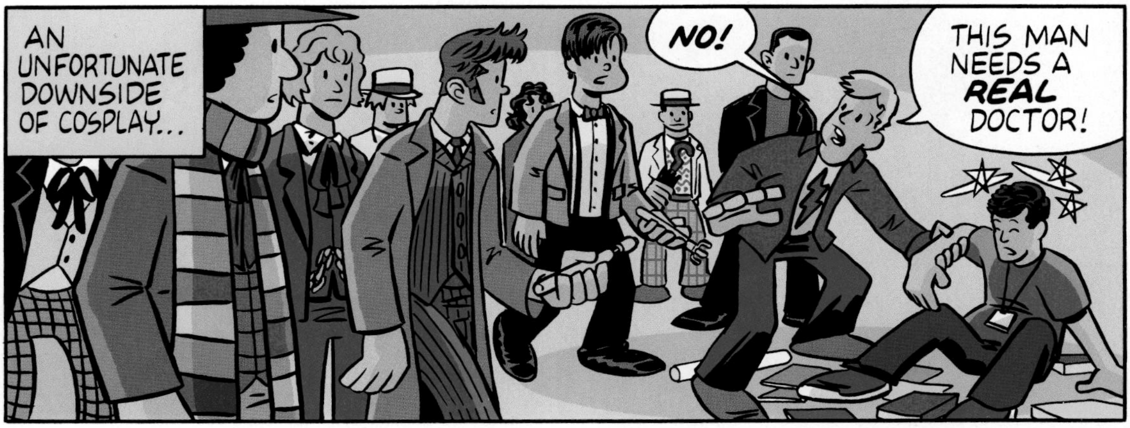
AN UNFORTUNATE DOWNSIDE OF COSPLAY...
NO!
THIS MAN NEEDS A REAL DOCTOR!

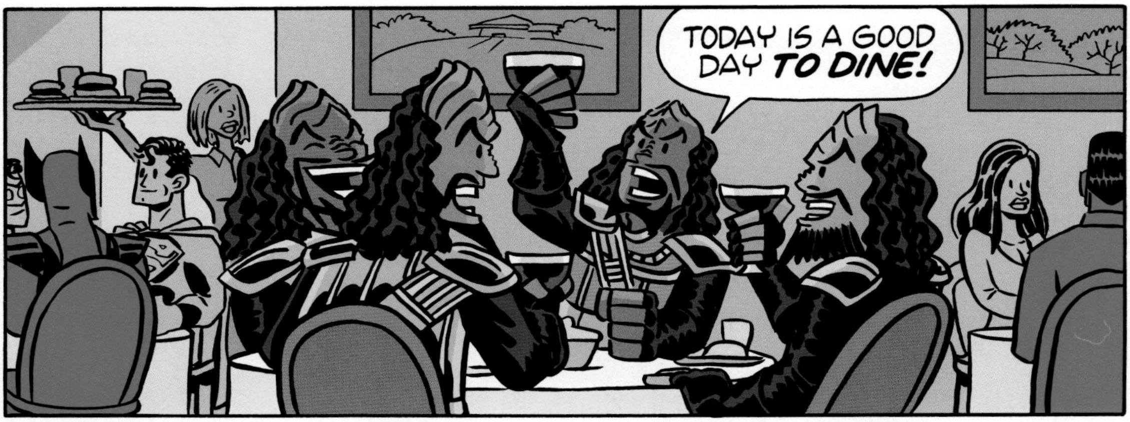
TODAY IS A GOOD DAY TO DINE!

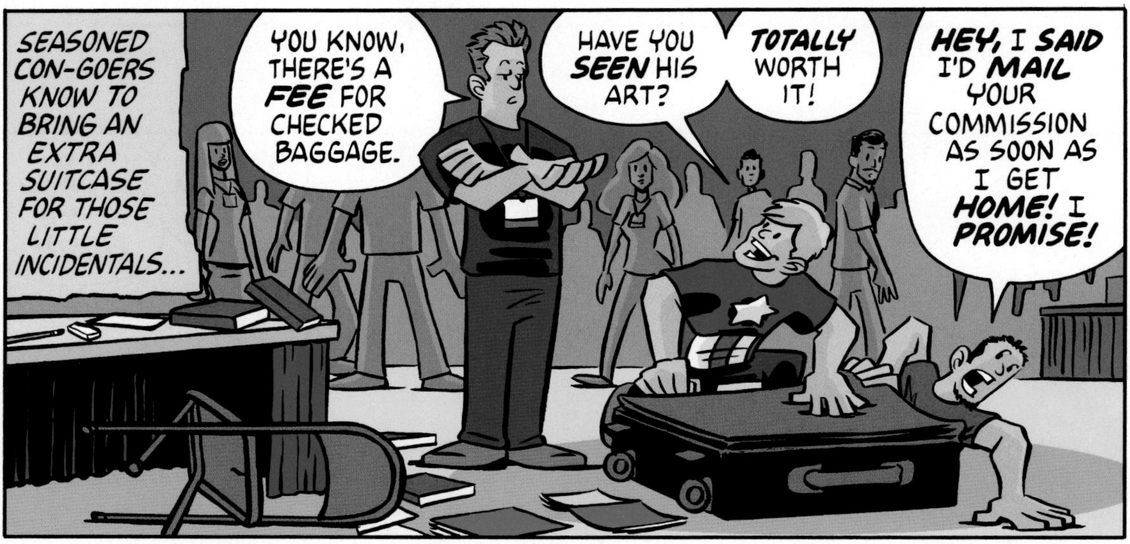
SEASONED CON-GOERS KNOW TO BRING AN EXTRA SUITCASE FOR THOSE LITTLE INCIDENTALS...
YOU KNOW, THERE'S A FEE FOR CHECKED BAGGAGE.
HAVE YOU SEEN HIS ART?
TOTALLY WORTH IT!
HEY, I SAID I'D MAIL YOUR COMMISSION AS SOON AS I GET HOME! I PROMISE!

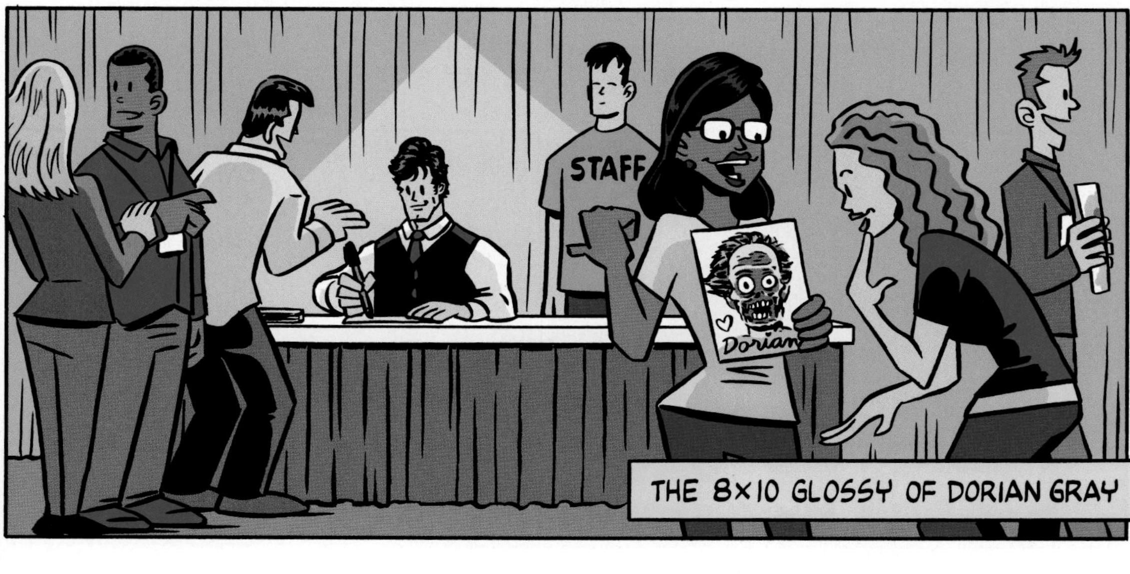
STAFF
Dorian
THE 8×10 GLOSSY OF DORIAN GRAY

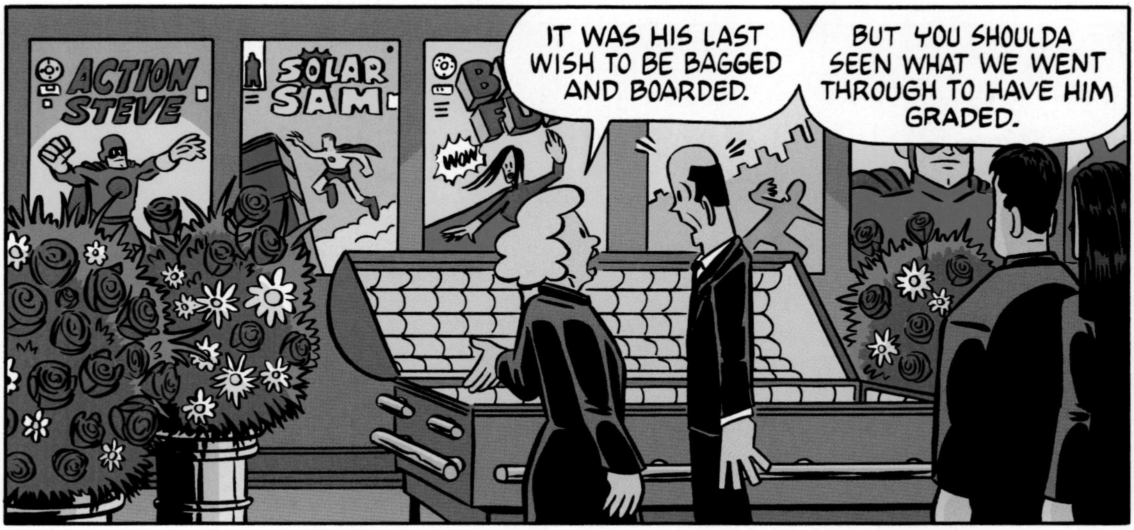
ACTION STEVE
SOLAR SAM
WOW
IT WAS HIS LAST WISH TO BE BAGGED AND BOARDED.
BUT YOU SHOULDA SEEN WHAT WE WENT THROUGH TO HAVE HIM GRADED.

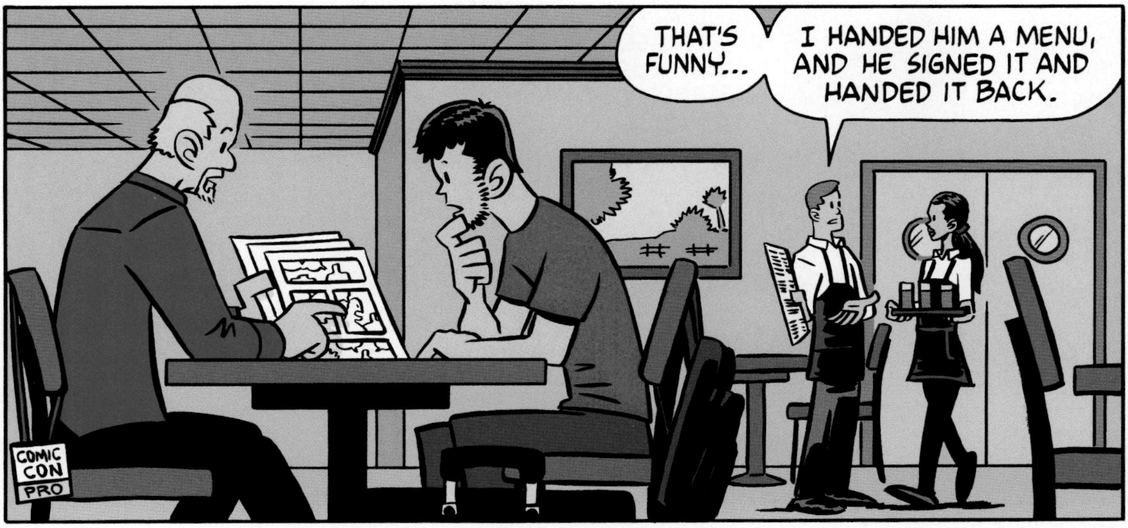
THAT'S FUNNY...
I HANDED HIM A MENU, AND HE SIGNED IT AND HANDED IT BACK.
COMIC CON PRO

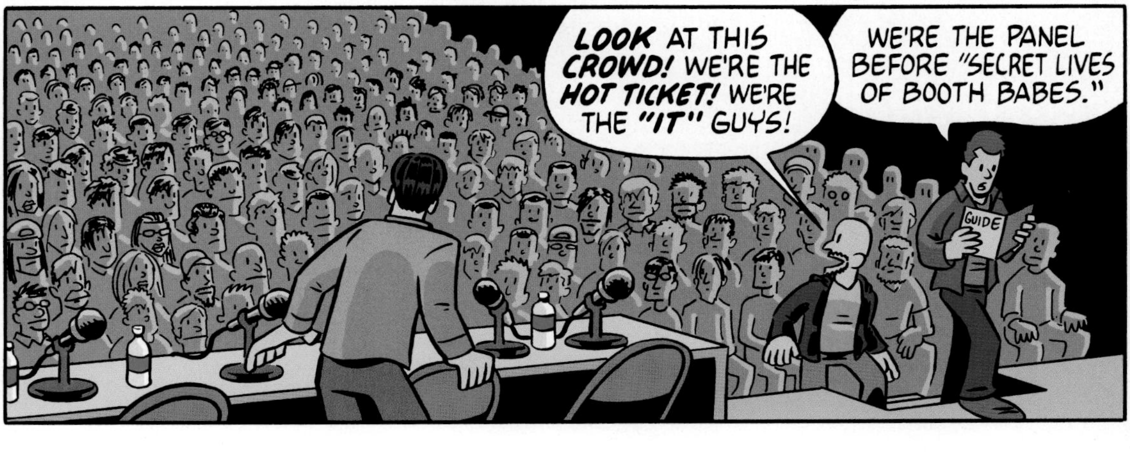
***LOOK*** AT THIS ***CROWD!*** WE'RE THE ***HOT TICKET!*** WE'RE THE ***"IT"*** GUYS!
WE'RE THE PANEL BEFORE "SECRET LIVES OF BOOTH BABES."
GUIDE

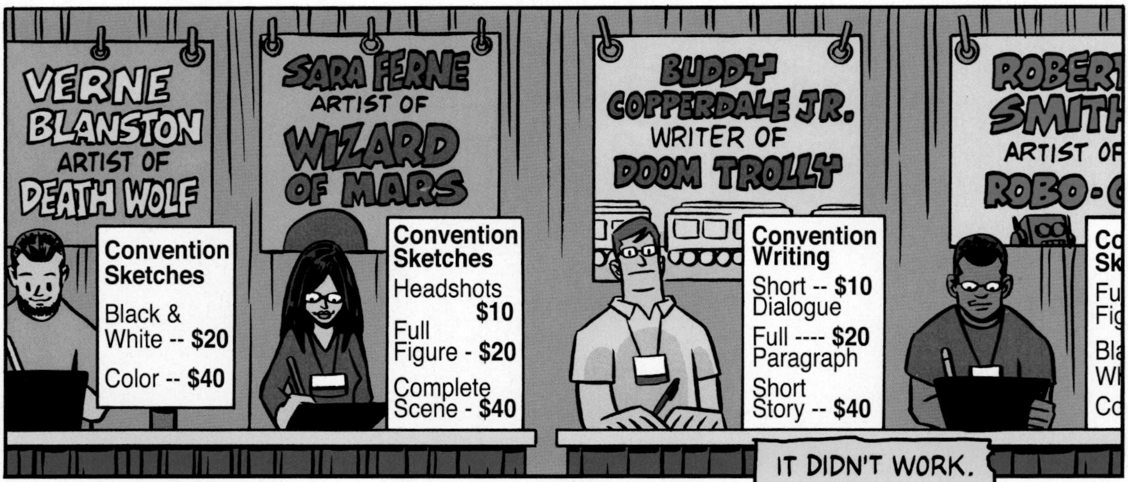
VERNE BLANSTON
ARTIST OF
DEATH WOLF
Convention Sketches
Black & White -- $20
Color -- $40
SARA FERNE
ARTIST OF
WIZARD OF MARS
Convention Sketches
Headshots $10
Full Figure - $20
Complete Scene - $40
BUDDY COPPERDALE JR.
WRITER OF
DOOM TROLLY
Convention Writing
Short Dialogue -- $10
Full Paragraph ---- $20
Short Story -- $40
IT DIDN'T WORK.

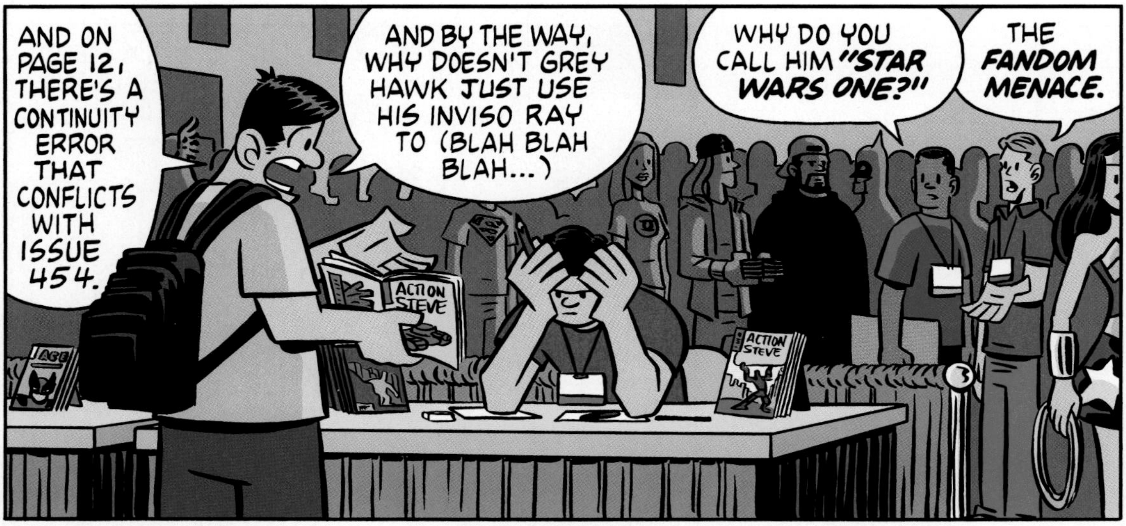
AND ON PAGE 12, THERE'S A CONTINUITY ERROR THAT CONFLICTS WITH ISSUE 454.
AND BY THE WAY, WHY DOESN'T GREY HAWK JUST USE HIS INVISO RAY TO (BLAH BLAH BLAH...)
WHY DO YOU CALL HIM "STAR WARS ONE?"
THE FANDOM MENACE.
ACTION STEVE
ACTION STEVE

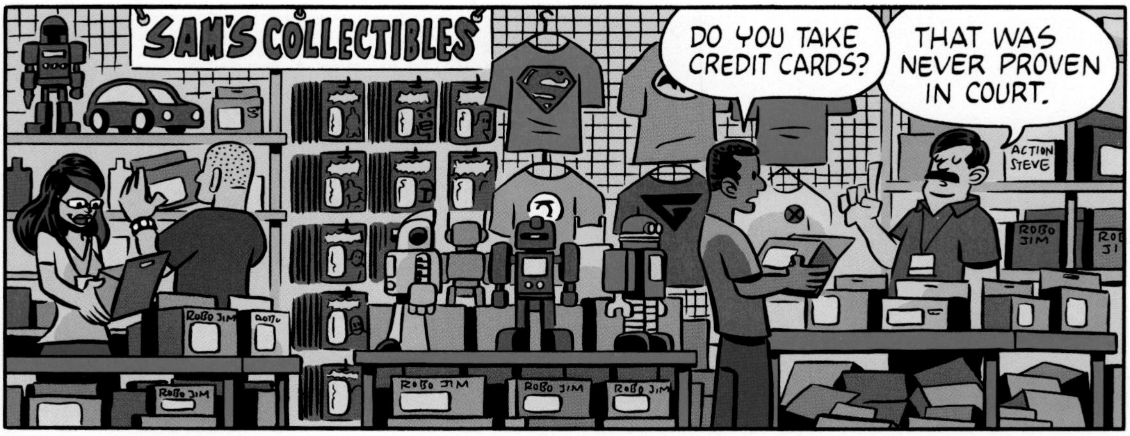
SAM'S COLLECTIBLES
DO YOU TAKE CREDIT CARDS?
THAT WAS NEVER PROVEN IN COURT.
ACTION STEVE
ROBO JIM
ROBO JIM
ROBO JIM
ROBO JIM
ROBO JIM
ROBO JIM

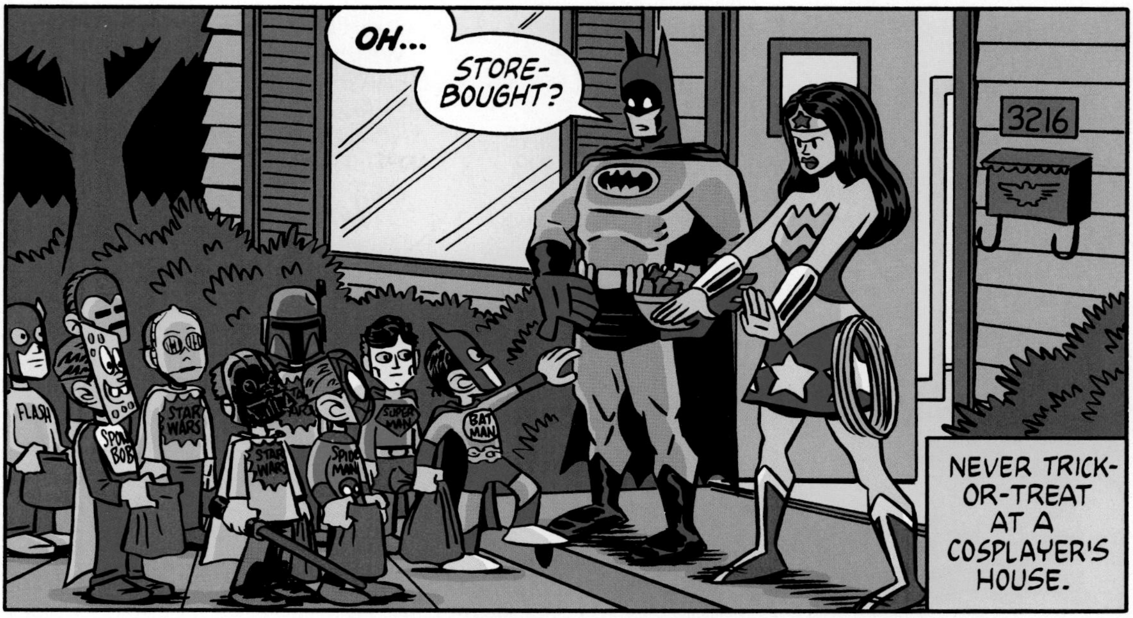
OH...
STORE-BOUGHT?
3216
NEVER TRICK-OR-TREAT AT A COSPLAYER'S HOUSE.

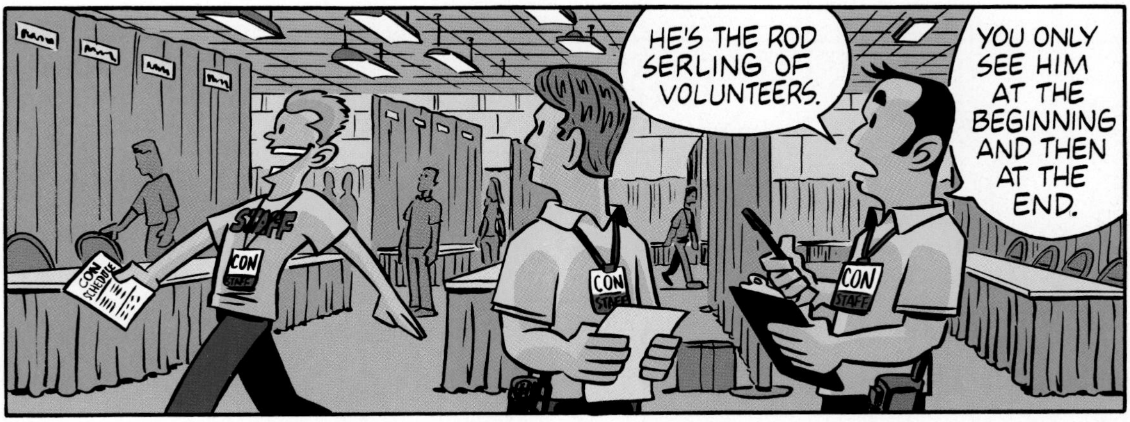
CON SCHEDULE
STAFF
CON STAFF
HE'S THE ROD SERLING OF VOLUNTEERS.
YOU ONLY SEE HIM AT THE BEGINNING AND THEN AT THE END.

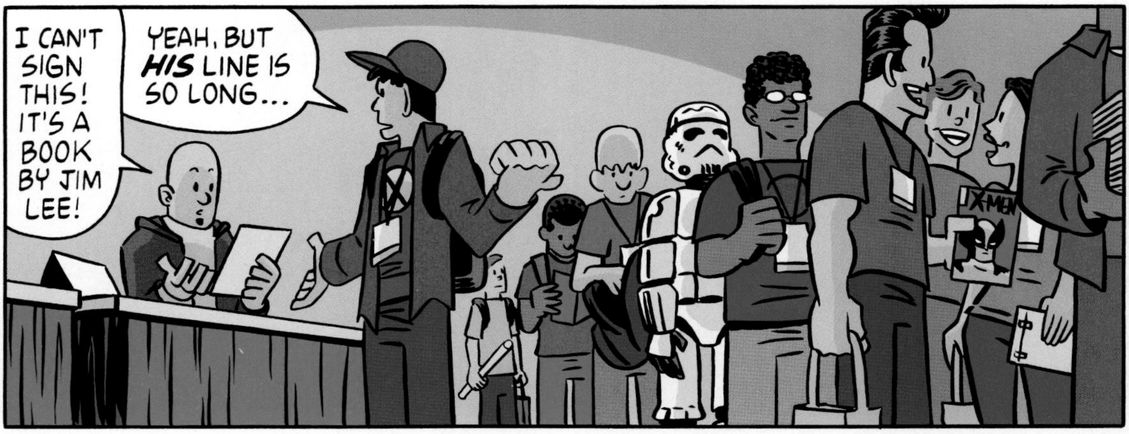
I CAN'T SIGN THIS! IT'S A BOOK BY JIM LEE!
YEAH, BUT ***HIS*** LINE IS SO LONG...

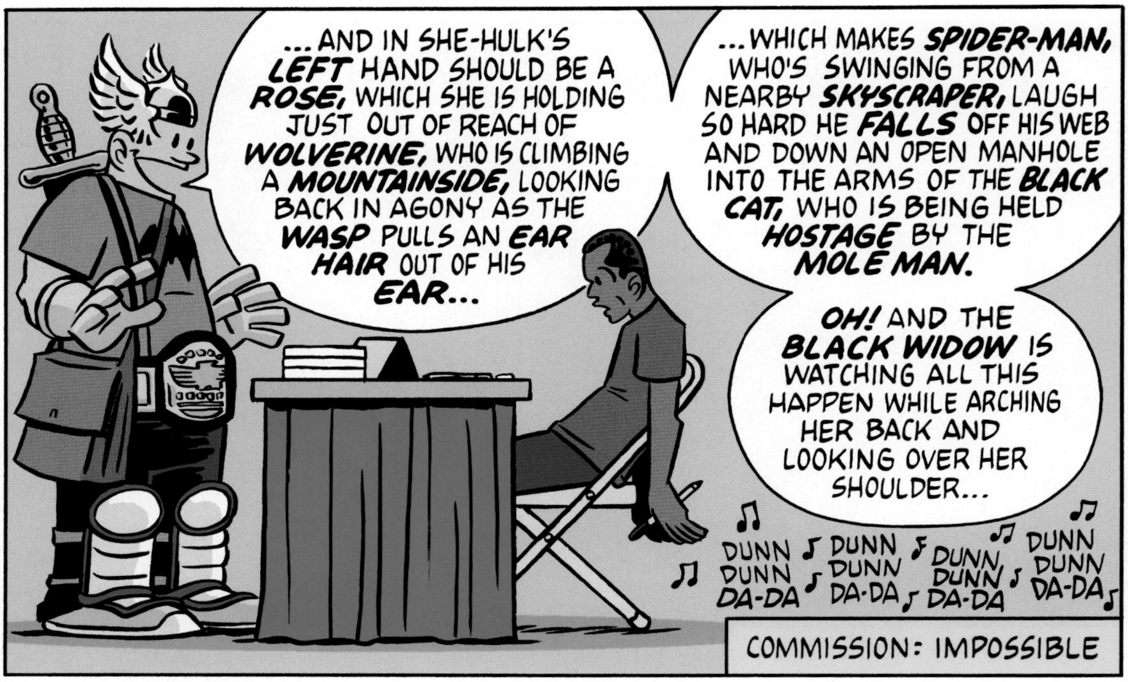
...AND IN SHE-HULK'S LEFT HAND SHOULD BE A ROSE, WHICH SHE IS HOLDING JUST OUT OF REACH OF WOLVERINE, WHO IS CLIMBING A MOUNTAINSIDE, LOOKING BACK IN AGONY AS THE WASP PULLS AN EAR HAIR OUT OF HIS EAR...
...WHICH MAKES SPIDER-MAN, WHO'S SWINGING FROM A NEARBY SKYSCRAPER, LAUGH SO HARD HE FALLS OFF HIS WEB AND DOWN AN OPEN MANHOLE INTO THE ARMS OF THE BLACK CAT, WHO IS BEING HELD HOSTAGE BY THE MOLE MAN.
OH! AND THE BLACK WIDOW IS WATCHING ALL THIS HAPPEN WHILE ARCHING HER BACK AND LOOKING OVER HER SHOULDER...
DUNN DUNN DA-DA
DUNN DUNN DA-DA
DUNN DUNN DA-DA
DUNN DUNN DA-DA
COMMISSION: IMPOSSIBLE

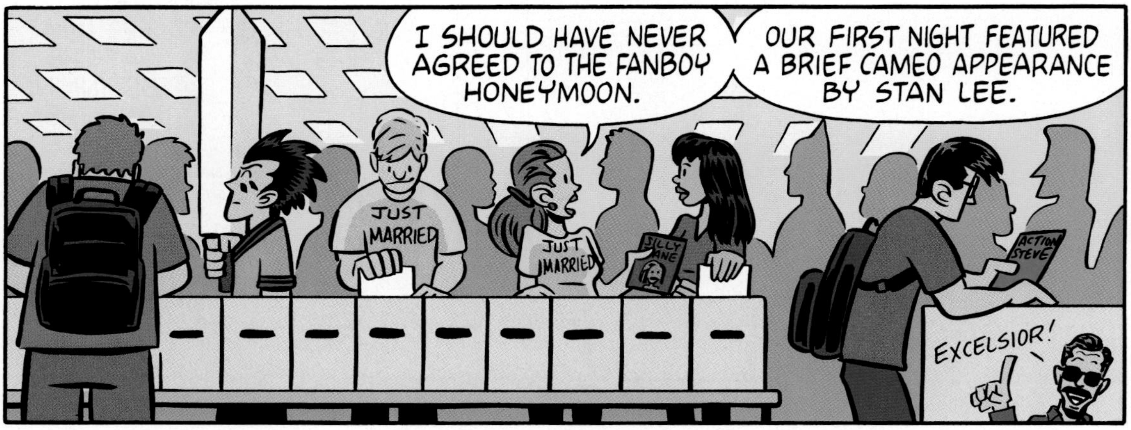
I SHOULD HAVE NEVER AGREED TO THE FANBOY HONEYMOON.
OUR FIRST NIGHT FEATURED A BRIEF CAMEO APPEARANCE BY STAN LEE.
JUST MARRIED
JUST MARRIED
ACTION STEVE
EXCELSIOR!

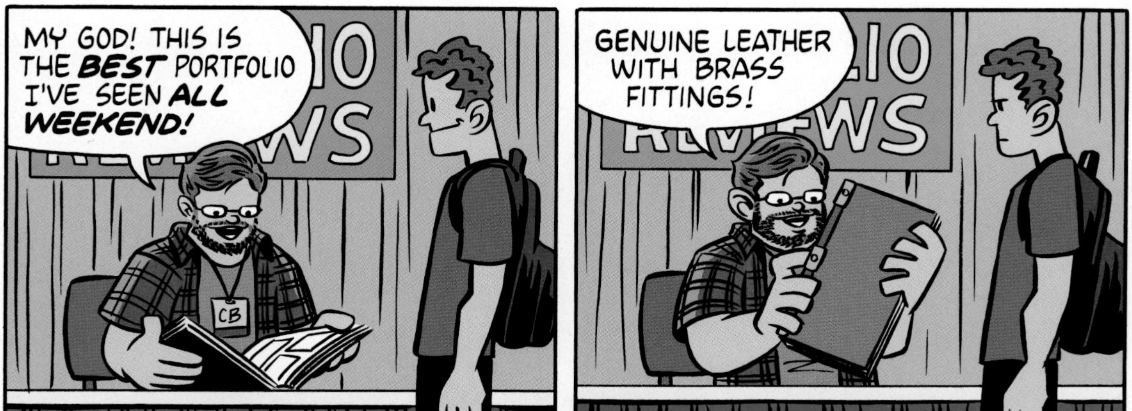
MY GOD! THIS IS THE BEST PORTFOLIO I'VE SEEN ALL WEEKEND!
CB
GENUINE LEATHER WITH BRASS FITTINGS!

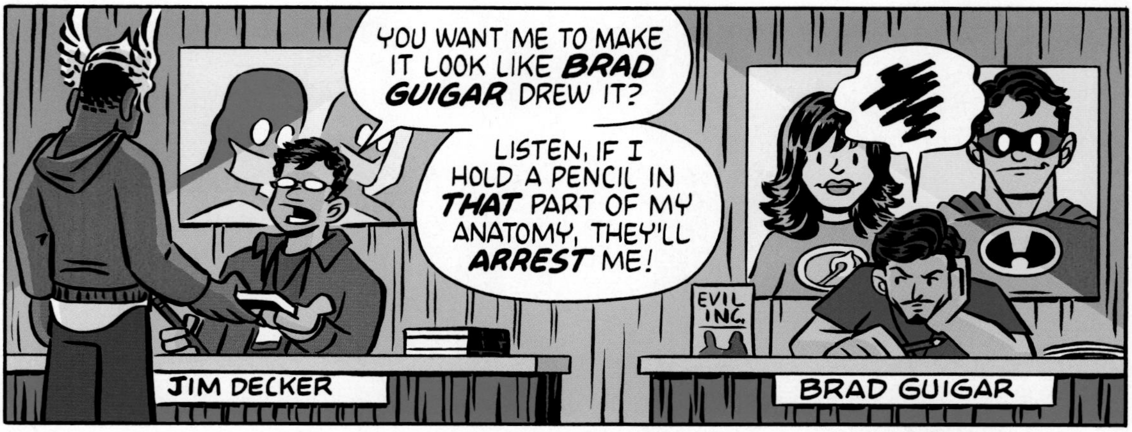
YOU WANT ME TO MAKE IT LOOK LIKE BRAD GUIGAR DREW IT?
LISTEN, IF I HOLD A PENCIL IN THAT PART OF MY ANATOMY, THEY'LL ARREST ME!
EVIL INC.
JIM DECKER
BRAD GUIGAR

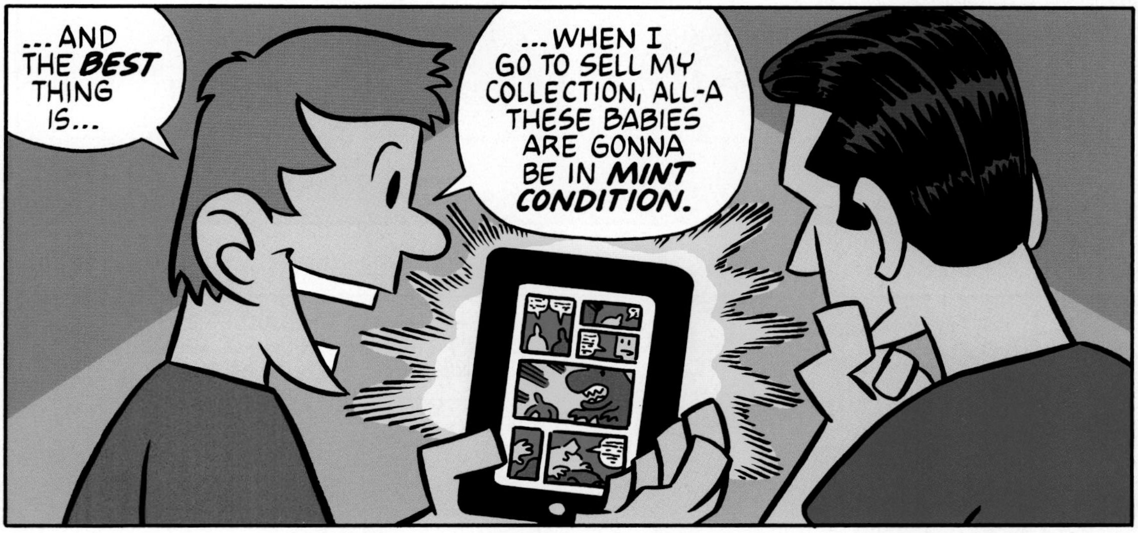
...AND THE BEST THING IS...
...WHEN I GO TO SELL MY COLLECTION, ALL-A THESE BABIES ARE GONNA BE IN MINT CONDITION.

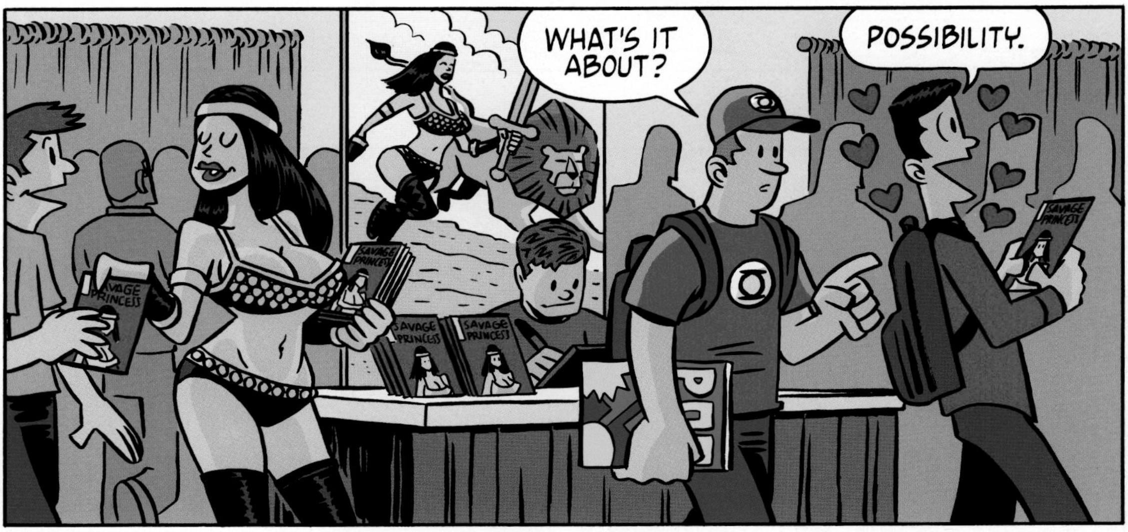
WHAT'S IT ABOUT?
POSSIBILITY.
SAVAGE PRINCESS

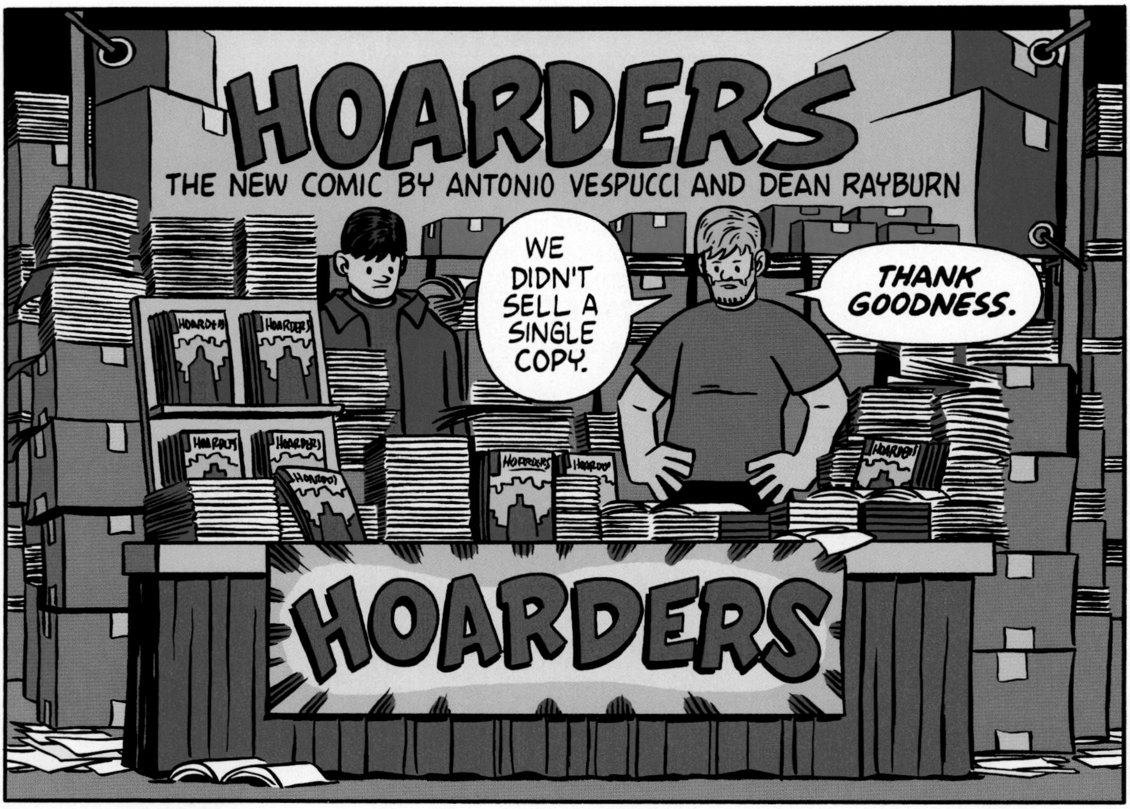
HOARDERS
THE NEW COMIC BY ANTONIO VESPUCCI AND DEAN RAYBURN
WE DIDN'T SELL A SINGLE COPY.
THANK GOODNESS.
HOARDERS

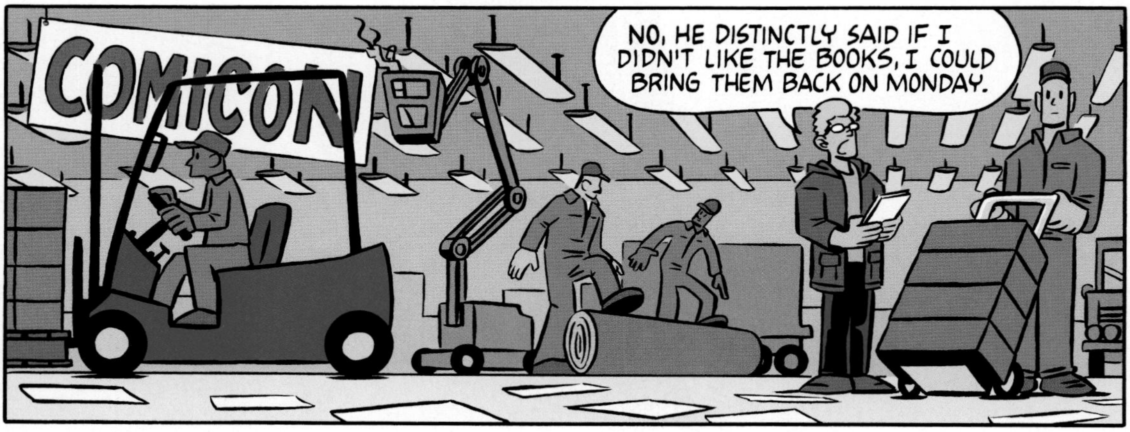
COMICON
NO, HE DISTINCTLY SAID IF I DIDN'T LIKE THE BOOKS, I COULD BRING THEM BACK ON MONDAY.

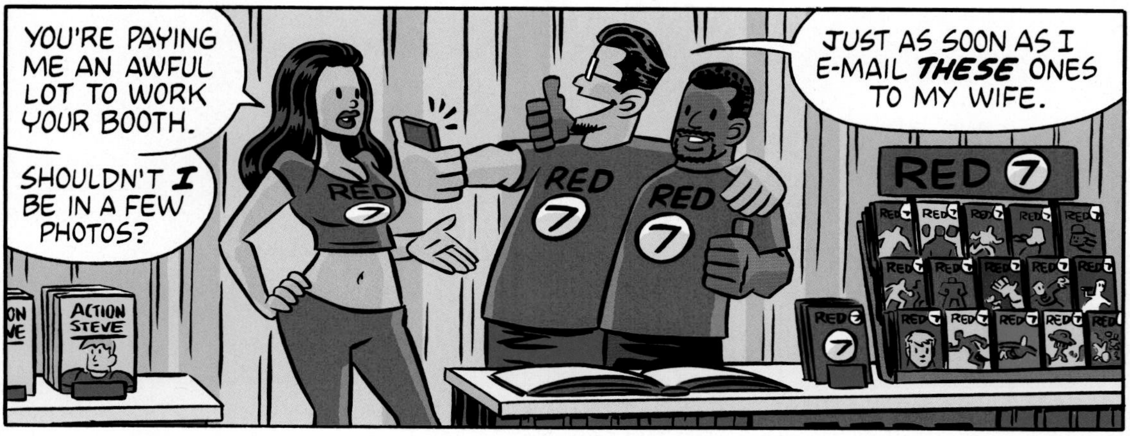
YOU'RE PAYING ME AN AWFUL LOT TO WORK YOUR BOOTH.
SHOULDN'T ***I*** BE IN A FEW PHOTOS?
JUST AS SOON AS I E-MAIL ***THESE*** ONES TO MY WIFE.
RED 7
ACTION STEVE

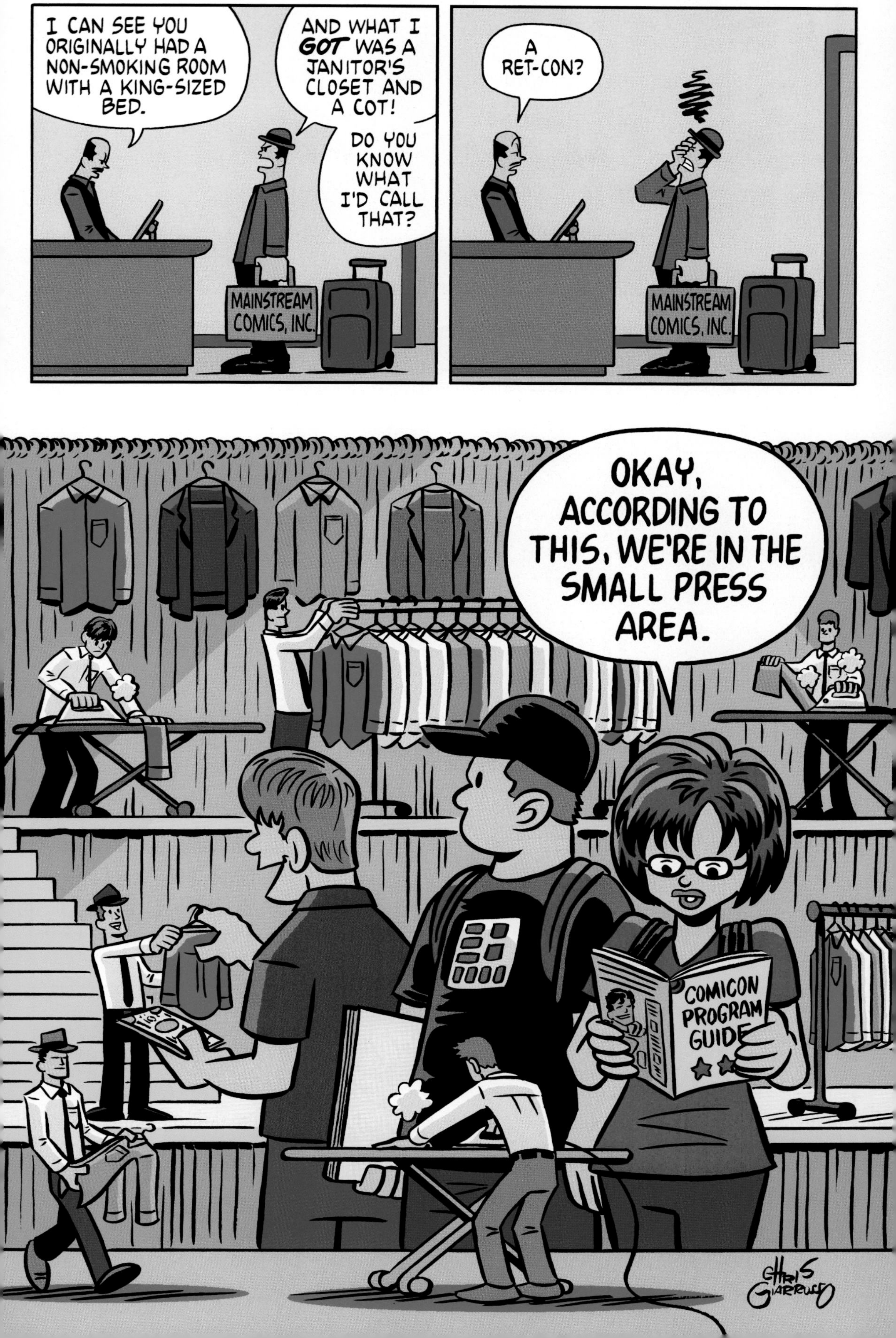
I CAN SEE YOU ORIGINALLY HAD A NON-SMOKING ROOM WITH A KING-SIZED BED.
AND WHAT I GOT WAS A JANITOR'S CLOSET AND A COT!
DO YOU KNOW WHAT I'D CALL THAT?
MAINSTREAM COMICS, INC.
A RET-CON?
MAINSTREAM COMICS, INC.
OKAY, ACCORDING TO THIS, WE'RE IN THE SMALL PRESS AREA.
COMICON PROGRAM GUIDE
CHRIS GIARRUSSO

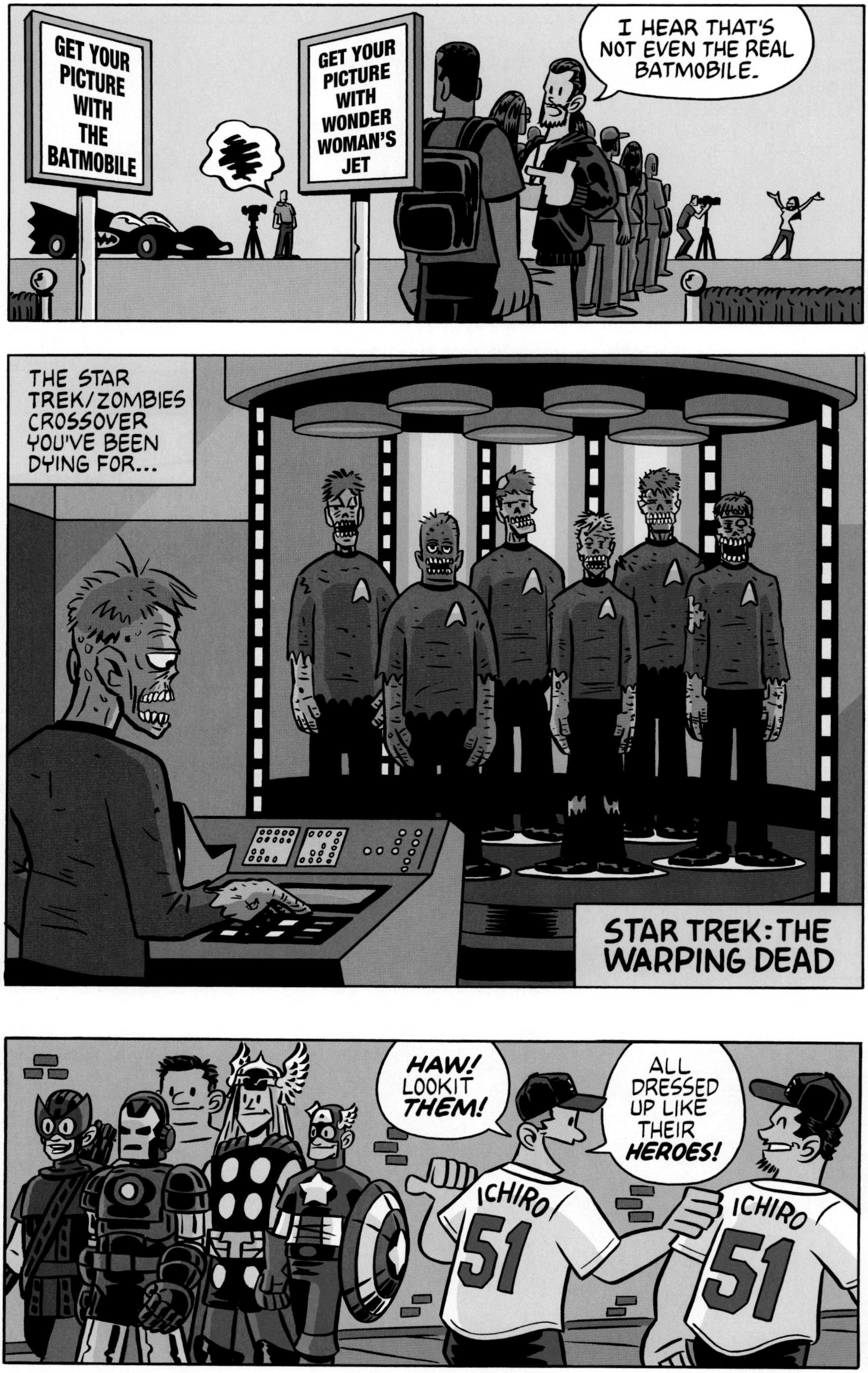
GET YOUR PICTURE WITH THE BATMOBILE
GET YOUR PICTURE WITH WONDER WOMAN'S JET
I HEAR THAT'S NOT EVEN THE REAL BATMOBILE.
THE STAR TREK/ZOMBIES CROSSOVER YOU'VE BEEN DYING FOR...
STAR TREK: THE WARPING DEAD
*HAW!* LOOKIT *THEM!*
ALL DRESSED UP LIKE THEIR *HEROES!*
ICHIRO 51
ICHIRO 51

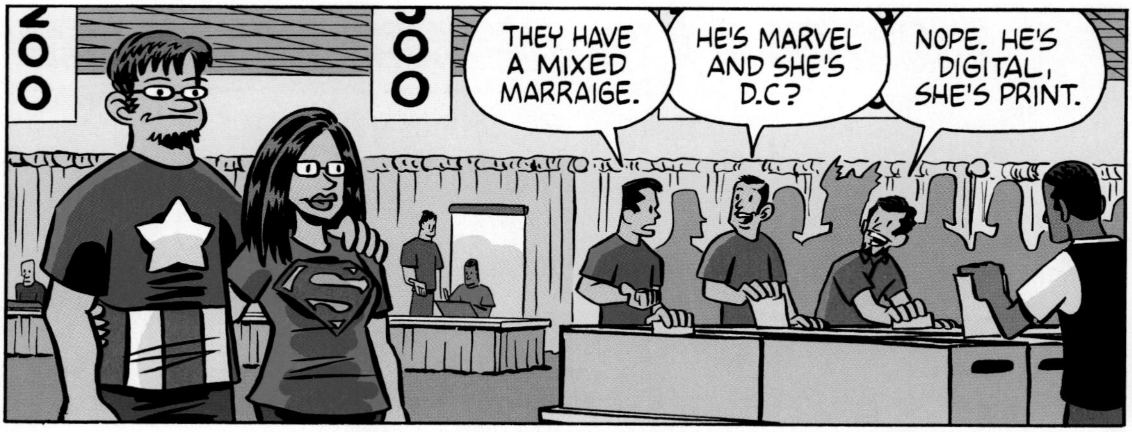
THEY HAVE A MIXED MARRAIGE.
HE'S MARVEL AND SHE'S D.C?
NOPE. HE'S DIGITAL, SHE'S PRINT.

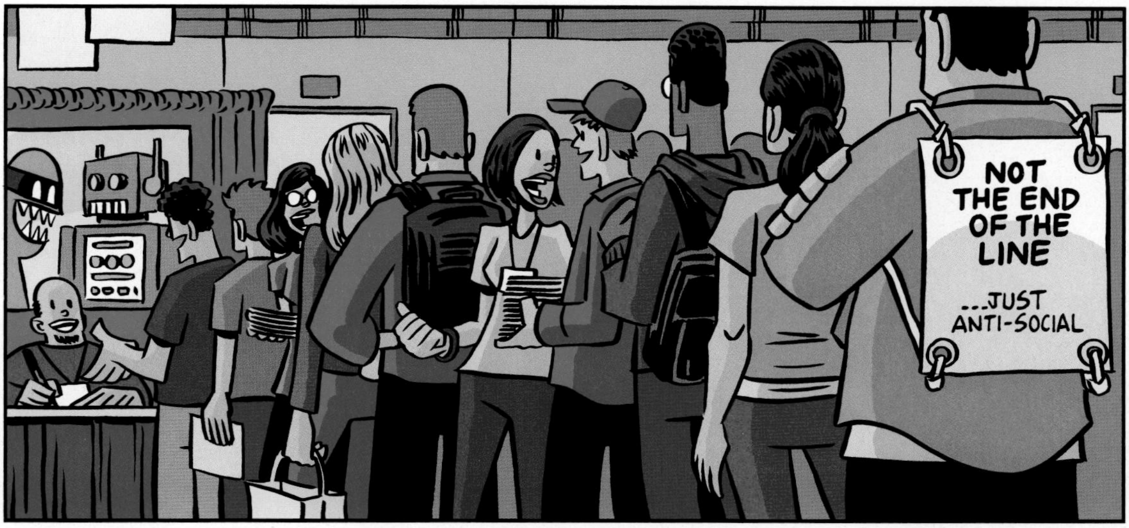
NOT THE END OF THE LINE
...JUST ANTI-SOCIAL

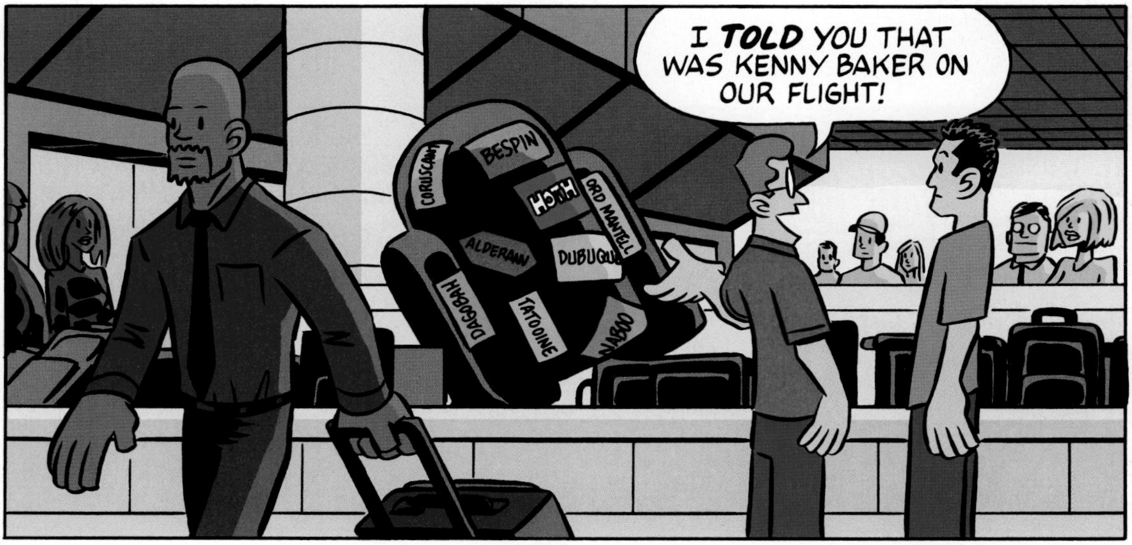
I TOLD YOU THAT WAS KENNY BAKER ON OUR FLIGHT!
CORUSCANT
BESPIN
HOTH
ORD MANTELL
ALDERAAN
DAGOBAH
TATOOINE
NABOO

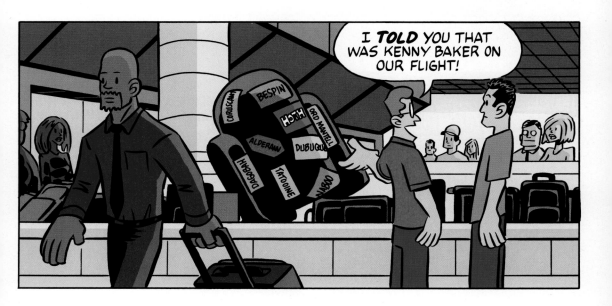

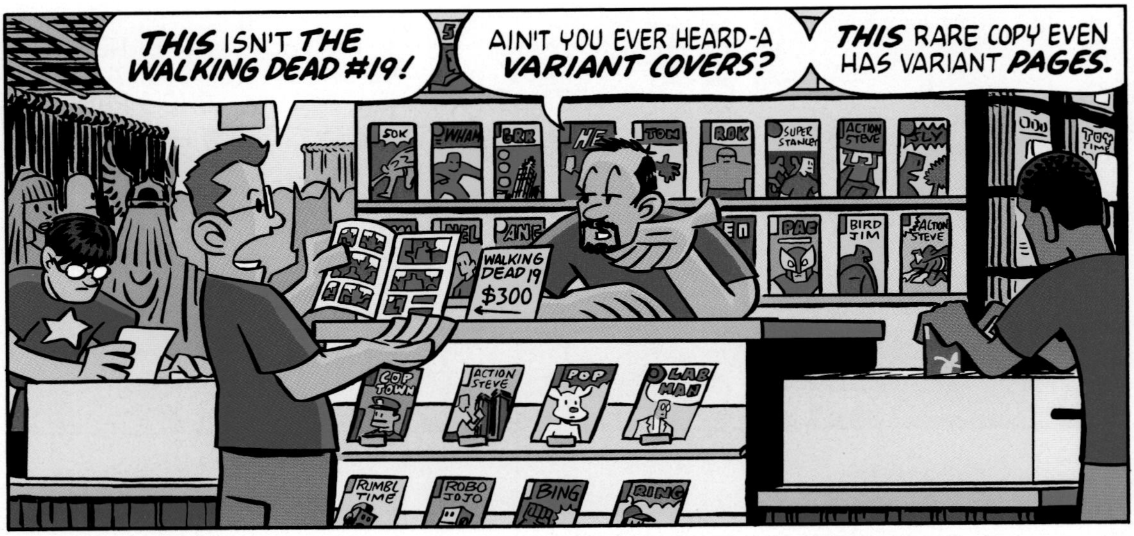
THIS ISN'T THE WALKING DEAD #19!
AIN'T YOU EVER HEARD-A VARIANT COVERS?
THIS RARE COPY EVEN HAS VARIANT PAGES.
WALKING DEAD 19 $300

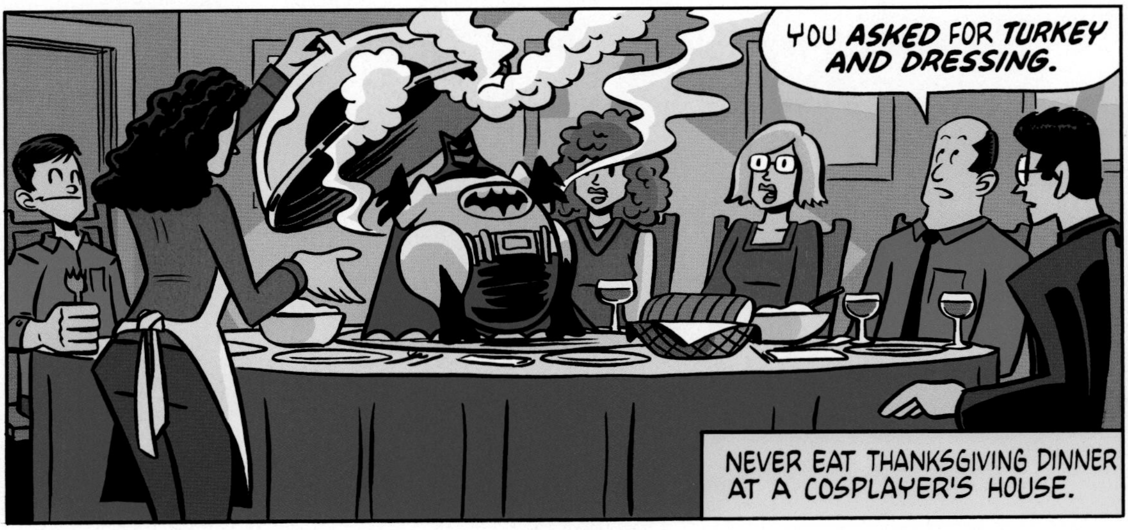
YOU ASKED FOR TURKEY AND DRESSING.
NEVER EAT THANKSGIVING DINNER AT A COSPLAYER'S HOUSE.

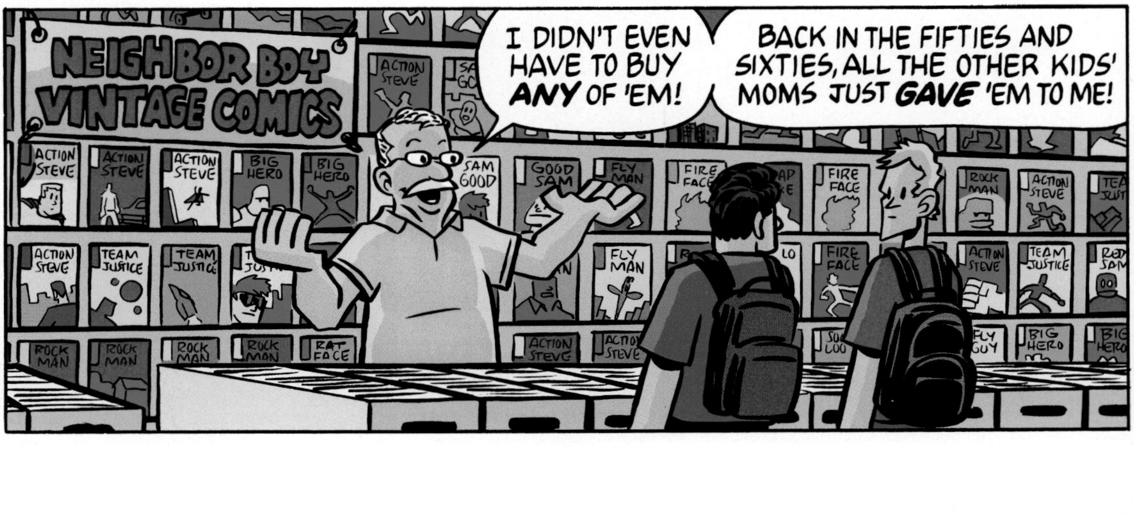
NEIGHBOR BOY VINTAGE COMICS
I DIDN'T EVEN HAVE TO BUY ANY OF 'EM!
BACK IN THE FIFTIES AND SIXTIES, ALL THE OTHER KIDS' MOMS JUST GAVE 'EM TO ME!

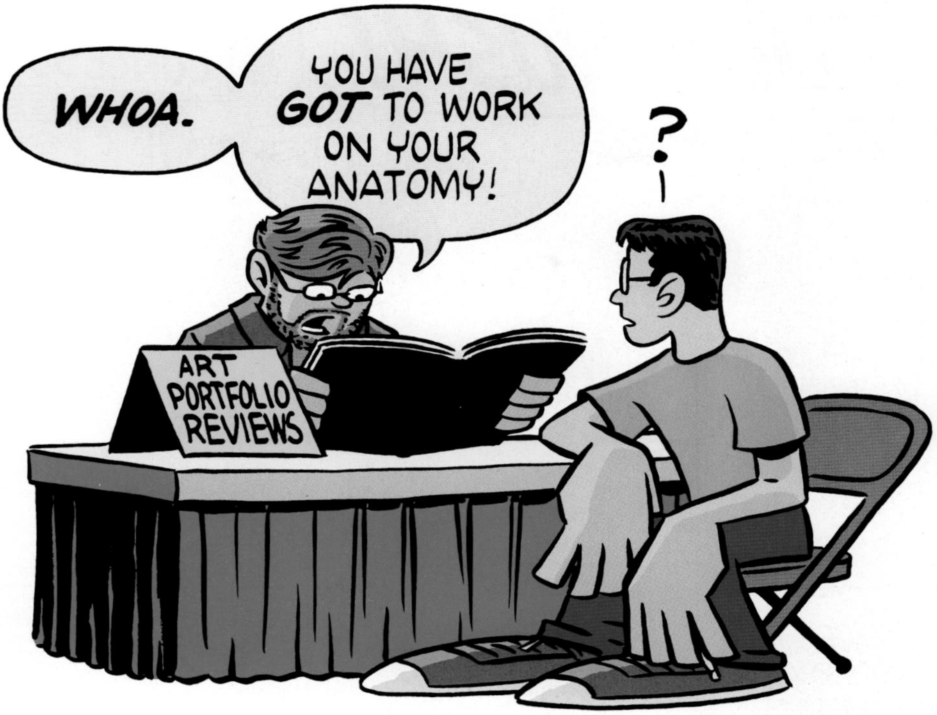
WHOA.
YOU HAVE GOT TO WORK ON YOUR ANATOMY!
?
ART PORTFOLIO REVIEWS

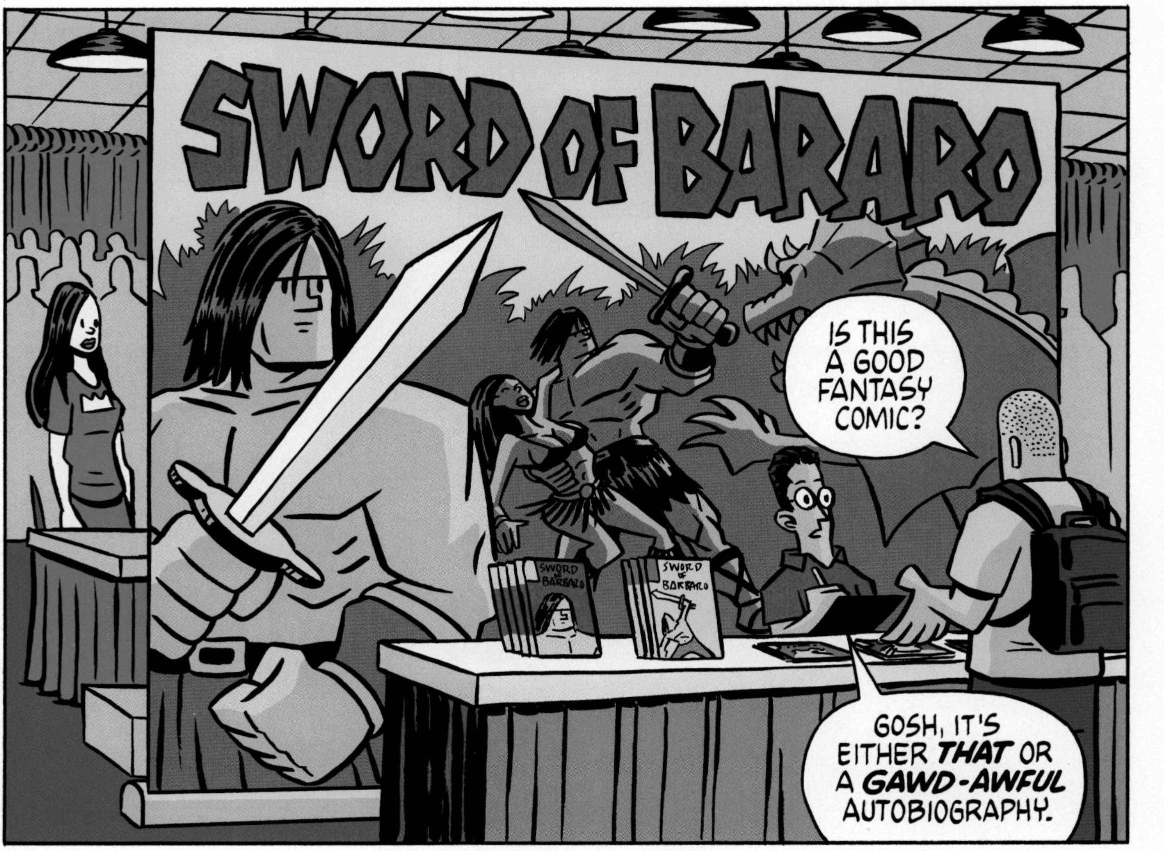
SWORD OF BARARO
SWORD OF BARBARO
SWORD OF BARBARO
IS THIS A GOOD FANTASY COMIC?
GOSH, IT'S EITHER THAT OR A GAWD-AWFUL AUTOBIOGRAPHY.

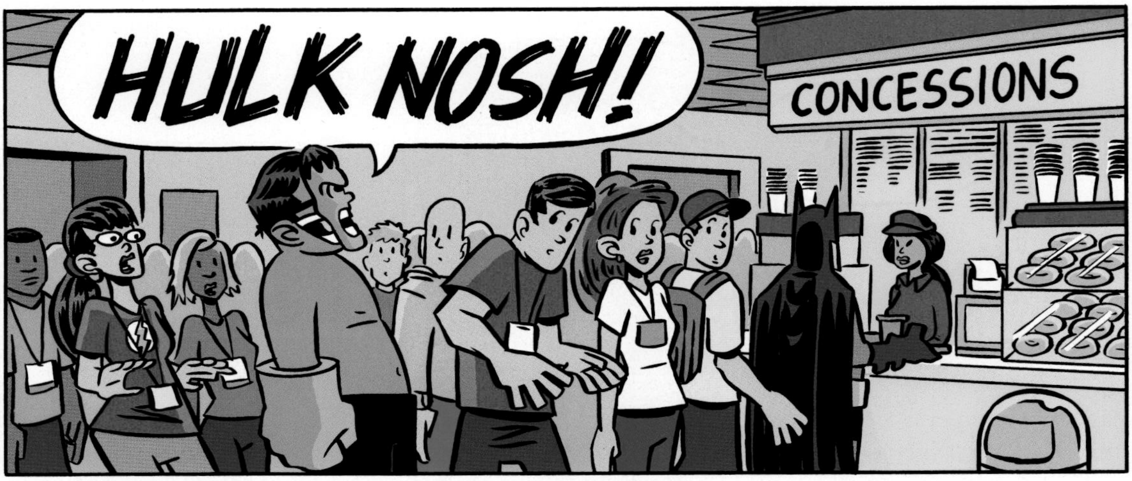
HULK NOSH!
CONCESSIONS

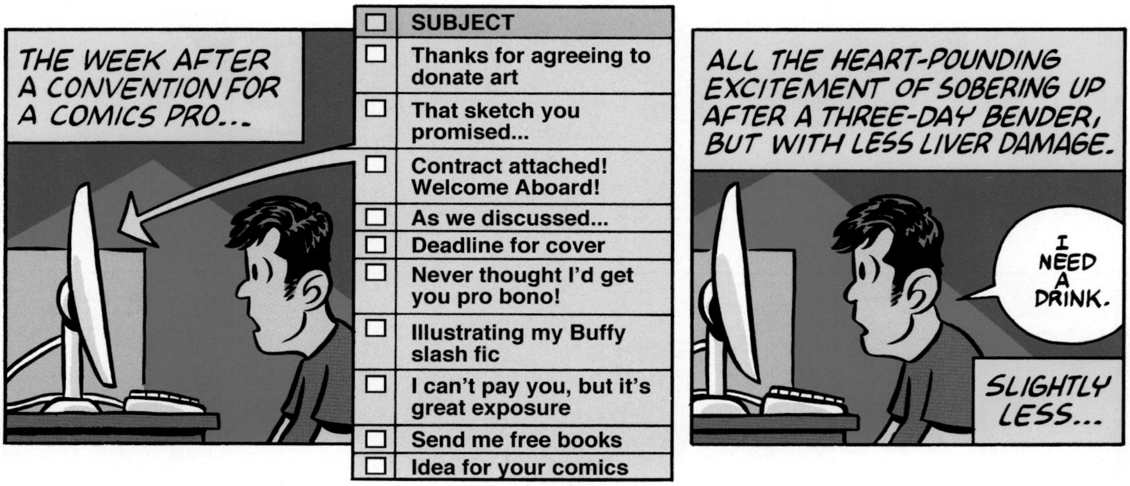
THE WEEK AFTER A CONVENTION FOR A COMICS PRO...
SUBJECT
Thanks for agreeing to donate art
That sketch you promised...
Contract attached! Welcome Aboard!
As we discussed...
Deadline for cover
Never thought I'd get you pro bono!
Illustrating my Buffy slash fic
I can't pay you, but it's great exposure
Send me free books
Idea for your comics
ALL THE HEART-POUNDING EXCITEMENT OF SOBERING UP AFTER A THREE-DAY BENDER, BUT WITH LESS LIVER DAMAGE.
I NEED A DRINK.
SLIGHTLY LESS...

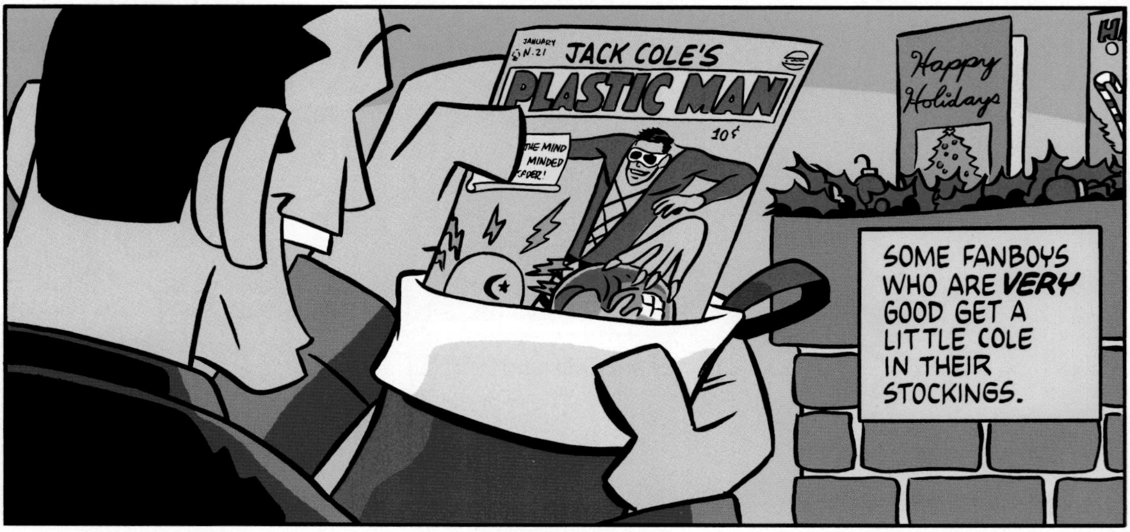
JANUARY N.21
JACK COLE'S
PLASTIC MAN
10¢
Happy Holidays
SOME FANBOYS WHO ARE VERY GOOD GET A LITTLE COLE IN THEIR STOCKINGS.

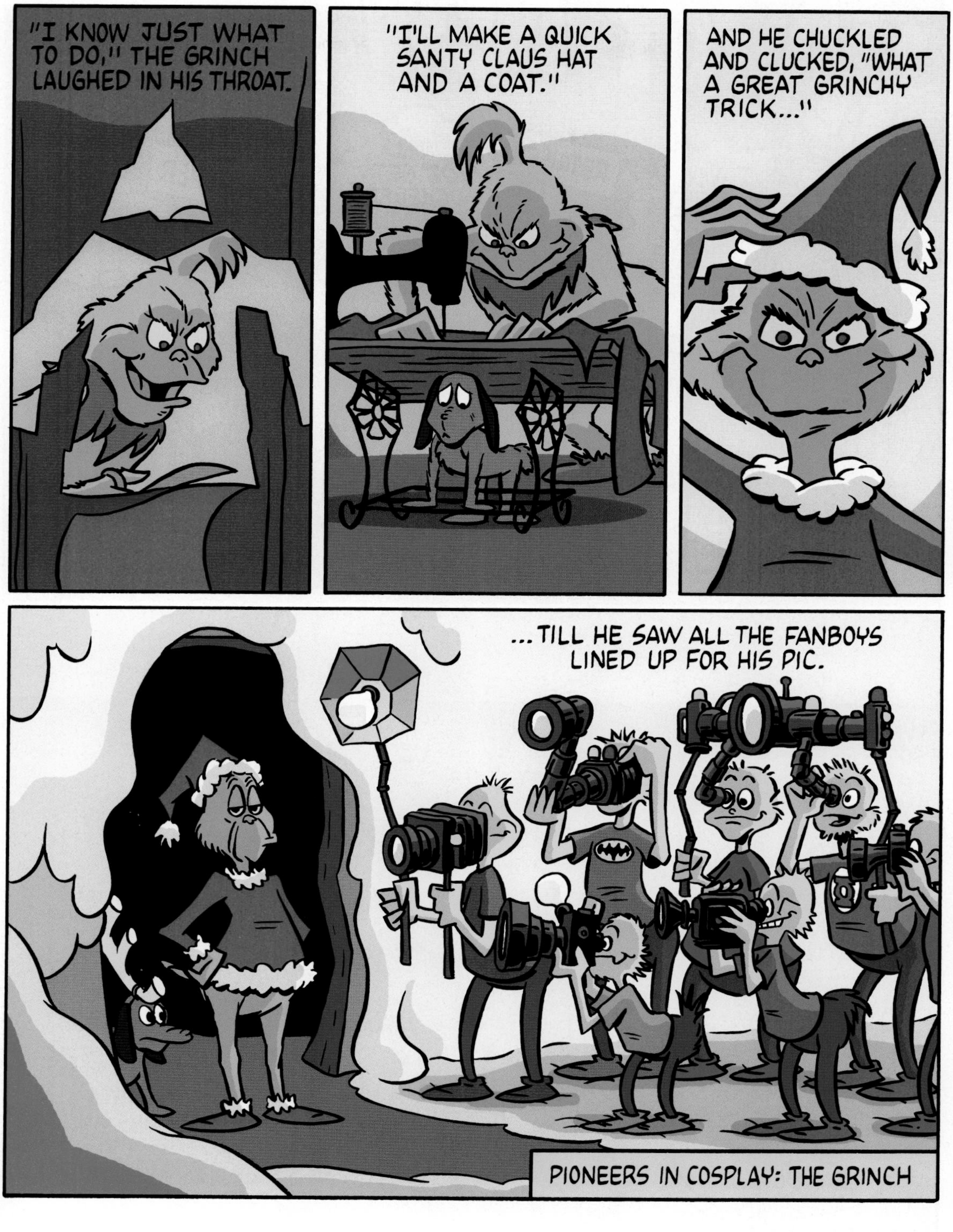
"I KNOW JUST WHAT TO DO," THE GRINCH LAUGHED IN HIS THROAT.
"I'LL MAKE A QUICK SANTY CLAUS HAT AND A COAT."
AND HE CHUCKLED AND CLUCKED, "WHAT A GREAT GRINCHY TRICK..."
...TILL HE SAW ALL THE FANBOYS LINED UP FOR HIS PIC.
PIONEERS IN COSPLAY: THE GRINCH

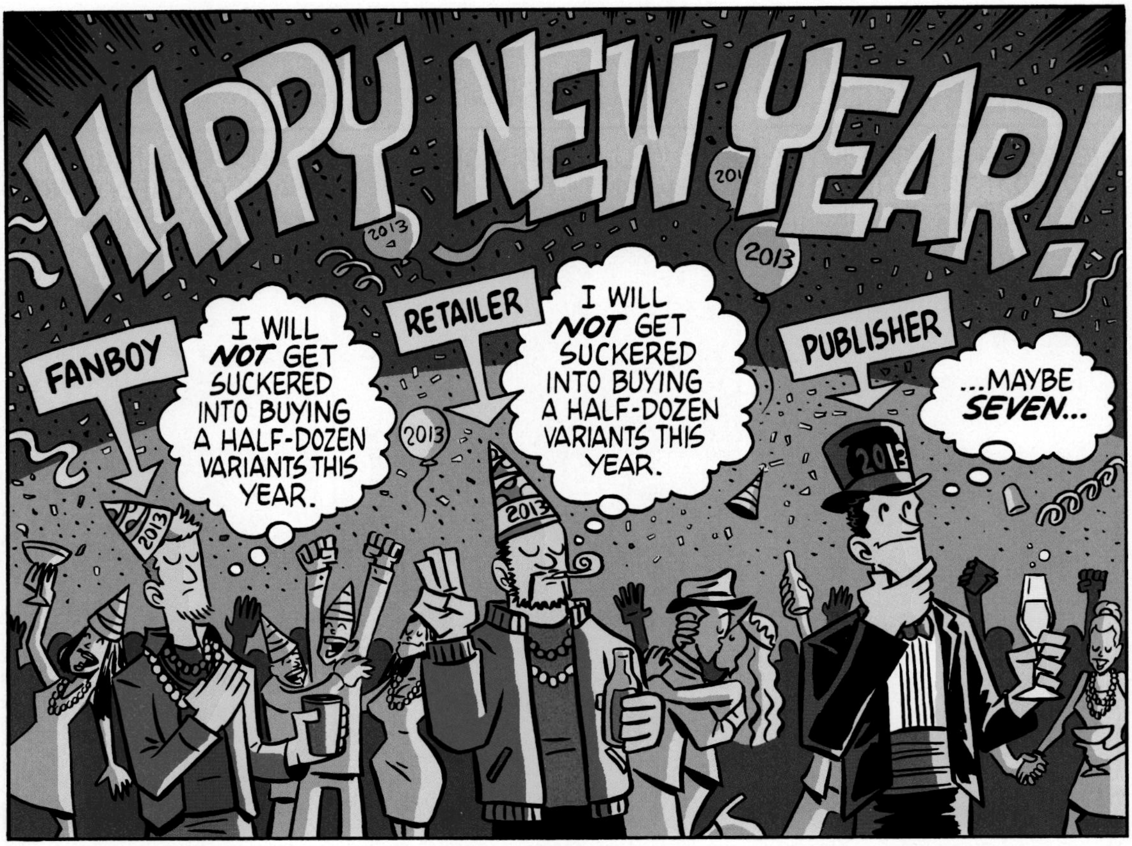
HAPPY NEW YEAR!
FANBOY
I WILL NOT GET SUCKERED INTO BUYING A HALF-DOZEN VARIANTS THIS YEAR.
RETAILER
I WILL NOT GET SUCKERED INTO BUYING A HALF-DOZEN VARIANTS THIS YEAR.
PUBLISHER
...MAYBE SEVEN...
2013

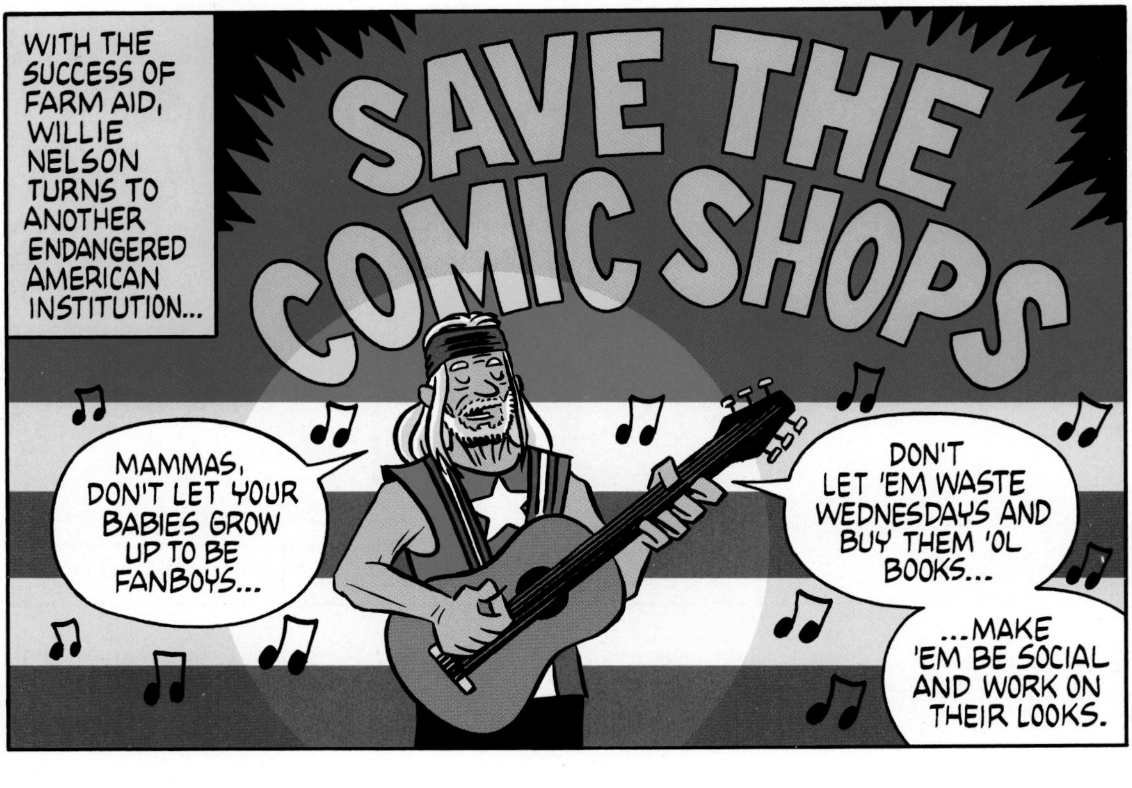
WITH THE SUCCESS OF FARM AID, WILLIE NELSON TURNS TO ANOTHER ENDANGERED AMERICAN INSTITUTION...
SAVE THE COMIC SHOPS
MAMMAS, DON'T LET YOUR BABIES GROW UP TO BE FANBOYS...
DON'T LET 'EM WASTE WEDNESDAYS AND BUY THEM 'OL BOOKS...
...MAKE 'EM BE SOCIAL AND WORK ON THEIR LOOKS.

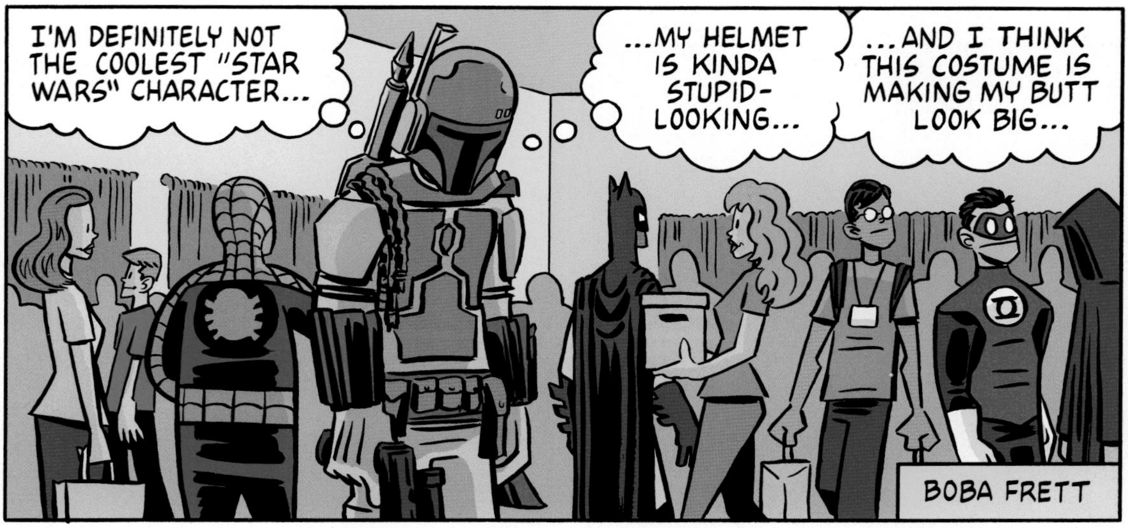
I'M DEFINITELY NOT THE COOLEST "STAR WARS" CHARACTER...
...MY HELMET IS KINDA STUPID-LOOKING...
...AND I THINK THIS COSTUME IS MAKING MY BUTT LOOK BIG...
BOBA FRETT

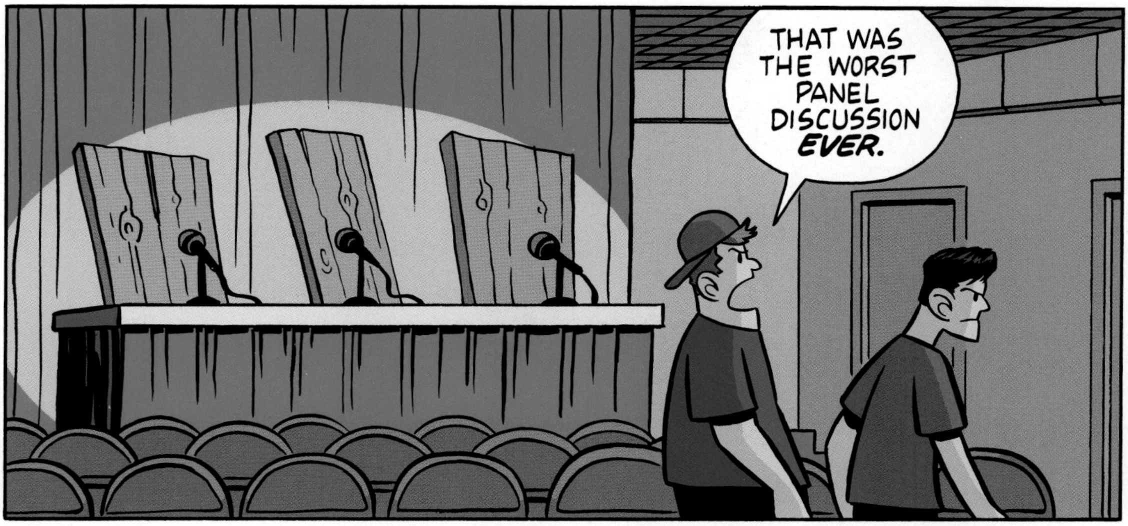
THAT WAS THE WORST PANEL DISCUSSION *EVER*.

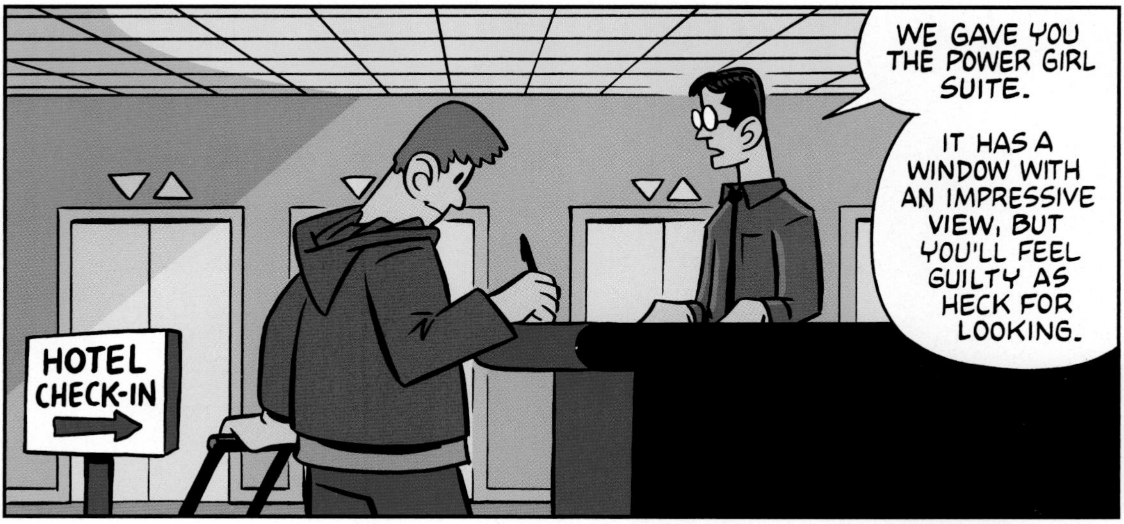
WE GAVE YOU THE POWER GIRL SUITE.
IT HAS A WINDOW WITH AN IMPRESSIVE VIEW, BUT YOU'LL FEEL GUILTY AS HECK FOR LOOKING.
HOTEL CHECK-IN

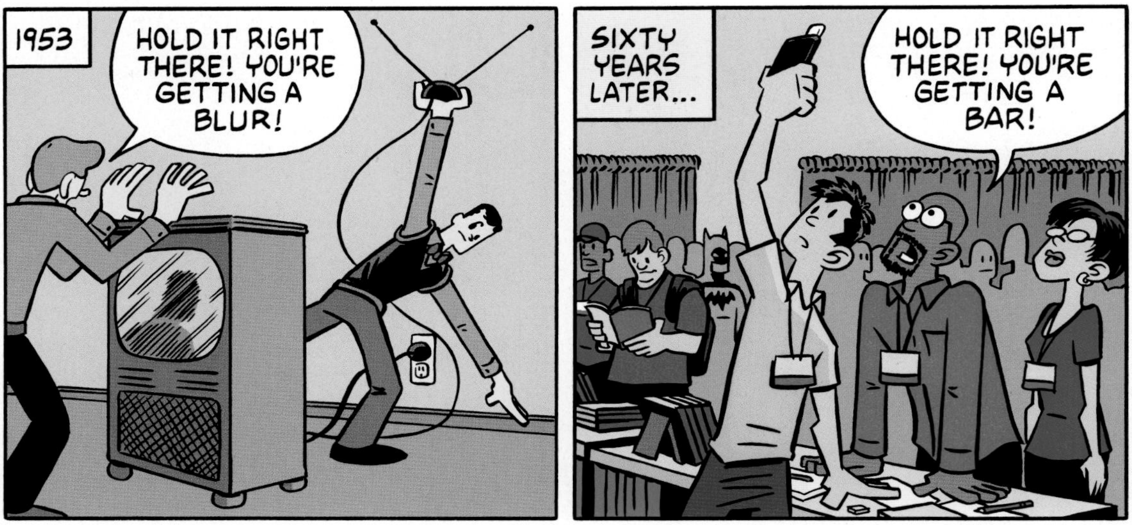
1953
HOLD IT RIGHT THERE! YOU'RE GETTING A BLUR!
SIXTY YEARS LATER...
HOLD IT RIGHT THERE! YOU'RE GETTING A BAR!

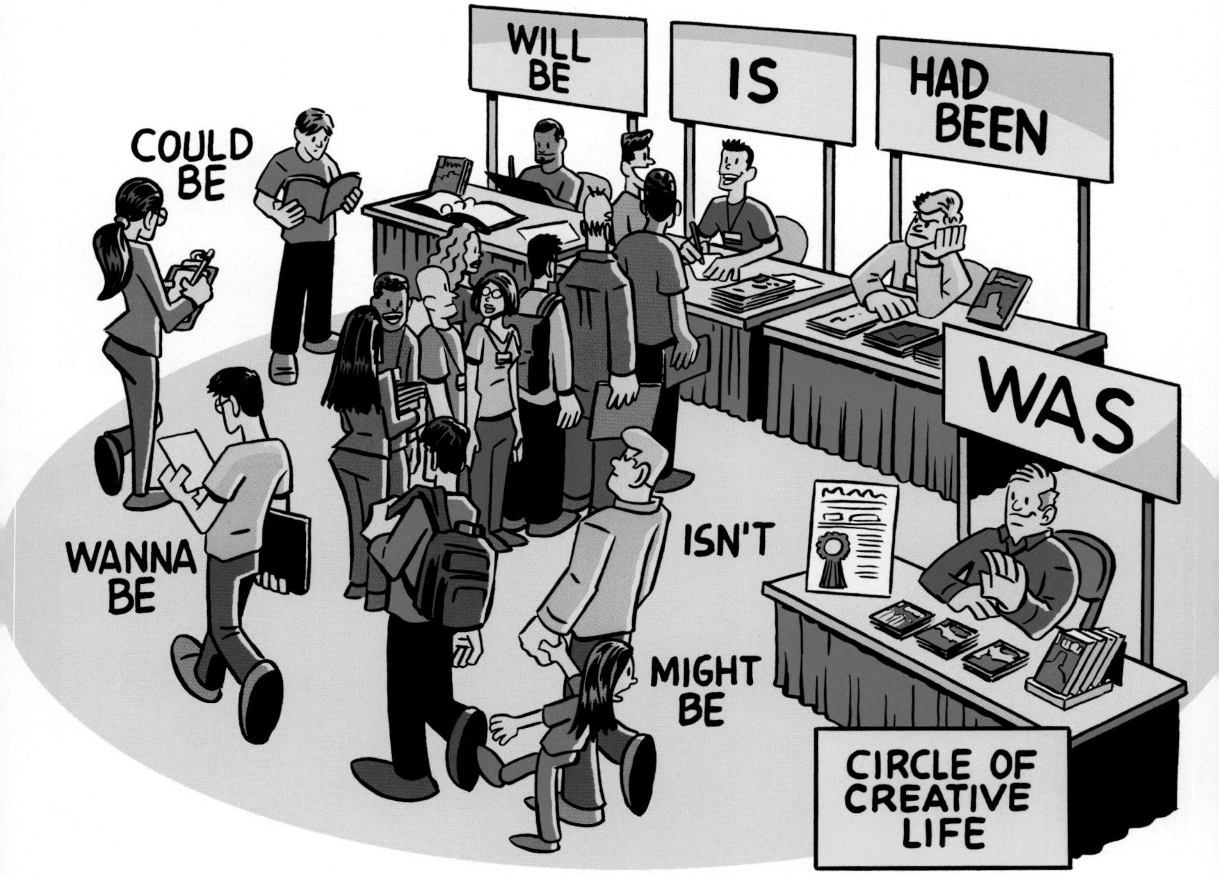
WILL BE
IS
HAD BEEN
WAS
COULD BE
WANNA BE
ISN'T
MIGHT BE
CIRCLE OF CREATIVE LIFE

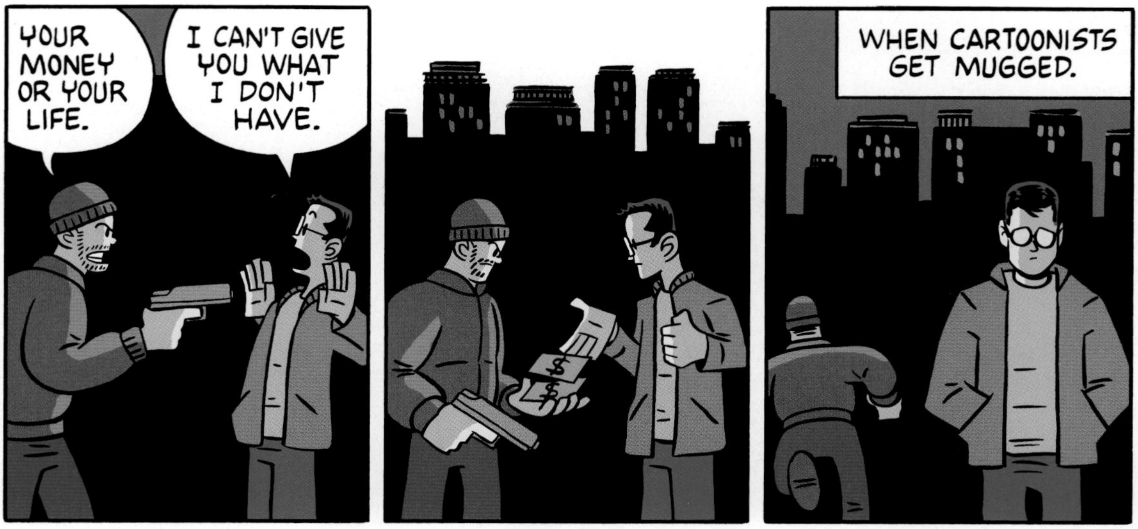
YOUR MONEY OR YOUR LIFE.
I CAN'T GIVE YOU WHAT I DON'T HAVE.
WHEN CARTOONISTS GET MUGGED.

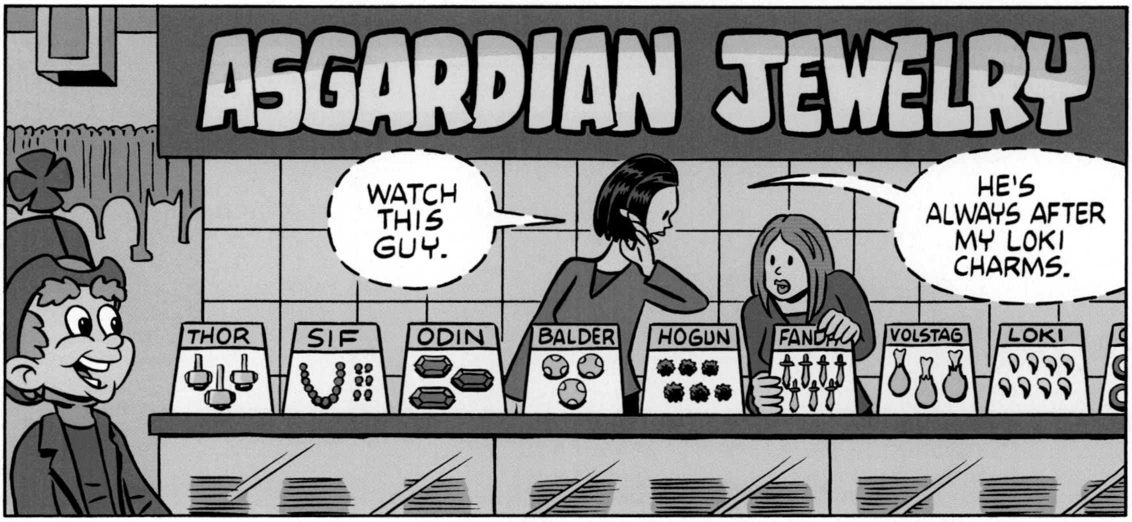
ASGARDIAN JEWELRY
WATCH THIS GUY.
HE'S ALWAYS AFTER MY LOKI CHARMS.
THOR
SIF
ODIN
BALDER
HOGUN
VOLSTAG
LOKI

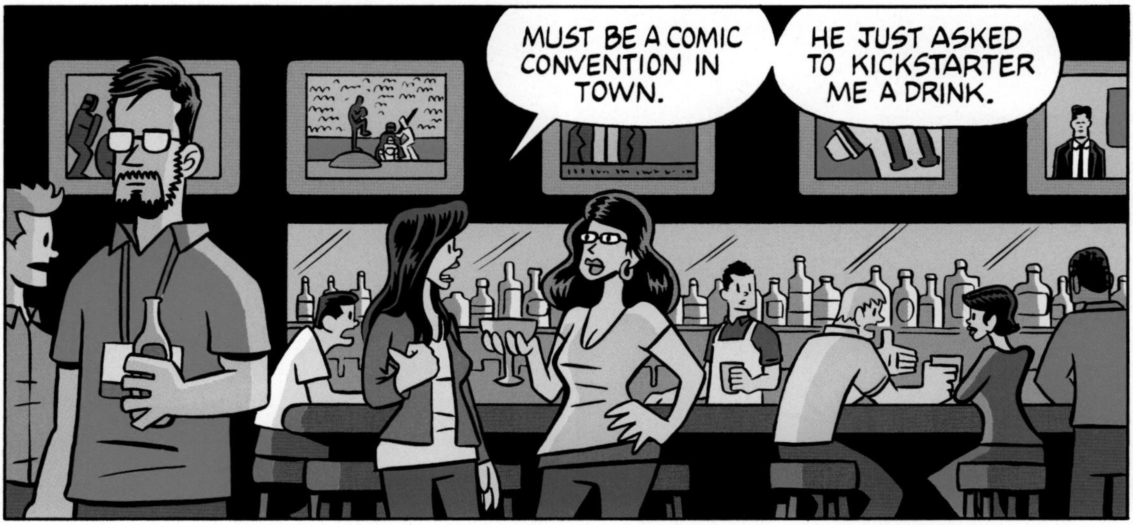
MUST BE A COMIC CONVENTION IN TOWN.
HE JUST ASKED TO KICKSTARTER ME A DRINK.

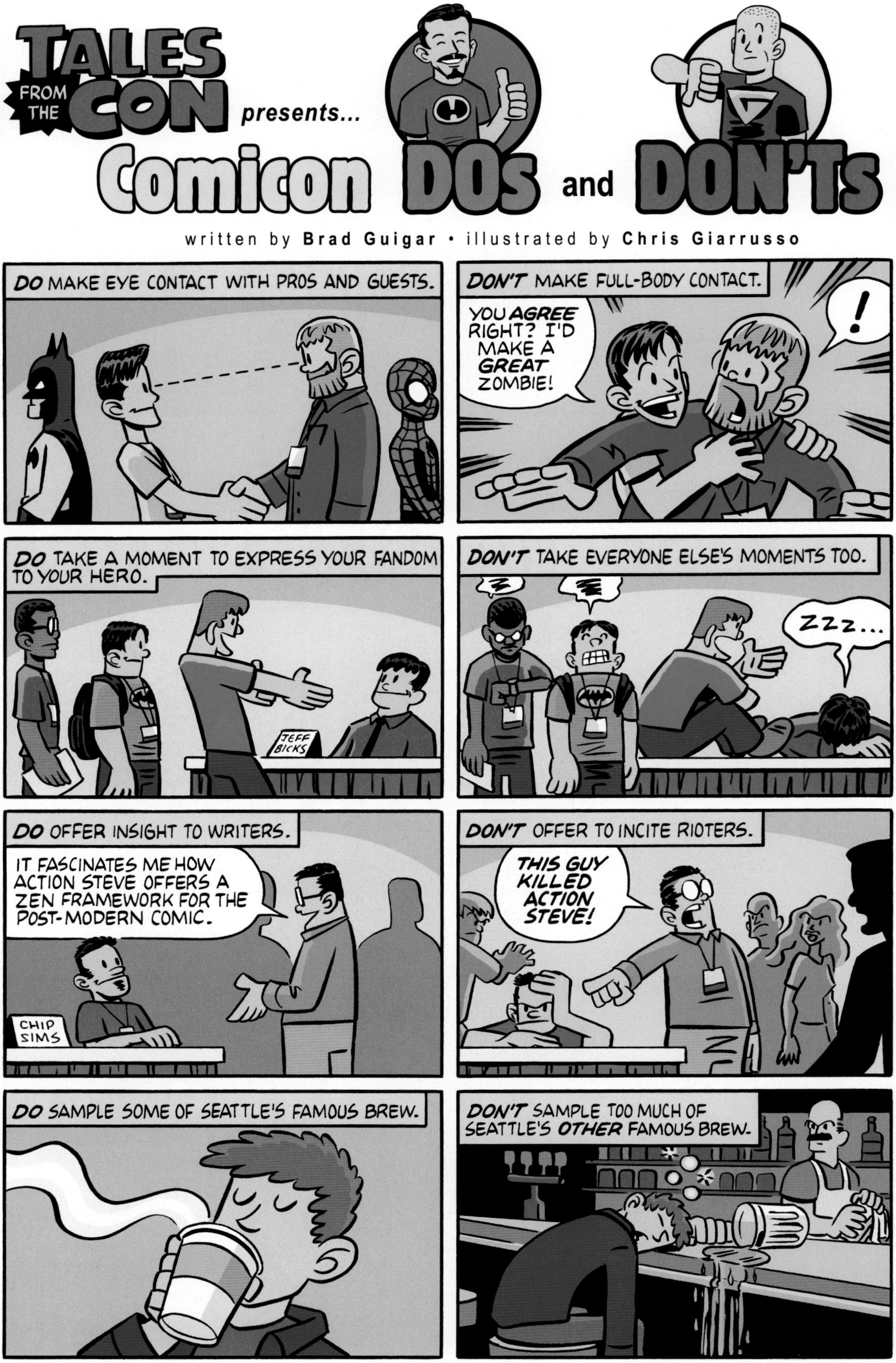
TALES FROM THE CON presents...
Comicon DOs and DON'Ts
written by Brad Guigar • illustrated by Chris Giarrusso
DO MAKE EYE CONTACT WITH PROS AND GUESTS.
DON'T MAKE FULL-BODY CONTACT.
YOU AGREE RIGHT? I'D MAKE A GREAT ZOMBIE!
!
DO TAKE A MOMENT TO EXPRESS YOUR FANDOM TO YOUR HERO.
JEFF BICKS
DON'T TAKE EVERYONE ELSE'S MOMENTS TOO.
ZZZ...
DO OFFER INSIGHT TO WRITERS.
IT FASCINATES ME HOW ACTION STEVE OFFERS A ZEN FRAMEWORK FOR THE POST-MODERN COMIC.
CHIP SIMS
DON'T OFFER TO INCITE RIOTERS.
THIS GUY KILLED ACTION STEVE!
DO SAMPLE SOME OF SEATTLE'S FAMOUS BREW.
DON'T SAMPLE TOO MUCH OF SEATTLE'S OTHER FAMOUS BREW.

# Common ComiConversation

by Chris Giarrusso

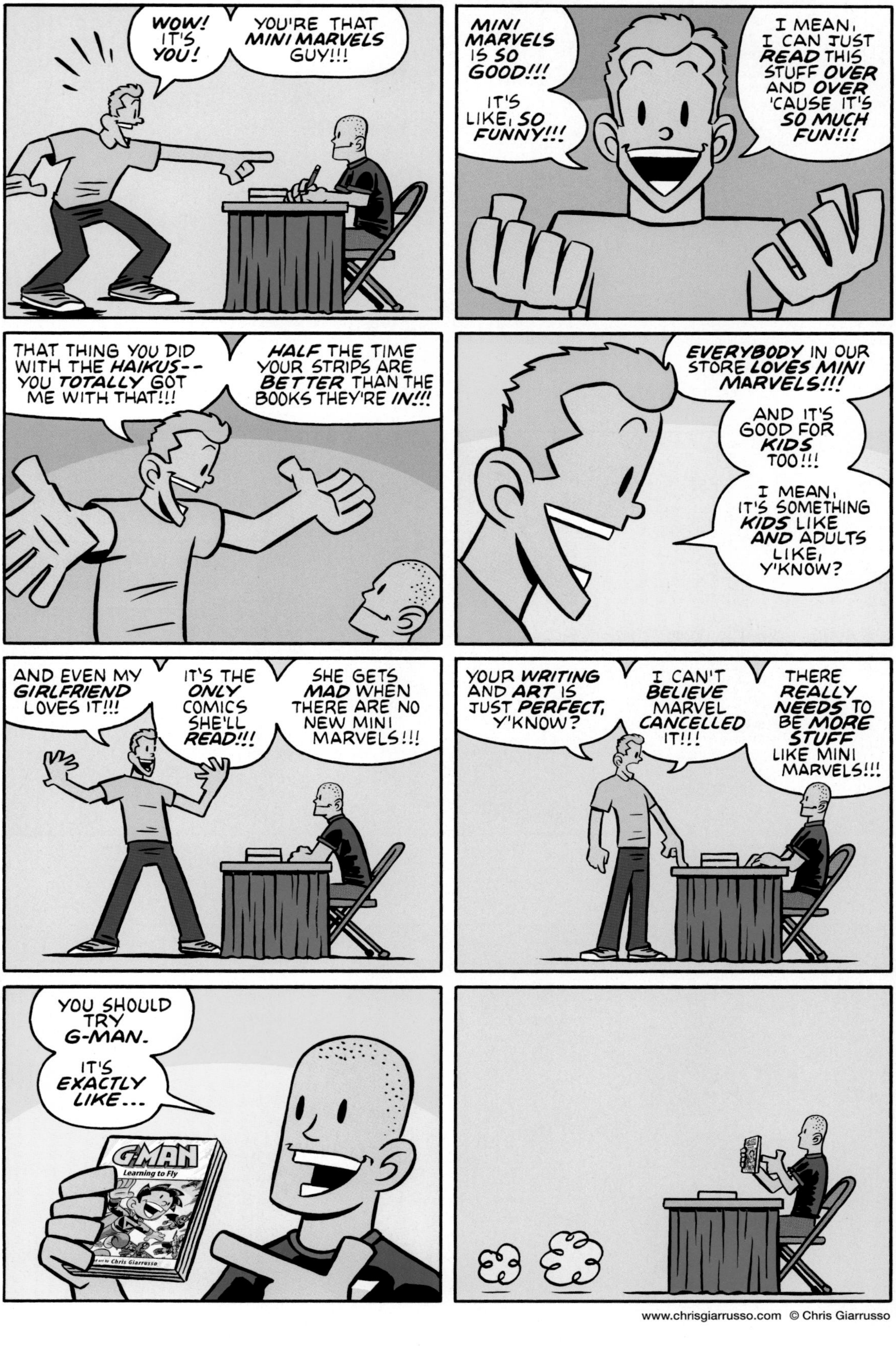

WOW! IT'S YOU!
YOU'RE THAT MINI MARVELS GUY!!!
MINI MARVELS IS SO GOOD!!!
IT'S LIKE, SO FUNNY!!!
I MEAN, I CAN JUST READ THIS STUFF OVER AND OVER 'CAUSE IT'S SO MUCH FUN!!!
THAT THING YOU DID WITH THE HAIKUS-- YOU TOTALLY GOT ME WITH THAT!!!
HALF THE TIME YOUR STRIPS ARE BETTER THAN THE BOOKS THEY'RE IN!!!
EVERYBODY IN OUR STORE LOVES MINI MARVELS!!!
AND IT'S GOOD FOR KIDS TOO!!!
I MEAN, IT'S SOMETHING KIDS LIKE AND ADULTS LIKE, Y'KNOW?
AND EVEN MY GIRLFRIEND LOVES IT!!!
IT'S THE ONLY COMICS SHE'LL READ!!!
SHE GETS MAD WHEN THERE ARE NO NEW MINI MARVELS!!!
YOUR WRITING AND ART IS JUST PERFECT, Y'KNOW?
I CAN'T BELIEVE MARVEL CANCELLED IT!!!
THERE REALLY NEEDS TO BE MORE STUFF LIKE MINI MARVELS!!!
YOU SHOULD TRY G-MAN.
IT'S EXACTLY LIKE...
G-MAN
Learning to Fly
Chris Giarrusso

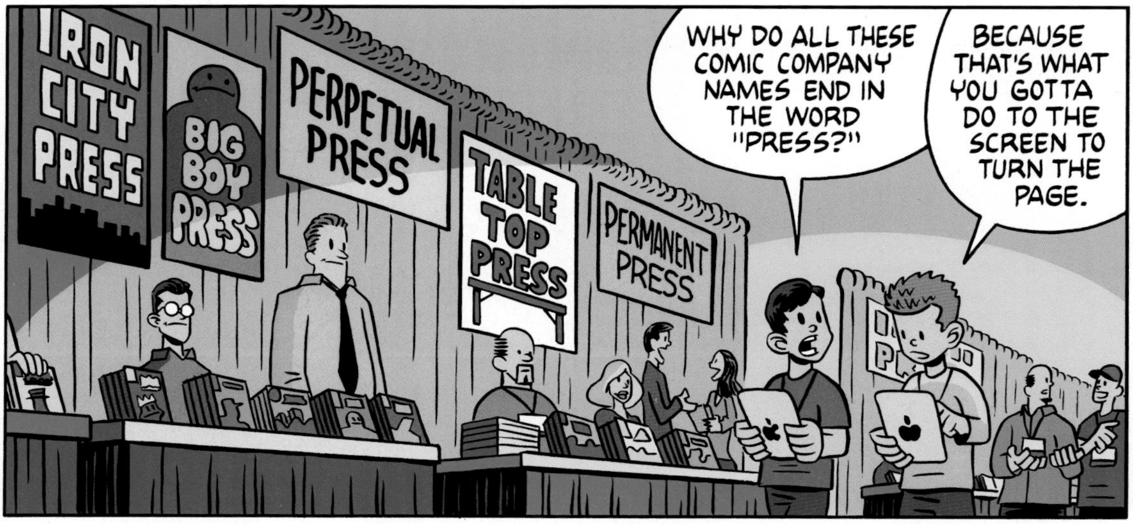
IRON CITY PRESS
BIG BOY PRESS
PERPETUAL PRESS
TABLE TOP PRESS
PERMANENT PRESS
WHY DO ALL THESE COMIC COMPANY NAMES END IN THE WORD "PRESS?"
BECAUSE THAT'S WHAT YOU GOTTA DO TO THE SCREEN TO TURN THE PAGE.

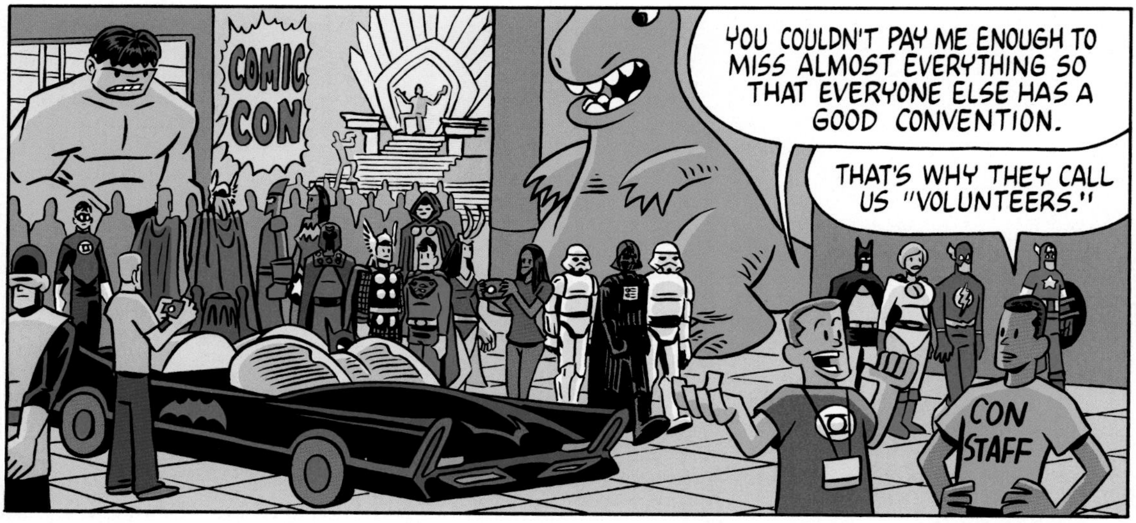
COMIC CON
YOU COULDN'T PAY ME ENOUGH TO MISS ALMOST EVERYTHING SO THAT EVERYONE ELSE HAS A GOOD CONVENTION.
THAT'S WHY THEY CALL US "VOLUNTEERS."
CON STAFF

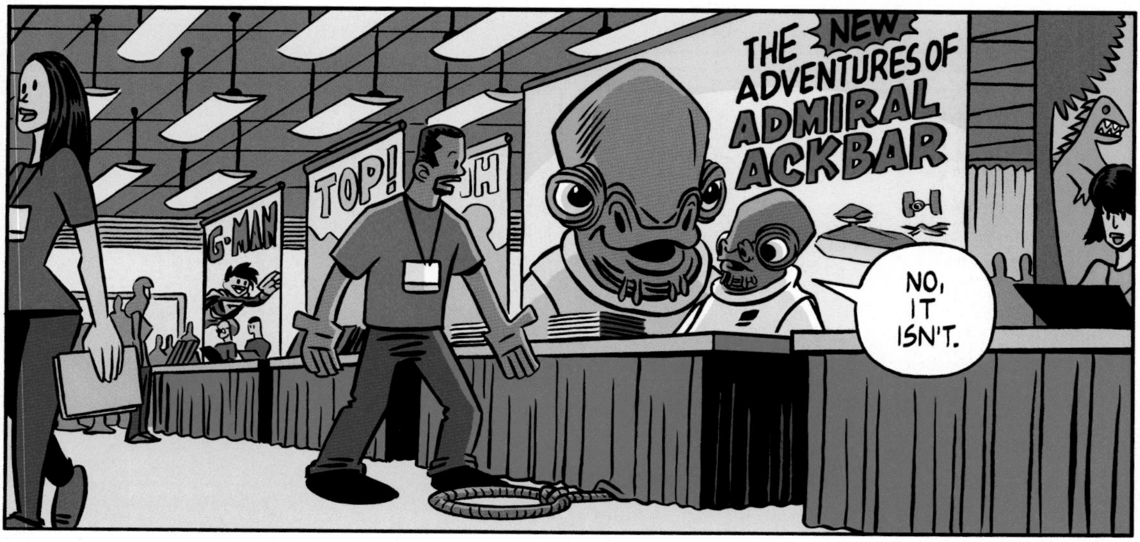
G-MAN
TOP!
THE NEW ADVENTURES OF ADMIRAL ACKBAR
NO, IT ISN'T.

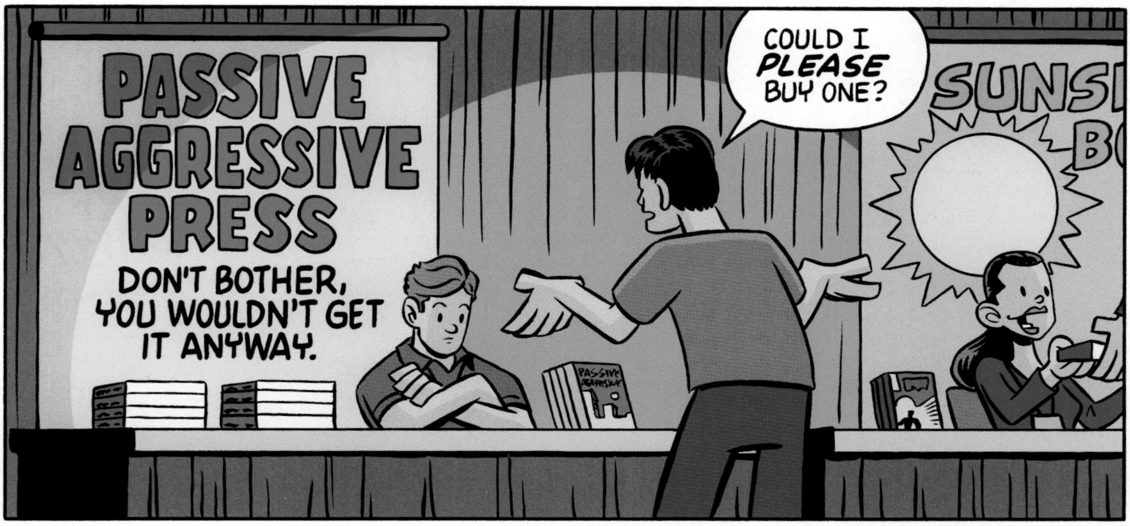
PASSIVE AGGRESSIVE PRESS
DON'T BOTHER, YOU WOULDN'T GET IT ANYWAY.
COULD I *PLEASE* BUY ONE?

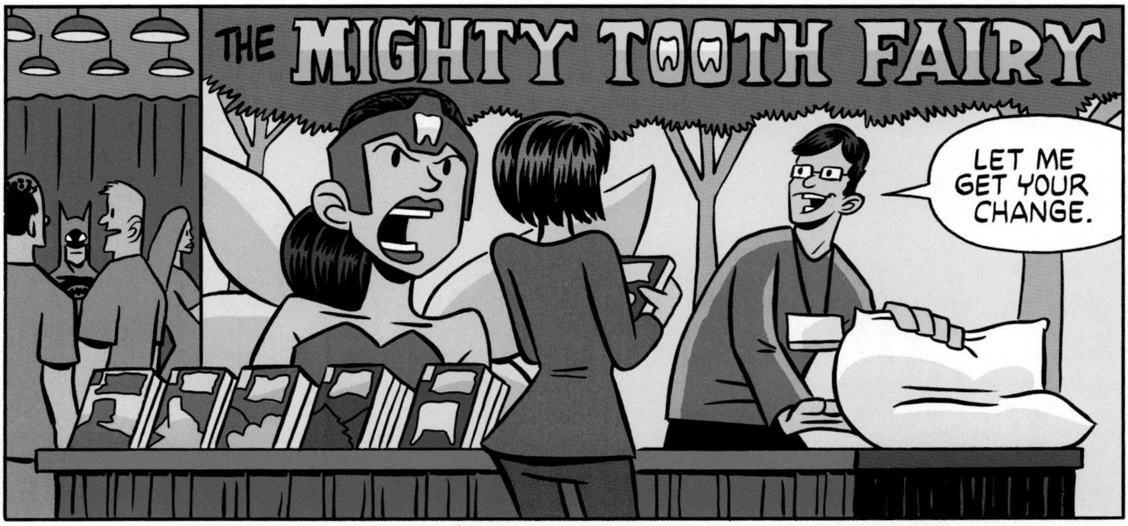
THE MIGHTY TOOTH FAIRY
LET ME GET YOUR CHANGE.

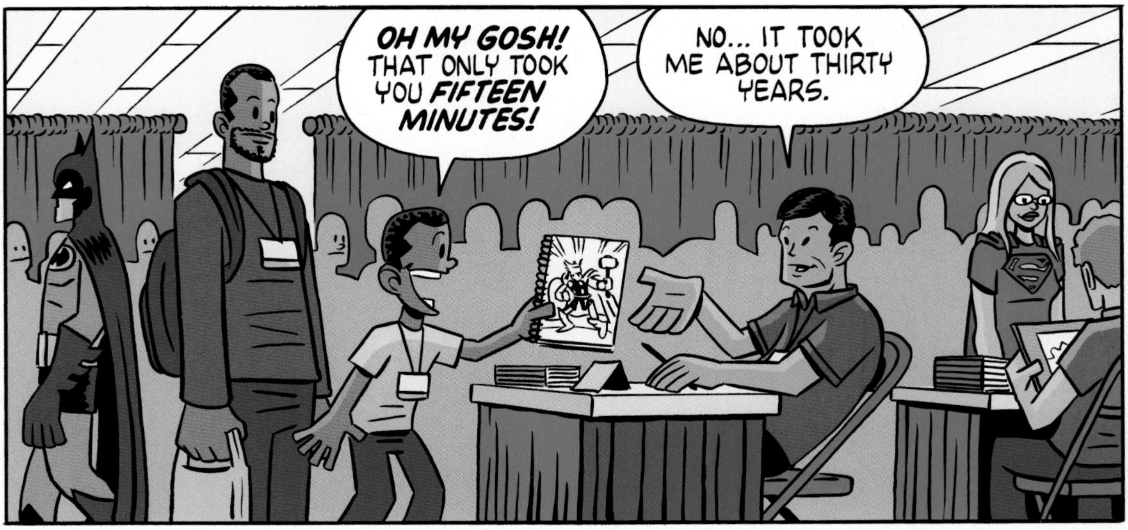
*OH MY GOSH!* THAT ONLY TOOK YOU *FIFTEEN MINUTES!*
NO... IT TOOK ME ABOUT THIRTY YEARS.

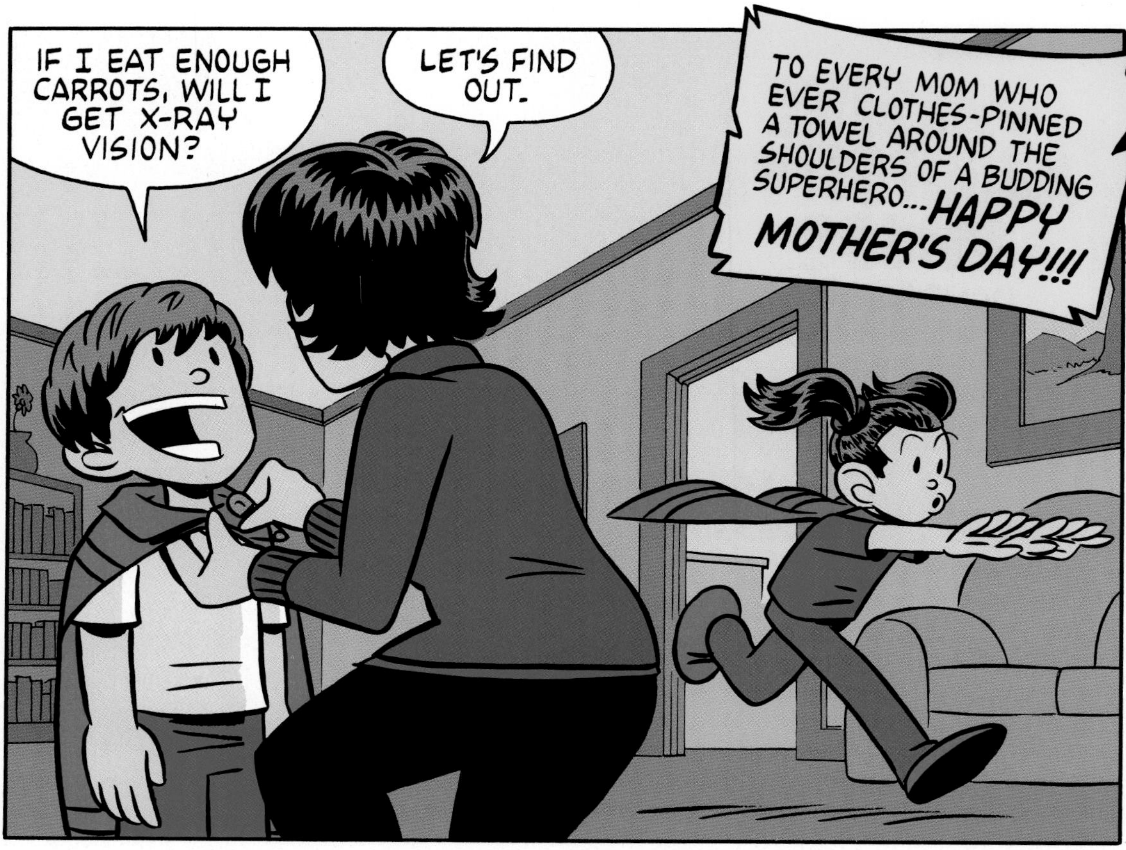
IF I EAT ENOUGH CARROTS, WILL I GET X-RAY VISION?
LET'S FIND OUT.
TO EVERY MOM WHO EVER CLOTHES-PINNED A TOWEL AROUND THE SHOULDERS OF A BUDDING SUPERHERO... HAPPY MOTHER'S DAY!!!

# CELEBRATE INDEPENDENTS DAY!

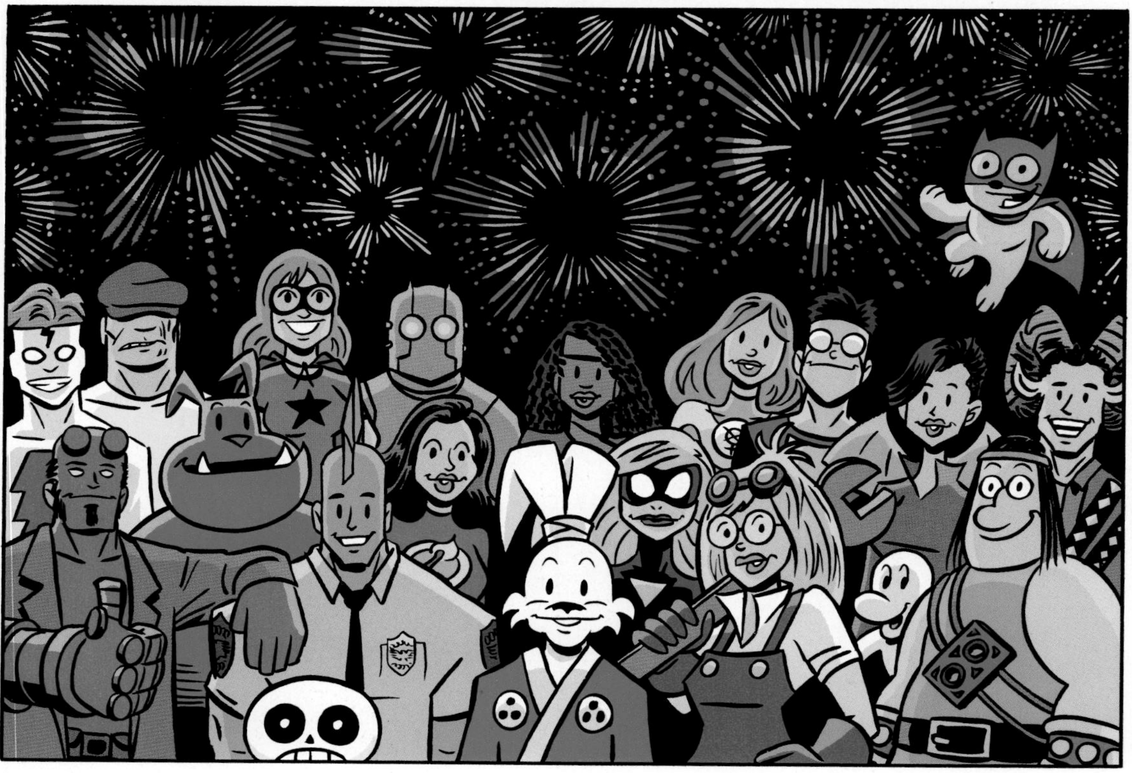

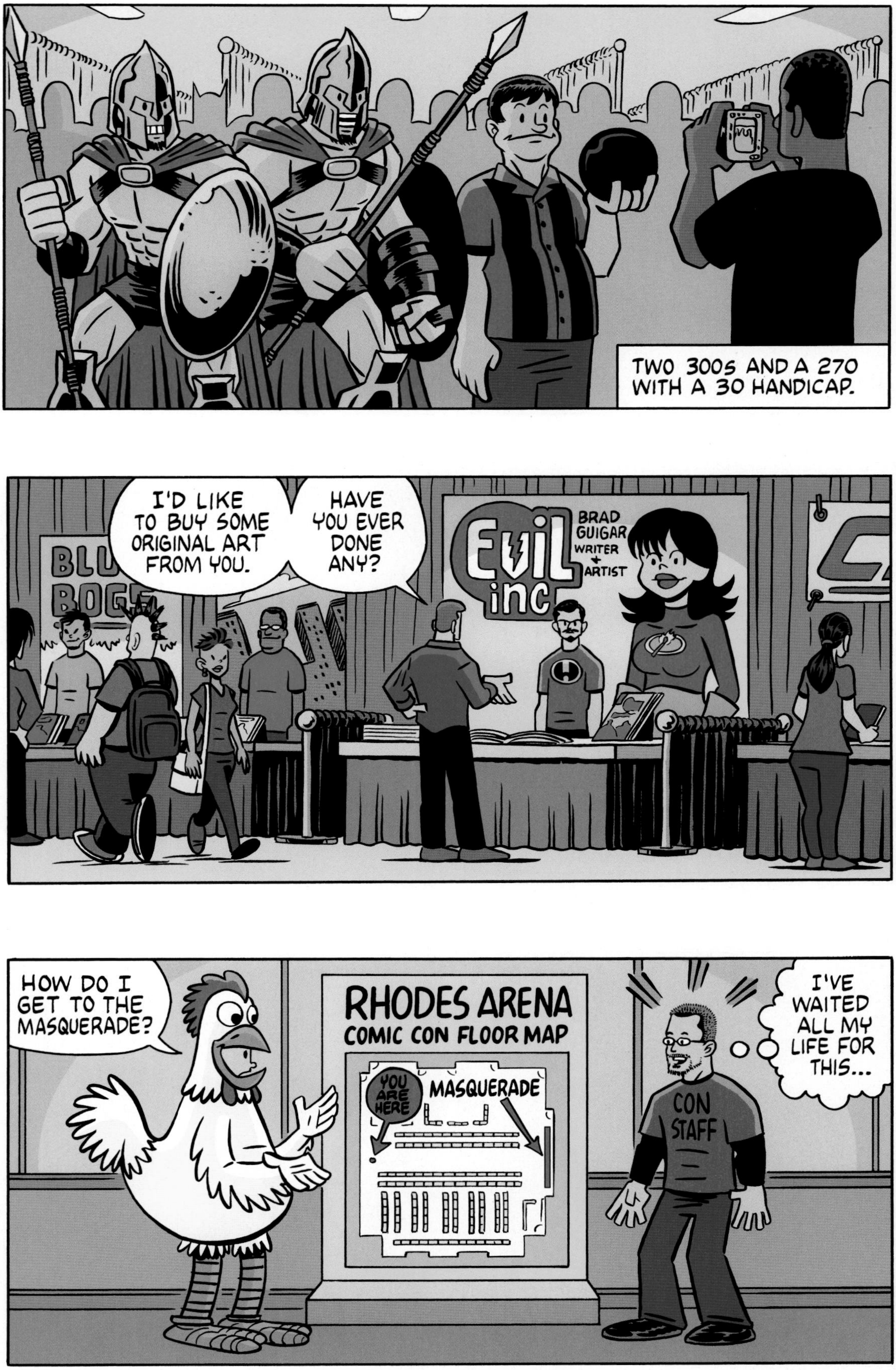
TWO 300S AND A 270 WITH A 30 HANDICAP.
I'D LIKE TO BUY SOME ORIGINAL ART FROM YOU.
HAVE YOU EVER DONE ANY?
Evil inc
BRAD GUIGAR WRITER + ARTIST
HOW DO I GET TO THE MASQUERADE?
RHODES ARENA
COMIC CON FLOOR MAP
YOU ARE HERE
MASQUERADE
CON STAFF
I'VE WAITED ALL MY LIFE FOR THIS...

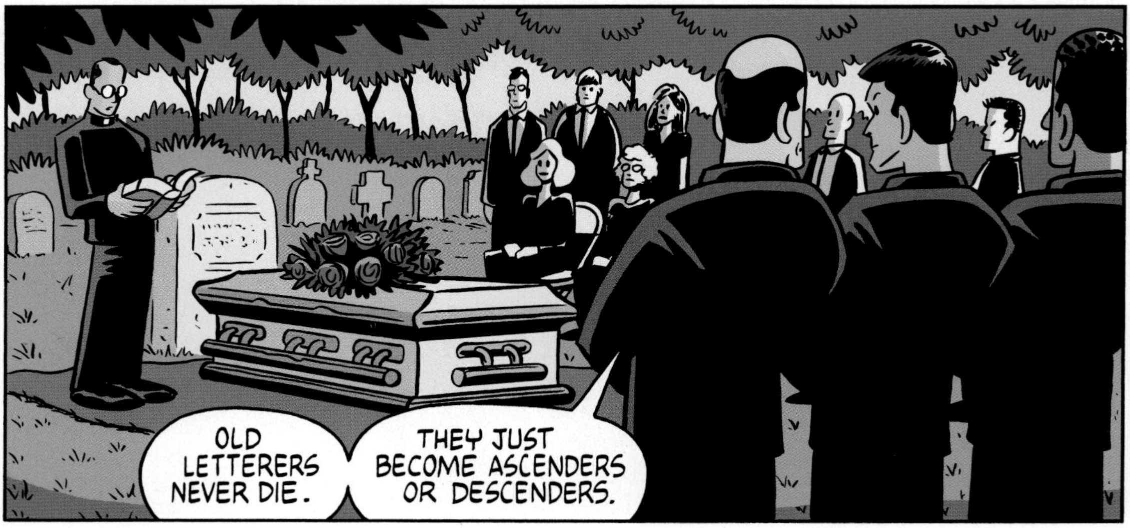
OLD LETTERERS NEVER DIE.
THEY JUST BECOME ASCENDERS OR DESCENDERS.

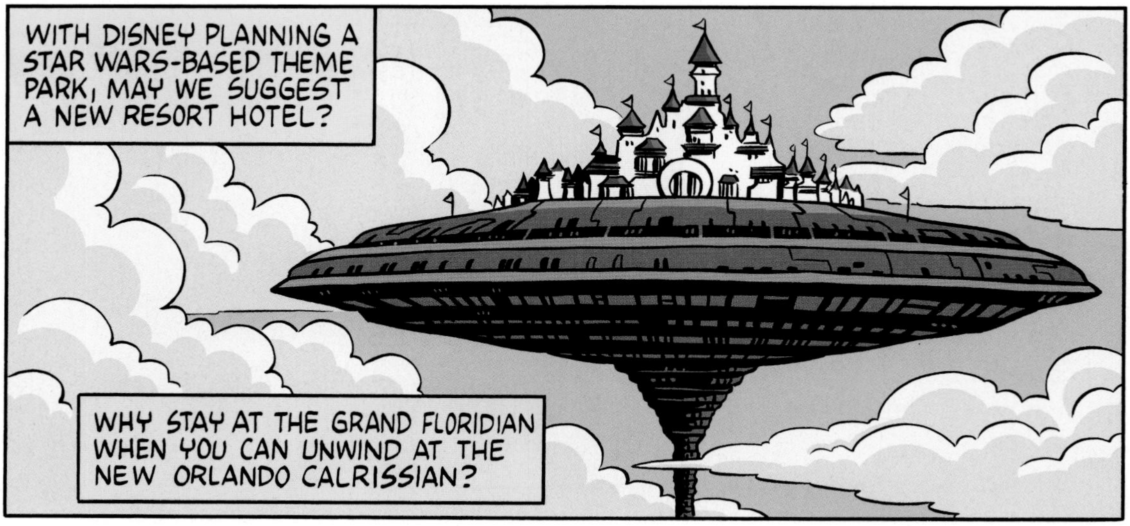
WITH DISNEY PLANNING A STAR WARS-BASED THEME PARK, MAY WE SUGGEST A NEW RESORT HOTEL?
WHY STAY AT THE GRAND FLORIDIAN WHEN YOU CAN UNWIND AT THE NEW ORLANDO CALRISSIAN?

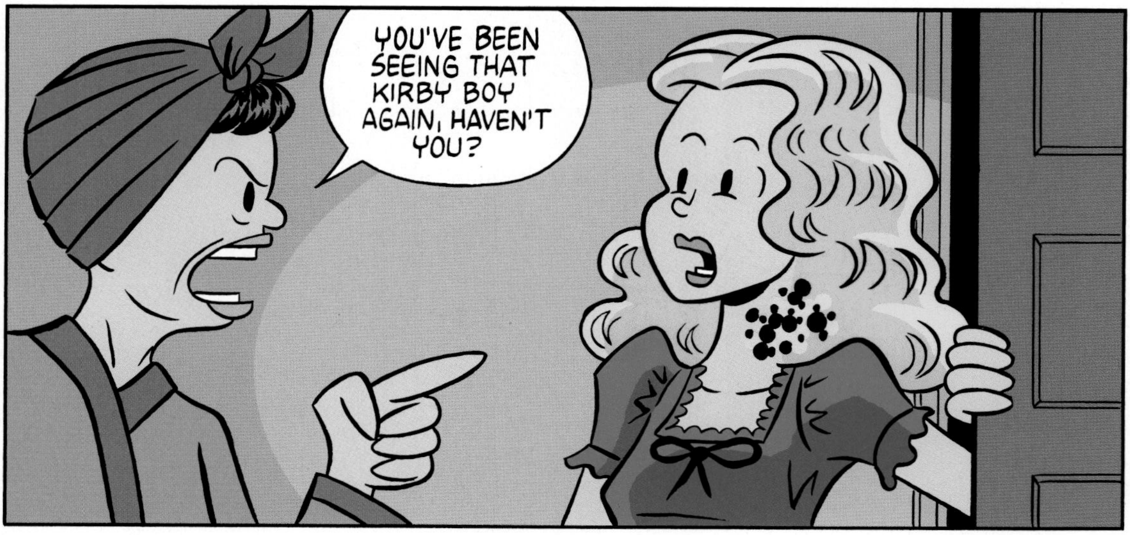
YOU'VE BEEN SEEING THAT KIRBY BOY AGAIN, HAVEN'T YOU?

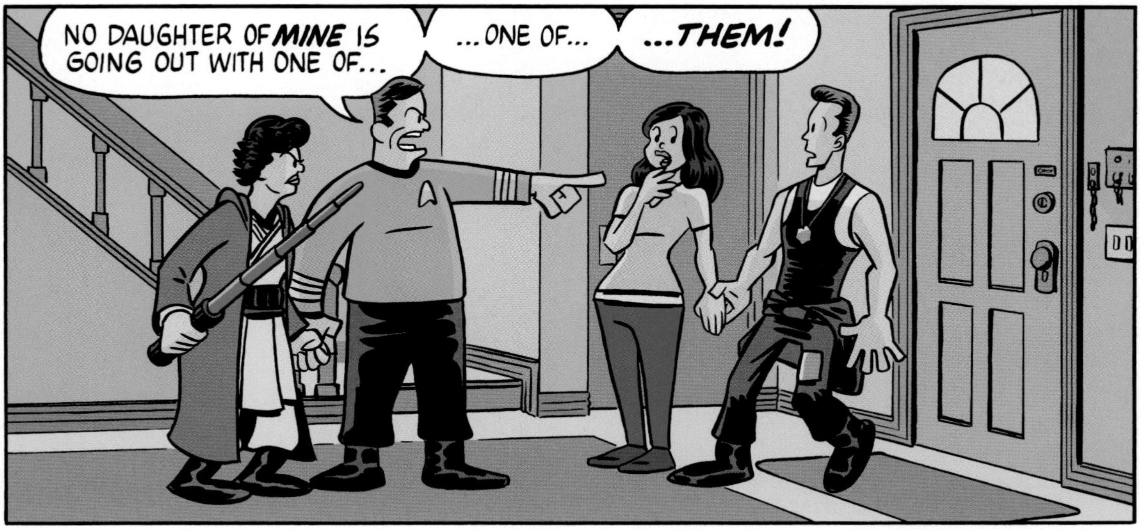
NO DAUGHTER OF *MINE* IS GOING OUT WITH ONE OF...
...ONE OF...
***...THEM!***

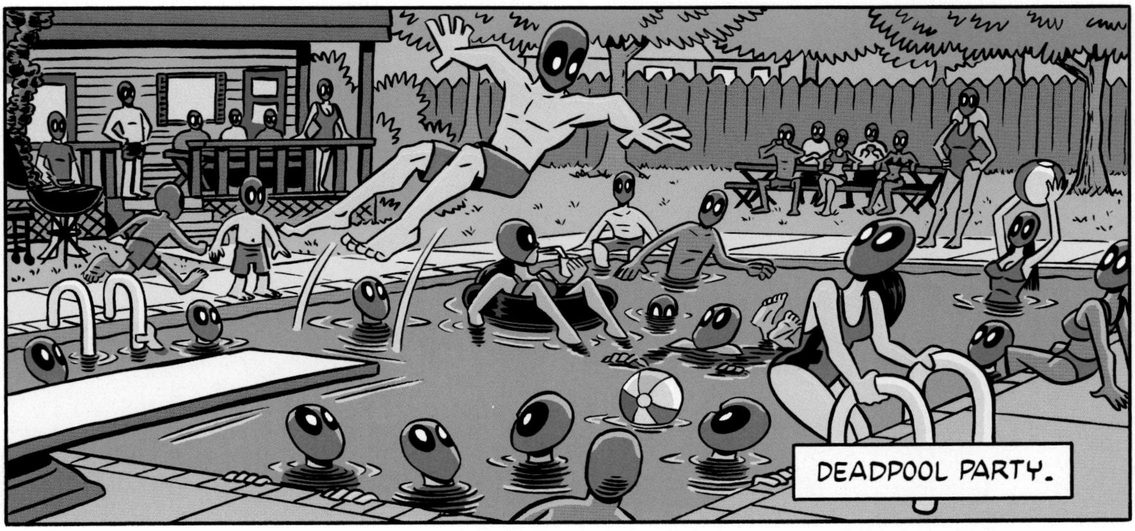
DEADPOOL PARTY.

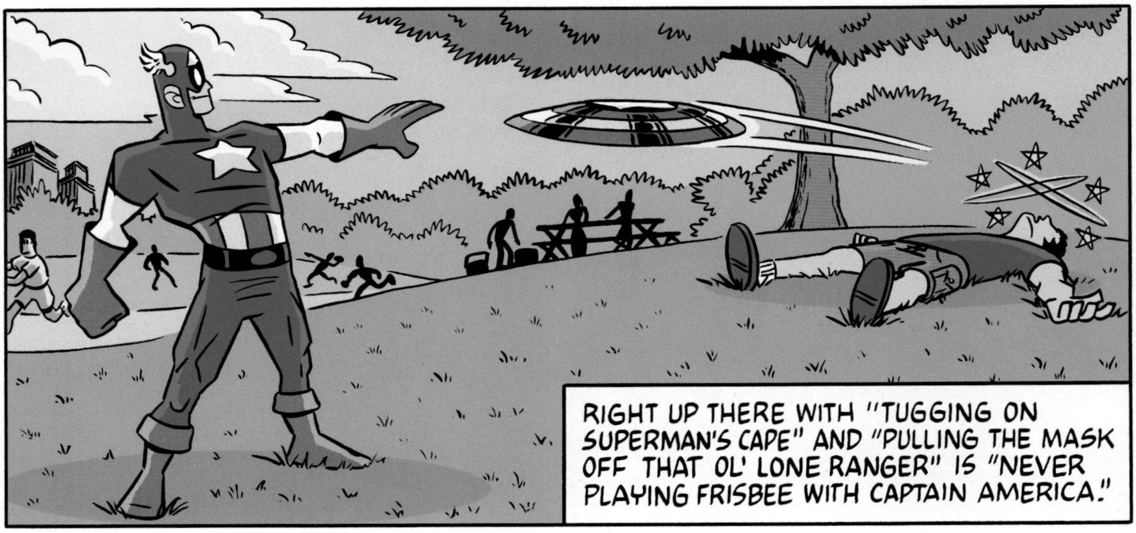
RIGHT UP THERE WITH "TUGGING ON SUPERMAN'S CAPE" AND "PULLING THE MASK OFF THAT OL' LONE RANGER" IS "NEVER PLAYING FRISBEE WITH CAPTAIN AMERICA."

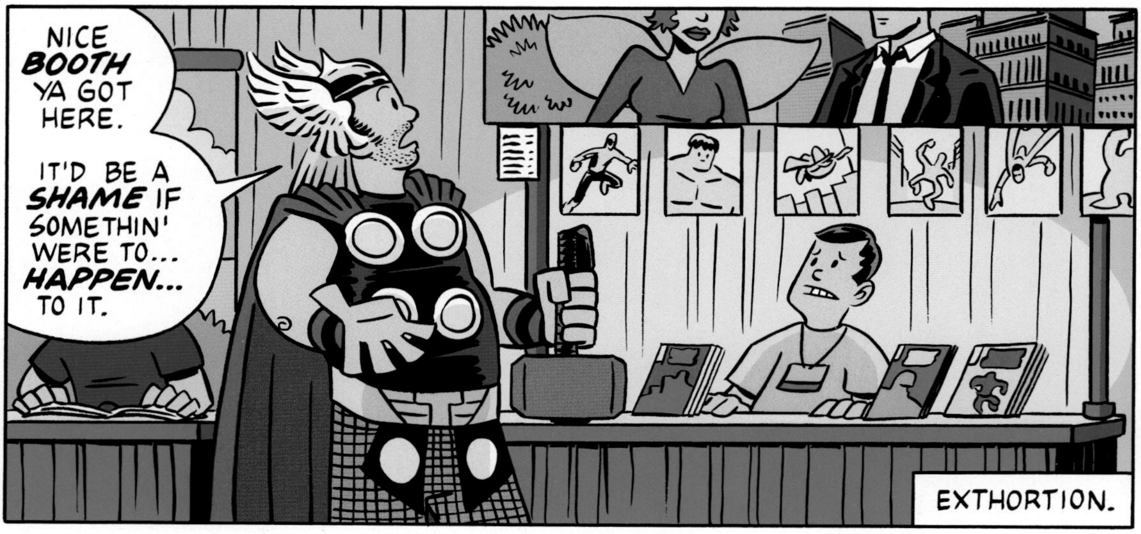
NICE **BOOTH** YA GOT HERE.
IT'D BE A **SHAME** IF SOMETHIN' WERE TO... **HAPPEN...** TO IT.
EXTHORTION.

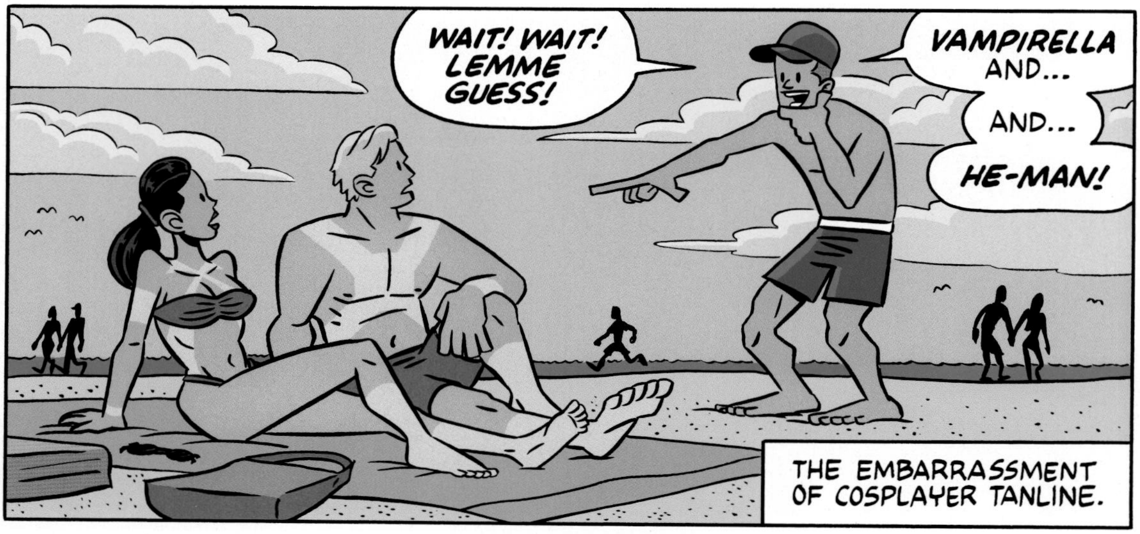
WAIT! WAIT! LEMME GUESS!
VAMPIRELLA AND...
AND...
HE-MAN!
THE EMBARRASSMENT OF COSPLAYER TANLINE.

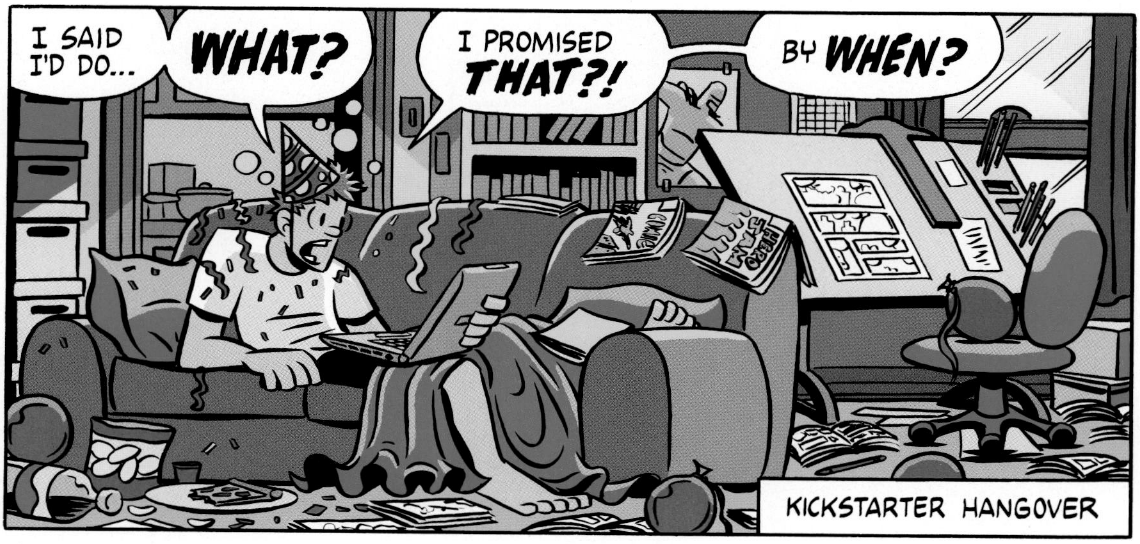
I SAID I'D DO...
**WHAT?**
I PROMISED **THAT?!**
BY **WHEN?**
KICKSTARTER HANGOVER

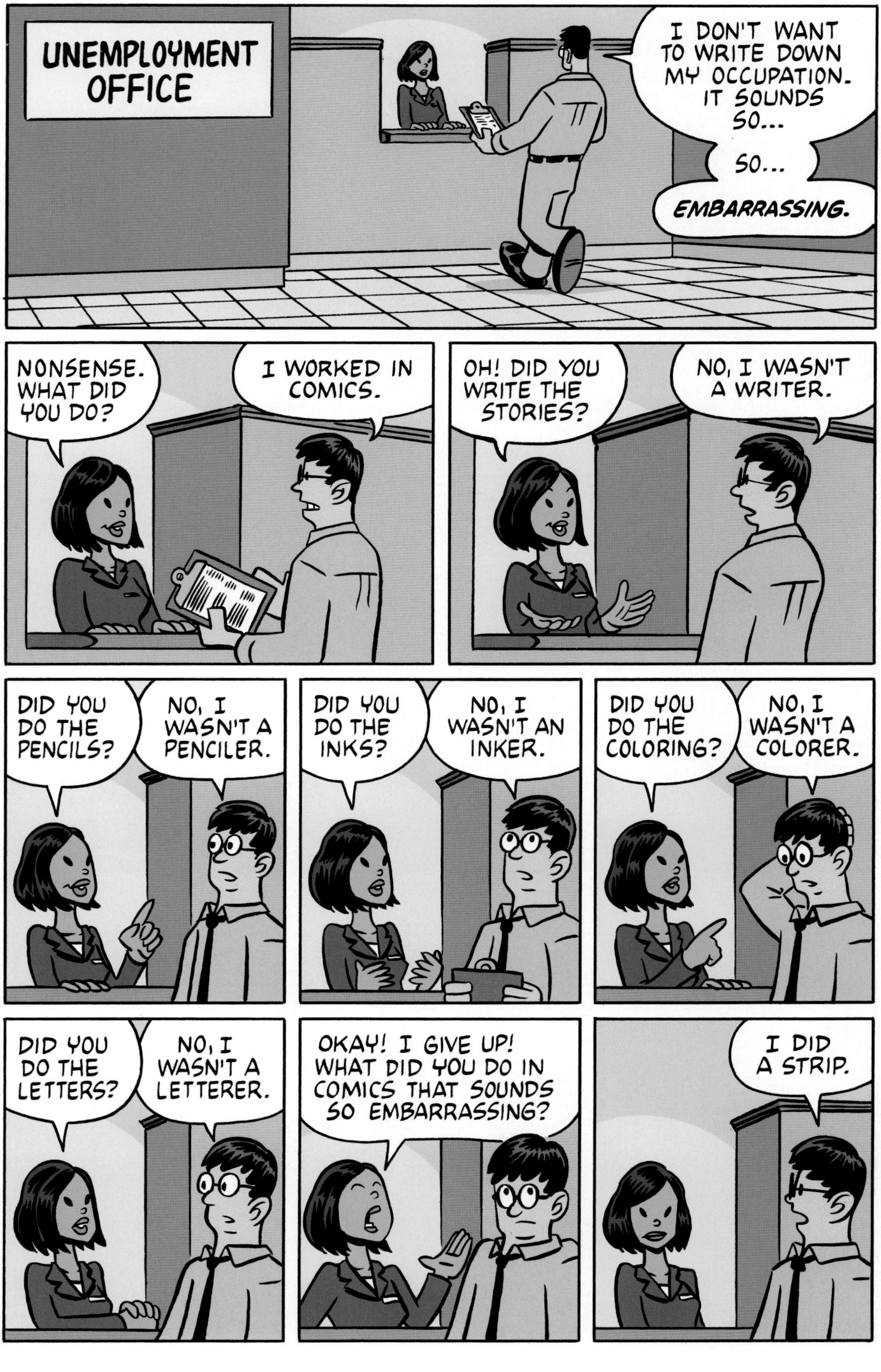
UNEMPLOYMENT OFFICE
I DON'T WANT TO WRITE DOWN MY OCCUPATION. IT SOUNDS SO...
SO...
EMBARRASSING.
NONSENSE. WHAT DID YOU DO?
I WORKED IN COMICS.
OH! DID YOU WRITE THE STORIES?
NO, I WASN'T A WRITER.
DID YOU DO THE PENCILS?
NO, I WASN'T A PENCILER.
DID YOU DO THE INKS?
NO, I WASN'T AN INKER.
DID YOU DO THE COLORING?
NO, I WASN'T A COLORER.
DID YOU DO THE LETTERS?
NO, I WASN'T A LETTERER.
OKAY! I GIVE UP! WHAT DID YOU DO IN COMICS THAT SOUNDS SO EMBARRASSING?
I DID A STRIP.

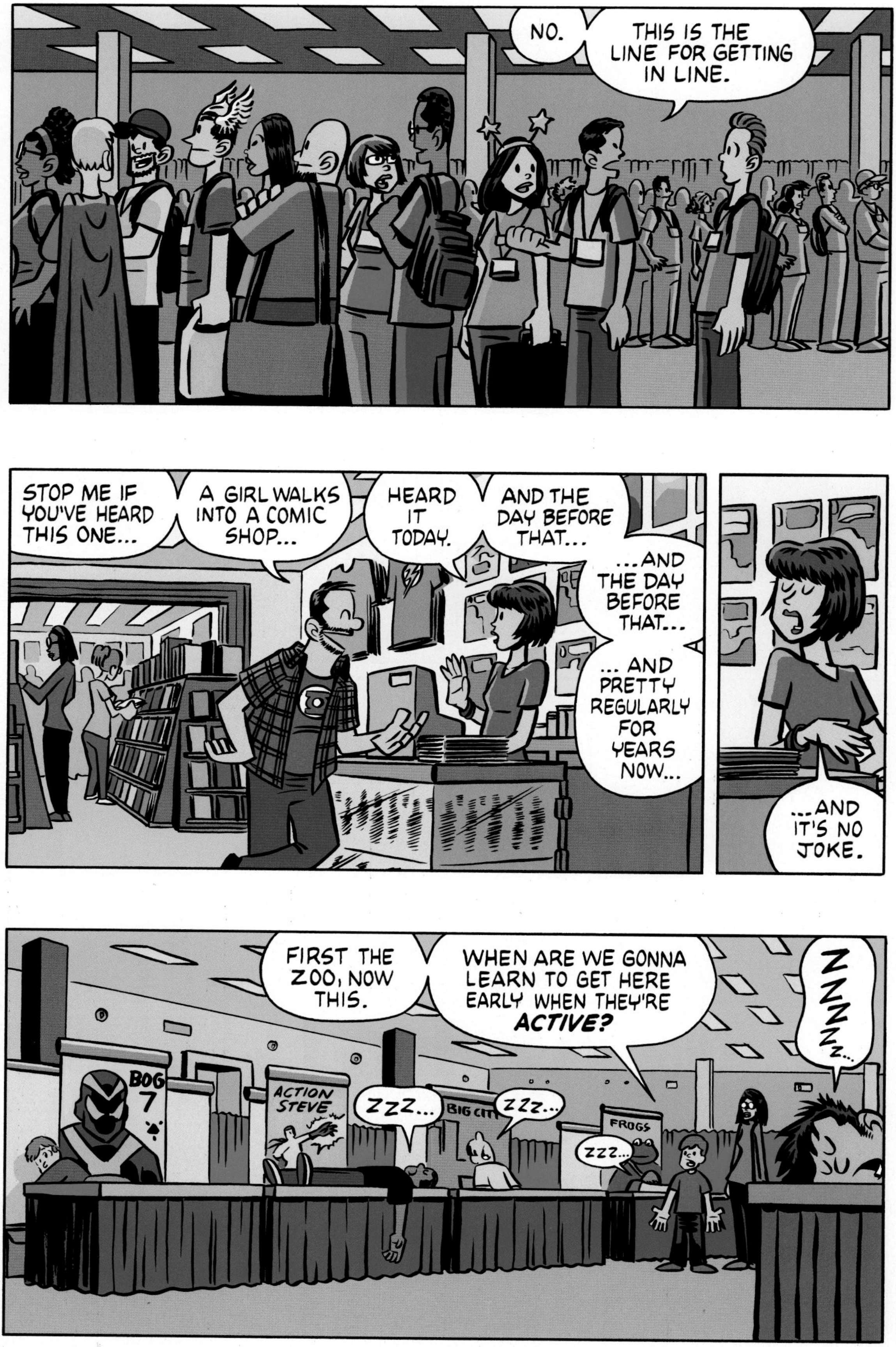
NO.
THIS IS THE LINE FOR GETTING IN LINE.
STOP ME IF YOU'VE HEARD THIS ONE...
A GIRL WALKS INTO A COMIC SHOP...
HEARD IT TODAY.
AND THE DAY BEFORE THAT...
...AND THE DAY BEFORE THAT...
... AND PRETTY REGULARLY FOR YEARS NOW...
...AND IT'S NO JOKE.
FIRST THE ZOO, NOW THIS.
WHEN ARE WE GONNA LEARN TO GET HERE EARLY WHEN THEY'RE *ACTIVE?*
ZZZZz...
BOG 7
ACTION STEVE
ZZZ...
BIG CITY
ZZz...
FROGS
ZZZ...

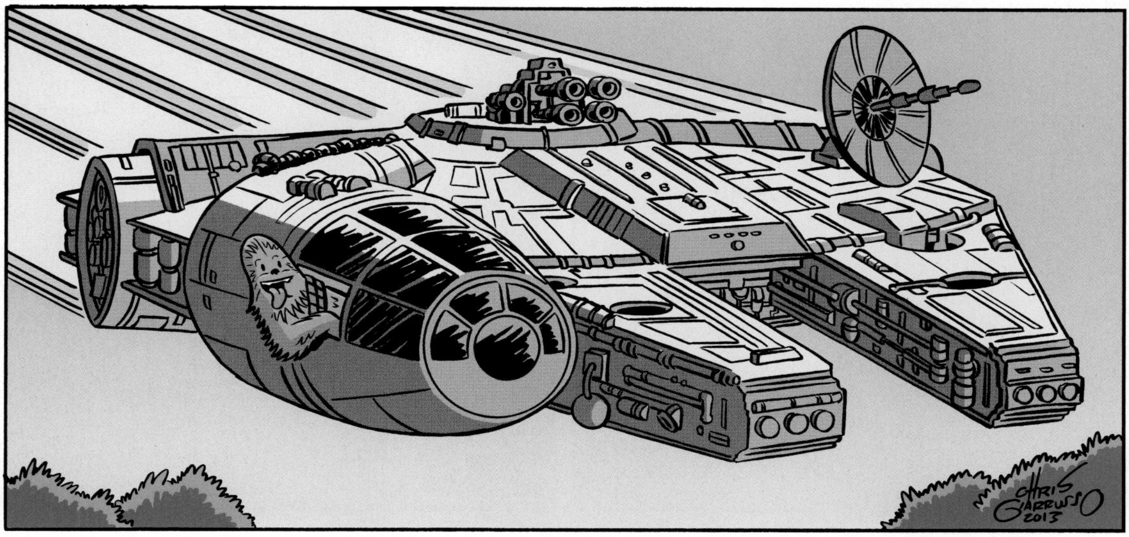
CHRIS GIARRUSSO 2013

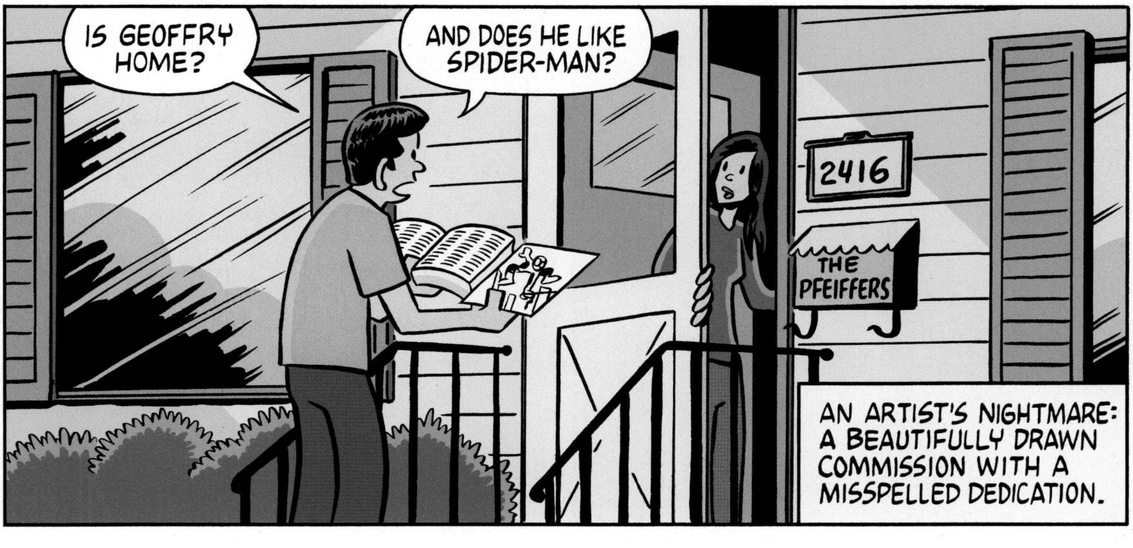
IS GEOFFRY HOME?
AND DOES HE LIKE SPIDER-MAN?
2416
THE PFEIFFERS
AN ARTIST'S NIGHTMARE: A BEAUTIFULLY DRAWN COMMISSION WITH A MISSPELLED DEDICATION.

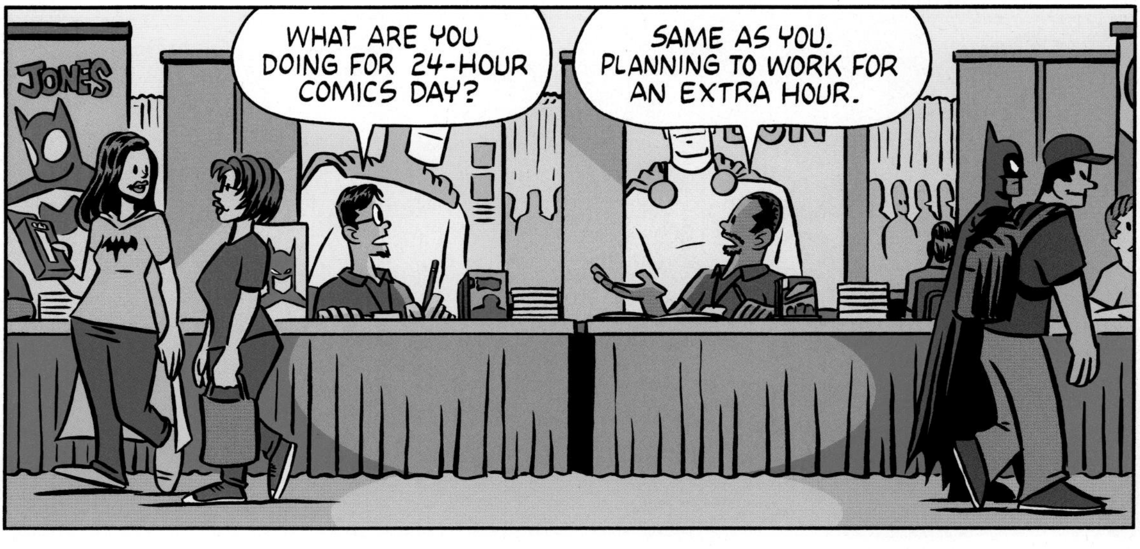
JONES
WHAT ARE YOU DOING FOR 24-HOUR COMICS DAY?
SAME AS YOU. PLANNING TO WORK FOR AN EXTRA HOUR.

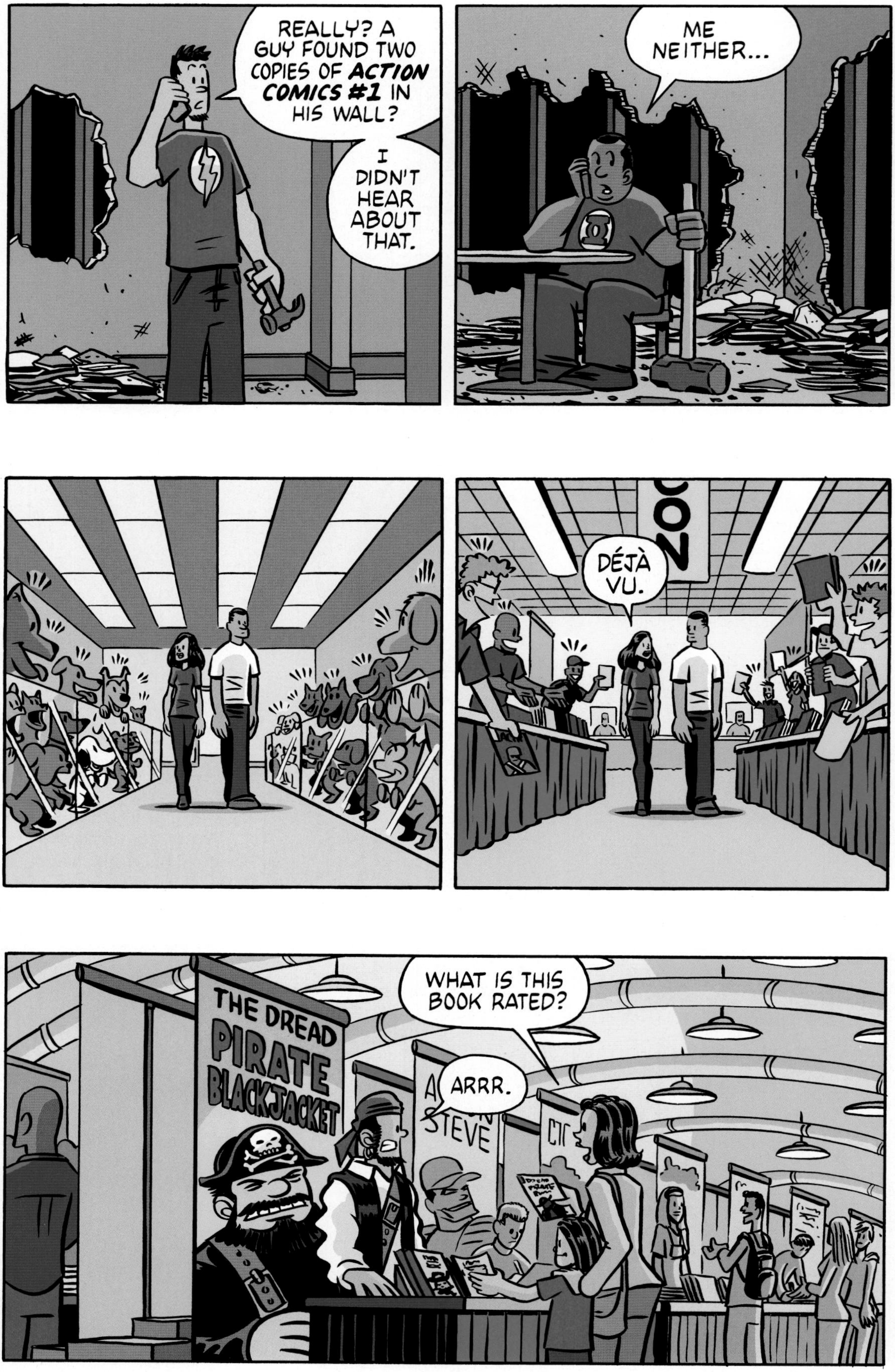
REALLY? A GUY FOUND TWO COPIES OF ACTION COMICS #1 IN HIS WALL?
I DIDN'T HEAR ABOUT THAT.
ME NEITHER...
DÉJÀ VU.
THE DREAD PIRATE BLACKJACKET
WHAT IS THIS BOOK RATED?
ARRR.

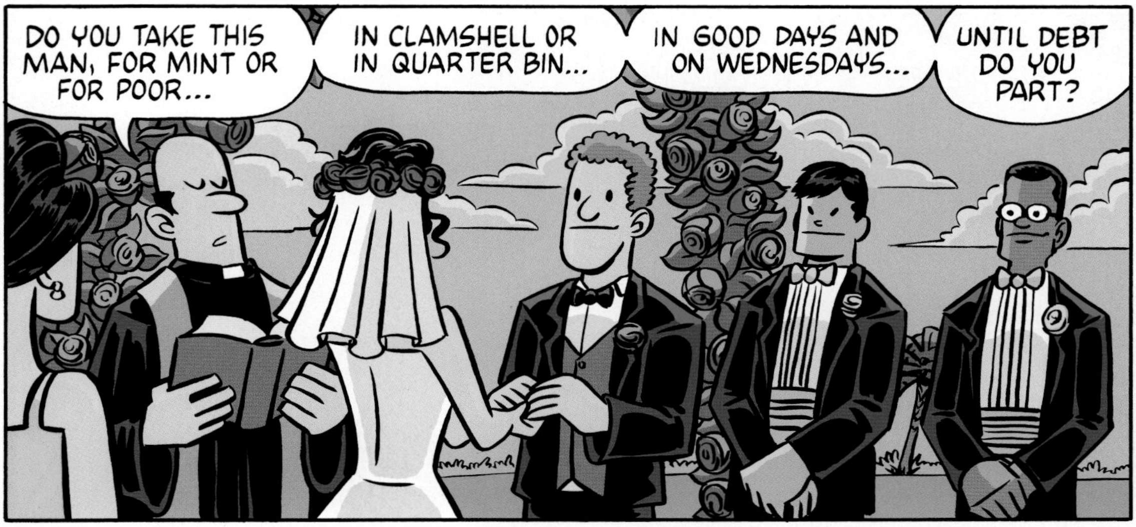
DO YOU TAKE THIS MAN, FOR MINT OR FOR POOR...
IN CLAMSHELL OR IN QUARTER BIN...
IN GOOD DAYS AND ON WEDNESDAYS...
UNTIL DEBT DO YOU PART?

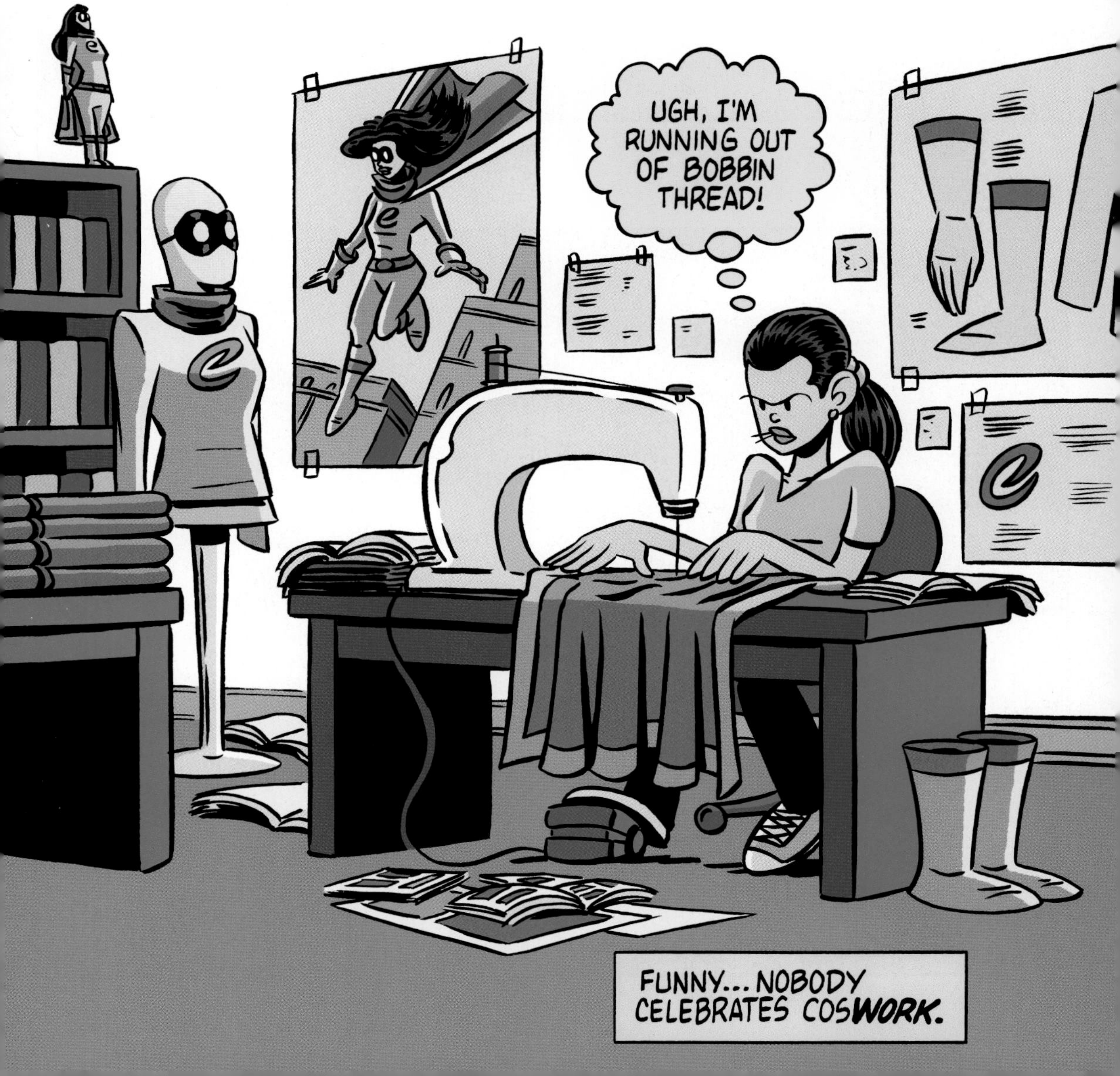
UGH, I'M RUNNING OUT OF BOBBIN THREAD!
FUNNY... NOBODY CELEBRATES COS**WORK.**

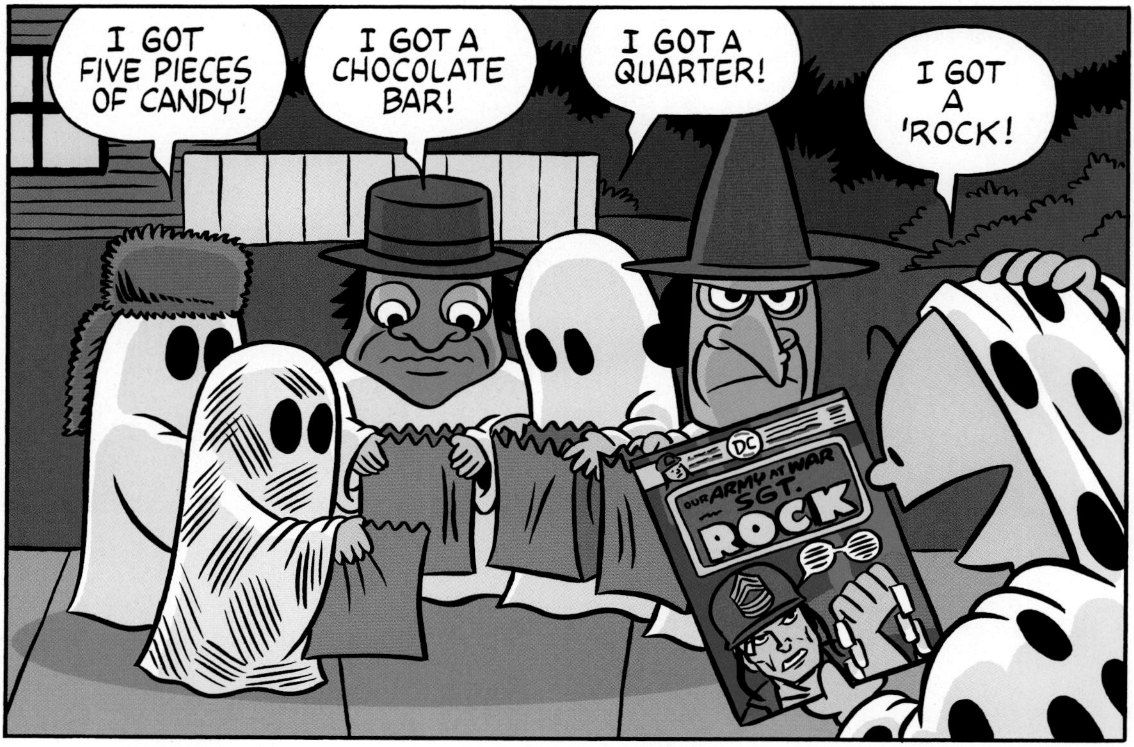
I GOT FIVE PIECES OF CANDY!
I GOT A CHOCOLATE BAR!
I GOT A QUARTER!
I GOT A 'ROCK!
DC
OUR ARMY AT WAR
SGT. ROCK

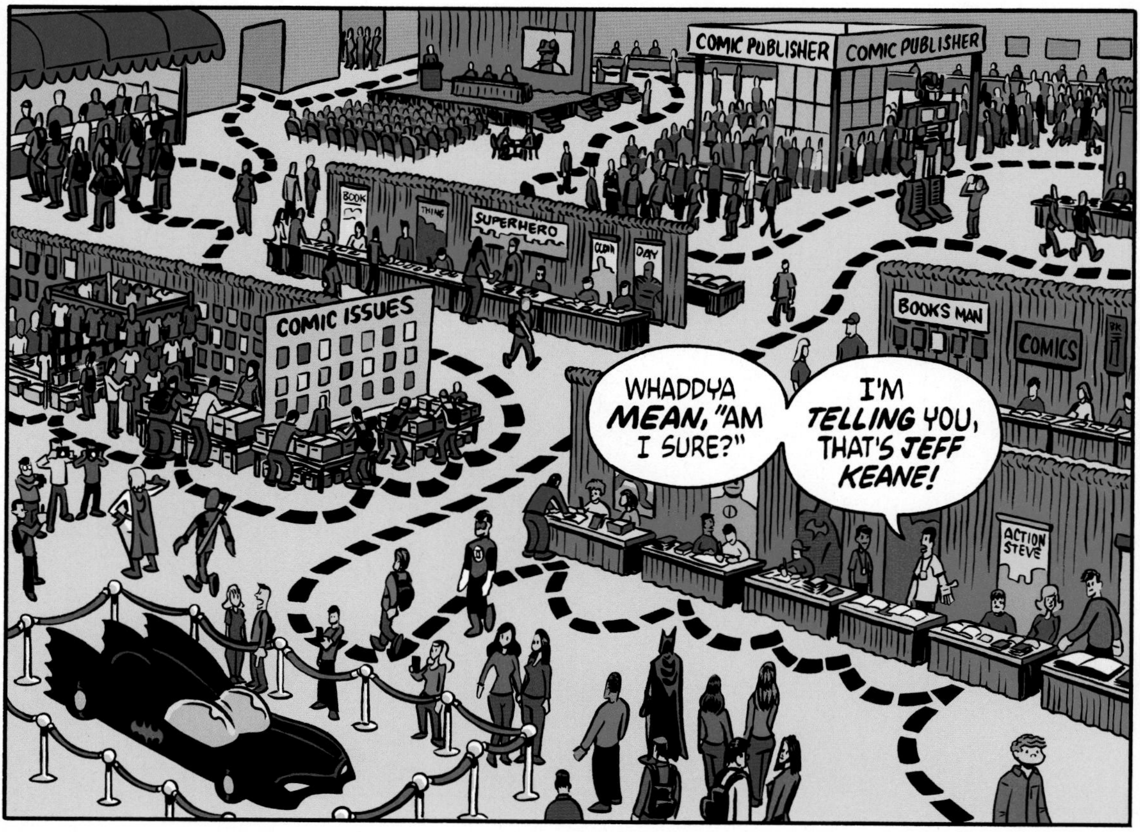
COMIC PUBLISHER
COMIC PUBLISHER
BOOK
THING
SUPERHERO
CLOWN
DAY
COMIC ISSUES
BOOKS MAN
COMICS
ACTION STEVE
WHADDYA MEAN, "AM I SURE?"
I'M TELLING YOU, THAT'S JEFF KEANE!

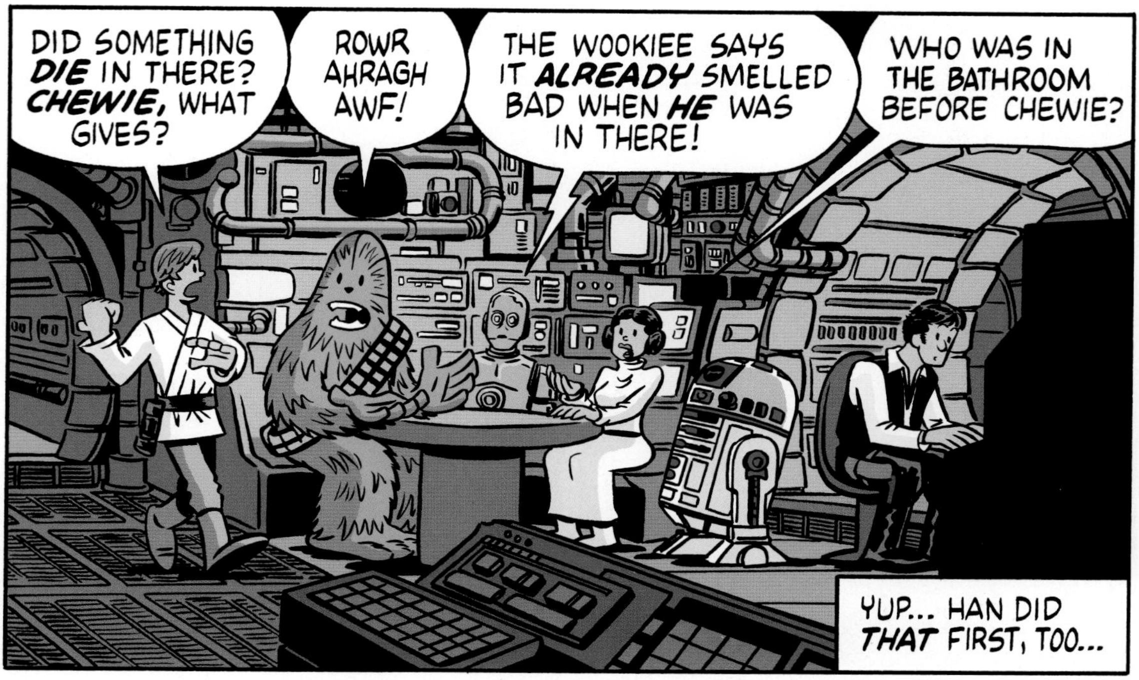
DID SOMETHING *DIE* IN THERE? *CHEWIE,* WHAT GIVES?
ROWR AHRAGH AWF!
THE WOOKIEE SAYS IT *ALREADY* SMELLED BAD WHEN *HE* WAS IN THERE!
WHO WAS IN THE BATHROOM BEFORE CHEWIE?
YUP... HAN DID *THAT* FIRST, TOO...

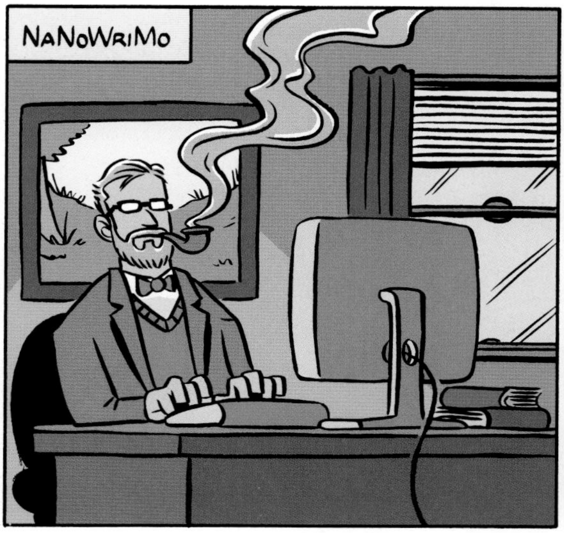
NANOWRIMO

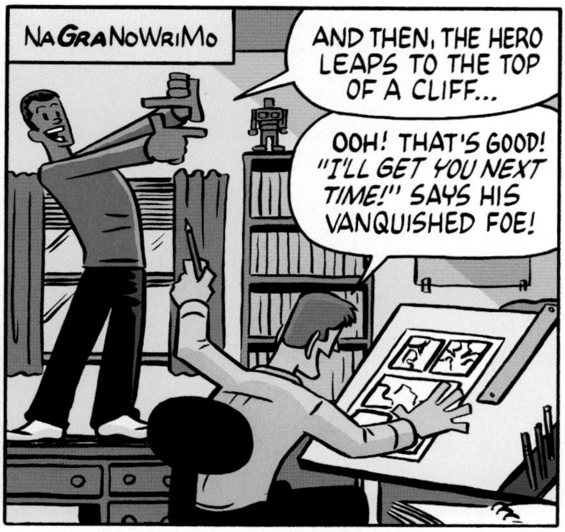
NAGRANOWRIMO
AND THEN, THE HERO LEAPS TO THE TOP OF A CLIFF...
OOH! THAT'S GOOD! *"I'LL GET YOU NEXT TIME!"* SAYS HIS VANQUISHED FOE!

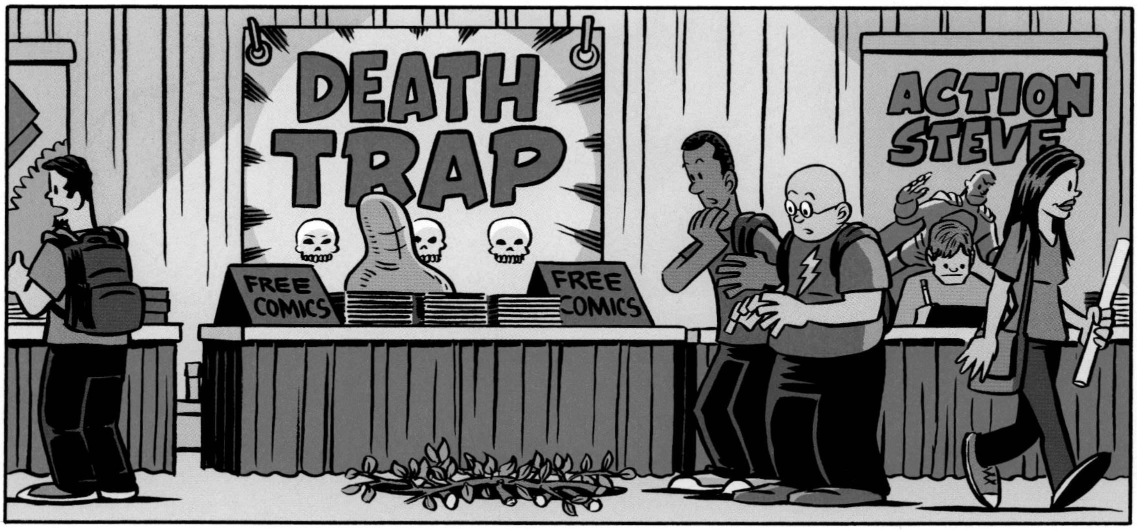
DEATH TRAP
FREE COMICS
FREE COMICS
ACTION STEVE

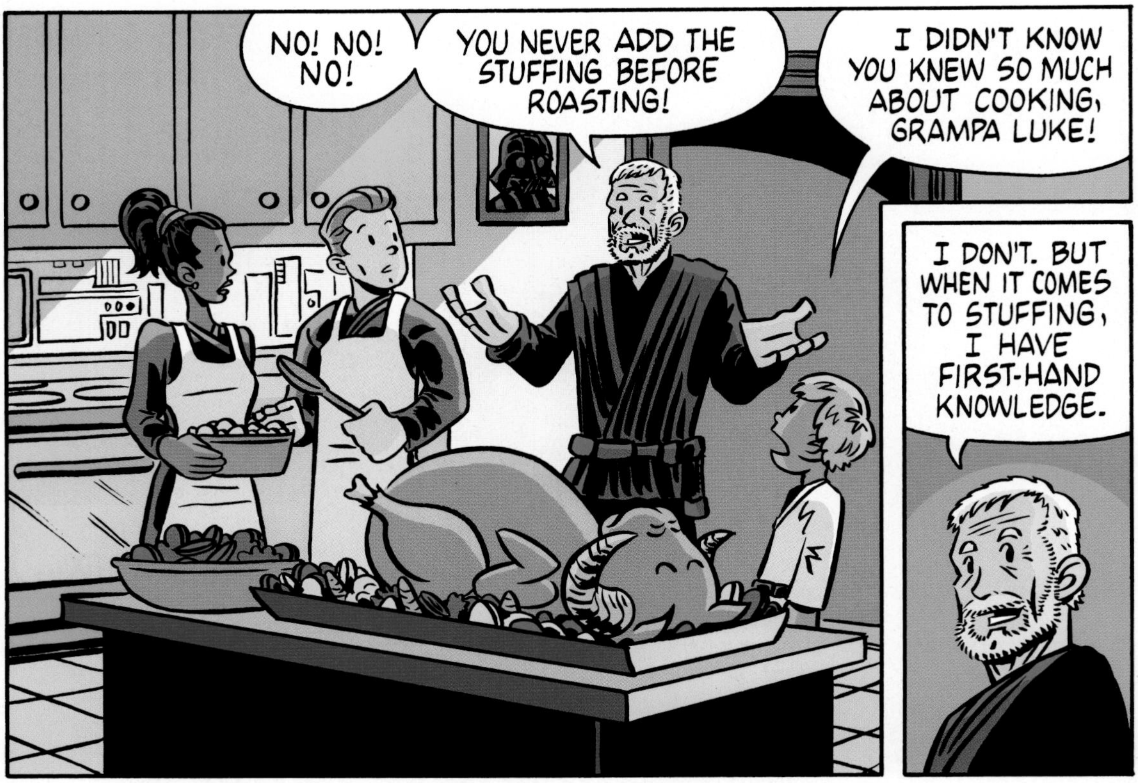
NO! NO! NO!
YOU NEVER ADD THE STUFFING BEFORE ROASTING!
I DIDN'T KNOW YOU KNEW SO MUCH ABOUT COOKING, GRAMPA LUKE!
I DON'T. BUT WHEN IT COMES TO STUFFING, I HAVE FIRST-HAND KNOWLEDGE.

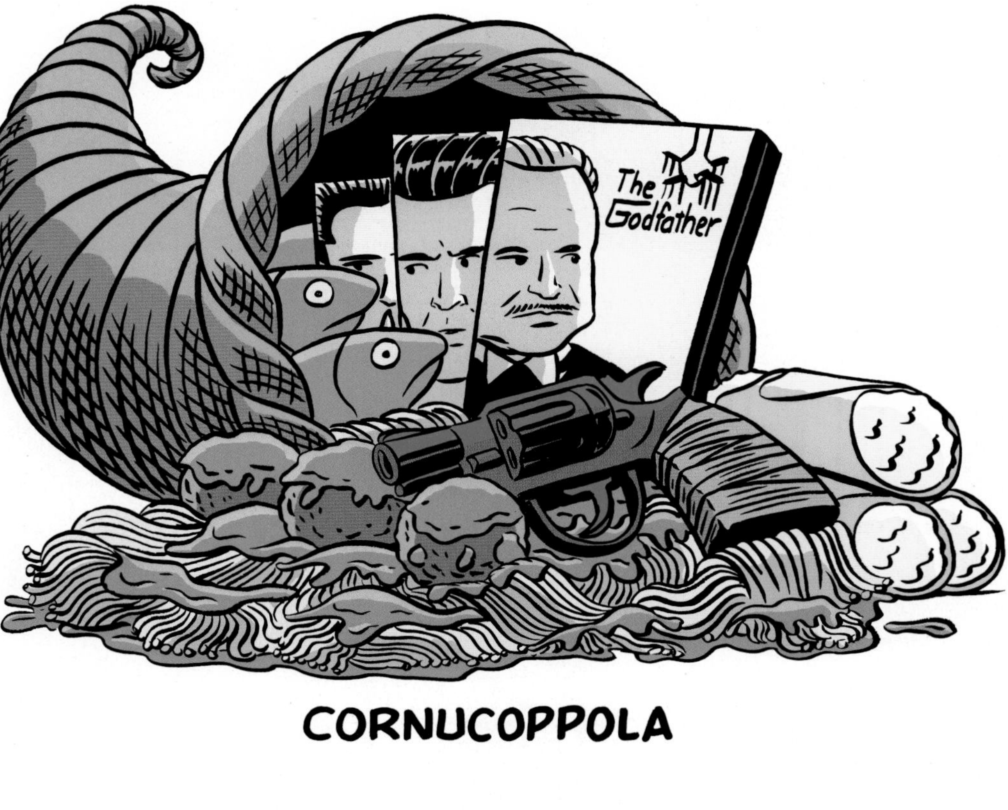
The Godfather

**CORNUCOPPOLA**

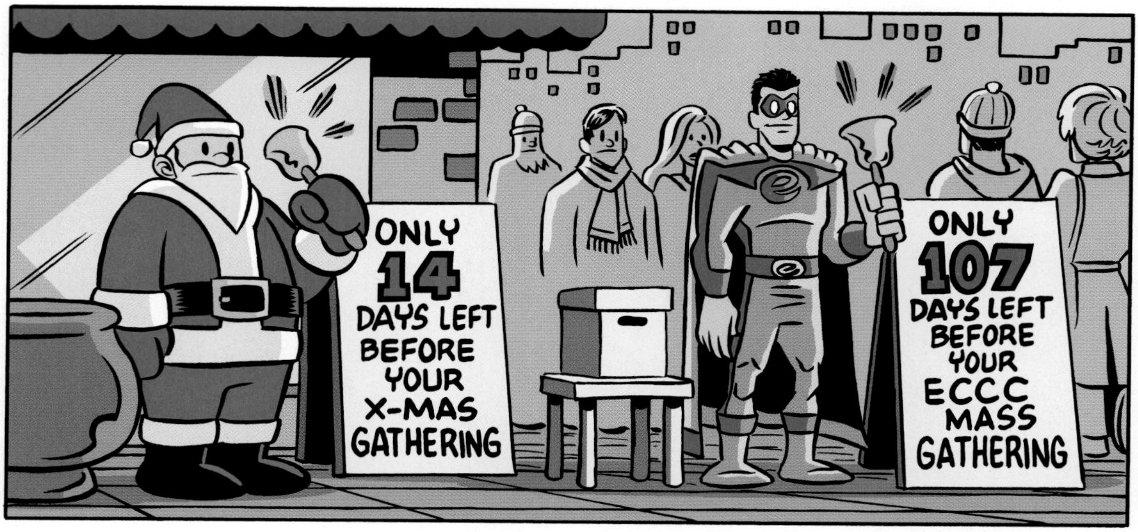
ONLY 14 DAYS LEFT BEFORE YOUR X-MAS GATHERING
ONLY 107 DAYS LEFT BEFORE YOUR ECCC MASS GATHERING

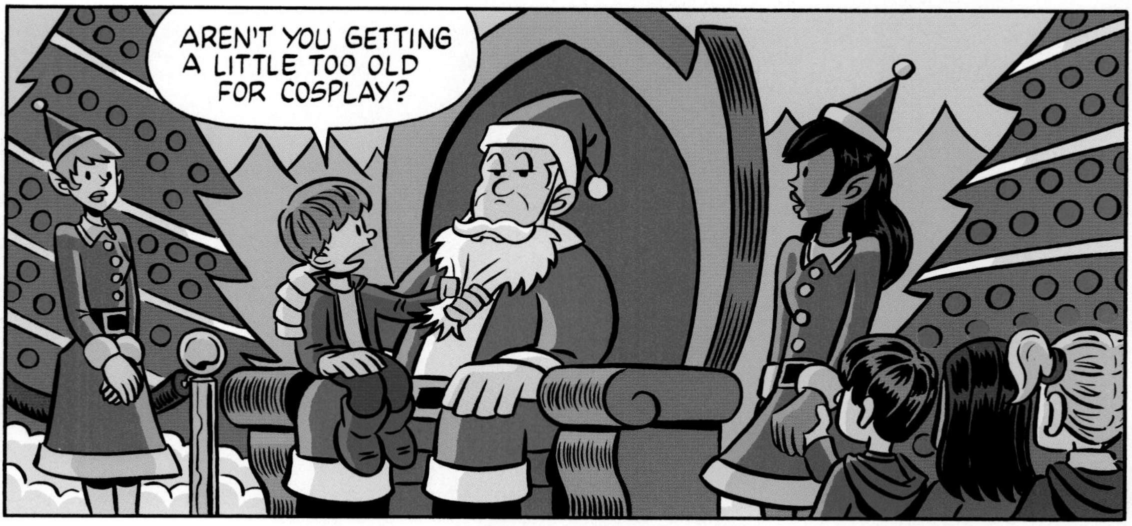
AREN'T YOU GETTING A LITTLE TOO OLD FOR COSPLAY?

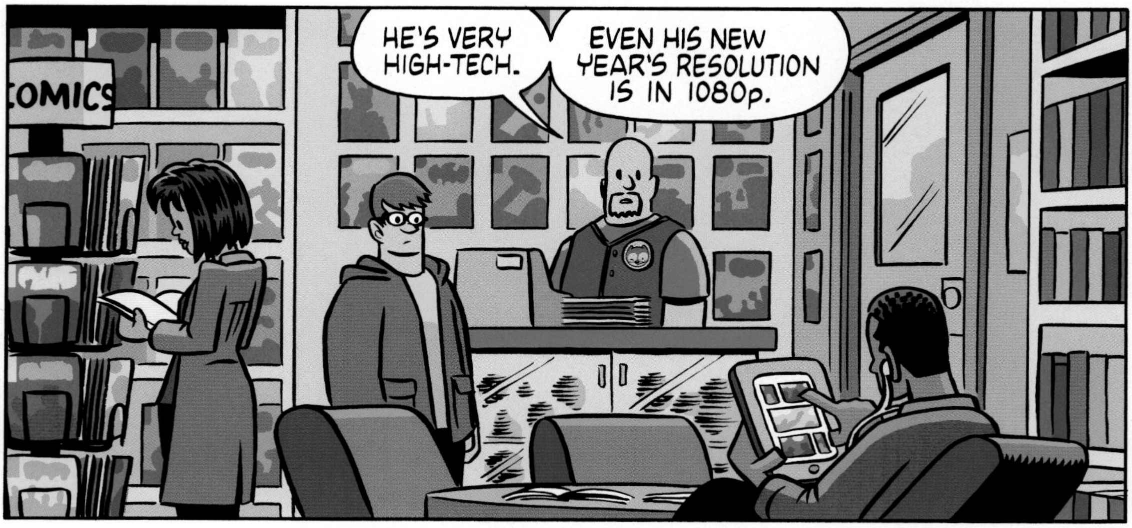
COMICS
HE'S VERY HIGH-TECH.
EVEN HIS NEW YEAR'S RESOLUTION IS IN 1080p.

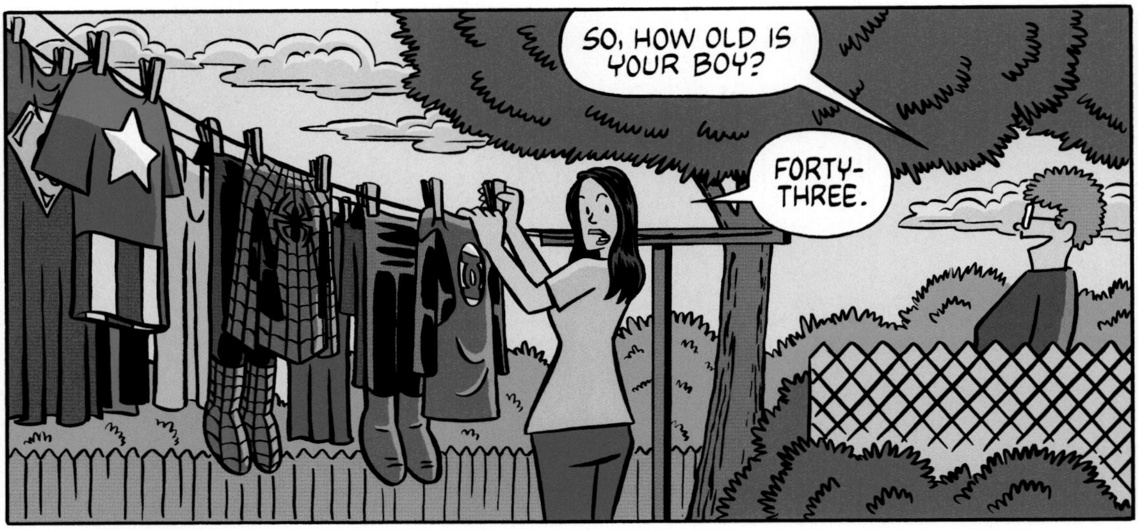
SO, HOW OLD IS YOUR BOY?
FORTY-THREE.

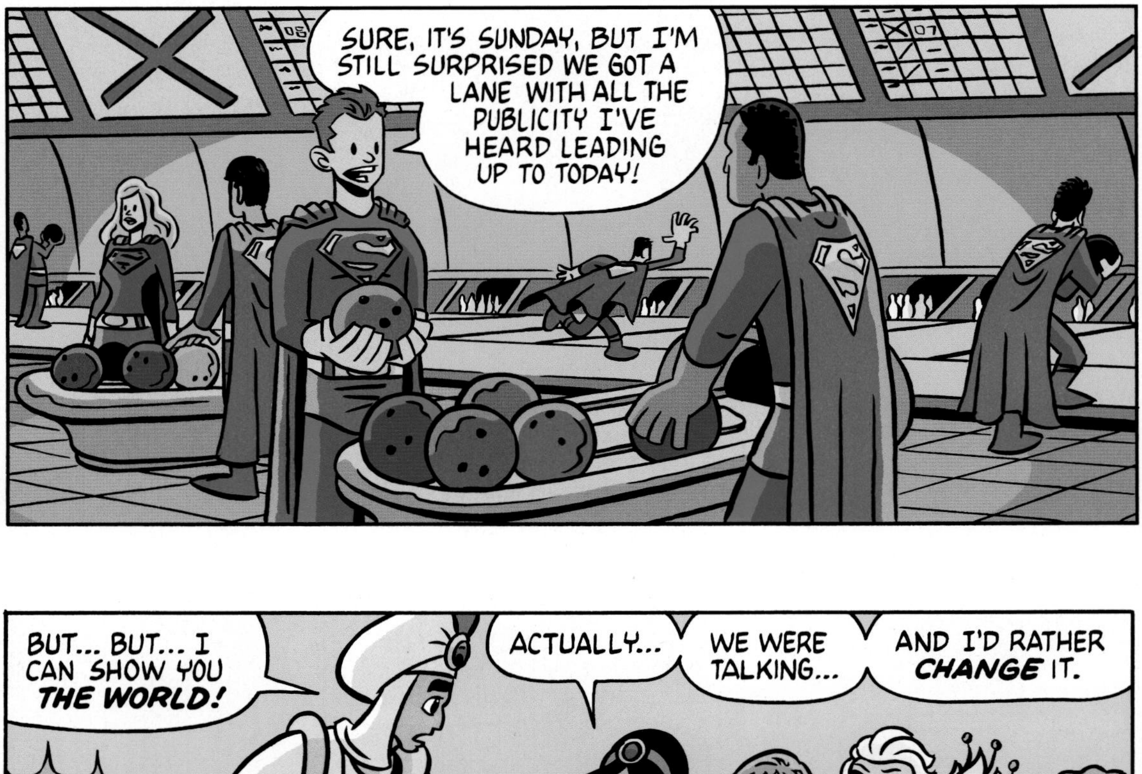
SURE, IT'S SUNDAY, BUT I'M STILL SURPRISED WE GOT A LANE WITH ALL THE PUBLICITY I'VE HEARD LEADING UP TO TODAY!

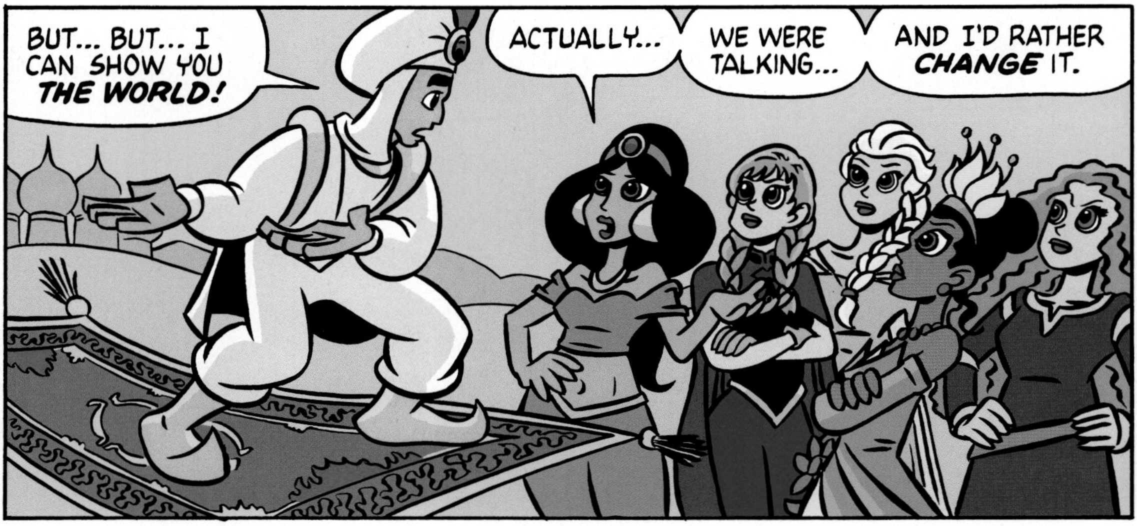
BUT... BUT... I CAN SHOW YOU **THE WORLD!**
ACTUALLY...
WE WERE TALKING...
AND I'D RATHER ***CHANGE*** IT.

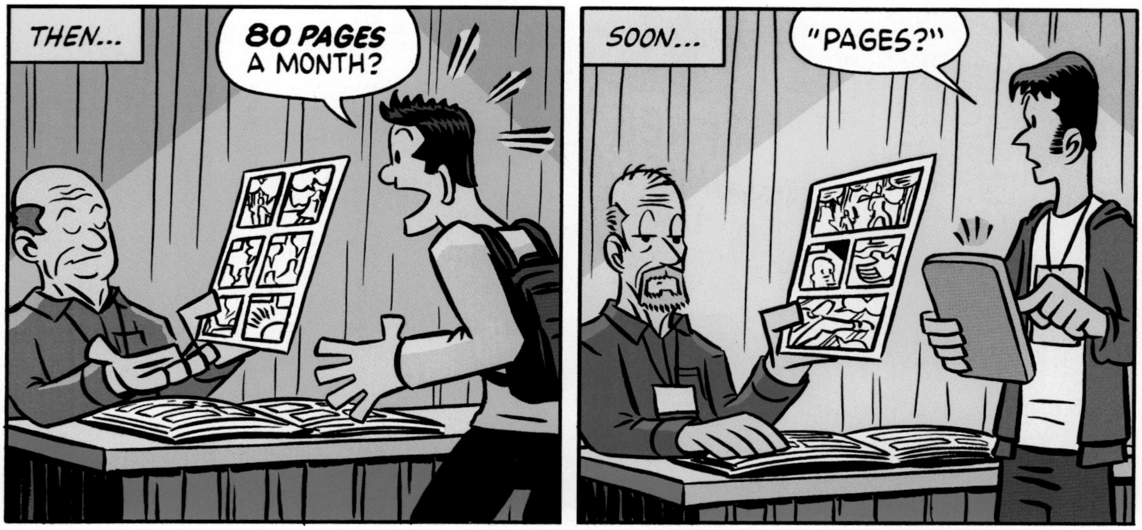
THEN...
80 PAGES A MONTH?
SOON...
"PAGES?"

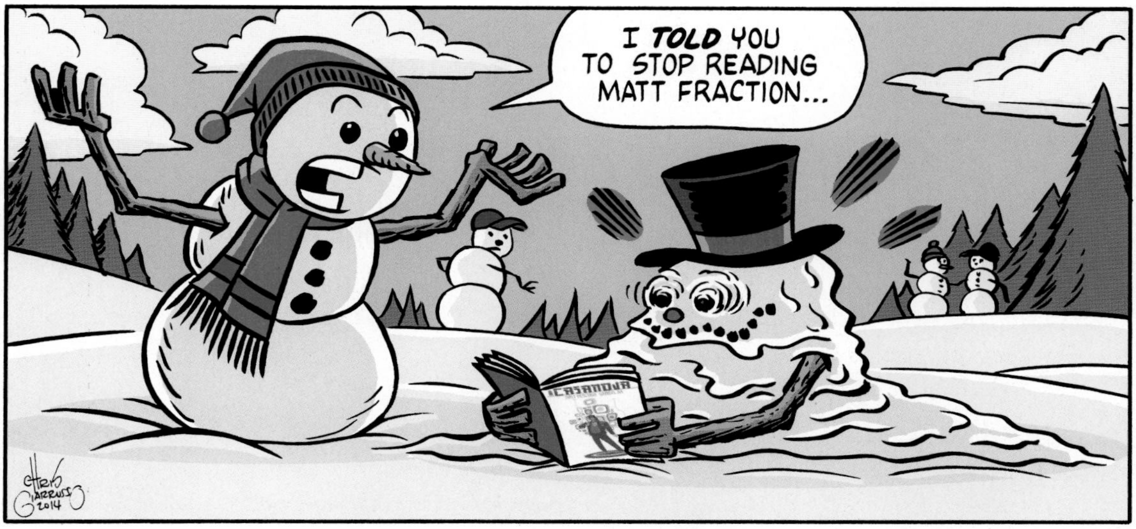
I TOLD YOU TO STOP READING MATT FRACTION...

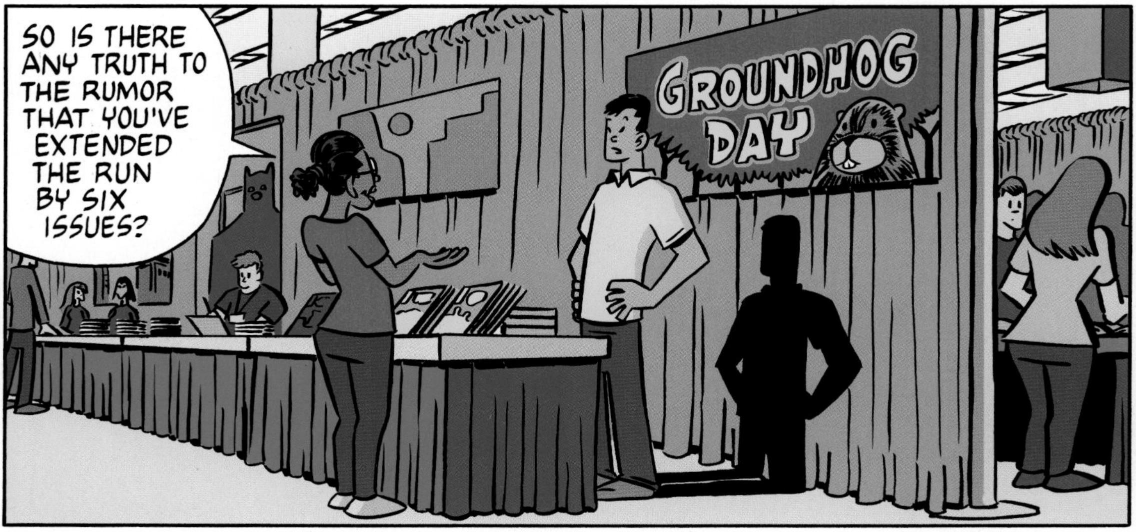
SO IS THERE ANY TRUTH TO THE RUMOR THAT YOU'VE EXTENDED THE RUN BY SIX ISSUES?
GROUNDHOG DAY

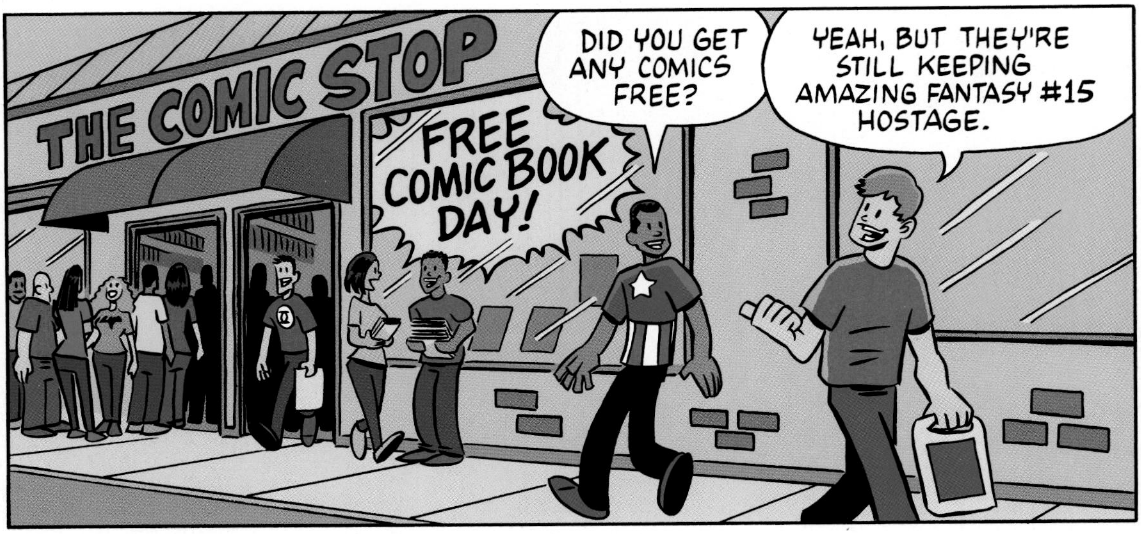
THE COMIC STOP
FREE COMIC BOOK DAY!
DID YOU GET ANY COMICS FREE?
YEAH, BUT THEY'RE STILL KEEPING AMAZING FANTASY #15 HOSTAGE.

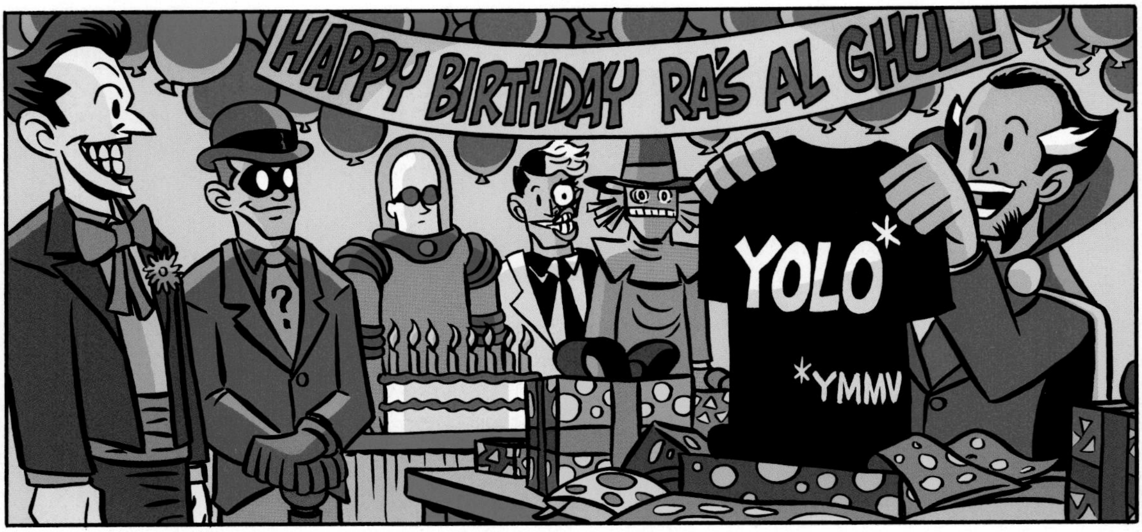
HAPPY BIRTHDAY RA'S AL GHUL!
YOLO*
*YMMV

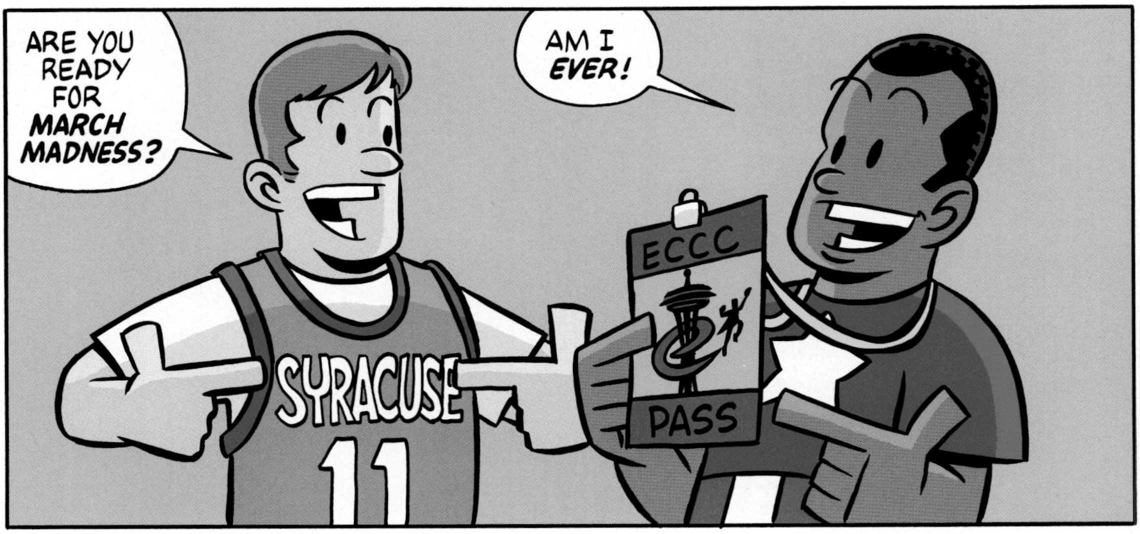
ARE YOU READY FOR MARCH MADNESS?
AM I EVER!
ECCC
PASS
SYRACUSE
11

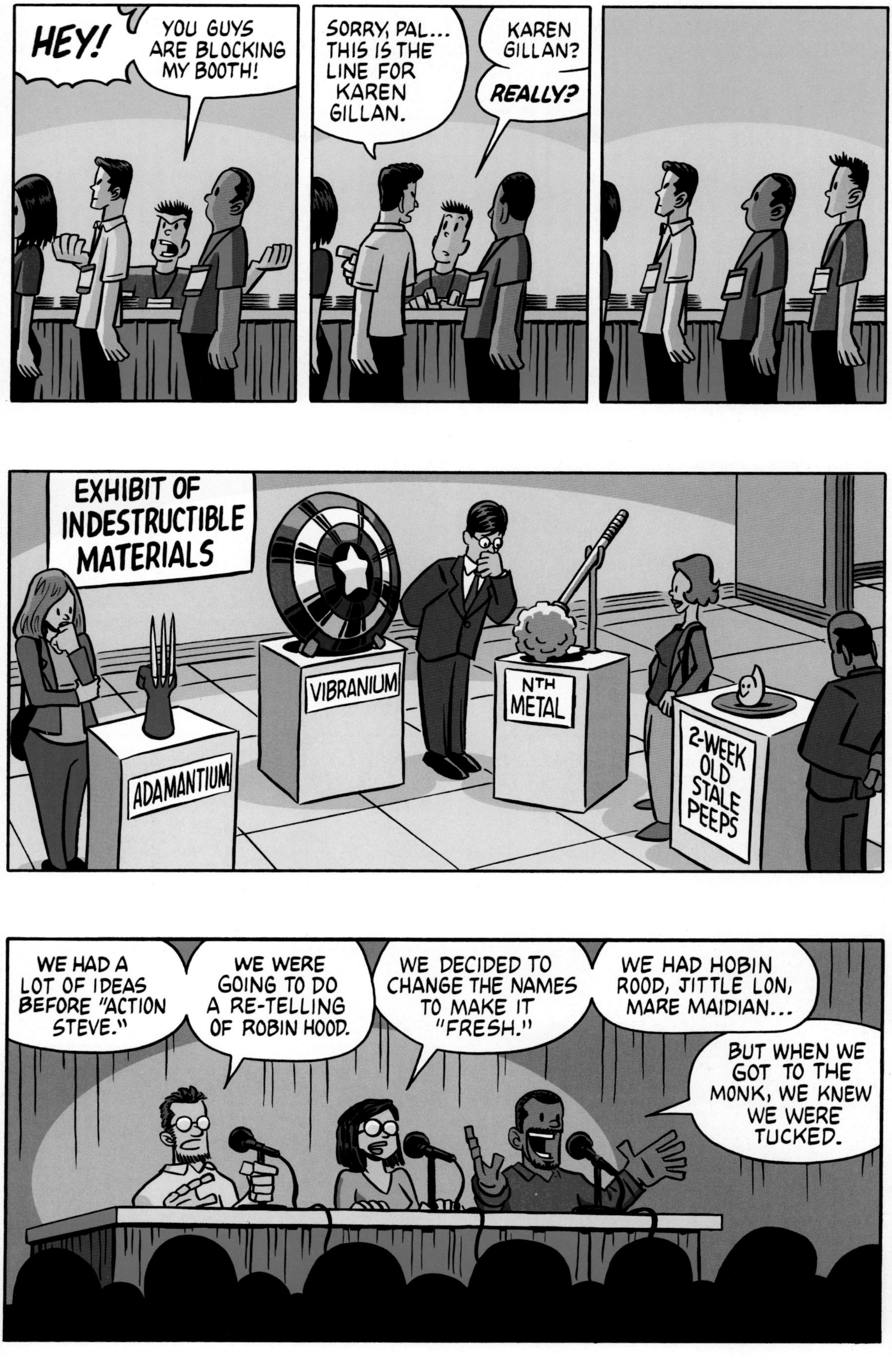
HEY!
YOU GUYS ARE BLOCKING MY BOOTH!
SORRY, PAL... THIS IS THE LINE FOR KAREN GILLAN.
KAREN GILLAN? REALLY?
EXHIBIT OF INDESTRUCTIBLE MATERIALS
ADAMANTIUM
VIBRANIUM
NTH METAL
2-WEEK OLD STALE PEEPS
WE HAD A LOT OF IDEAS BEFORE "ACTION STEVE."
WE WERE GOING TO DO A RE-TELLING OF ROBIN HOOD.
WE DECIDED TO CHANGE THE NAMES TO MAKE IT "FRESH."
WE HAD HOBIN ROOD, JITTLE LON, MARE MAIDIAN...
BUT WHEN WE GOT TO THE MONK, WE KNEW WE WERE TUCKED.

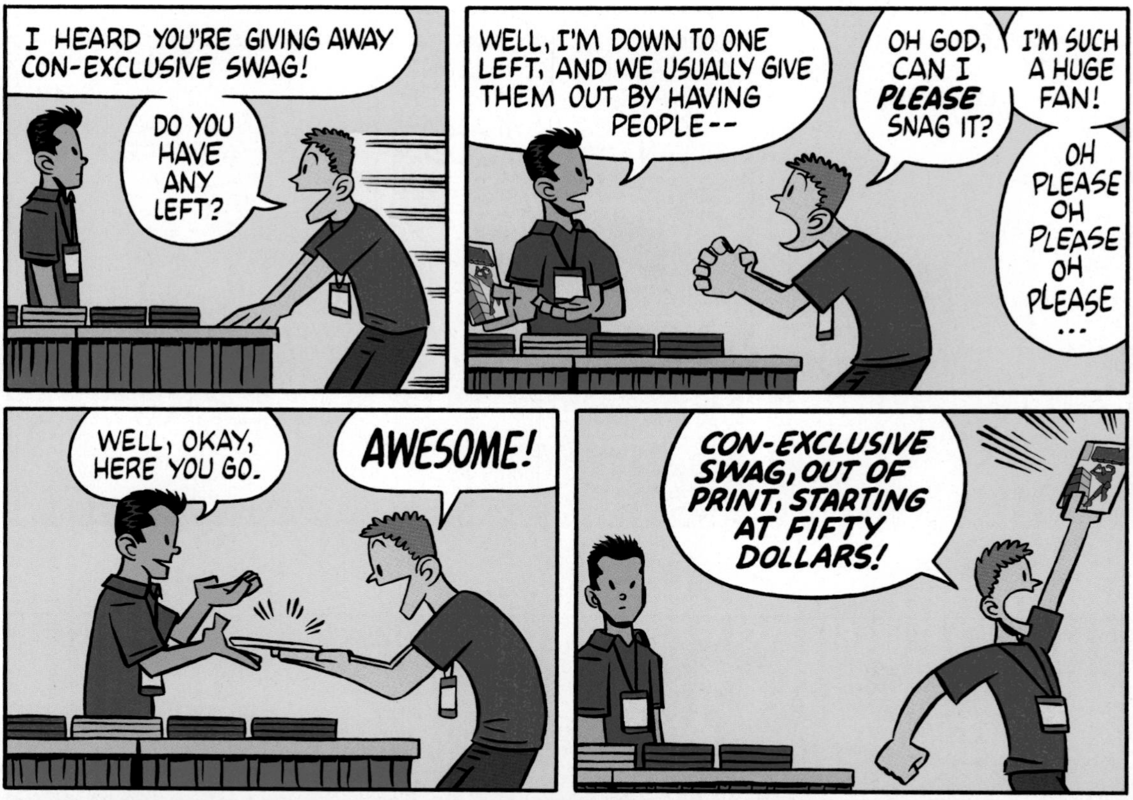
I HEARD YOU'RE GIVING AWAY CON-EXCLUSIVE SWAG!
DO YOU HAVE ANY LEFT?
WELL, I'M DOWN TO ONE LEFT, AND WE USUALLY GIVE THEM OUT BY HAVING PEOPLE--
OH GOD, CAN I PLEASE SNAG IT?
I'M SUCH A HUGE FAN!
OH PLEASE OH PLEASE OH PLEASE ...
WELL, OKAY, HERE YOU GO.
AWESOME!
CON-EXCLUSIVE SWAG, OUT OF PRINT, STARTING AT FIFTY DOLLARS!

**Written by Chris Hanel as part of the Kickstarter campaign for "The Webcomics Handbook."**

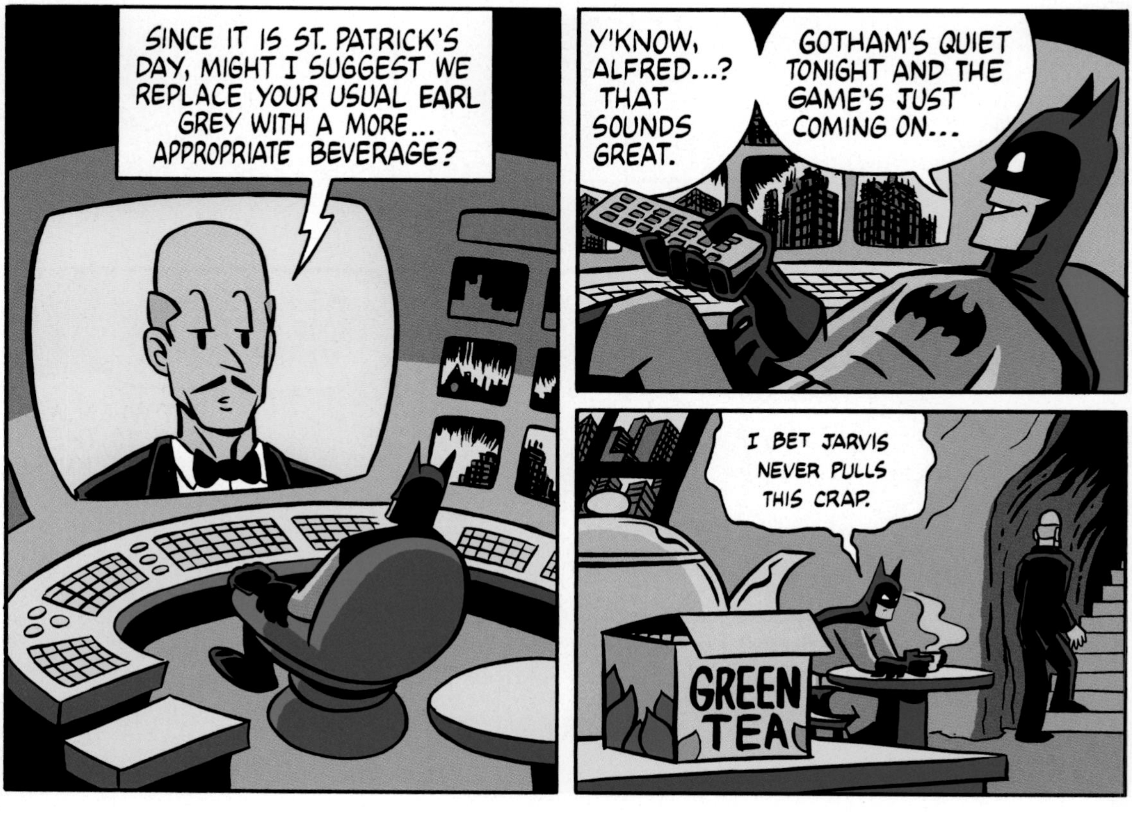
SINCE IT IS ST. PATRICK'S DAY, MIGHT I SUGGEST WE REPLACE YOUR USUAL EARL GREY WITH A MORE... APPROPRIATE BEVERAGE?
GOTHAM'S QUIET TONIGHT AND THE GAME'S JUST COMING ON...
Y'KNOW, ALFRED...? THAT SOUNDS GREAT.
I BET JARVIS NEVER PULLS THIS CRAP.
GREEN TEA

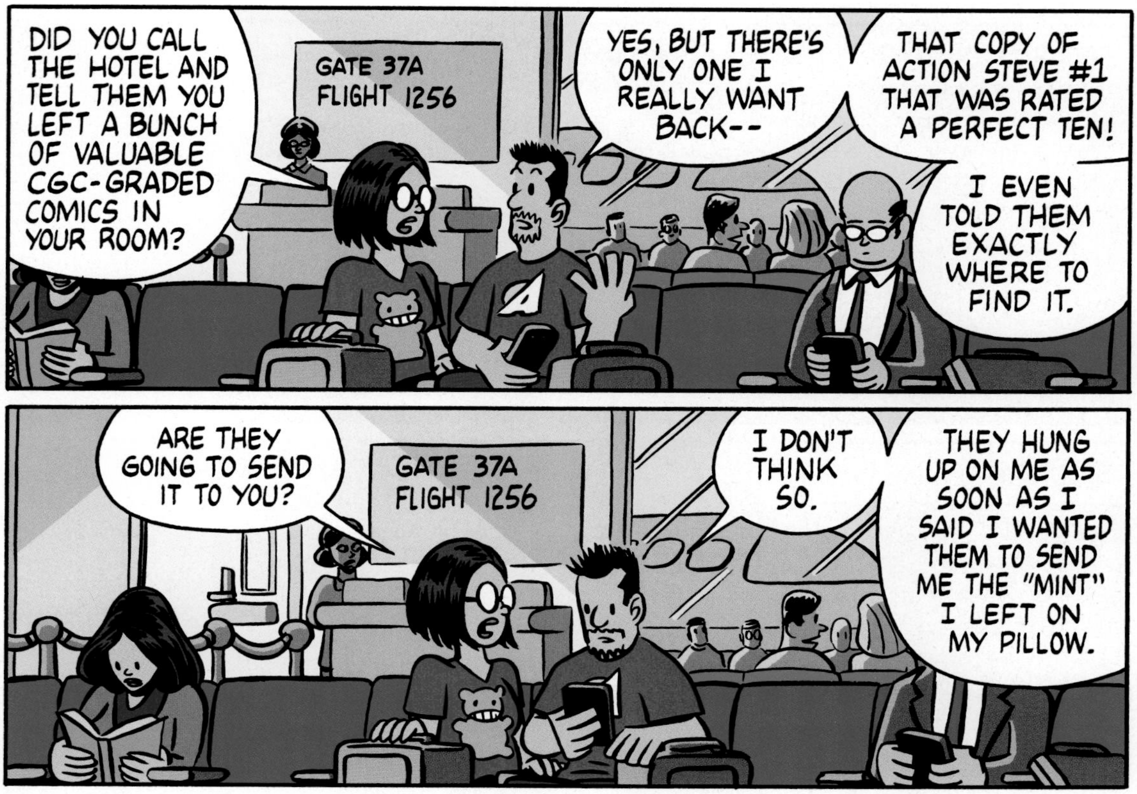
DID YOU CALL THE HOTEL AND TELL THEM YOU LEFT A BUNCH OF VALUABLE CGC-GRADED COMICS IN YOUR ROOM?
GATE 37A
FLIGHT 1256
YES, BUT THERE'S ONLY ONE I REALLY WANT BACK--
THAT COPY OF ACTION STEVE #1 THAT WAS RATED A PERFECT TEN!
I EVEN TOLD THEM EXACTLY WHERE TO FIND IT.
ARE THEY GOING TO SEND IT TO YOU?
GATE 37A
FLIGHT 1256
I DON'T THINK SO.
THEY HUNG UP ON ME AS SOON AS I SAID I WANTED THEM TO SEND ME THE "MINT" I LEFT ON MY PILLOW.

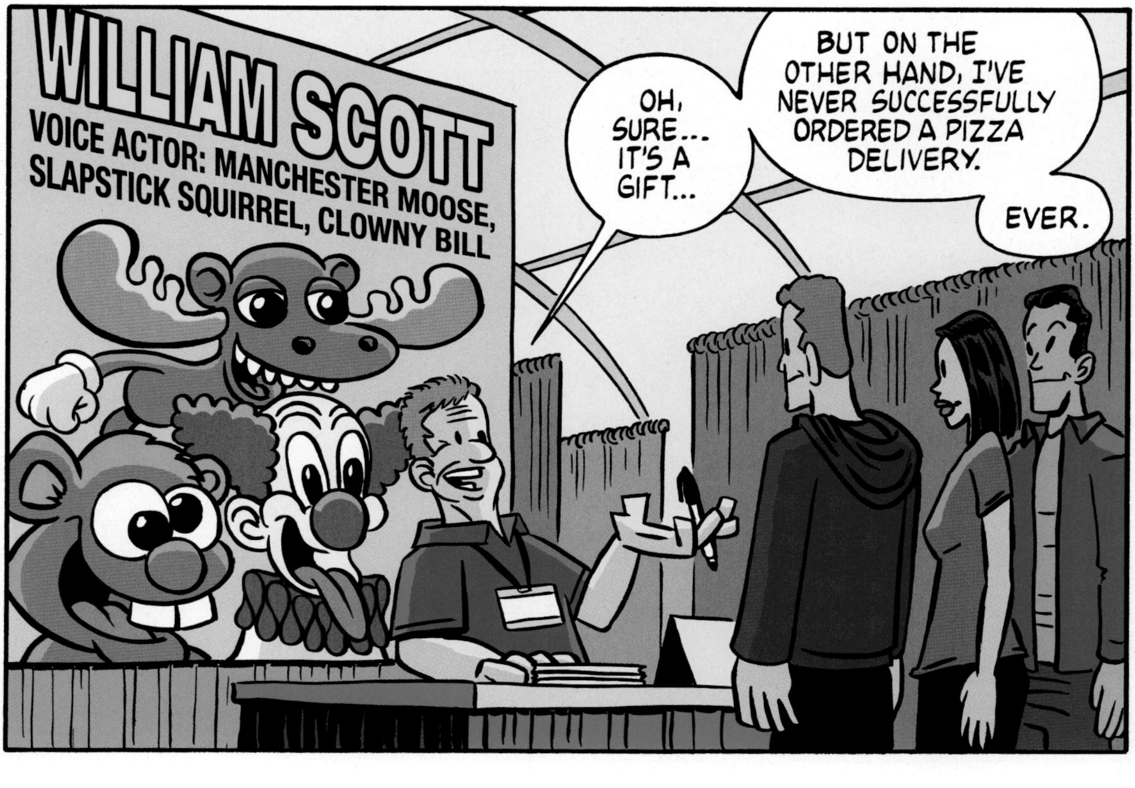
WILLIAM SCOTT
VOICE ACTOR: MANCHESTER MOOSE, SLAPSTICK SQUIRREL, CLOWNY BILL
OH, SURE... IT'S A GIFT...
BUT ON THE OTHER HAND, I'VE NEVER SUCCESSFULLY ORDERED A PIZZA DELIVERY.
EVER.

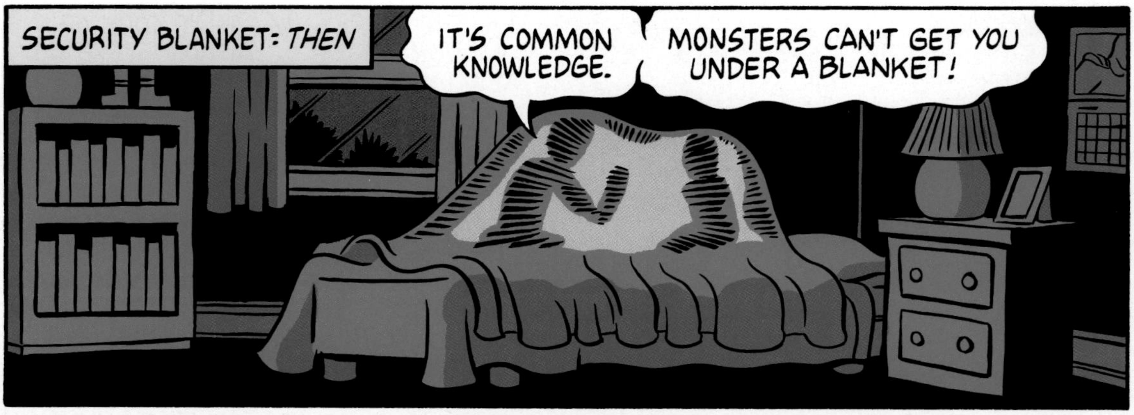
SECURITY BLANKET: *THEN*
IT'S COMMON KNOWLEDGE.
MONSTERS CAN'T GET YOU UNDER A BLANKET!

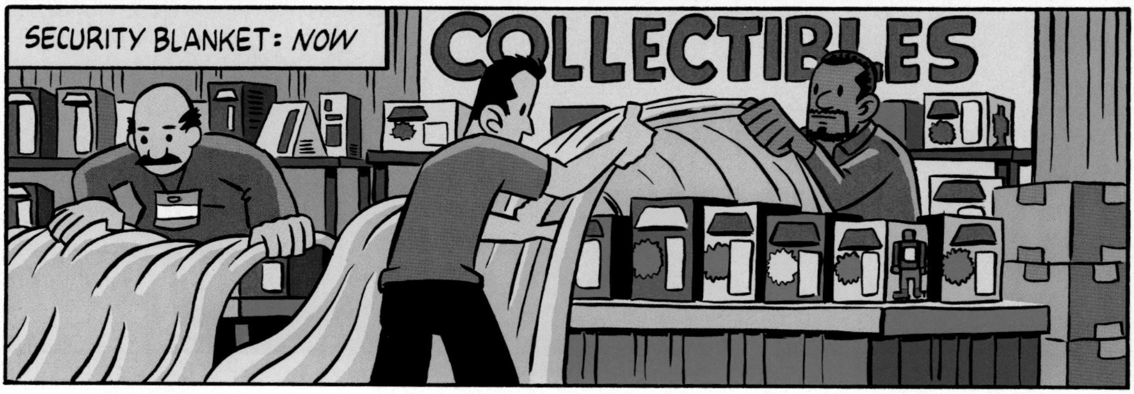
SECURITY BLANKET: *NOW*
COLLECTIBLES

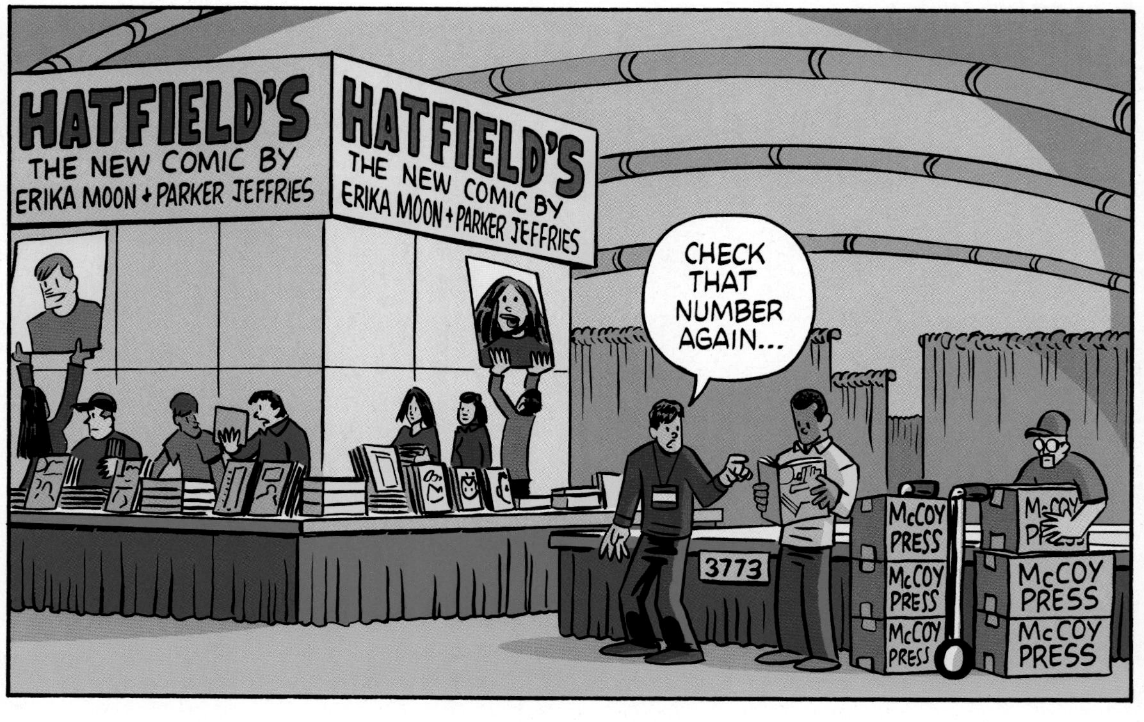
HATFIELD'S
THE NEW COMIC BY
ERIKA MOON + PARKER JEFFRIES
HATFIELD'S
THE NEW COMIC BY
ERIKA MOON + PARKER JEFFRIES
CHECK THAT NUMBER AGAIN...
3773
McCOY PRESS
McCOY PRESS
McCOY PRESS
McCOY PRESS
McCOY PRESS
McCOY PRESS

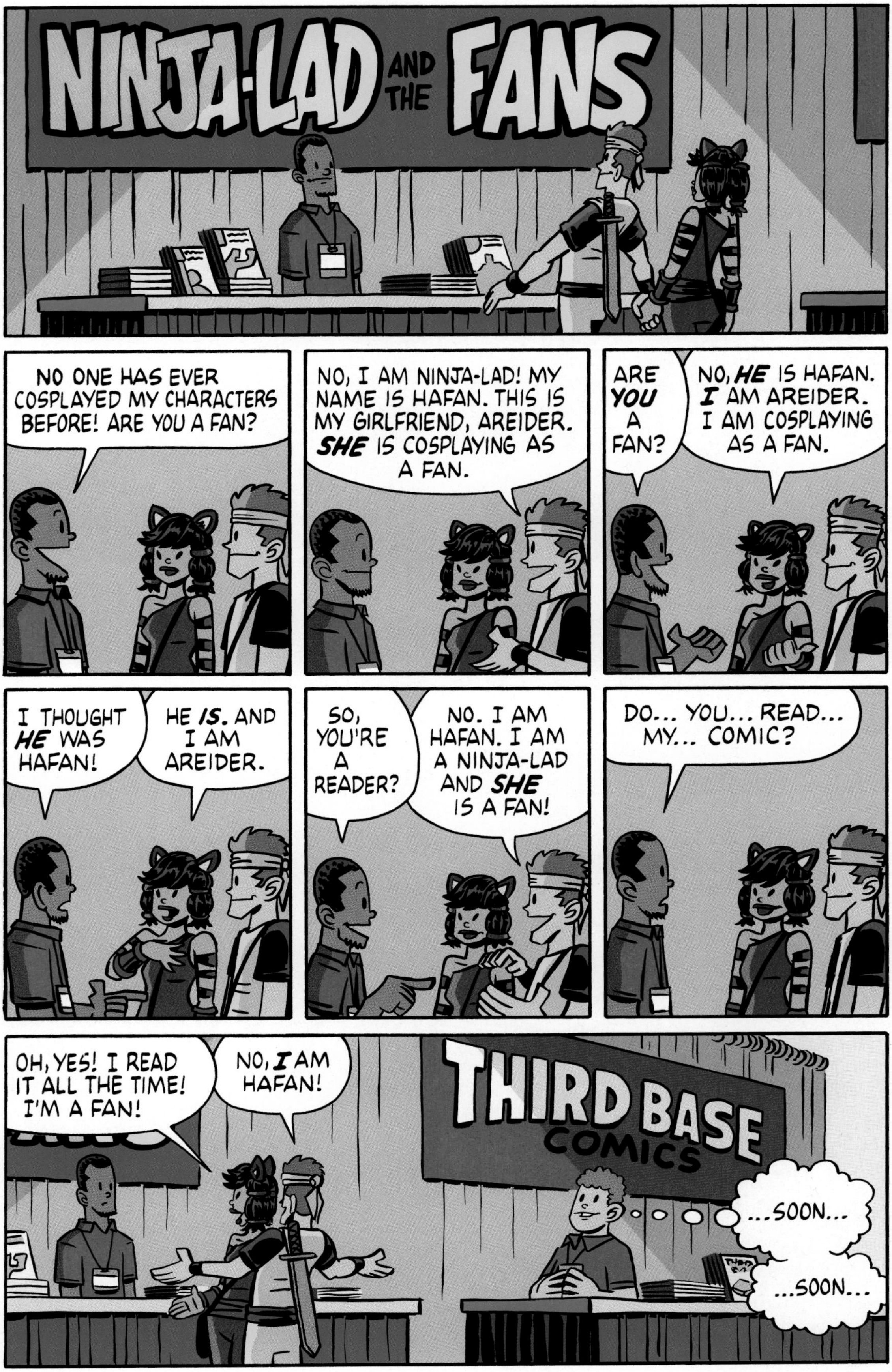
NINJA-LAD AND THE FANS
NO ONE HAS EVER COSPLAYED MY CHARACTERS BEFORE! ARE YOU A FAN?
NO, I AM NINJA-LAD! MY NAME IS HAFAN. THIS IS MY GIRLFRIEND, AREIDER. SHE IS COSPLAYING AS A FAN.
ARE YOU A FAN?
NO, HE IS HAFAN. I AM AREIDER. I AM COSPLAYING AS A FAN.
I THOUGHT HE WAS HAFAN!
HE IS. AND I AM AREIDER.
SO, YOU'RE A READER?
NO. I AM HAFAN. I AM A NINJA-LAD AND SHE IS A FAN!
DO... YOU... READ... MY... COMIC?
OH, YES! I READ IT ALL THE TIME! I'M A FAN!
NO, I AM HAFAN!
THIRD BASE COMICS
...SOON...
...SOON...

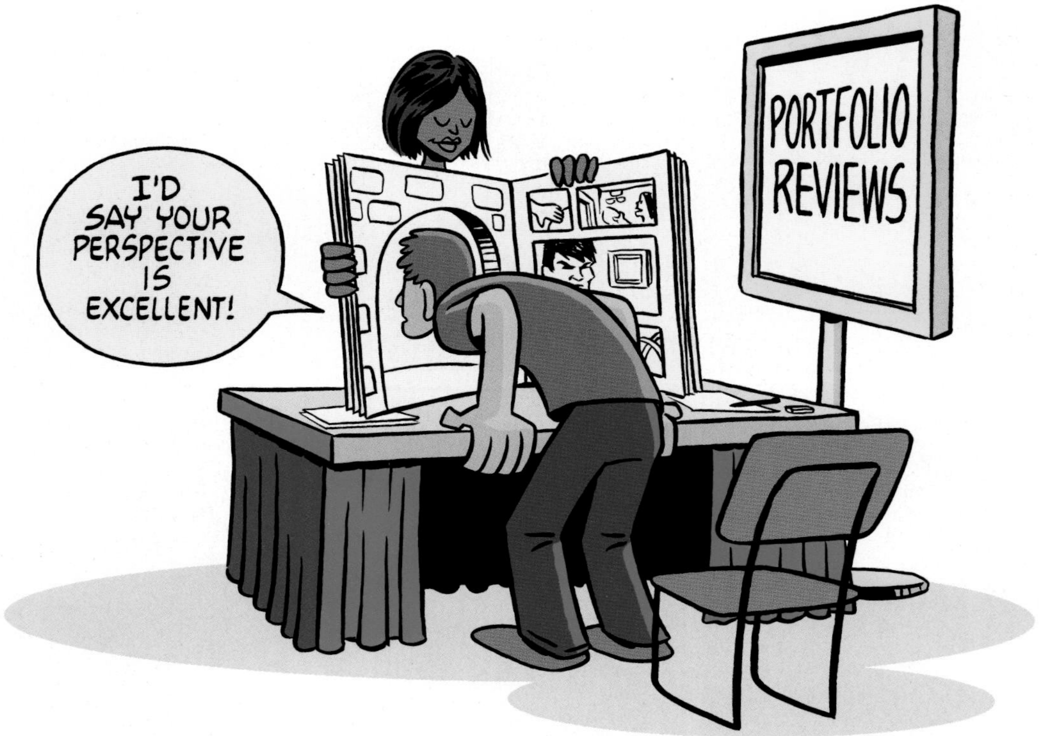
I'D SAY YOUR PERSPECTIVE IS EXCELLENT!
PORTFOLIO REVIEWS

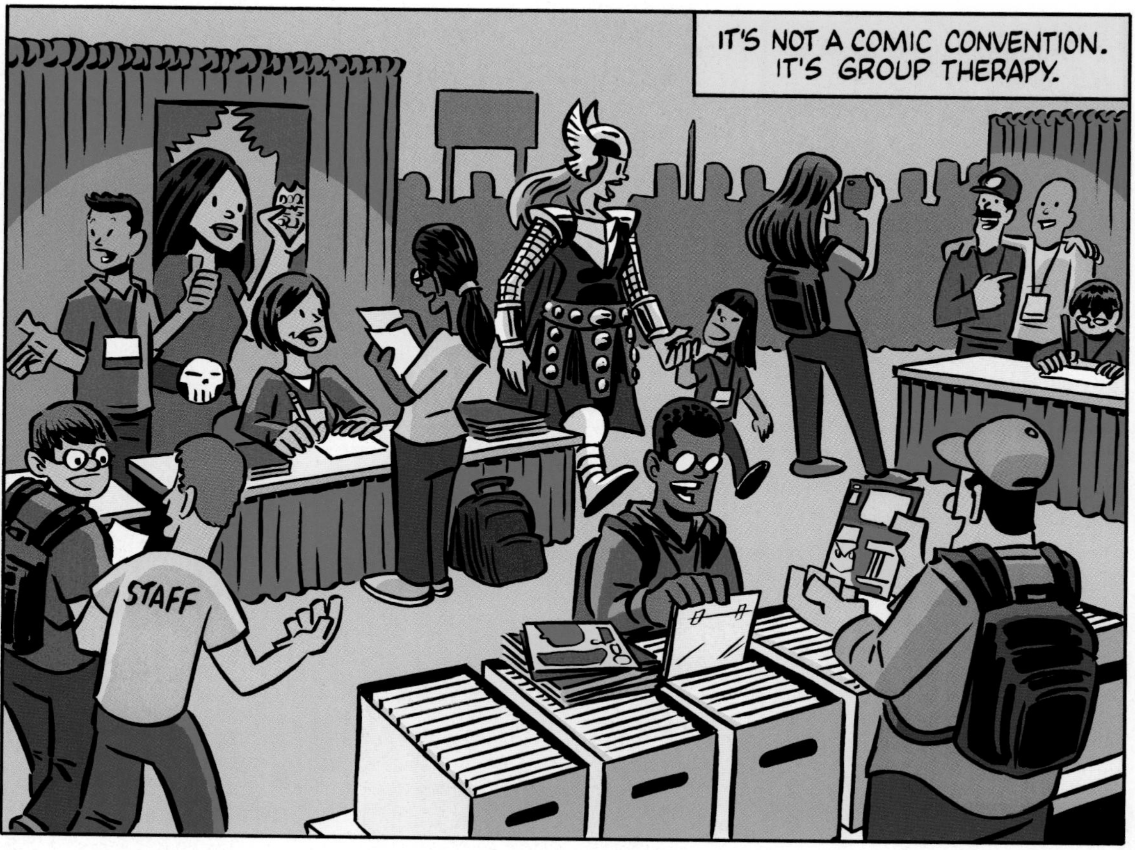
IT'S NOT A COMIC CONVENTION. IT'S GROUP THERAPY.
STAFF

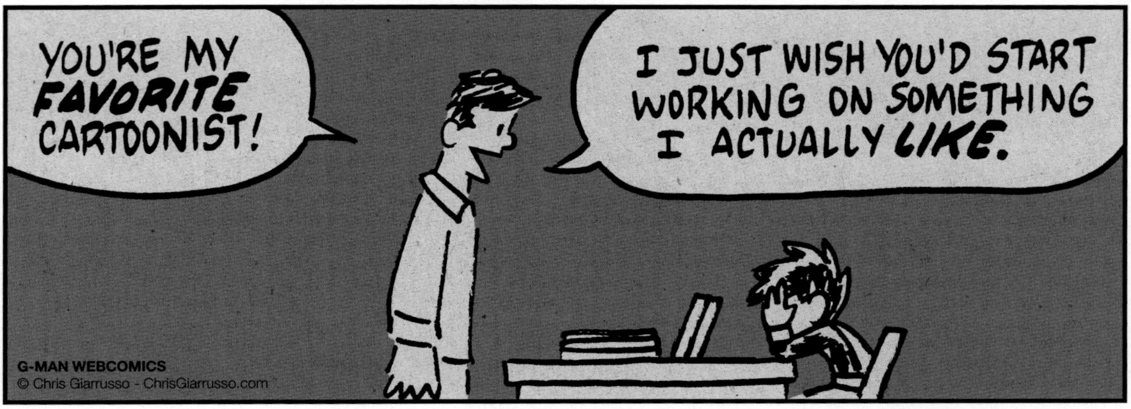
YOU'RE MY FAVORITE CARTOONIST!
I JUST WISH YOU'D START WORKING ON SOMETHING I ACTUALLY LIKE.
G-MAN WEBCOMICS
© Chris Giarrusso - ChrisGiarrusso.com

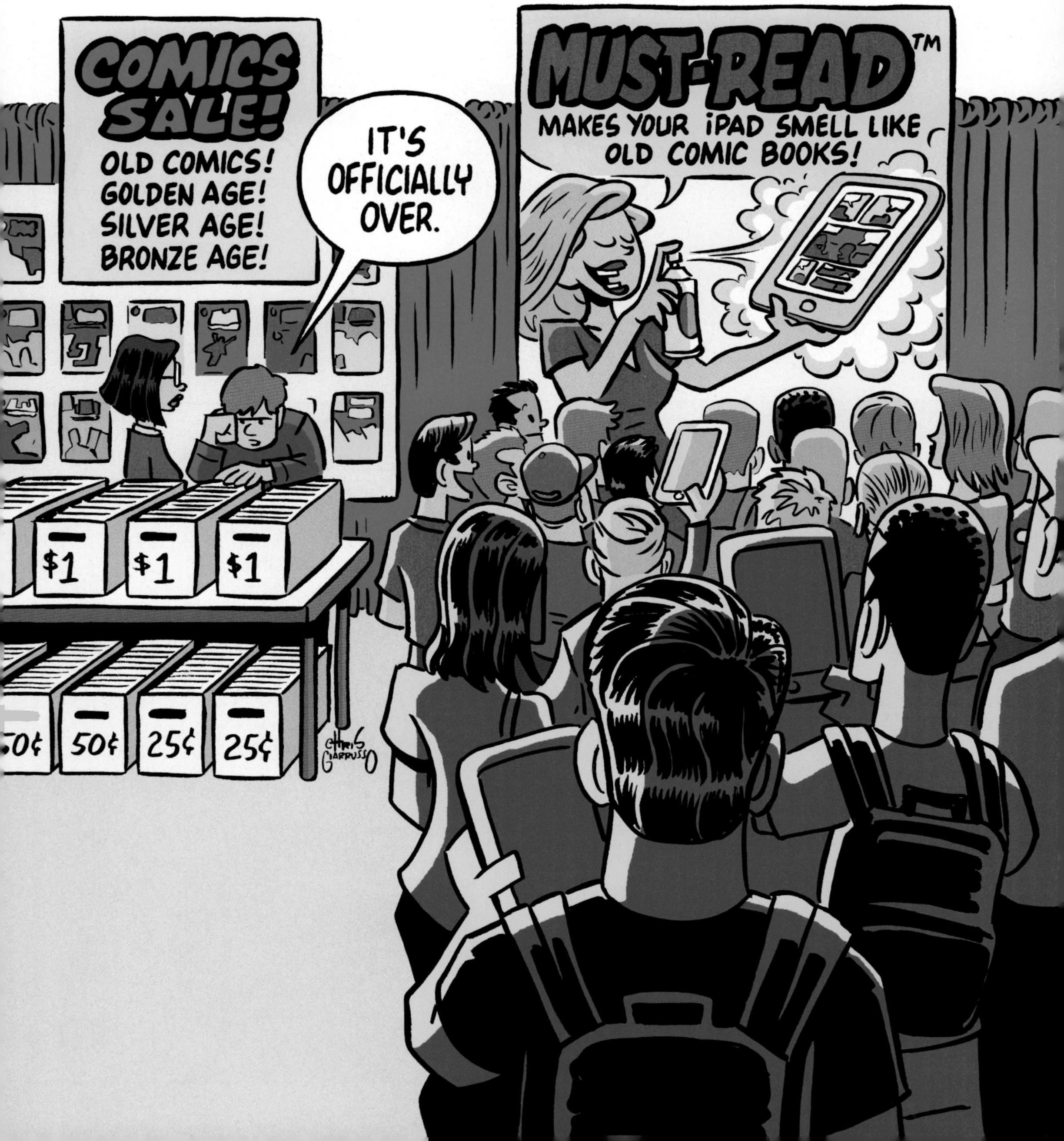
COMICS SALE!
OLD COMICS!
GOLDEN AGE!
SILVER AGE!
BRONZE AGE!
IT'S OFFICIALLY OVER.
MUST-READ™
MAKES YOUR iPAD SMELL LIKE OLD COMIC BOOKS!
$1
$1
$1
50¢
50¢
25¢
25¢
CHRIS GIARRUSSO

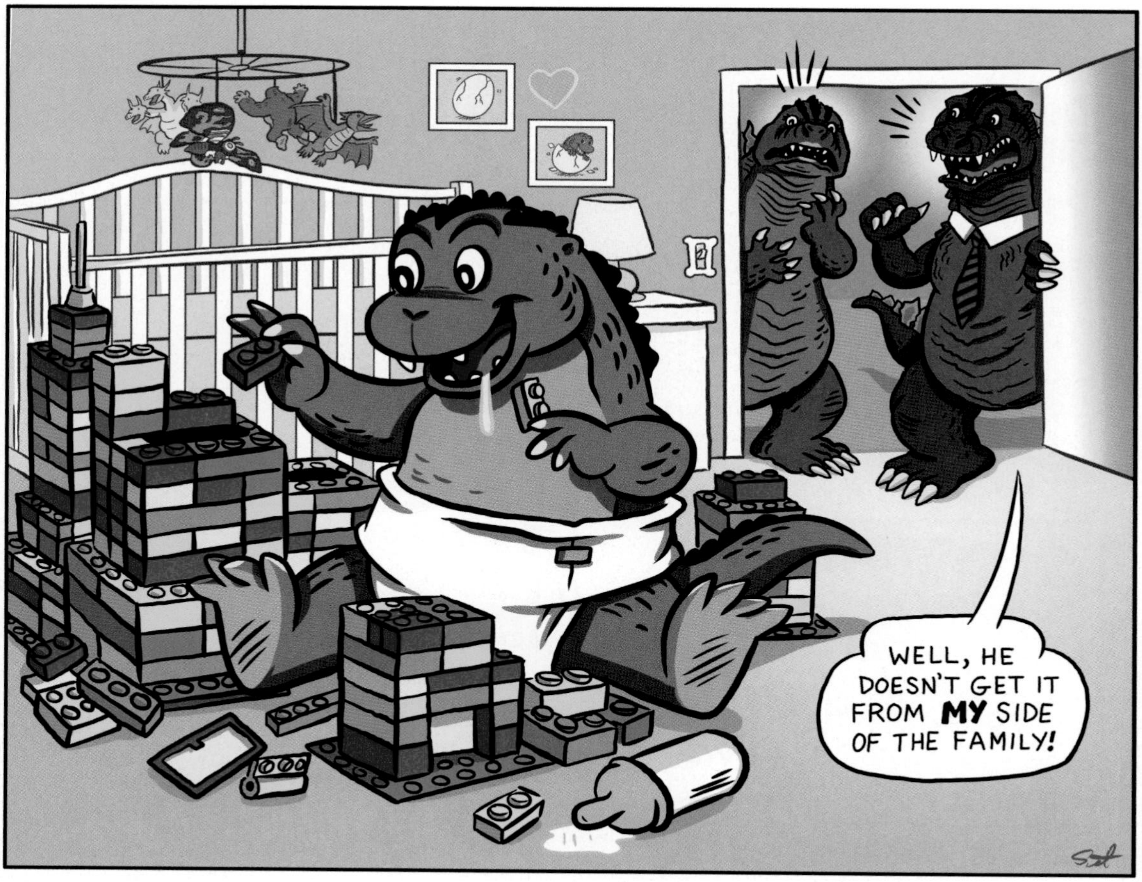
WELL, HE DOESN'T GET IT FROM **MY** SIDE OF THE FAMILY!

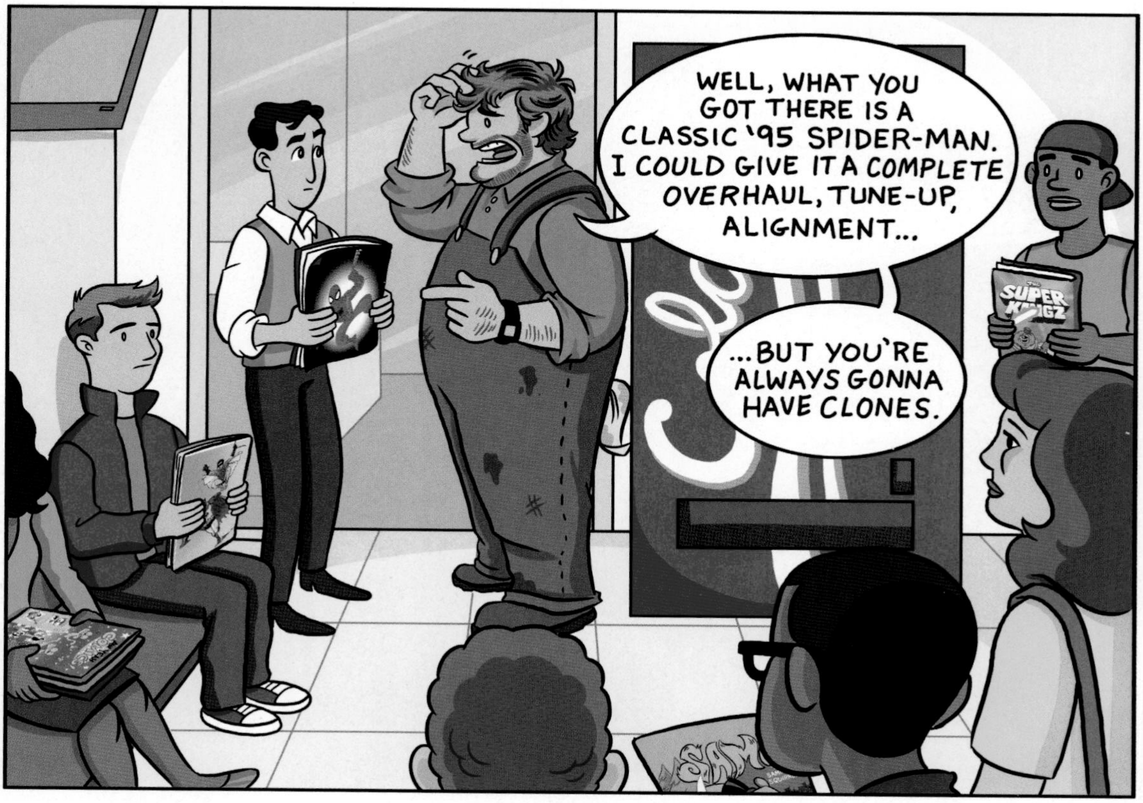
WELL, WHAT YOU GOT THERE IS A CLASSIC '95 SPIDER-MAN. I COULD GIVE IT A COMPLETE OVERHAUL, TUNE-UP, ALIGNMENT...
...BUT YOU'RE ALWAYS GONNA HAVE CLONES.
SUPER KINGZ

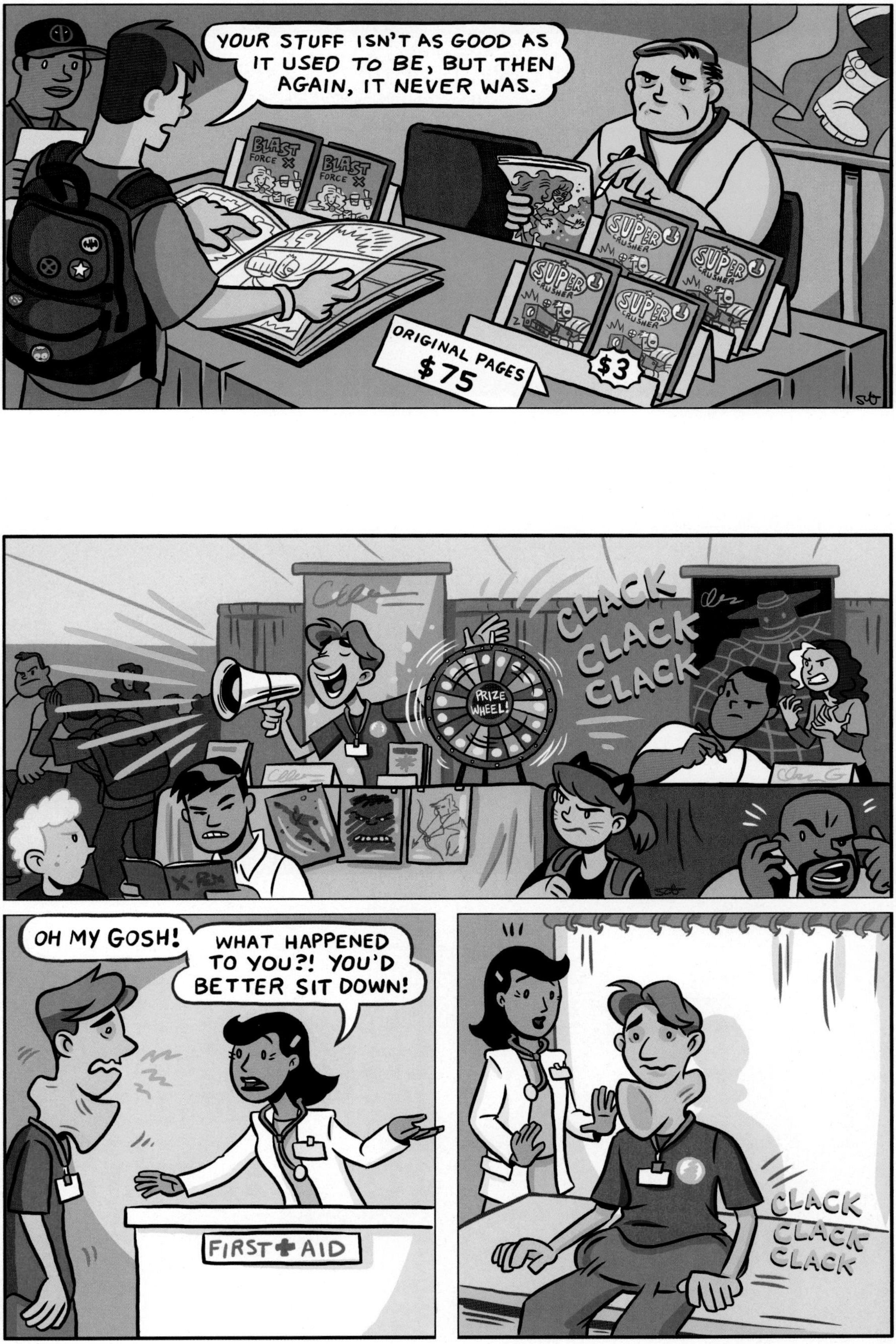
YOUR STUFF ISN'T AS GOOD AS IT USED TO BE, BUT THEN AGAIN, IT NEVER WAS.
BLAST FORCE X
SUPER CRUSHER
ORIGINAL PAGES $75
$3
PRIZE WHEEL!
CLACK CLACK CLACK
OH MY GOSH!
WHAT HAPPENED TO YOU?! YOU'D BETTER SIT DOWN!
FIRST AID
CLACK CLACK CLACK

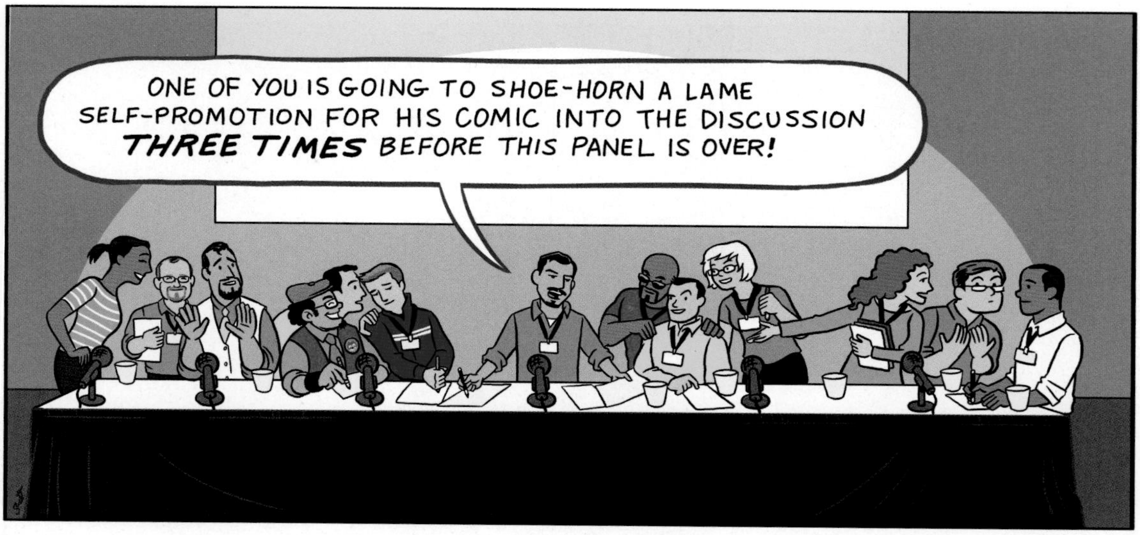
ONE OF YOU IS GOING TO SHOE-HORN A LAME SELF-PROMOTION FOR HIS COMIC INTO THE DISCUSSION ***THREE TIMES*** BEFORE THIS PANEL IS OVER!

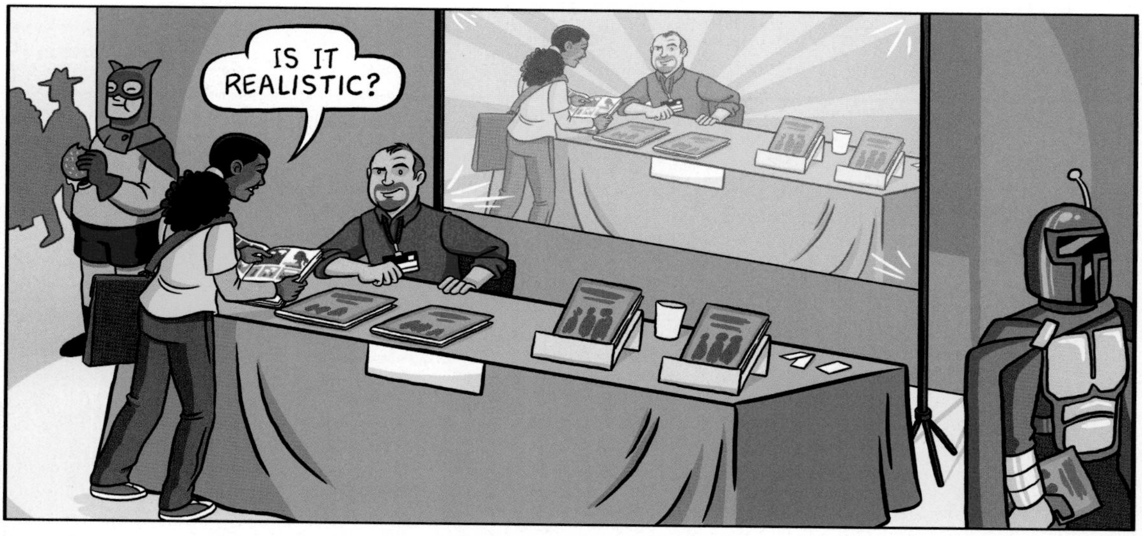
IS IT REALISTIC?

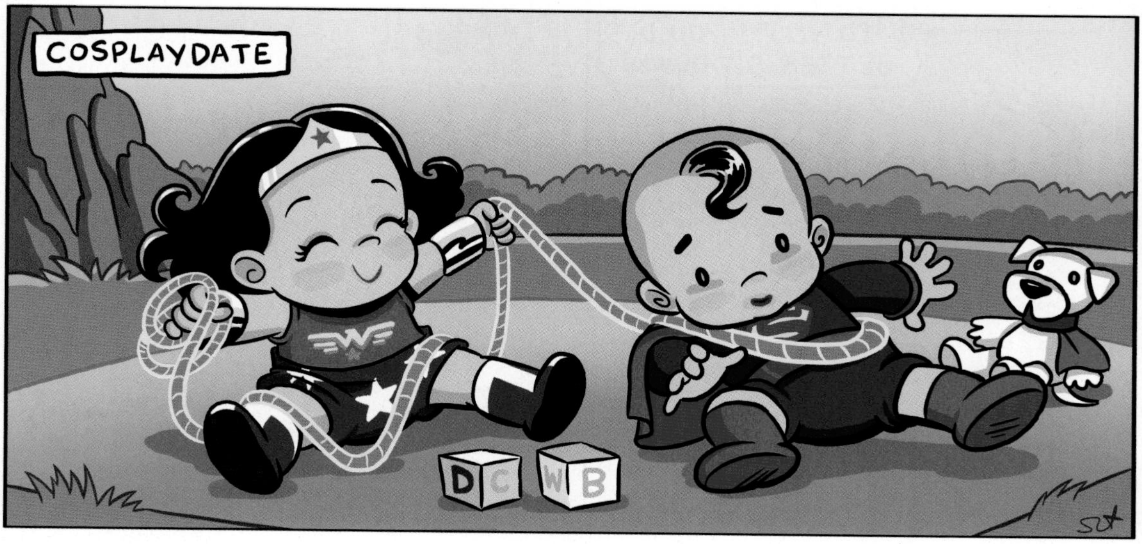
COSPLAYDATE
D C W B

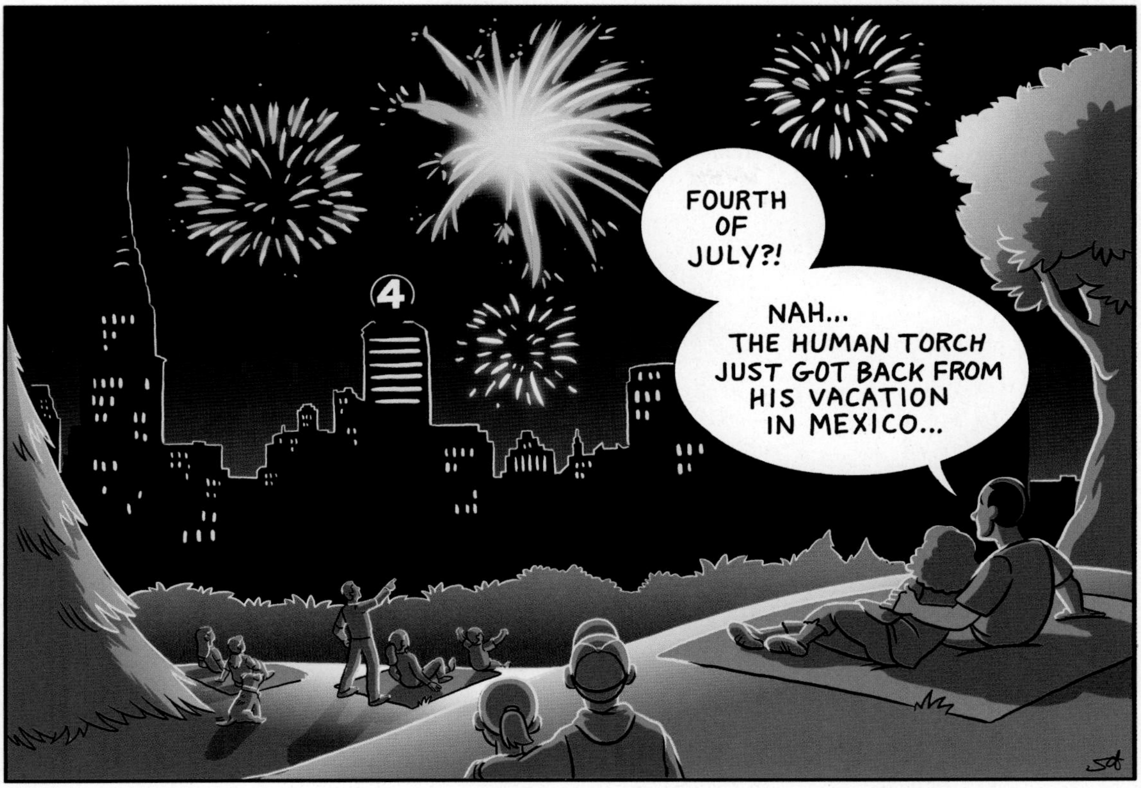
FOURTH OF JULY?!
NAH... THE HUMAN TORCH JUST GOT BACK FROM HIS VACATION IN MEXICO...

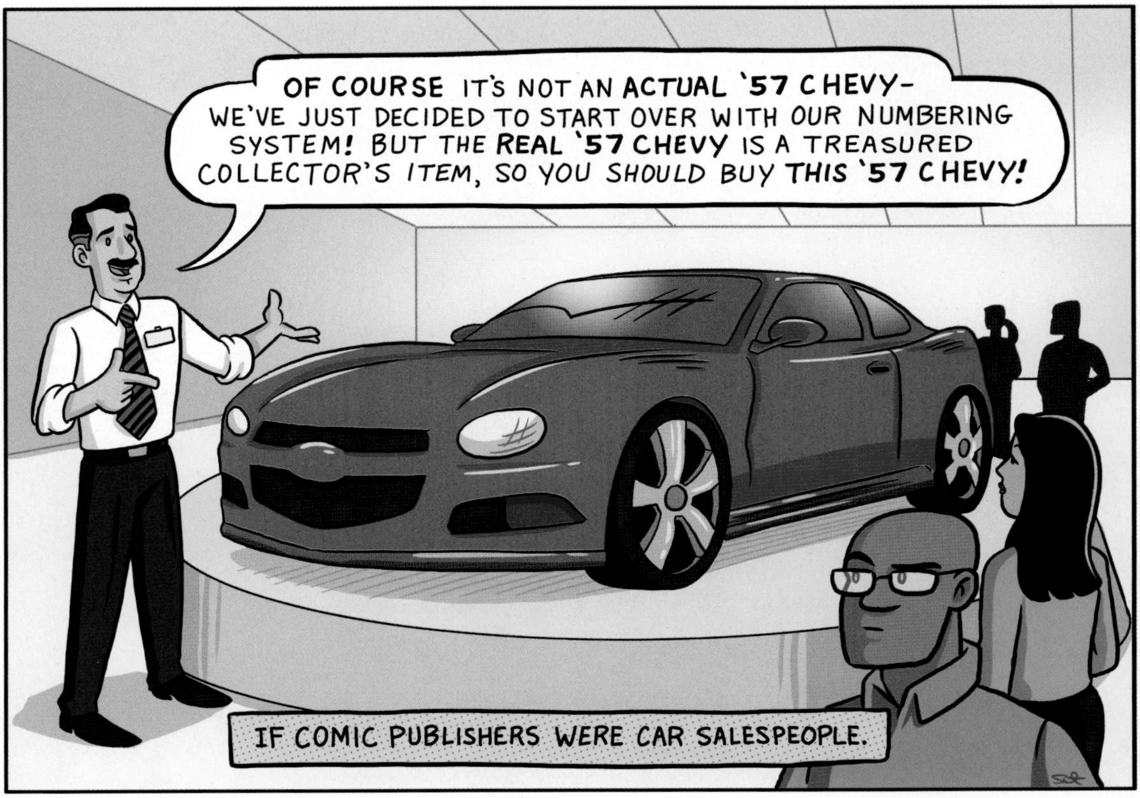
OF COURSE IT'S NOT AN ACTUAL '57 CHEVY- WE'VE JUST DECIDED TO START OVER WITH OUR NUMBERING SYSTEM! BUT THE REAL '57 CHEVY IS A TREASURED COLLECTOR'S ITEM, SO YOU SHOULD BUY THIS '57 CHEVY!
IF COMIC PUBLISHERS WERE CAR SALESPEOPLE.

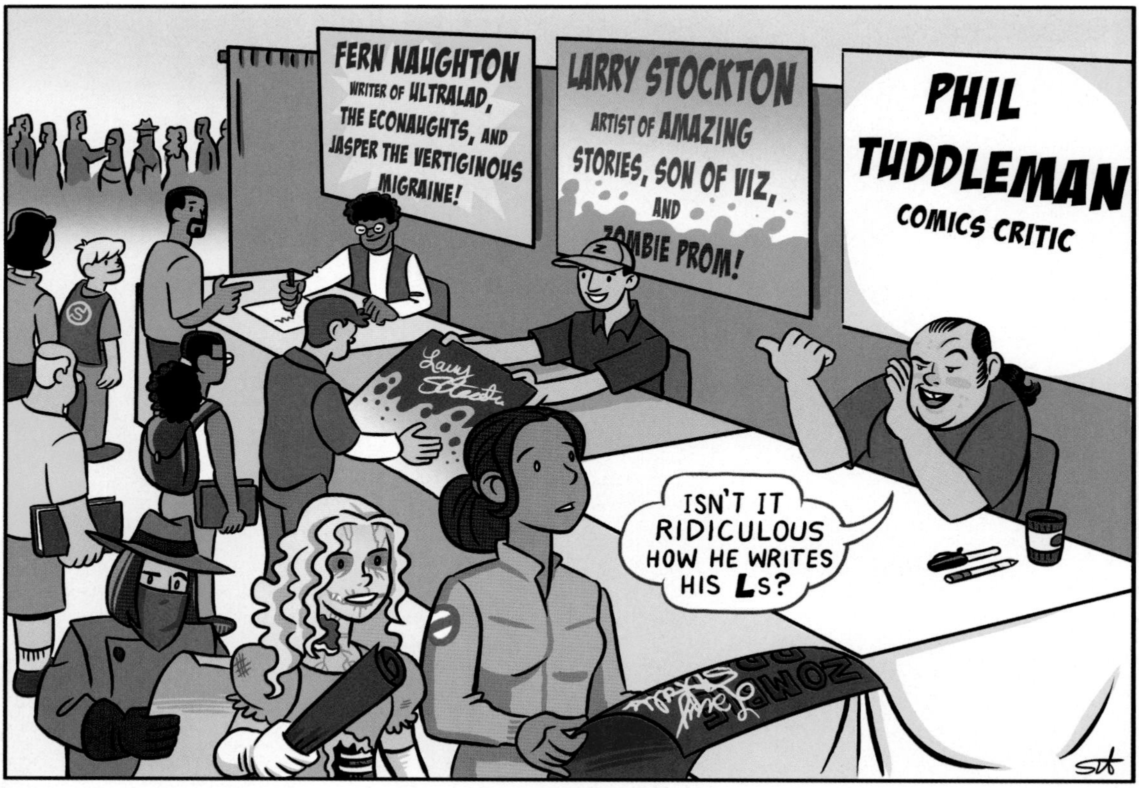
FERN NAUGHTON
WRITER OF ULTRALAD, THE ECONAUGHTS, AND JASPER THE VERTIGINOUS MIGRAINE!
LARRY STOCKTON
ARTIST OF AMAZING STORIES, SON OF VIZ, AND ZOMBIE PROM!
PHIL TUDDLEMAN
COMICS CRITIC
ISN'T IT RIDICULOUS HOW HE WRITES HIS Ls?

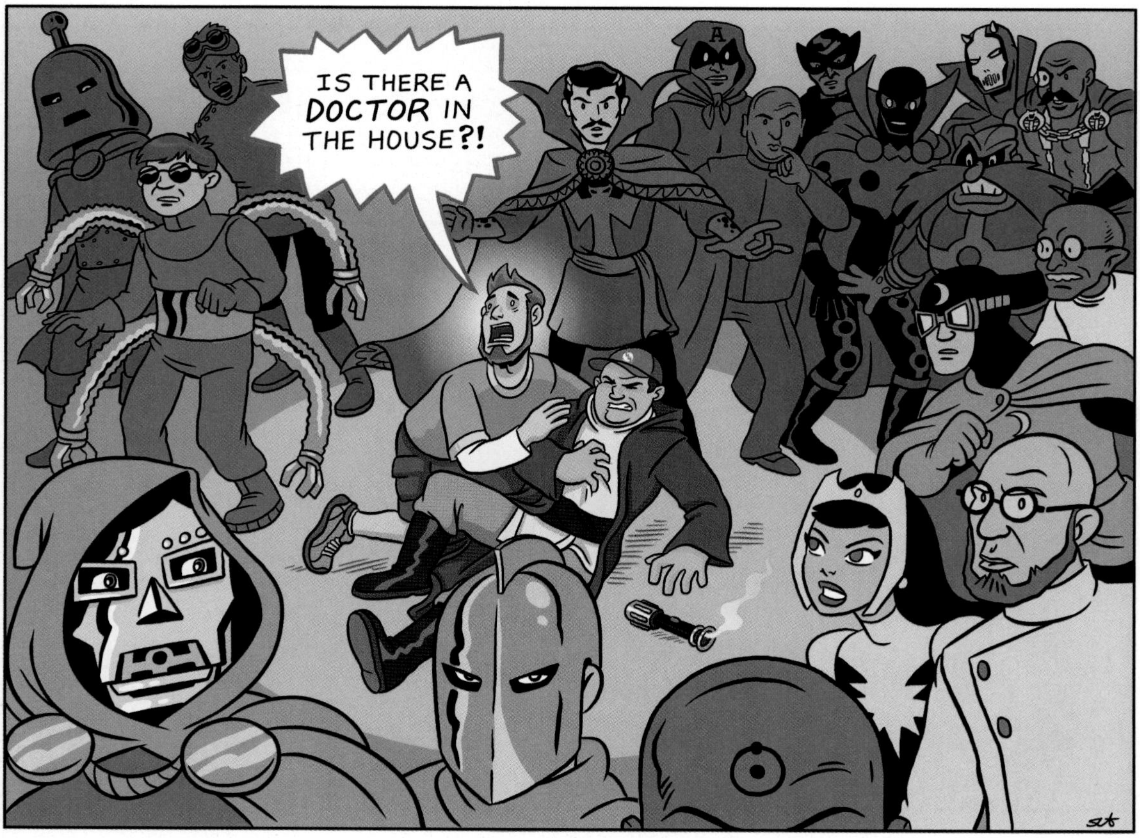
IS THERE A DOCTOR IN THE HOUSE?!

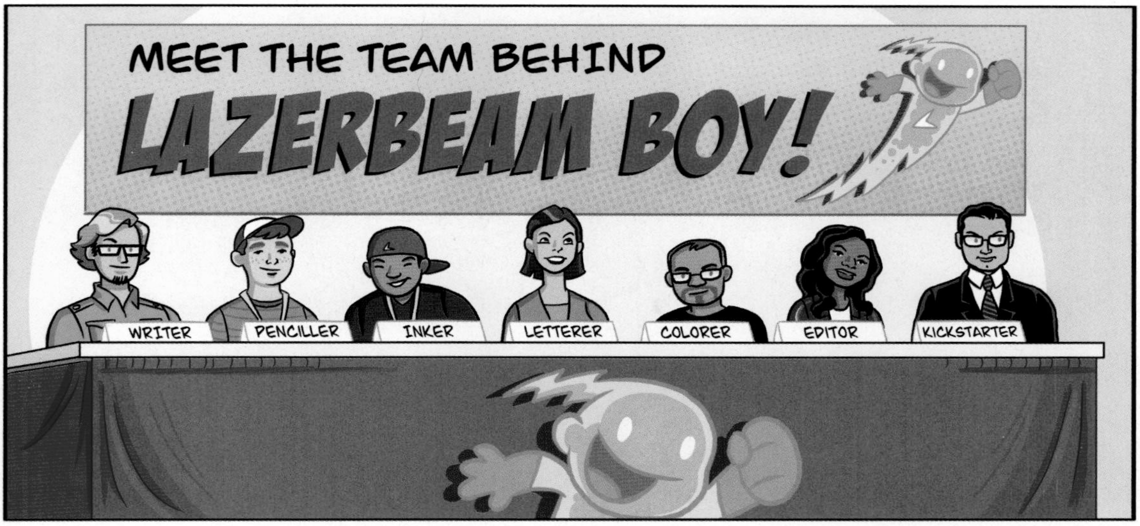
MEET THE TEAM BEHIND
LAZERBEAM BOY!
WRITER
PENCILLER
INKER
LETTERER
COLORER
EDITOR
KICKSTARTER

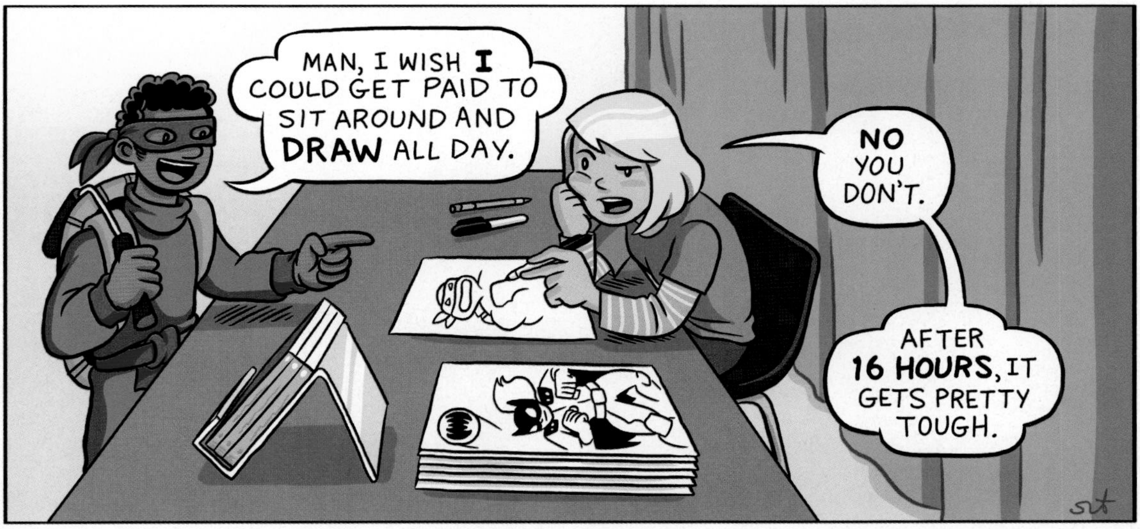
MAN, I WISH I COULD GET PAID TO SIT AROUND AND DRAW ALL DAY.
NO YOU DON'T.
AFTER 16 HOURS, IT GETS PRETTY TOUGH.

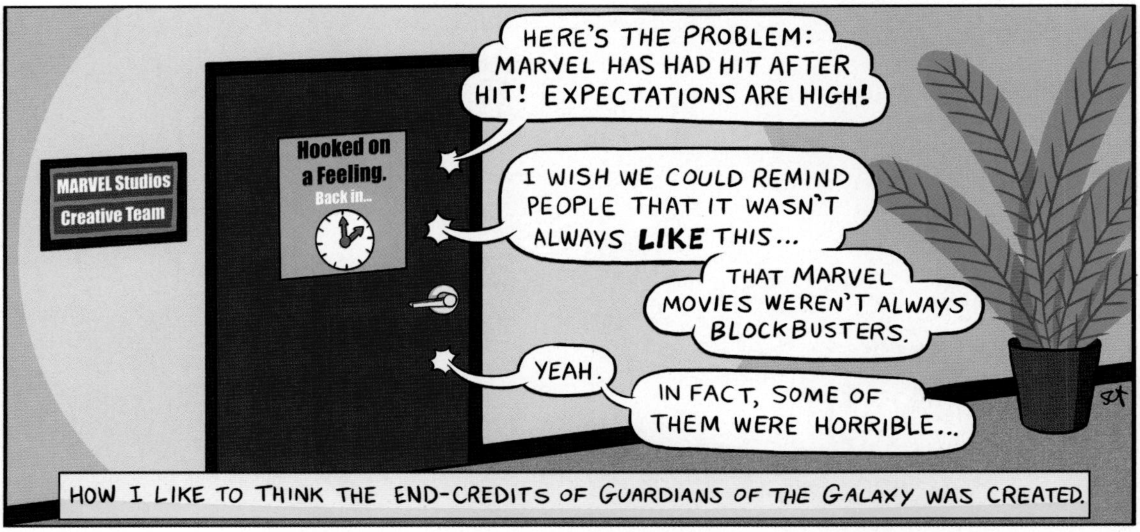
MARVEL Studios
Creative Team
Hooked on a Feeling.
Back in...
HERE'S THE PROBLEM: MARVEL HAS HAD HIT AFTER HIT! EXPECTATIONS ARE HIGH!
I WISH WE COULD REMIND PEOPLE THAT IT WASN'T ALWAYS LIKE THIS...
THAT MARVEL MOVIES WEREN'T ALWAYS BLOCKBUSTERS.
YEAH.
IN FACT, SOME OF THEM WERE HORRIBLE...
HOW I LIKE TO THINK THE END-CREDITS OF GUARDIANS OF THE GALAXY WAS CREATED.

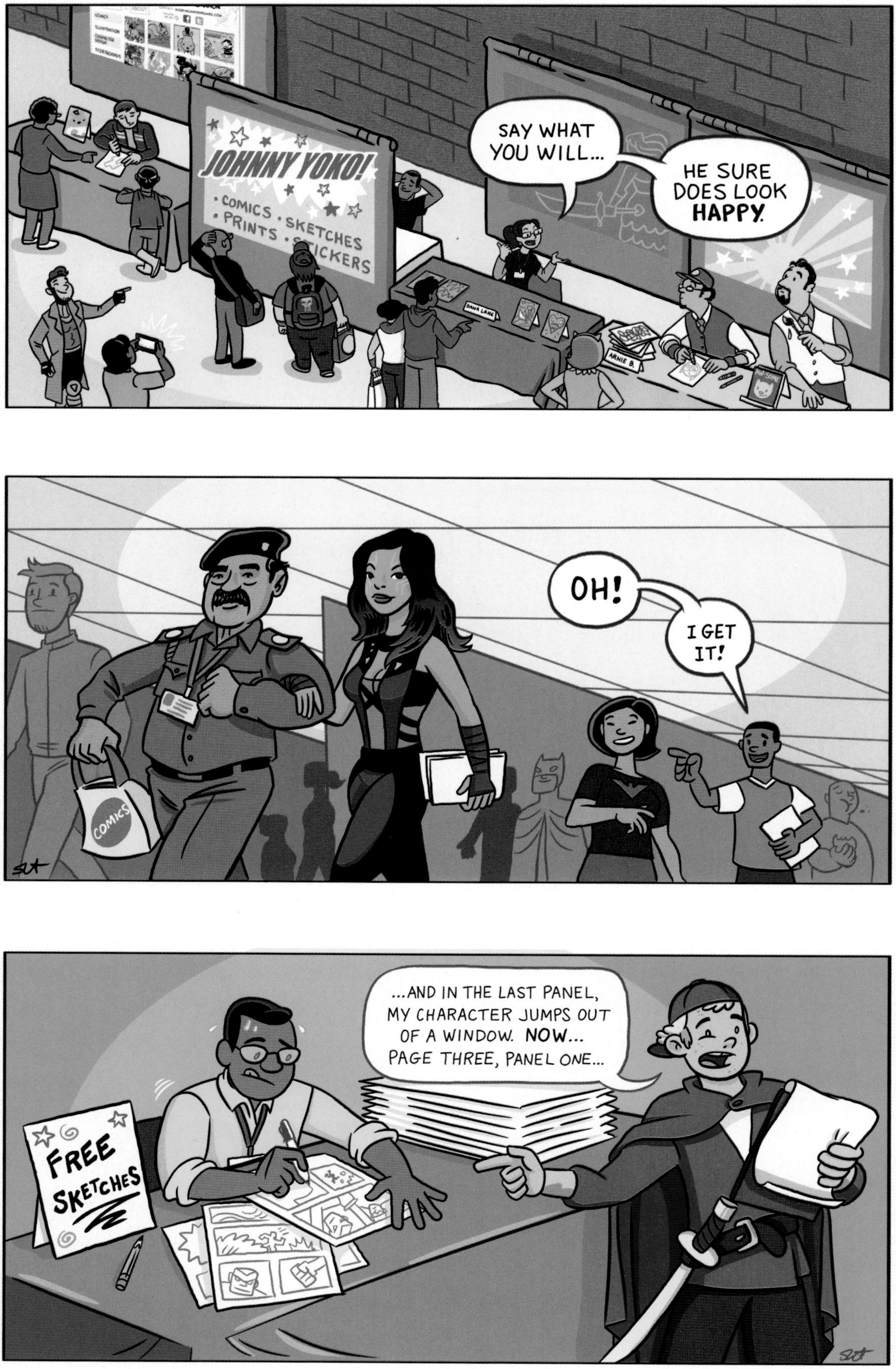
JOHNNY YOKO!
• COMICS • SKETCHES
• PRINTS • STICKERS
SAY WHAT YOU WILL...
HE SURE DOES LOOK **HAPPY**.
OH!
I GET IT!
COMICS
...AND IN THE LAST PANEL, MY CHARACTER JUMPS OUT OF A WINDOW. **NOW...** PAGE THREE, PANEL ONE...
FREE SKETCHES

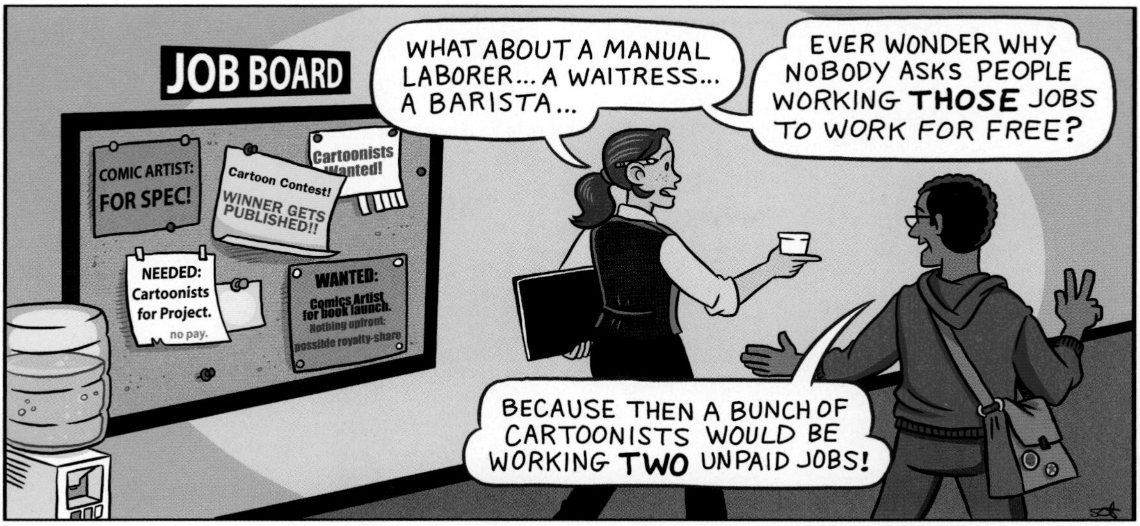
JOB BOARD
COMIC ARTIST: FOR SPEC!
Cartoon Contest! WINNER GETS PUBLISHED!!
Cartoonists Wanted!
NEEDED: Cartoonists for Project. no pay.
WANTED: Comics Artist for book launch. Nothing upfront; possible royalty-share
WHAT ABOUT A MANUAL LABORER... A WAITRESS... A BARISTA...
EVER WONDER WHY NOBODY ASKS PEOPLE WORKING THOSE JOBS TO WORK FOR FREE?
BECAUSE THEN A BUNCH OF CARTOONISTS WOULD BE WORKING TWO UNPAID JOBS!

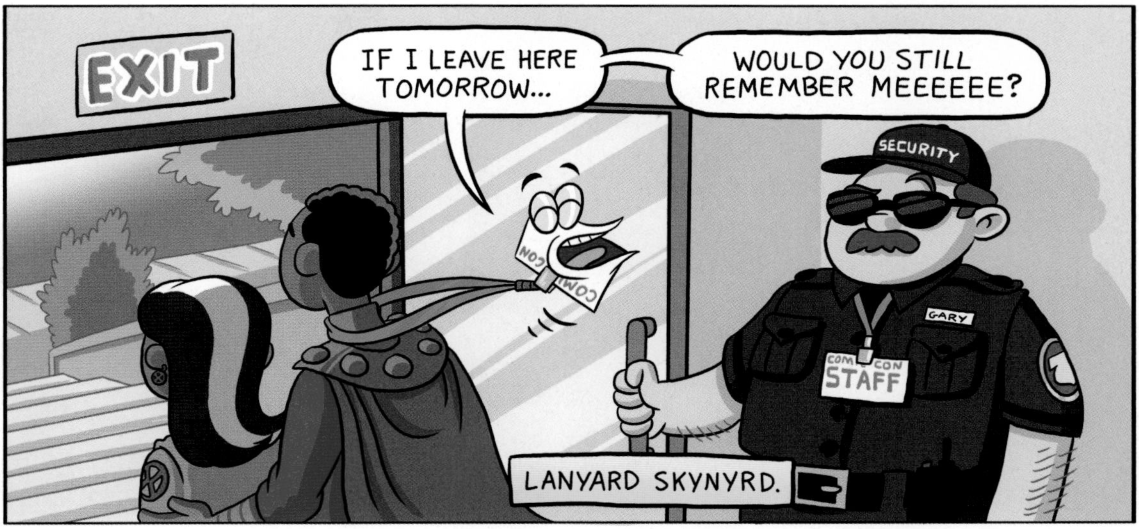
EXIT
IF I LEAVE HERE TOMORROW...
WOULD YOU STILL REMEMBER MEEEEEE?
SECURITY
GARY
COM CON STAFF
LANYARD SKYNYRD.

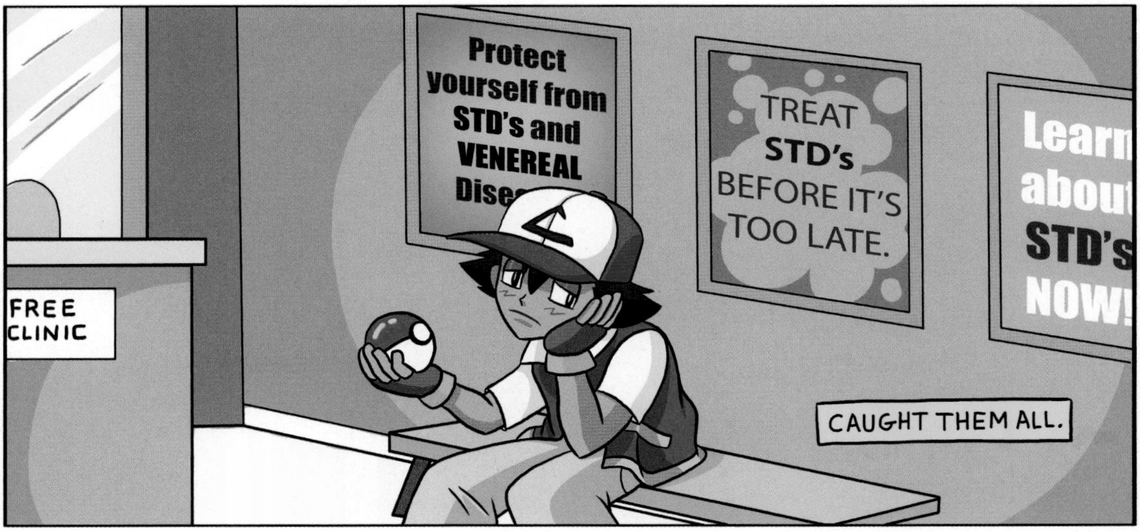
FREE CLINIC
Protect yourself from STD's and VENEREAL
TREAT STD's BEFORE IT'S TOO LATE.
STD's NOW!
CAUGHT THEM ALL.

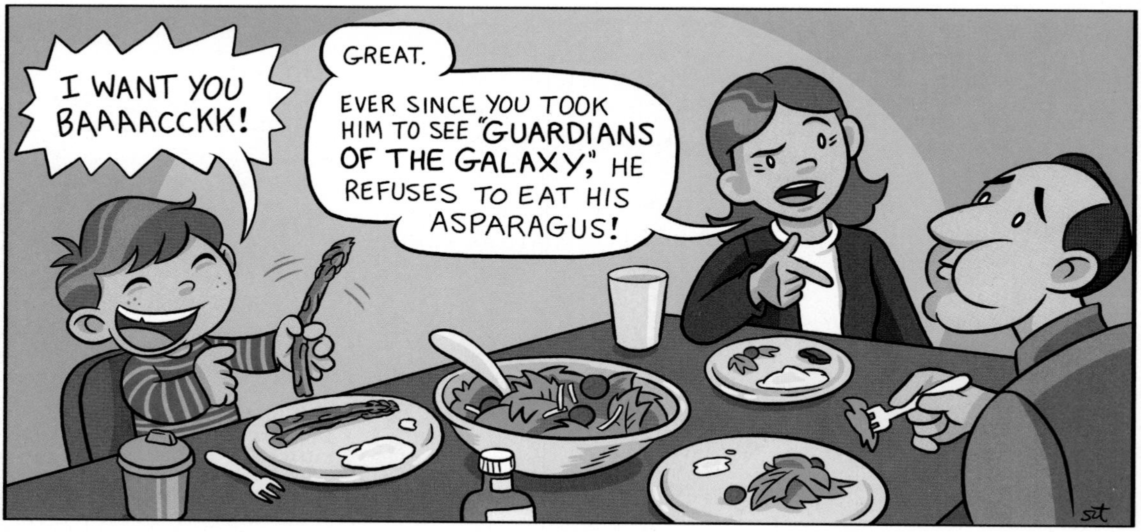
I WANT YOU BAAAACCKK!
GREAT.
EVER SINCE YOU TOOK HIM TO SEE "GUARDIANS OF THE GALAXY," HE REFUSES TO EAT HIS ASPARAGUS!

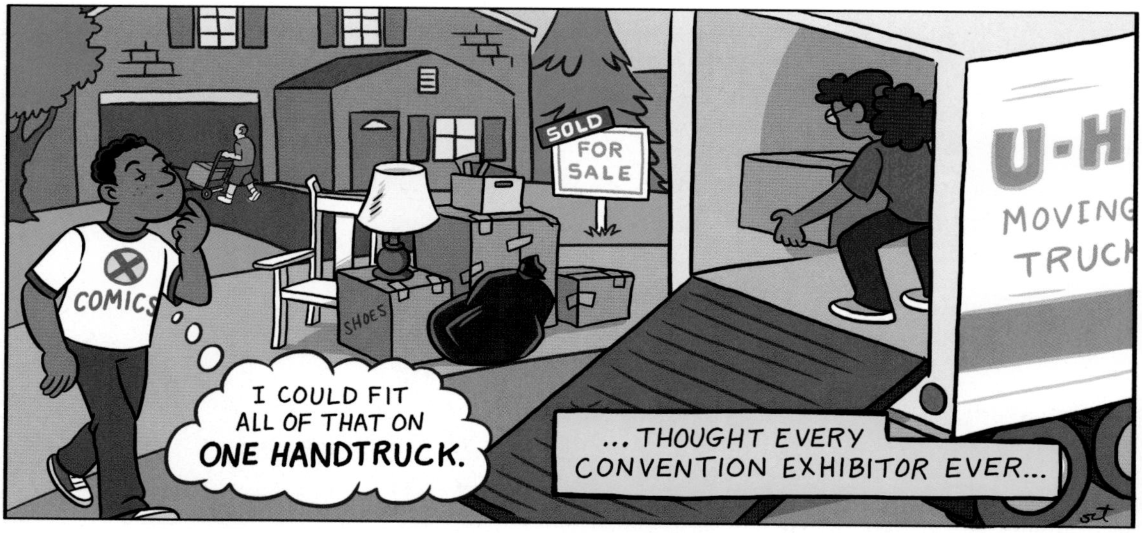
COMICS
SOLD
FOR SALE
SHOES
U-H
MOVIN
TRUC
I COULD FIT ALL OF THAT ON ONE HANDTRUCK.
... THOUGHT EVERY CONVENTION EXHIBITOR EVER...

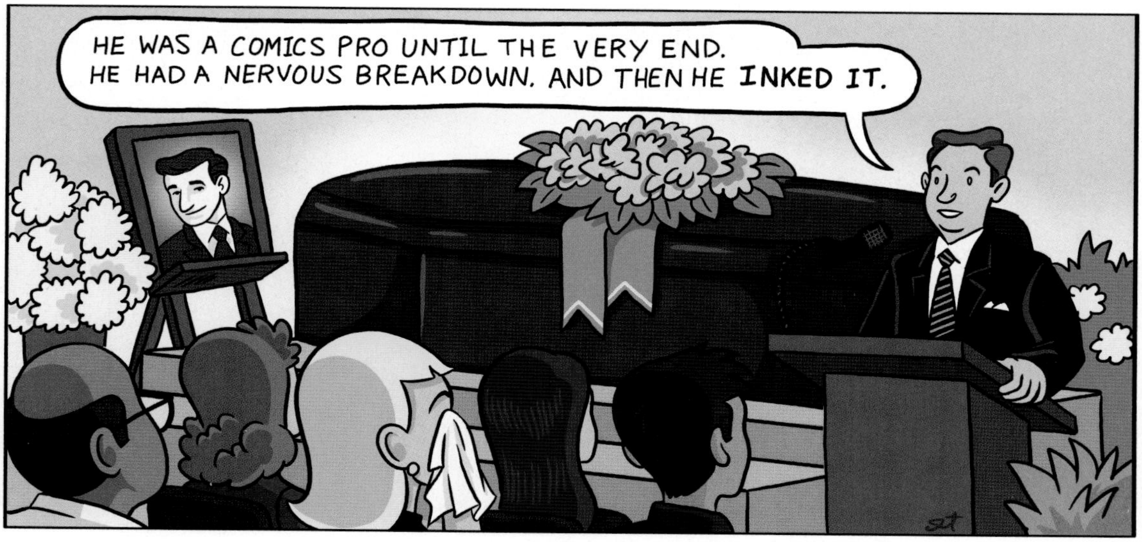
HE WAS A COMICS PRO UNTIL THE VERY END. HE HAD A NERVOUS BREAKDOWN, AND THEN HE INKED IT.

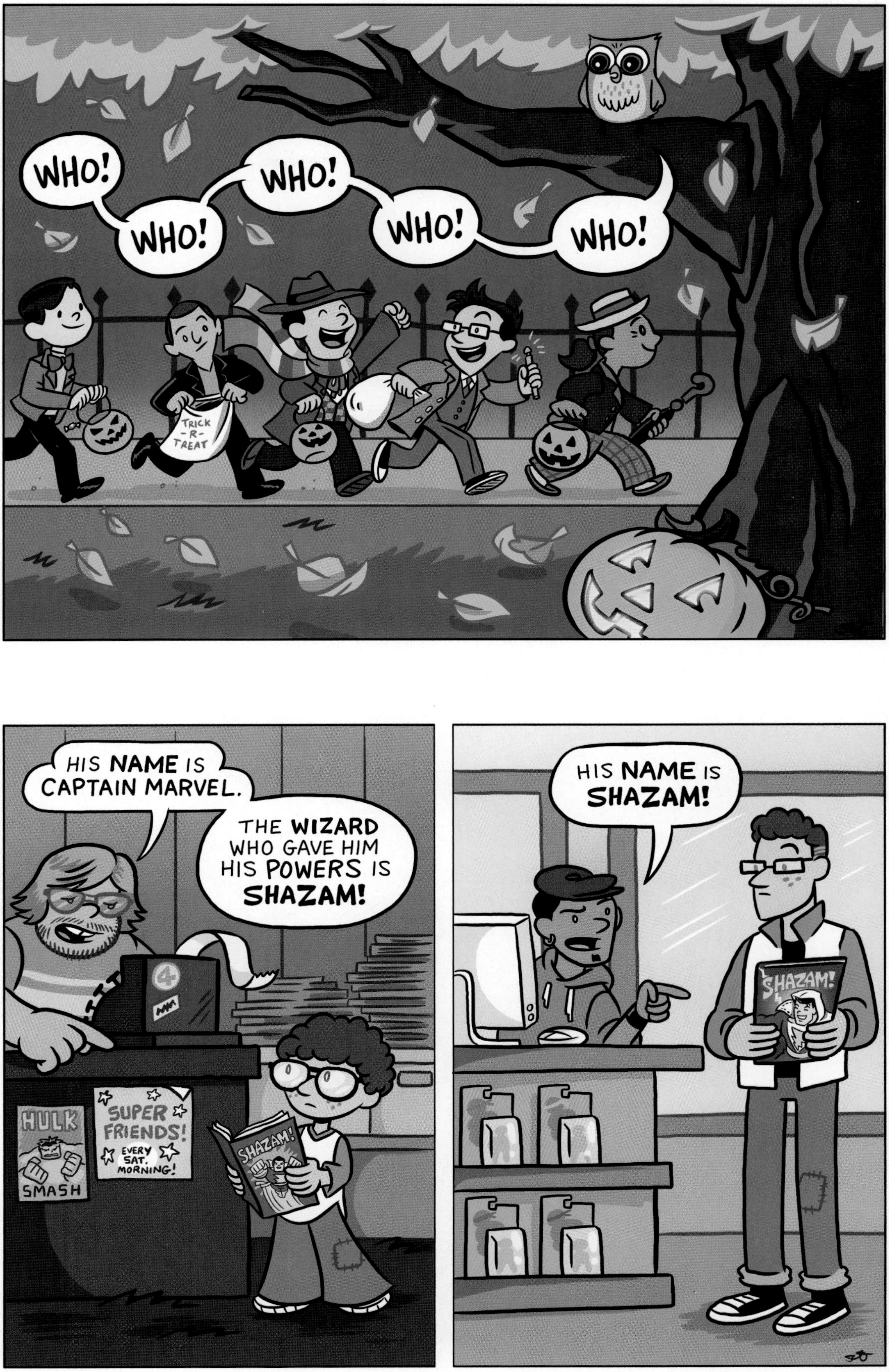
WHO!
WHO!
WHO!
WHO!
WHO!
TRICK -R- TREAT
HIS **NAME** IS CAPTAIN MARVEL.
THE **WIZARD** WHO GAVE HIM HIS **POWERS** IS **SHAZAM!**
HULK
SMASH
SUPER FRIENDS!
EVERY SAT. MORNING!
SHAZAM!
HIS **NAME** IS **SHAZAM!**
SHAZAM!

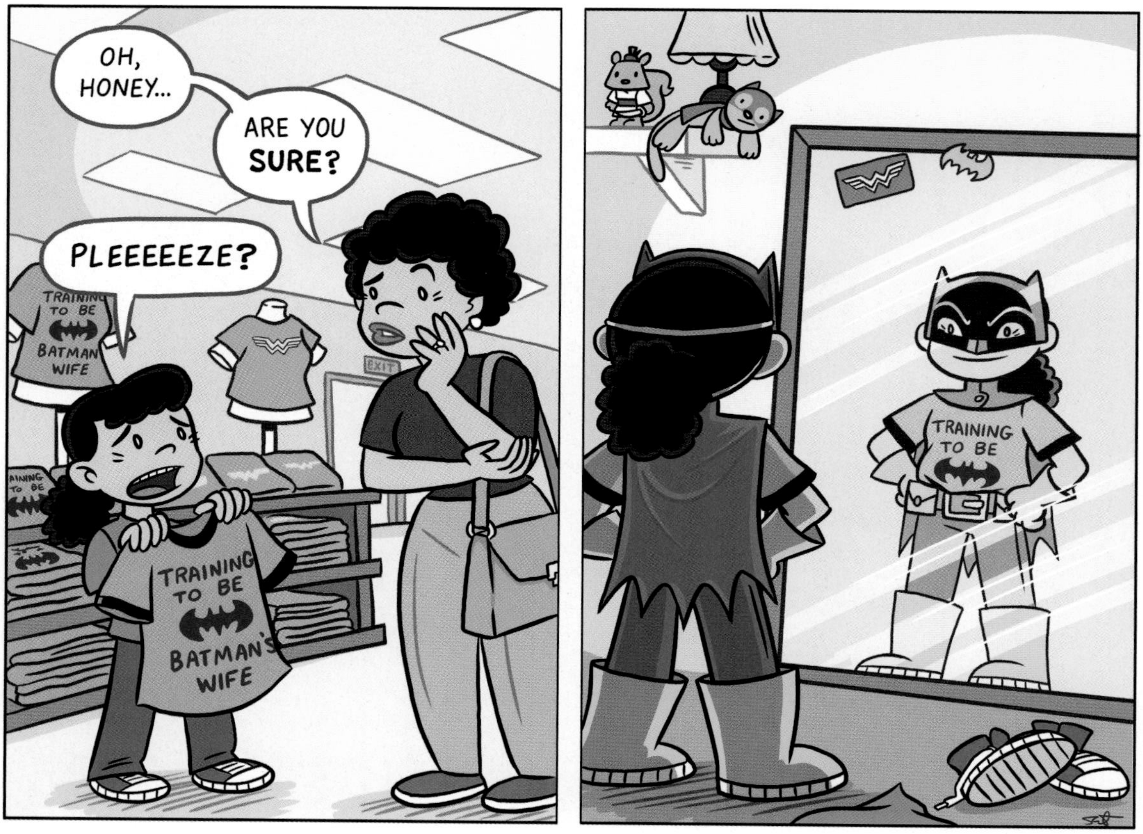
OH, HONEY...
ARE YOU **SURE?**
PLEEEEEZE?
TRAINING TO BE BATMAN'S WIFE
EXIT
TRAINING TO BE

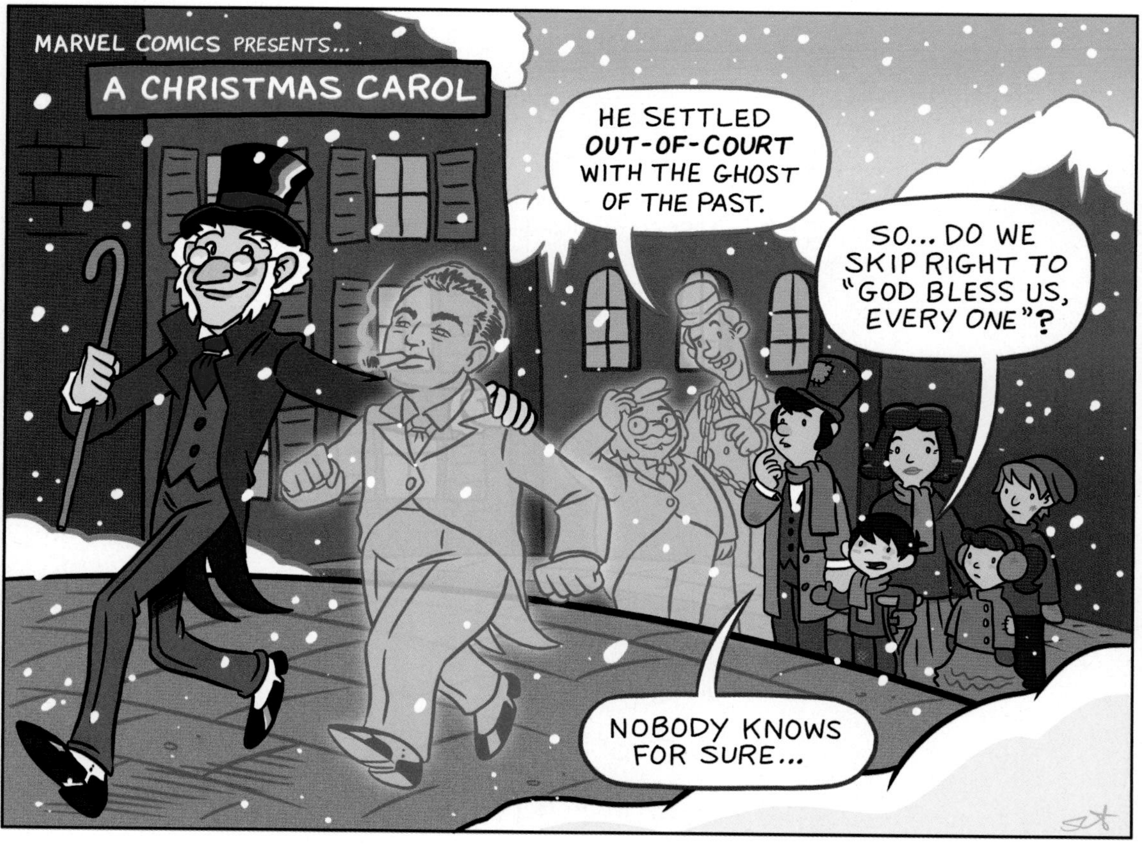
MARVEL COMICS PRESENTS...
A CHRISTMAS CAROL
HE SETTLED **OUT-OF-COURT** WITH THE GHOST OF THE PAST.
SO... DO WE SKIP RIGHT TO "GOD BLESS US, EVERY ONE"?
NOBODY KNOWS FOR SURE...

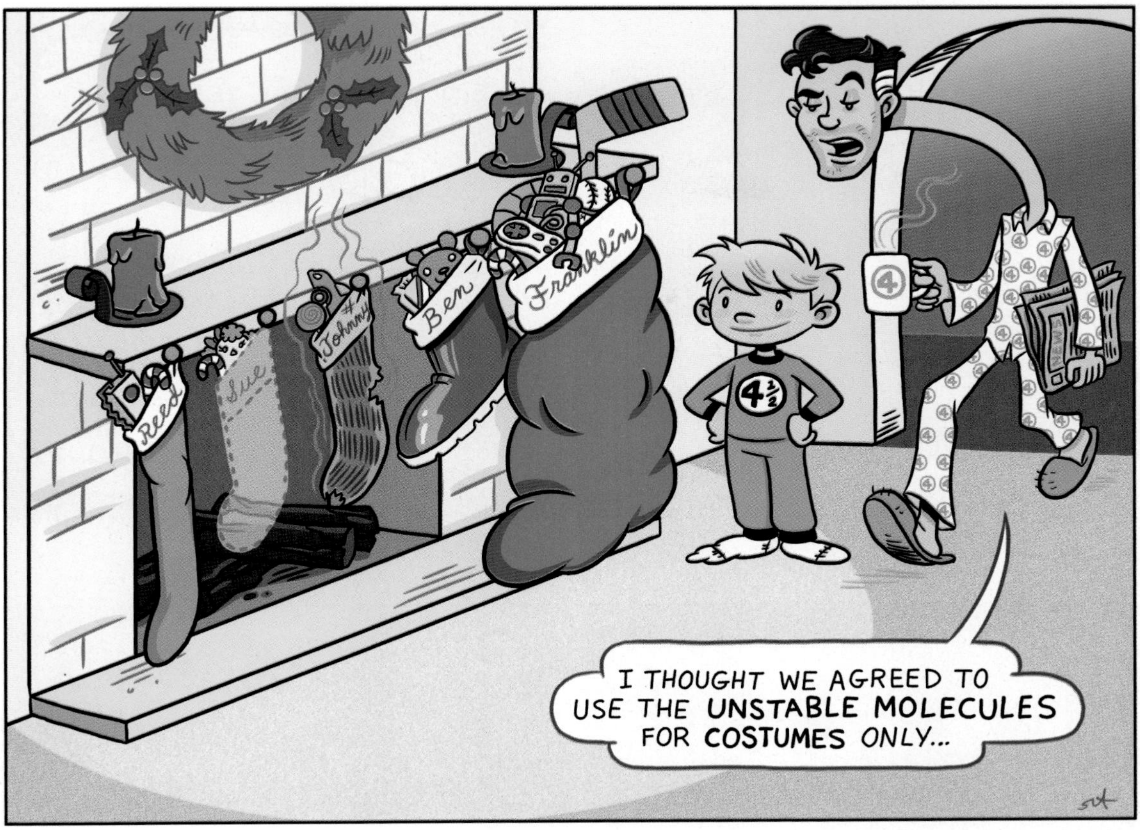
Reed
Sue
Johnny
Ben
Franklin
I THOUGHT WE AGREED TO USE THE UNSTABLE MOLECULES FOR COSTUMES ONLY...

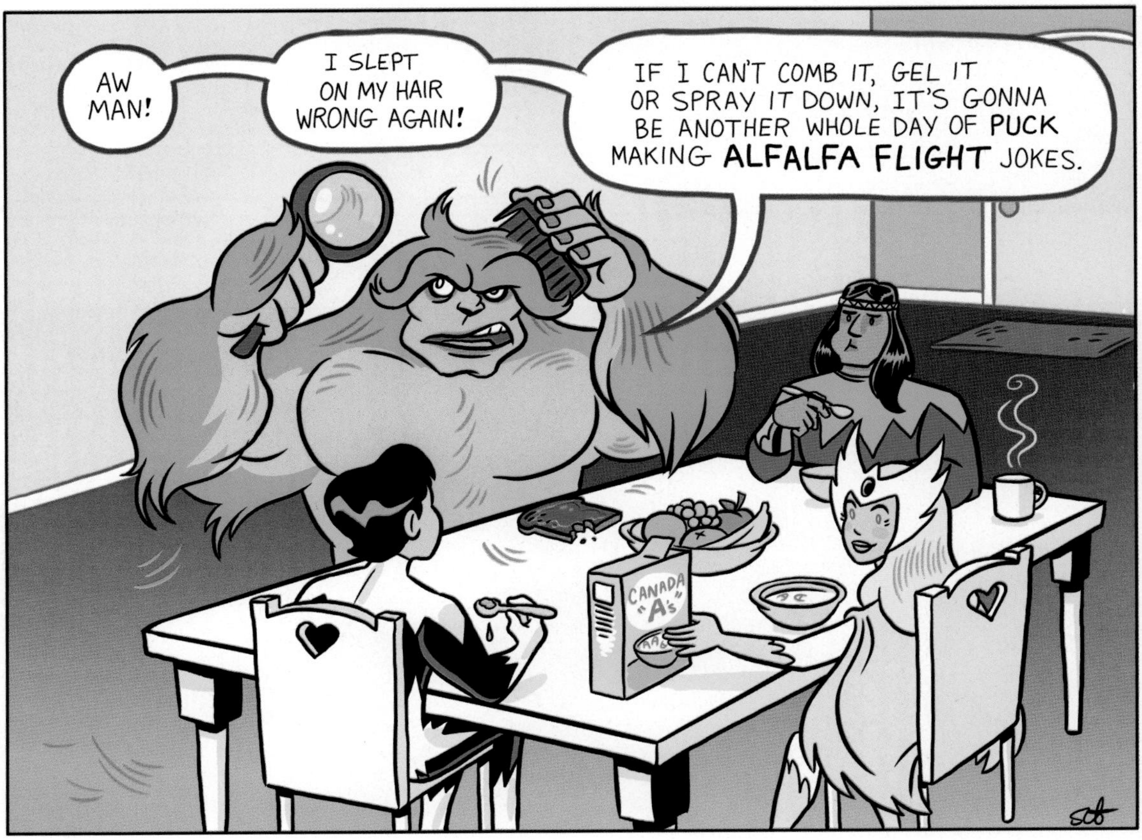
AW MAN!
I SLEPT ON MY HAIR WRONG AGAIN!
IF I CAN'T COMB IT, GEL IT OR SPRAY IT DOWN, IT'S GONNA BE ANOTHER WHOLE DAY OF PUCK MAKING ALFALFA FLIGHT JOKES.
CANADA "A"'s

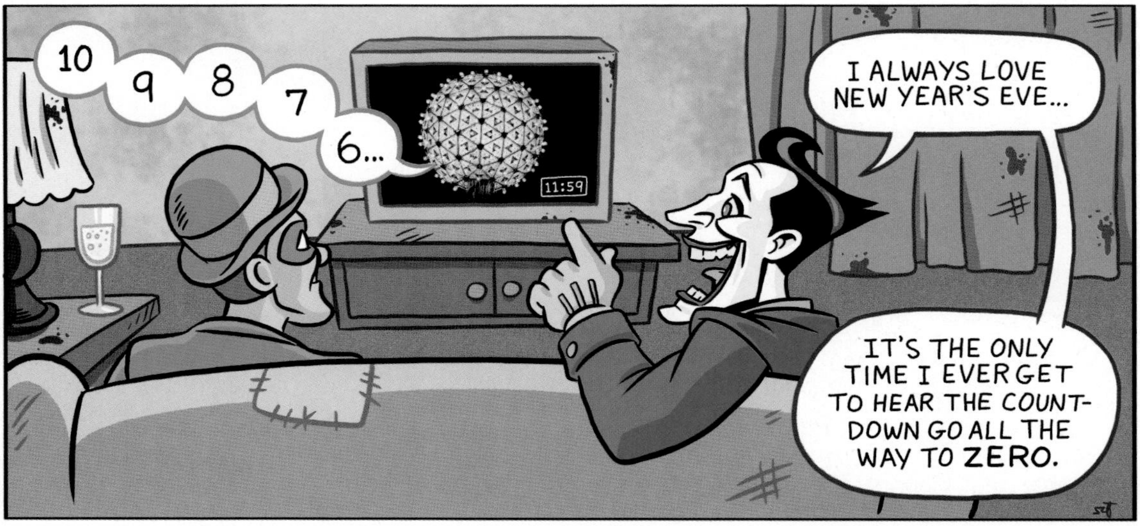
10
9
8
7
6...
11:59
I ALWAYS LOVE NEW YEAR'S EVE...
IT'S THE ONLY TIME I EVER GET TO HEAR THE COUNT-DOWN GO ALL THE WAY TO ZERO.

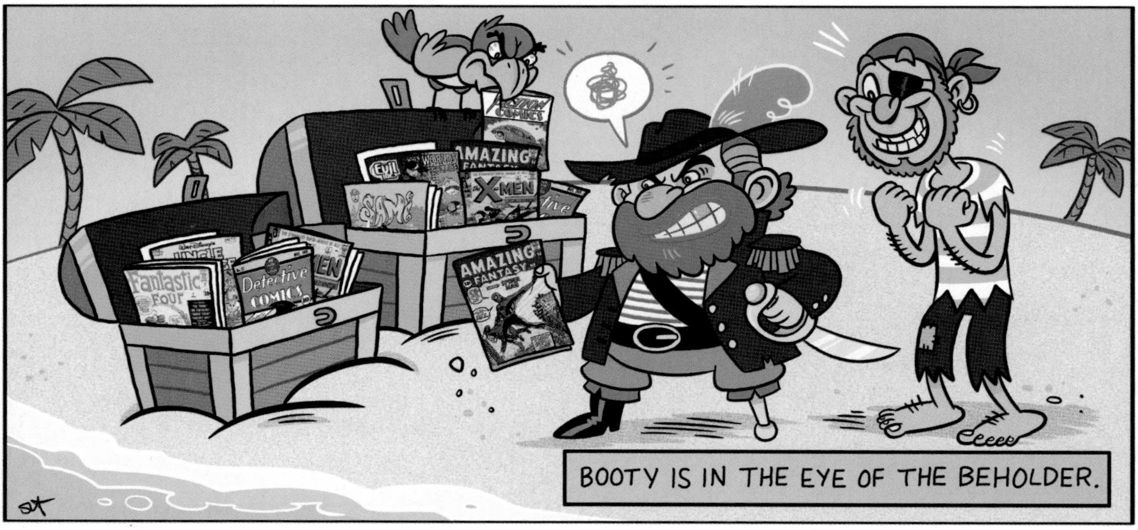
BOOTY IS IN THE EYE OF THE BEHOLDER.

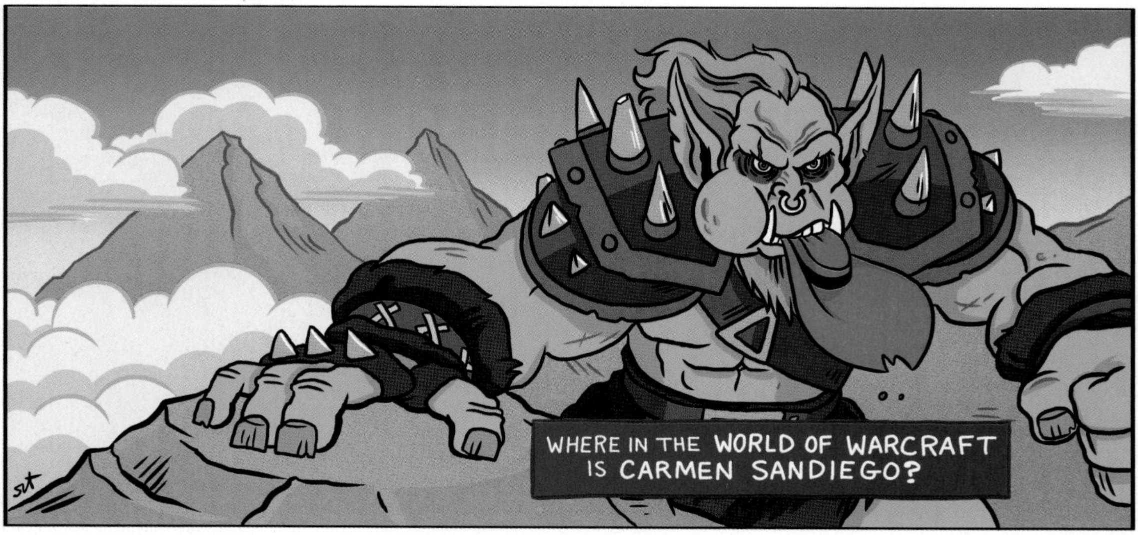
WHERE IN THE WORLD OF WARCRAFT IS CARMEN SANDIEGO?

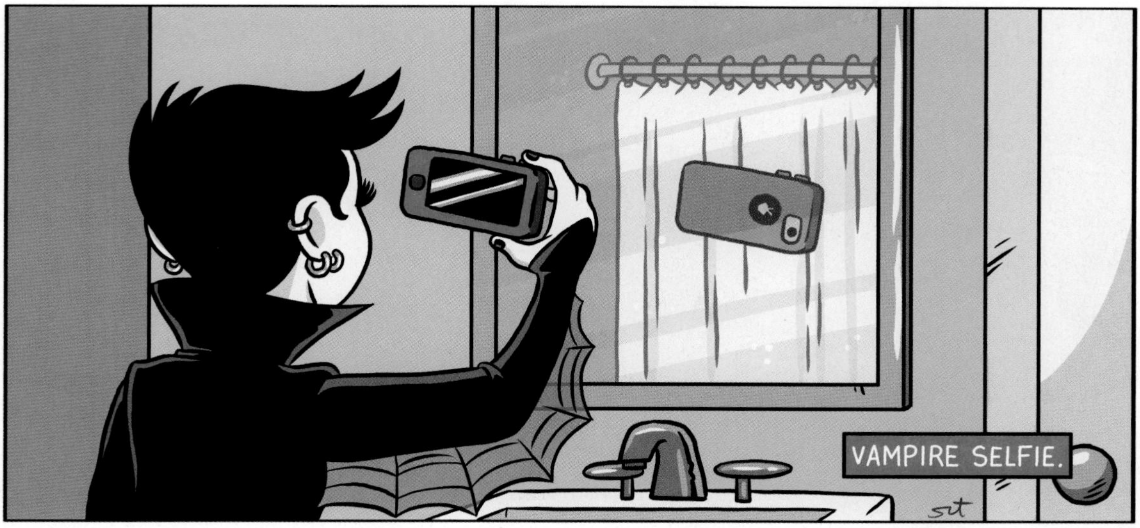
VAMPIRE SELFIE.

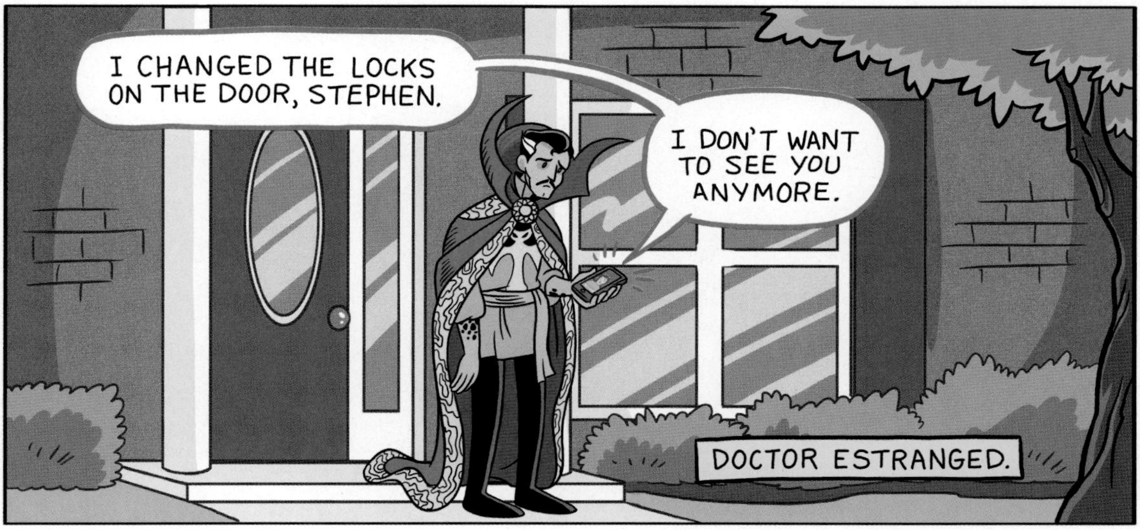
I CHANGED THE LOCKS ON THE DOOR, STEPHEN.
I DON'T WANT TO SEE YOU ANYMORE.
DOCTOR ESTRANGED.

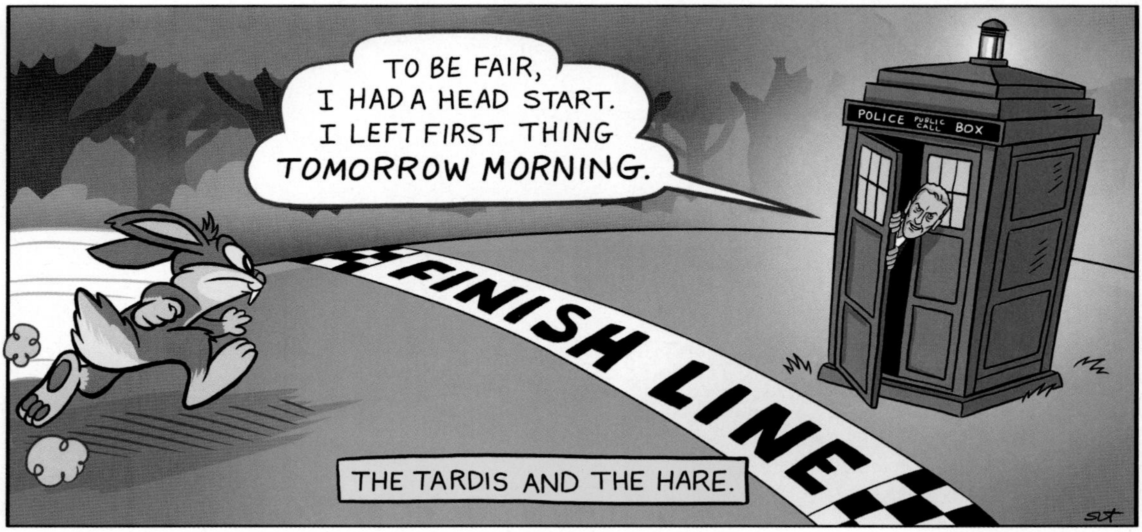
TO BE FAIR, I HAD A HEAD START. I LEFT FIRST THING TOMORROW MORNING.
POLICE PUBLIC CALL BOX
FINISH LINE
THE TARDIS AND THE HARE.

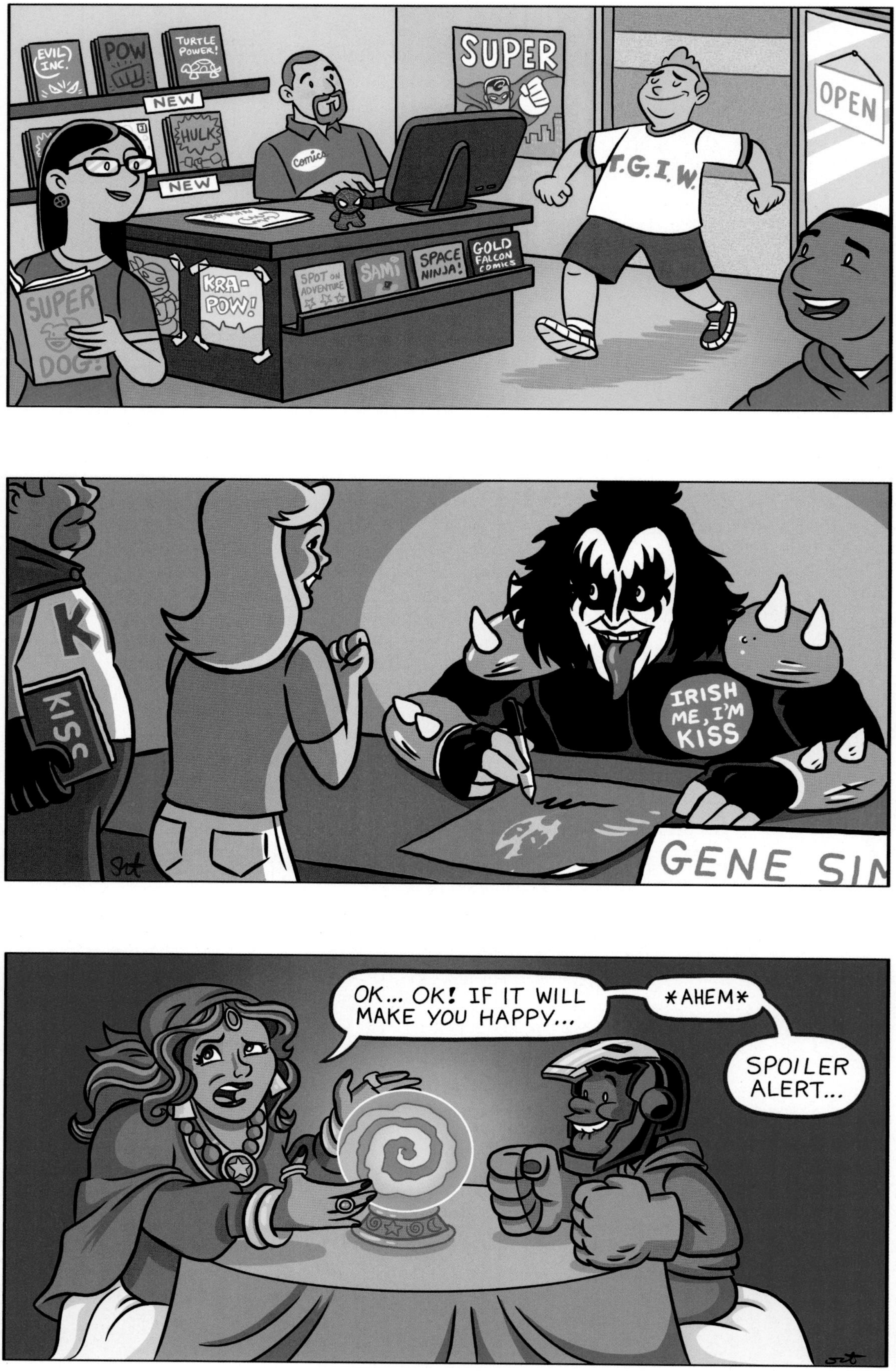
EVIL INC.
POW
TURTLE POWER!
NEW
HULK
NEW
Comics
SUPER
T.G.I.W.
OPEN
KRA-POW!
SUPER DOG!
SPOT ON ADVENTURE
SAMI
SPACE NINJA!
GOLD FALCON COMICS
K
KISS
IRISH ME, I'M KISS
GENE SI
OK... OK! IF IT WILL MAKE YOU HAPPY...
*AHEM*
SPOILER ALERT...

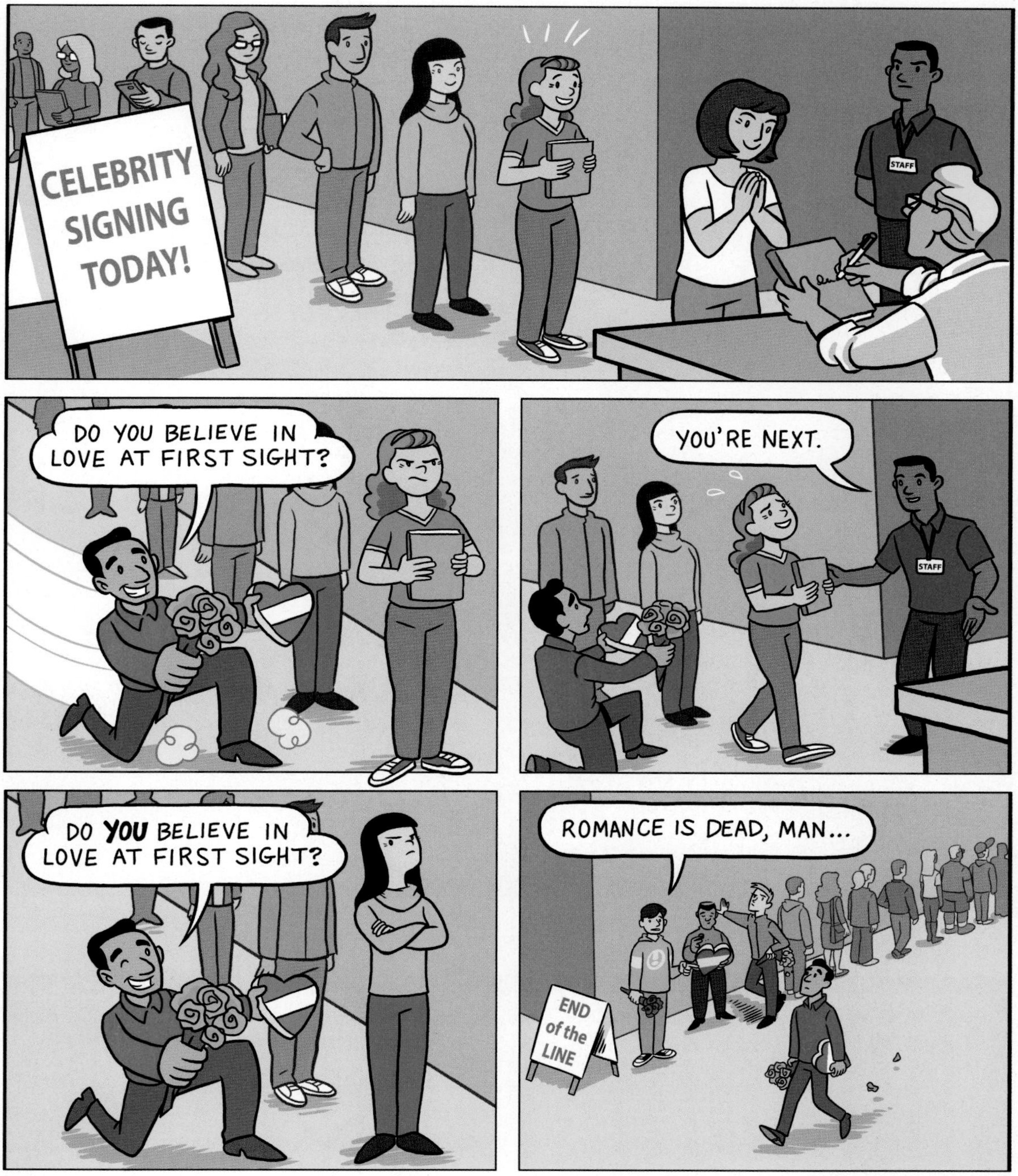
CELEBRITY SIGNING TODAY!
STAFF
DO YOU BELIEVE IN LOVE AT FIRST SIGHT?
YOU'RE NEXT.
STAFF
DO **YOU** BELIEVE IN LOVE AT FIRST SIGHT?
ROMANCE IS DEAD, MAN...
END of the LINE

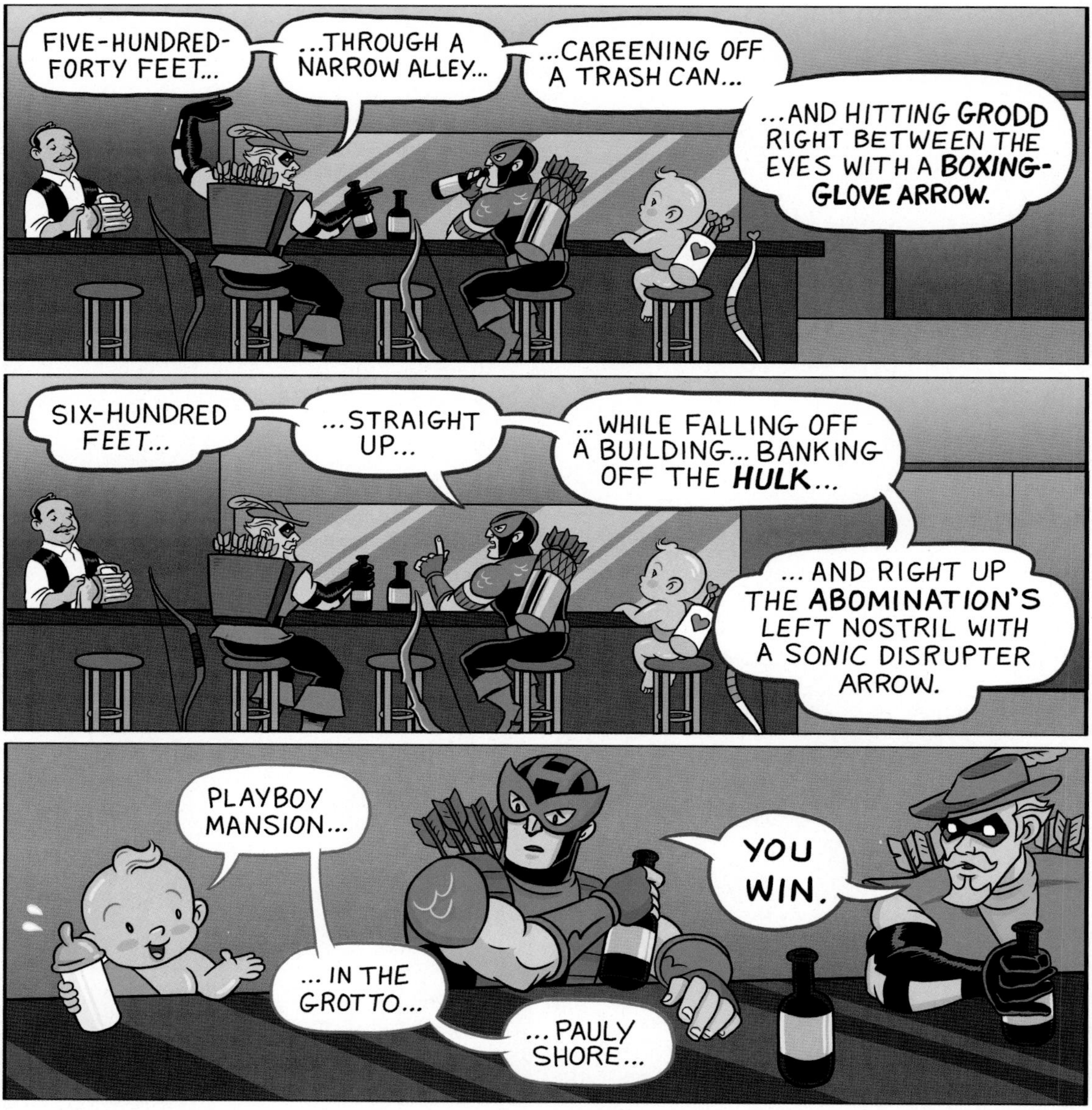
FIVE-HUNDRED-FORTY FEET...
...THROUGH A NARROW ALLEY...
...CAREENING OFF A TRASH CAN...
...AND HITTING GRODD RIGHT BETWEEN THE EYES WITH A BOXING-GLOVE ARROW.
SIX-HUNDRED FEET...
...STRAIGHT UP...
...WHILE FALLING OFF A BUILDING... BANKING OFF THE HULK...
...AND RIGHT UP THE ABOMINATION'S LEFT NOSTRIL WITH A SONIC DISRUPTER ARROW.
PLAYBOY MANSION...
...IN THE GROTTO...
...PAULY SHORE...
YOU WIN.

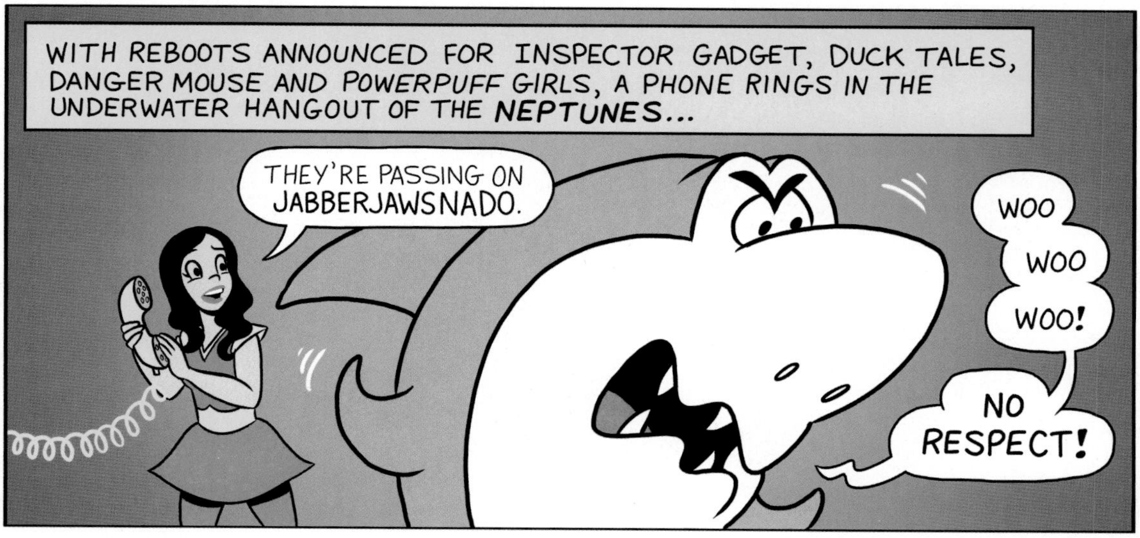
WITH REBOOTS ANNOUNCED FOR INSPECTOR GADGET, DUCK TALES, DANGER MOUSE AND POWERPUFF GIRLS, A PHONE RINGS IN THE UNDERWATER HANGOUT OF THE NEPTUNES...
THEY'RE PASSING ON JABBERJAWSNADO.
WOO
WOO
WOO!
NO RESPECT!

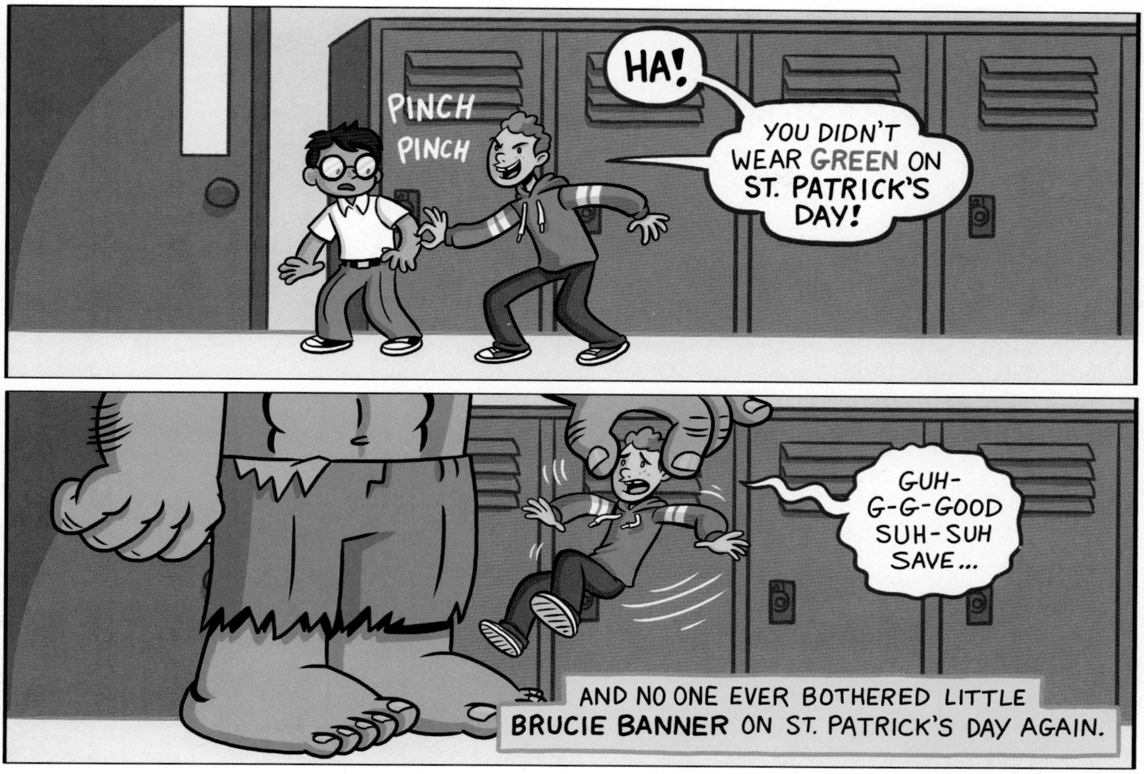
PINCH
PINCH
HA!
YOU DIDN'T WEAR GREEN ON ST. PATRICK'S DAY!
GUH- G-G-GOOD SUH-SUH SAVE...
AND NO ONE EVER BOTHERED LITTLE BRUCIE BANNER ON ST. PATRICK'S DAY AGAIN.

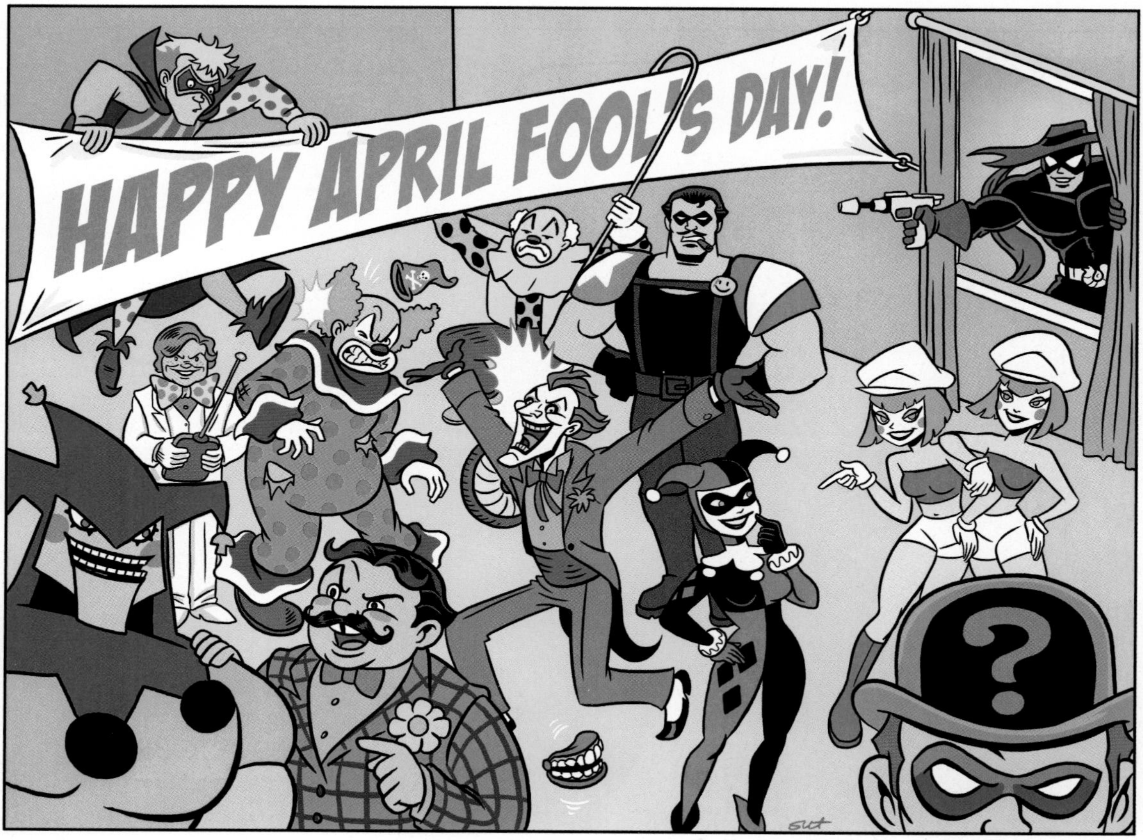
HAPPY APRIL FOOL'S DAY!

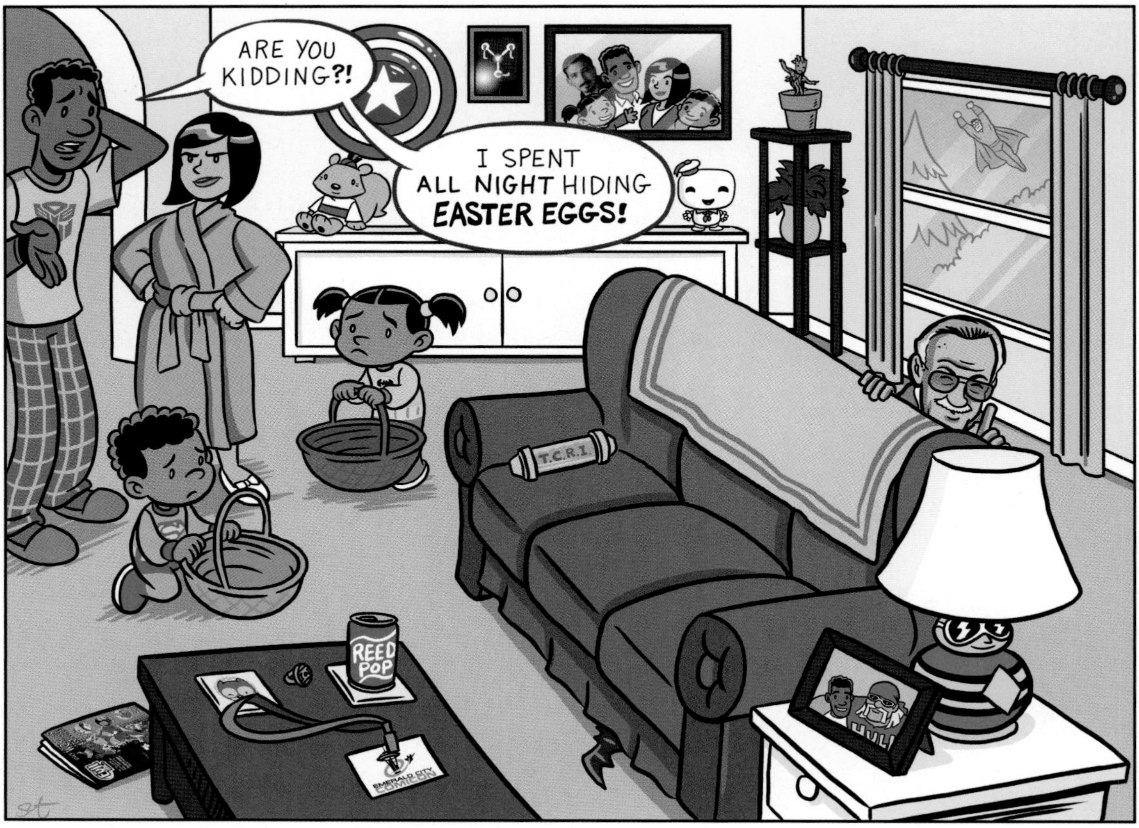
ARE YOU KIDDING?!
I SPENT ALL NIGHT HIDING EASTER EGGS!
T.C.R.I.
REED POP
EMERALD CITY COMICON

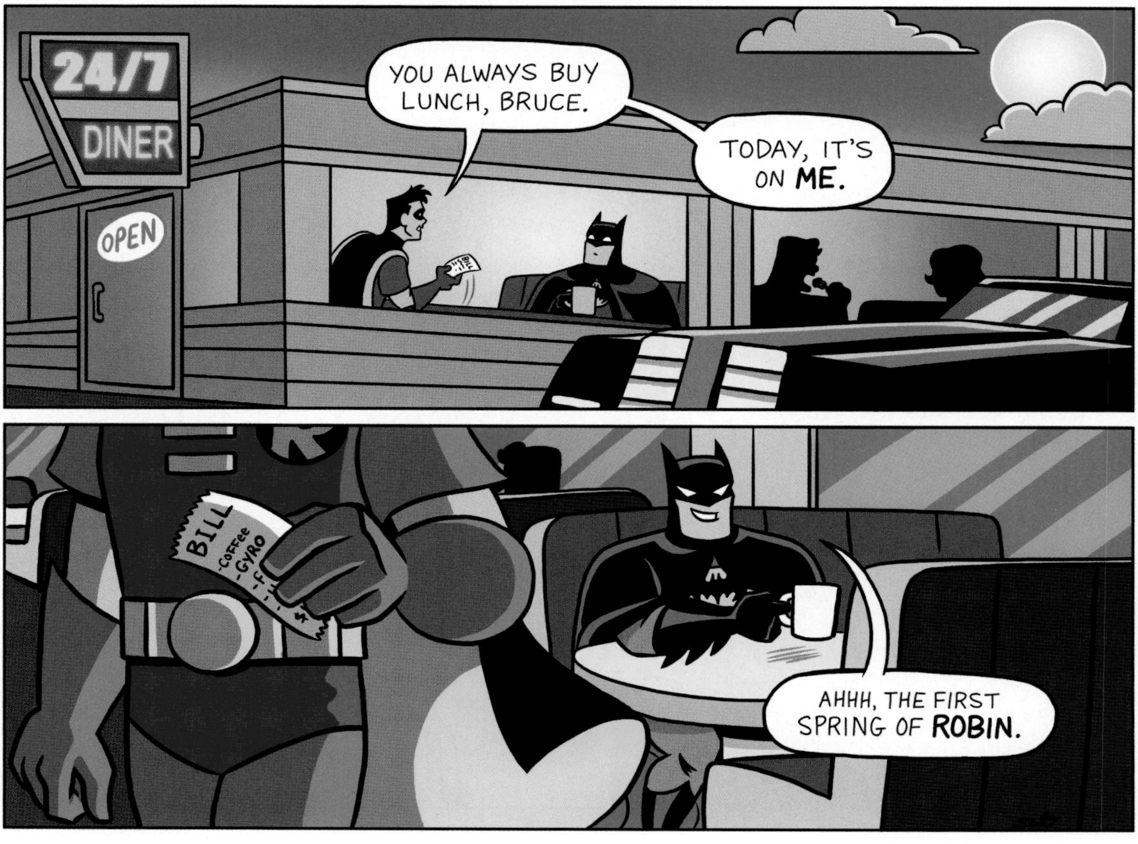
24/7
DINER
OPEN
YOU ALWAYS BUY LUNCH, BRUCE.
TODAY, IT'S ON ME.
BILL
-Coffee
-GYRO
AHHH, THE FIRST SPRING OF ROBIN.

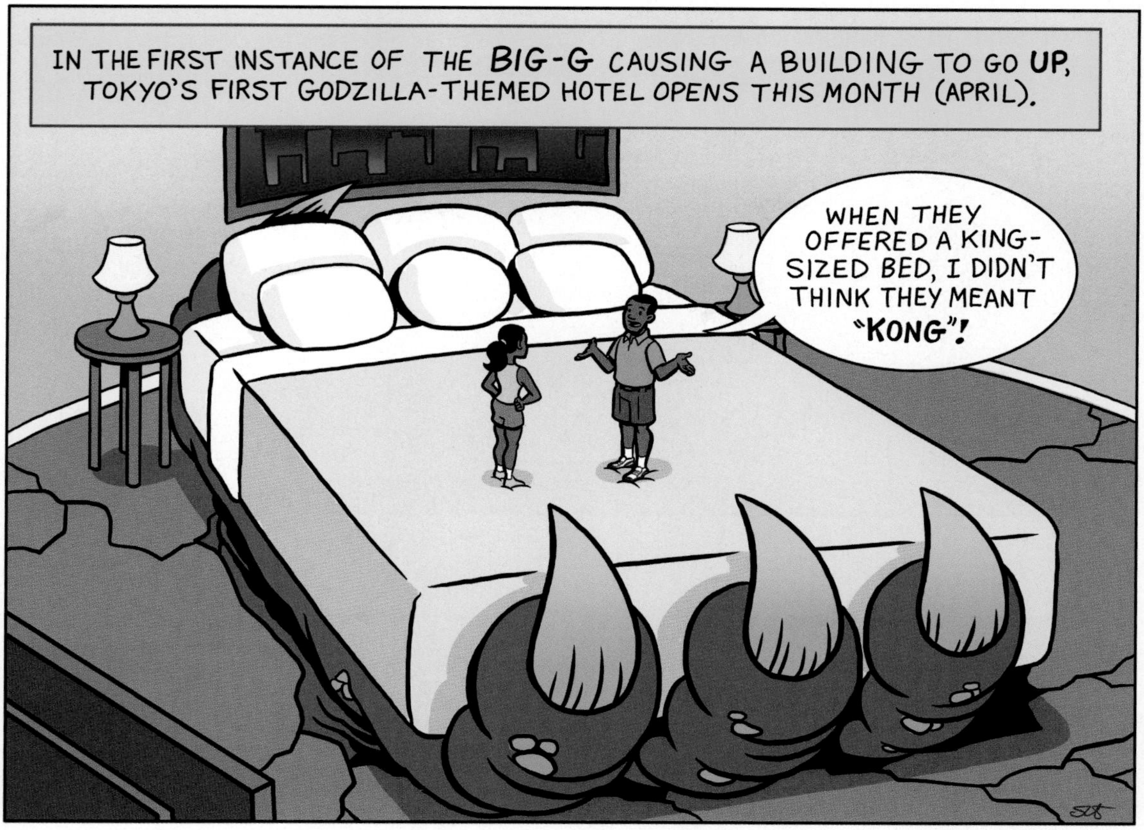
IN THE FIRST INSTANCE OF THE BIG-G CAUSING A BUILDING TO GO UP, TOKYO'S FIRST GODZILLA-THEMED HOTEL OPENS THIS MONTH (APRIL).
WHEN THEY OFFERED A KING-SIZED BED, I DIDN'T THINK THEY MEANT "KONG"!

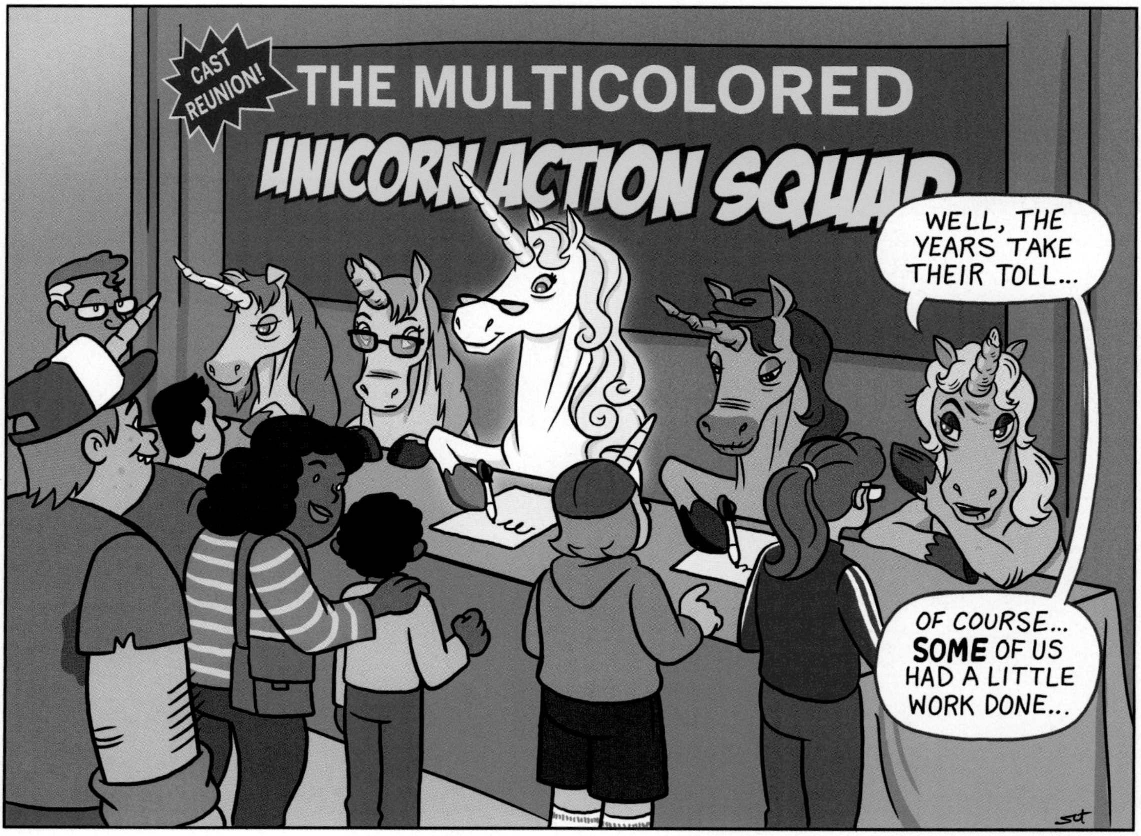
CAST REUNION!
THE MULTICOLORED
UNICORN ACTION SQUAD
WELL, THE YEARS TAKE THEIR TOLL...
OF COURSE... SOME OF US HAD A LITTLE WORK DONE...

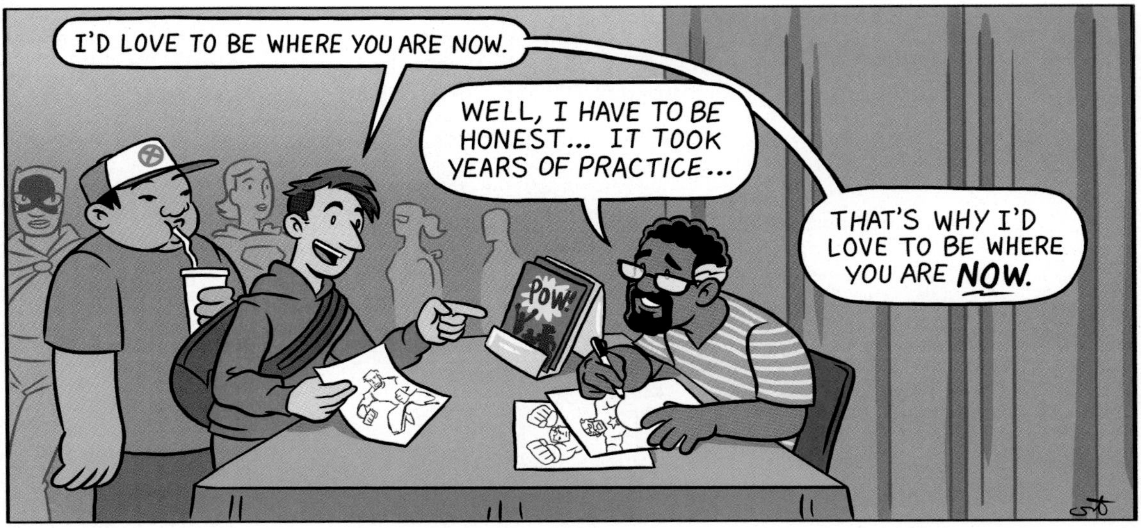
I'D LOVE TO BE WHERE YOU ARE NOW.
WELL, I HAVE TO BE HONEST... IT TOOK YEARS OF PRACTICE...
THAT'S WHY I'D LOVE TO BE WHERE YOU ARE NOW.
POW!

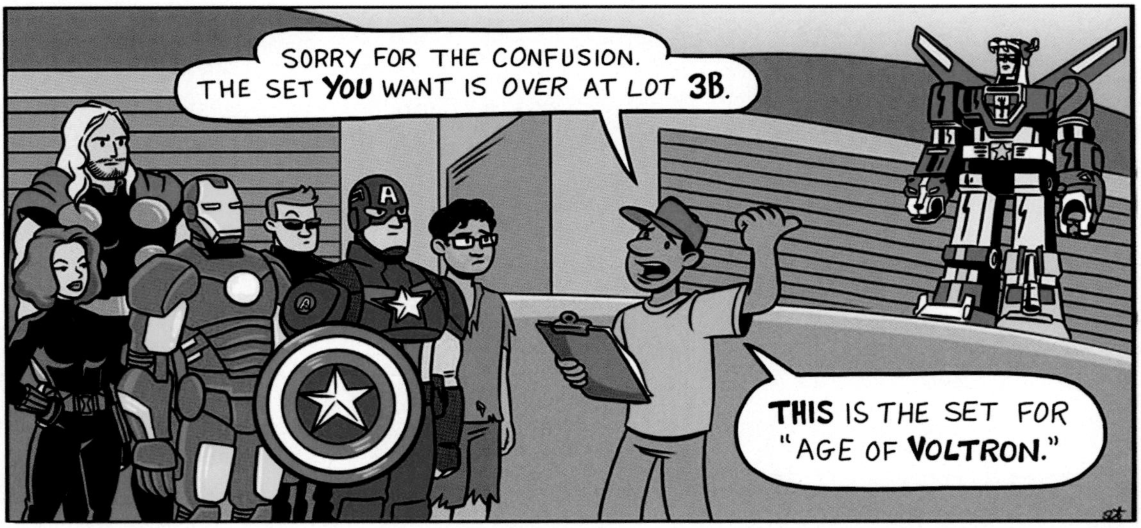
SORRY FOR THE CONFUSION. THE SET YOU WANT IS OVER AT LOT 3B.
THIS IS THE SET FOR "AGE OF VOLTRON."

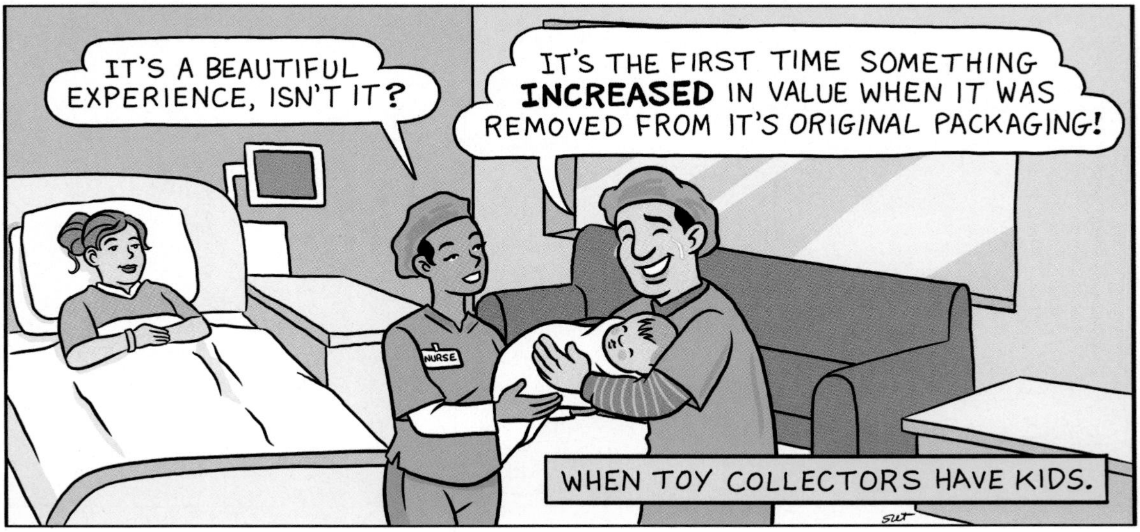
IT'S A BEAUTIFUL EXPERIENCE, ISN'T IT?
IT'S THE FIRST TIME SOMETHING INCREASED IN VALUE WHEN IT WAS REMOVED FROM IT'S ORIGINAL PACKAGING!
NURSE
WHEN TOY COLLECTORS HAVE KIDS.

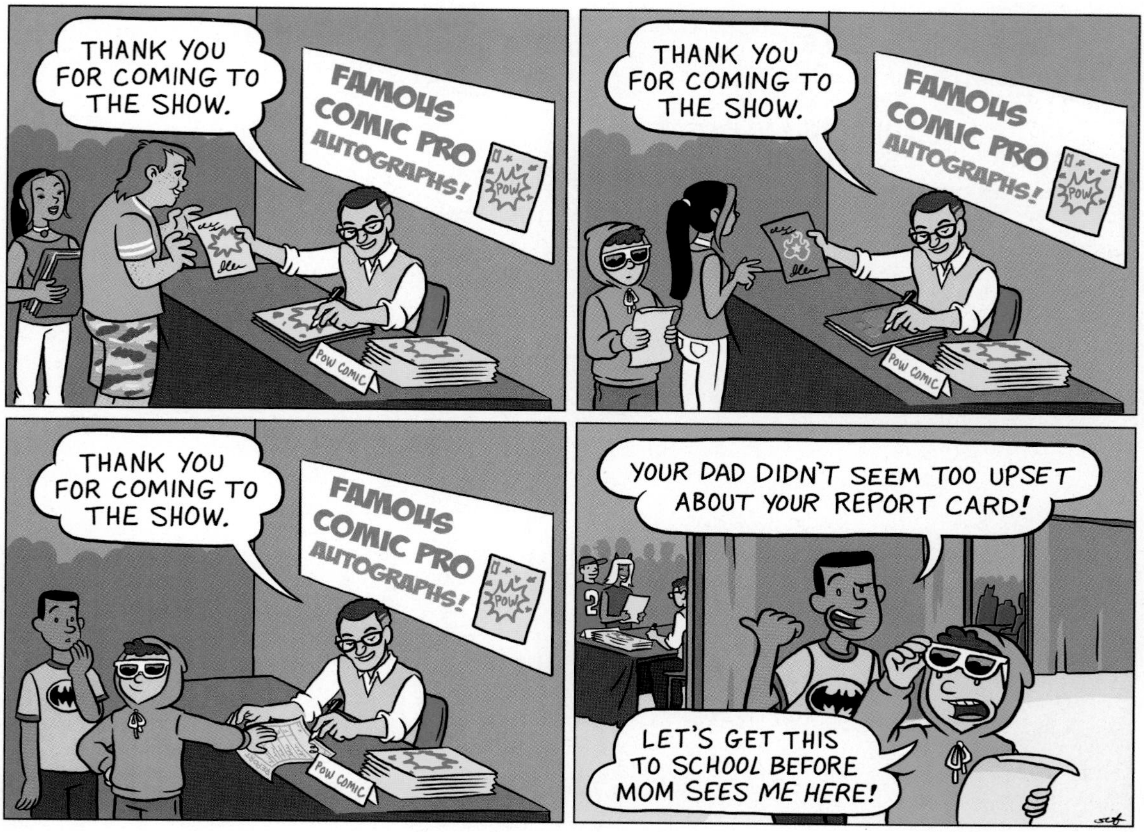
THANK YOU FOR COMING TO THE SHOW.
FAMOUS COMIC PRO AUTOGRAPHS!
POW
POW COMIC
THANK YOU FOR COMING TO THE SHOW.
FAMOUS COMIC PRO AUTOGRAPHS!
POW
POW COMIC
THANK YOU FOR COMING TO THE SHOW.
FAMOUS COMIC PRO AUTOGRAPHS!
POW
POW COMIC
YOUR DAD DIDN'T SEEM TOO UPSET ABOUT YOUR REPORT CARD!
LET'S GET THIS TO SCHOOL BEFORE MOM SEES ME HERE!

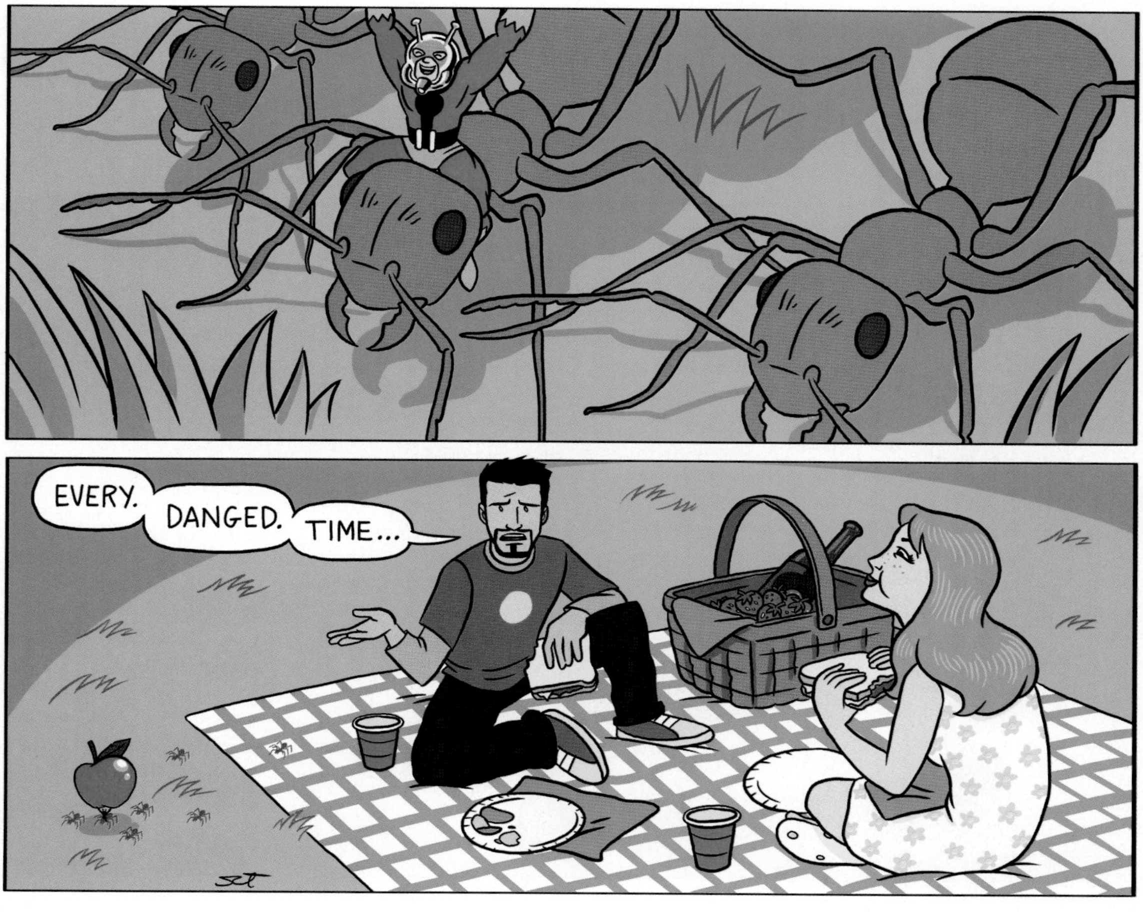
EVERY.
DANGED.
TIME...

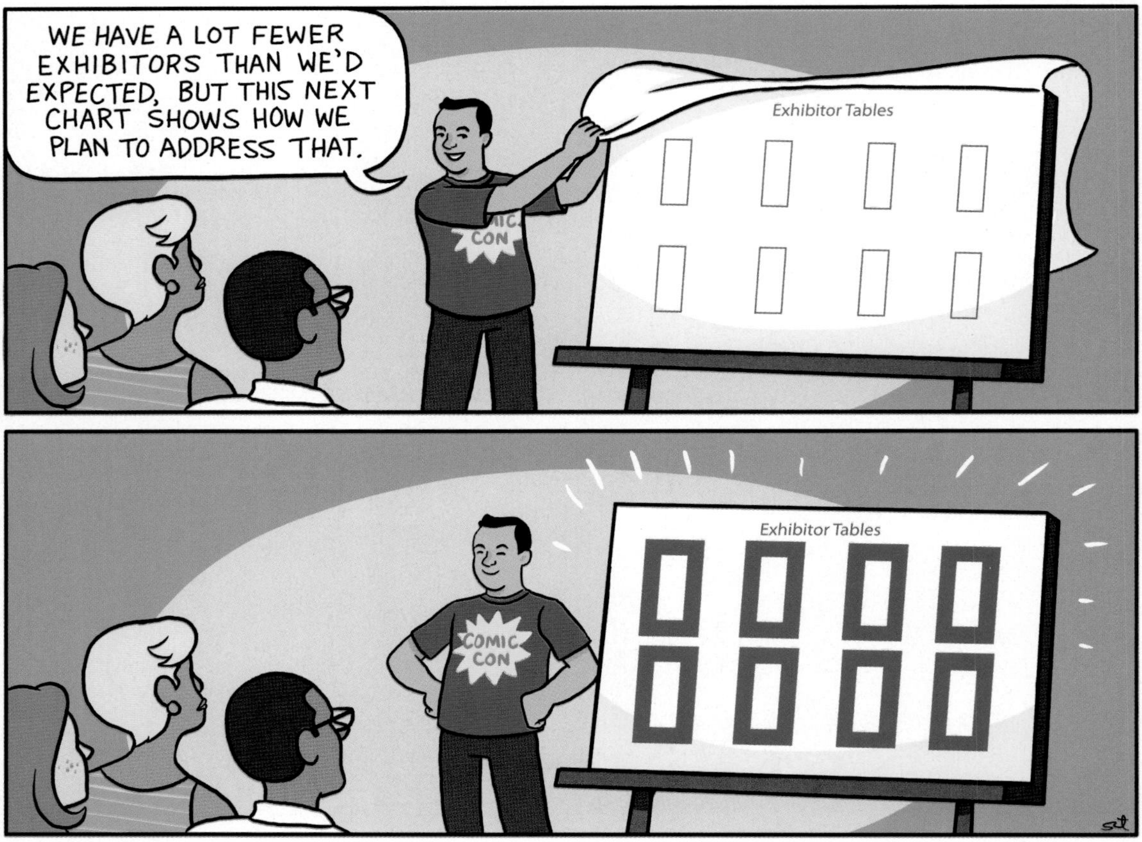
WE HAVE A LOT FEWER EXHIBITORS THAN WE'D EXPECTED, BUT THIS NEXT CHART SHOWS HOW WE PLAN TO ADDRESS THAT.
Exhibitor Tables
COMIC CON
Exhibitor Tables

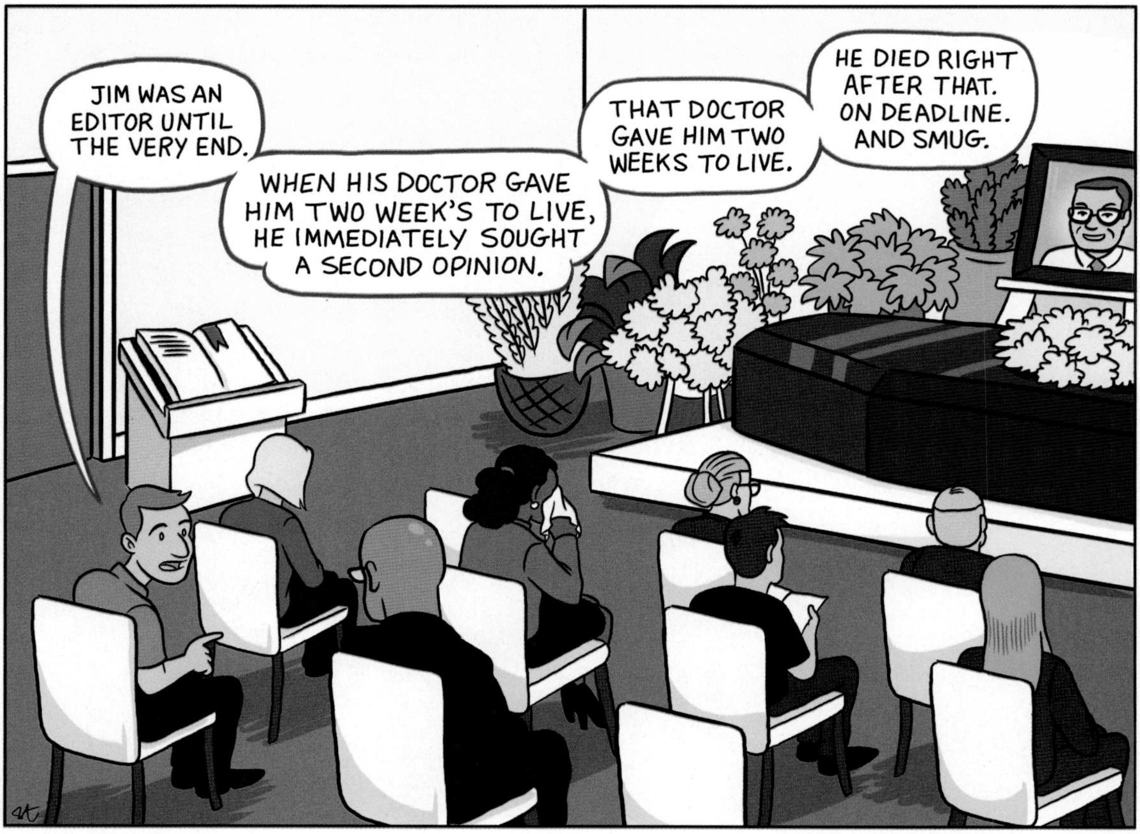
JIM WAS AN EDITOR UNTIL THE VERY END.
WHEN HIS DOCTOR GAVE HIM TWO WEEK'S TO LIVE, HE IMMEDIATELY SOUGHT A SECOND OPINION.
THAT DOCTOR GAVE HIM TWO WEEKS TO LIVE.
HE DIED RIGHT AFTER THAT. ON DEADLINE. AND SMUG.

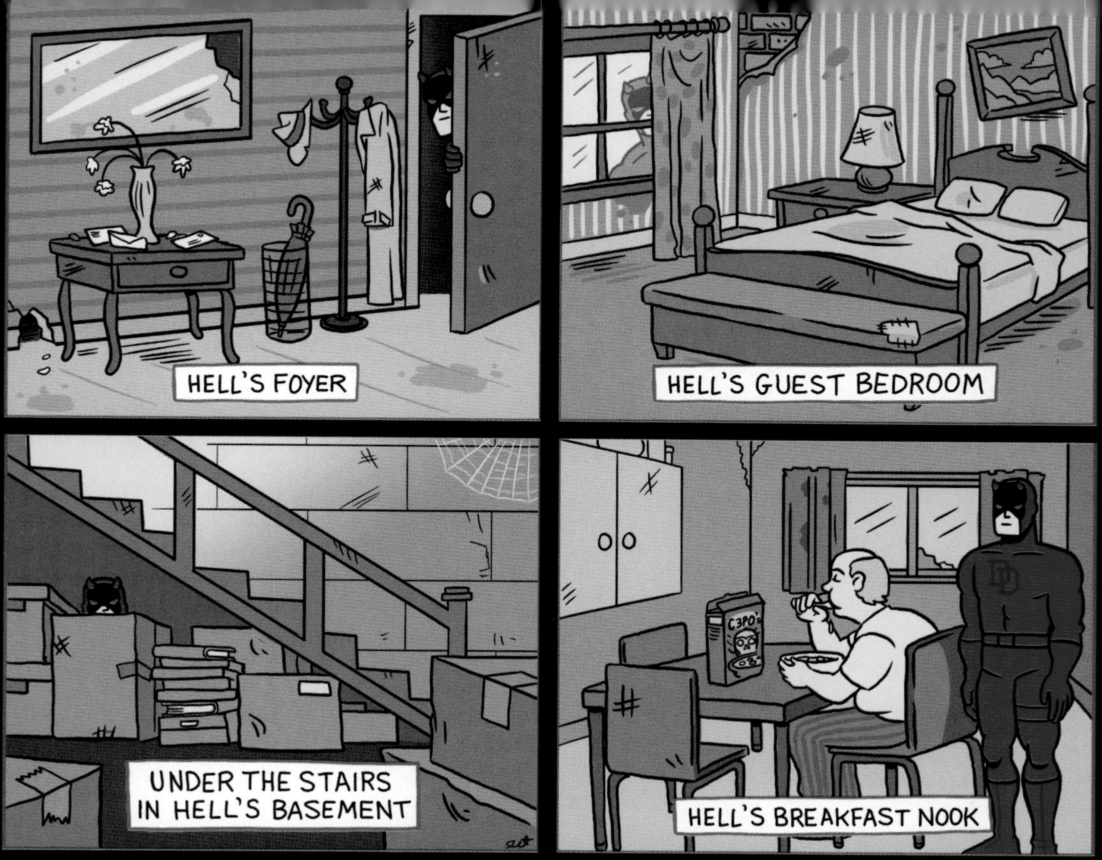
HELL'S FOYER
HELL'S GUEST BEDROOM
UNDER THE STAIRS IN HELL'S BASEMENT
HELL'S BREAKFAST NOOK

THE LESSER-KNOWN DAREDEVIL STORIES.

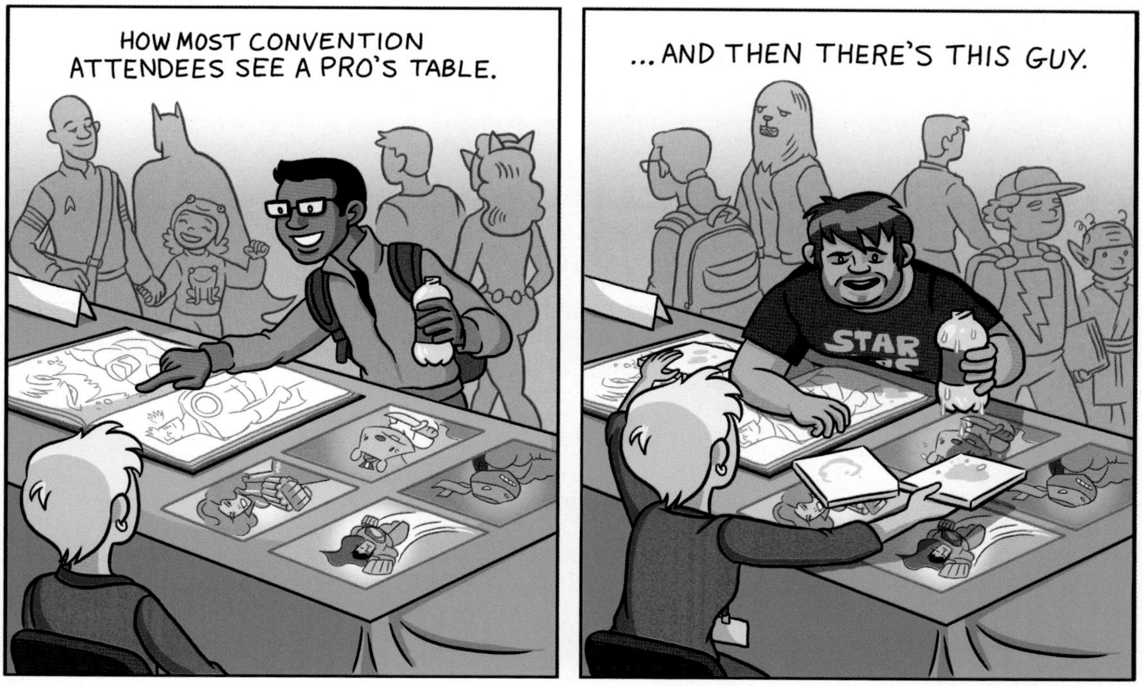
HOW MOST CONVENTION ATTENDEES SEE A PRO'S TABLE.
...AND THEN THERE'S THIS GUY.
STAR

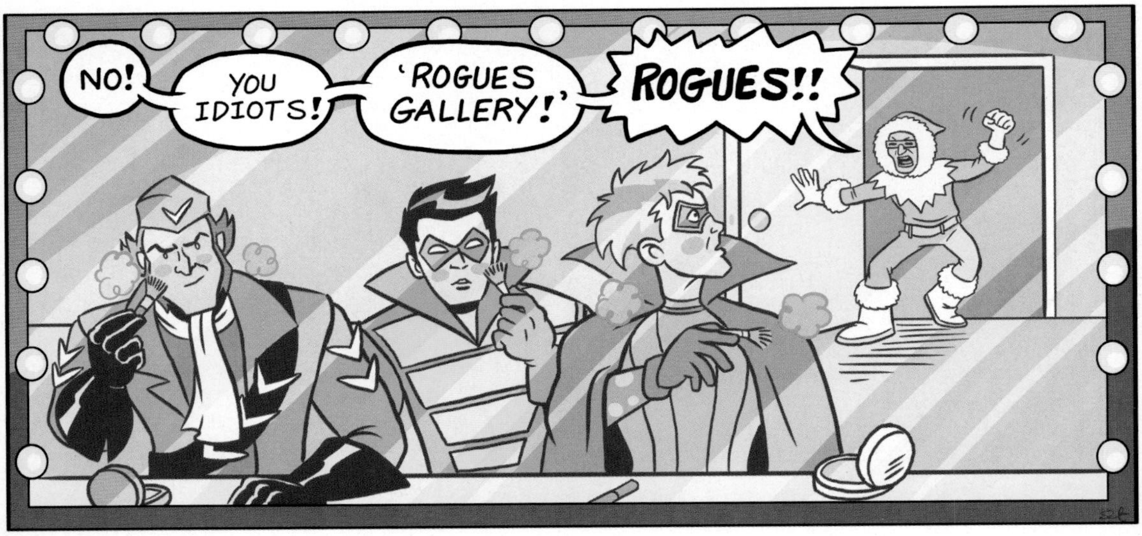
NO!
YOU IDIOTS!
'ROGUES GALLERY!'
ROGUES!!

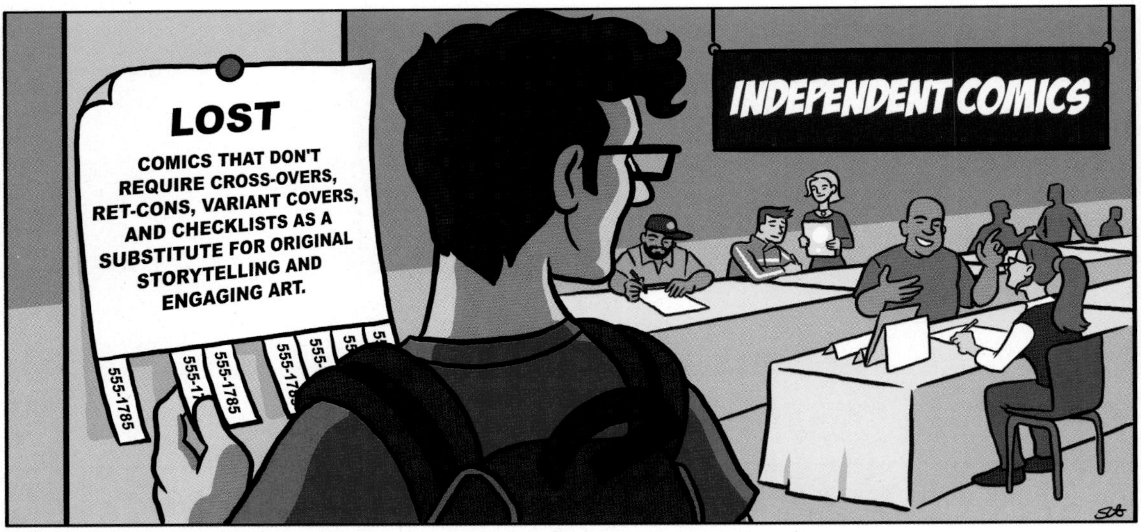
LOST
COMICS THAT DON'T REQUIRE CROSS-OVERS, RET-CONS, VARIANT COVERS, AND CHECKLISTS AS A SUBSTITUTE FOR ORIGINAL STORYTELLING AND ENGAGING ART.
555-1785
555-1785
INDEPENDENT COMICS

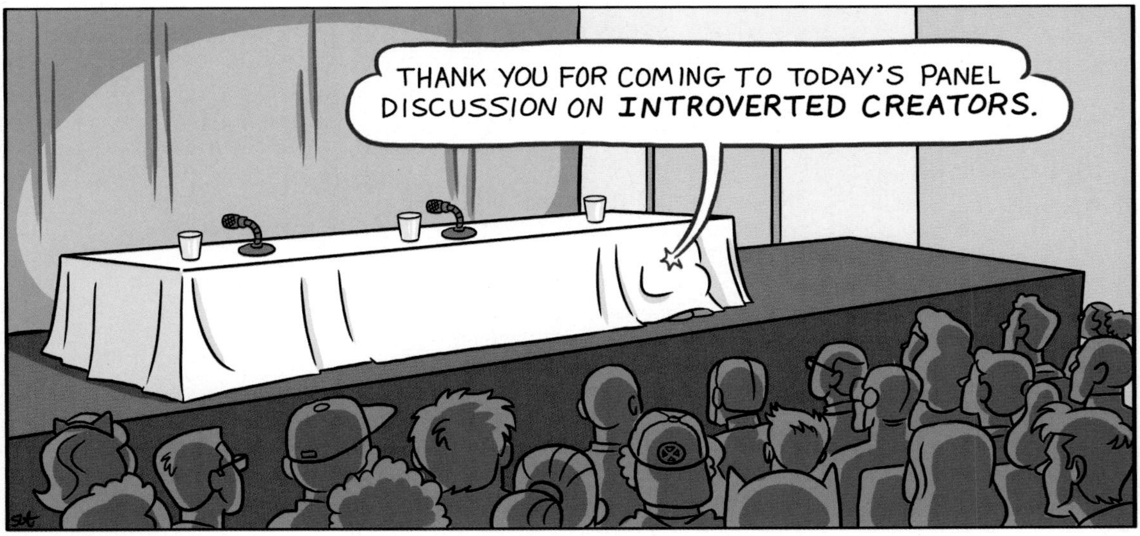
THANK YOU FOR COMING TO TODAY'S PANEL DISCUSSION ON INTROVERTED CREATORS.

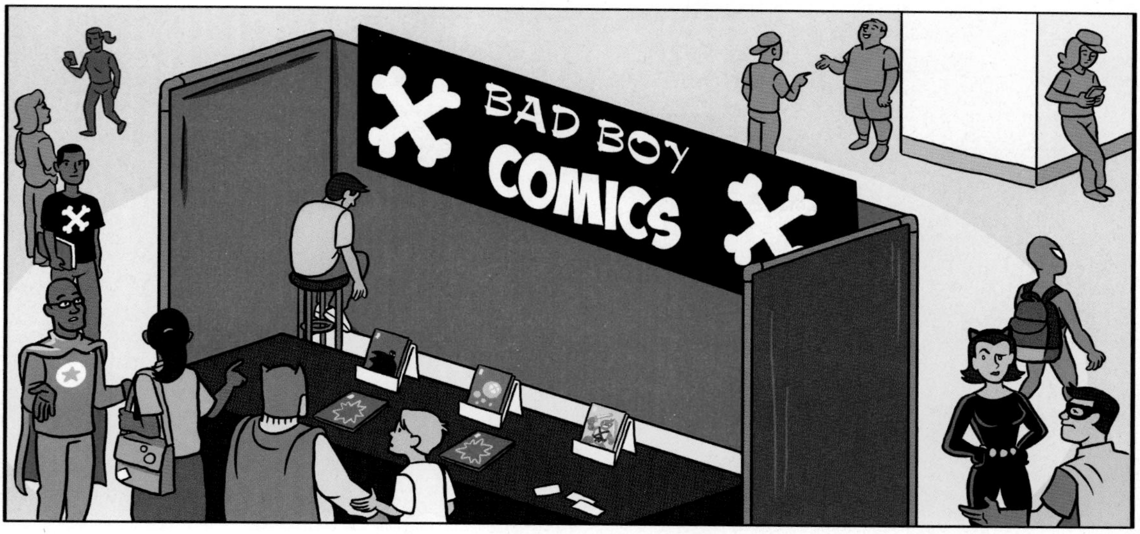
BAD BOY
COMICS

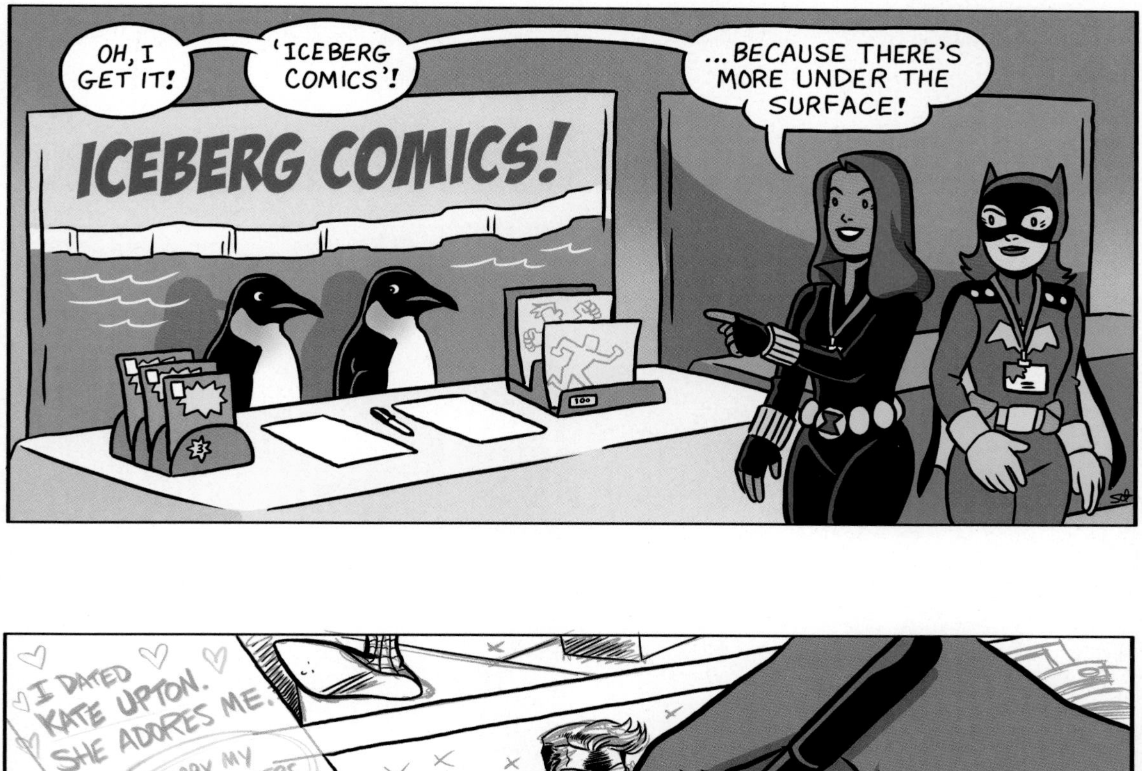
OH, I GET IT!
'ICEBERG COMICS'!
...BECAUSE THERE'S MORE UNDER THE SURFACE!
ICEBERG COMICS!

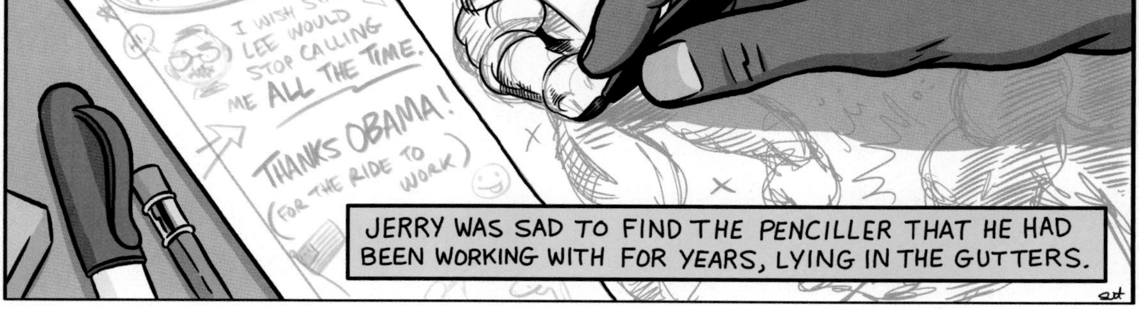
I DATED KATE UPTON. SHE ADORES ME.
SO HAPPY MY LOTTERY NUMBERS FINALLY HIT!
I WISH STAN LEE WOULD STOP CALLING ME ALL THE TIME.
THANKS OBAMA! (FOR THE RIDE TO WORK)
JERRY WAS SAD TO FIND THE PENCILLER THAT HE HAD BEEN WORKING WITH FOR YEARS, LYING IN THE GUTTERS.

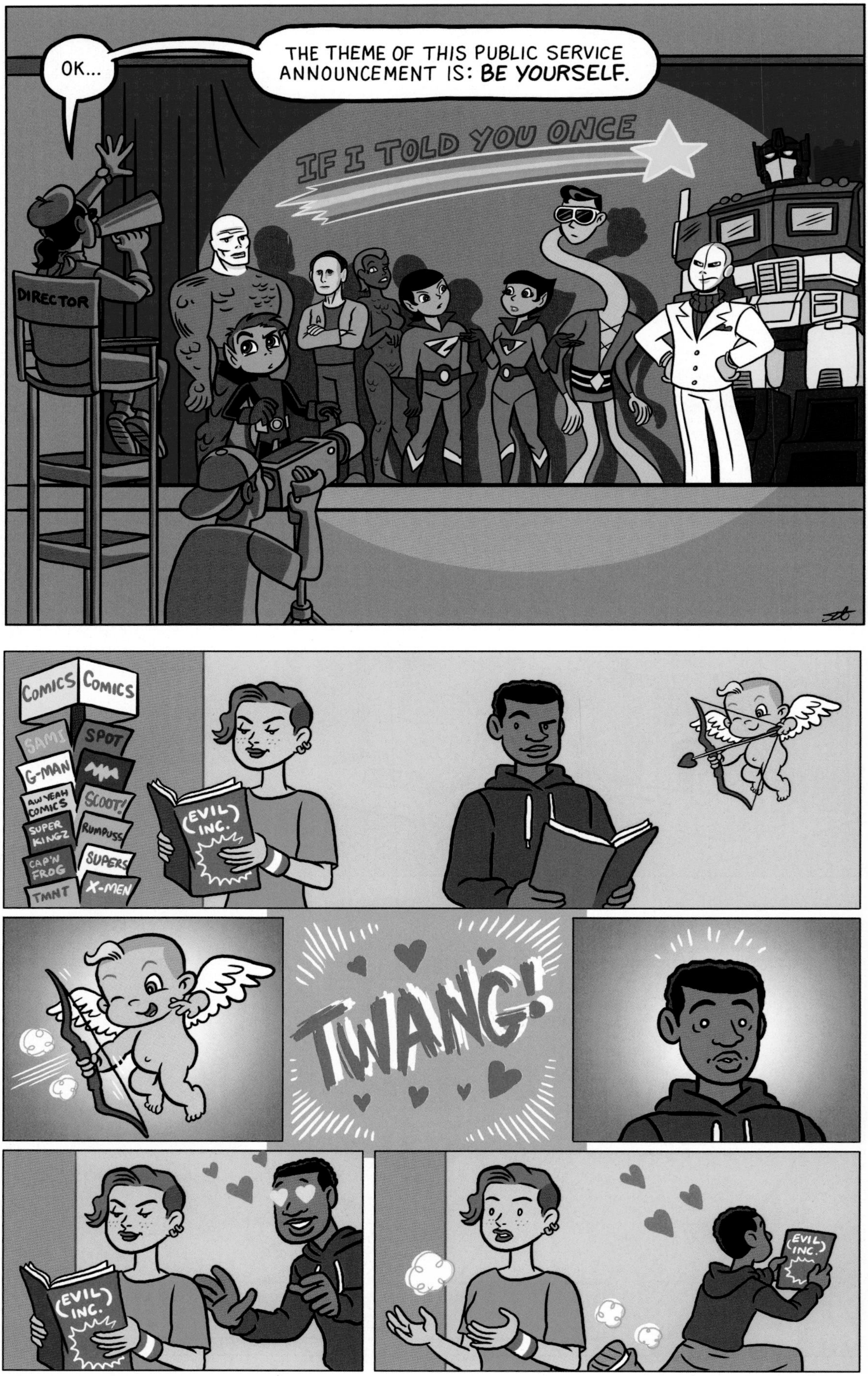
OK...
THE THEME OF THIS PUBLIC SERVICE ANNOUNCEMENT IS: BE YOURSELF.
IF I TOLD YOU ONCE
DIRECTOR
COMICS
COMICS
SAMI
SPOT
G-MAN
AW YEAH COMICS
SCOOT!
SUPER KINGZ
RUMPUSS
CAP'N FROG
SUPERS
TMNT
X-MEN
EVIL INC.
TWANG!
EVIL INC.
EVIL INC.

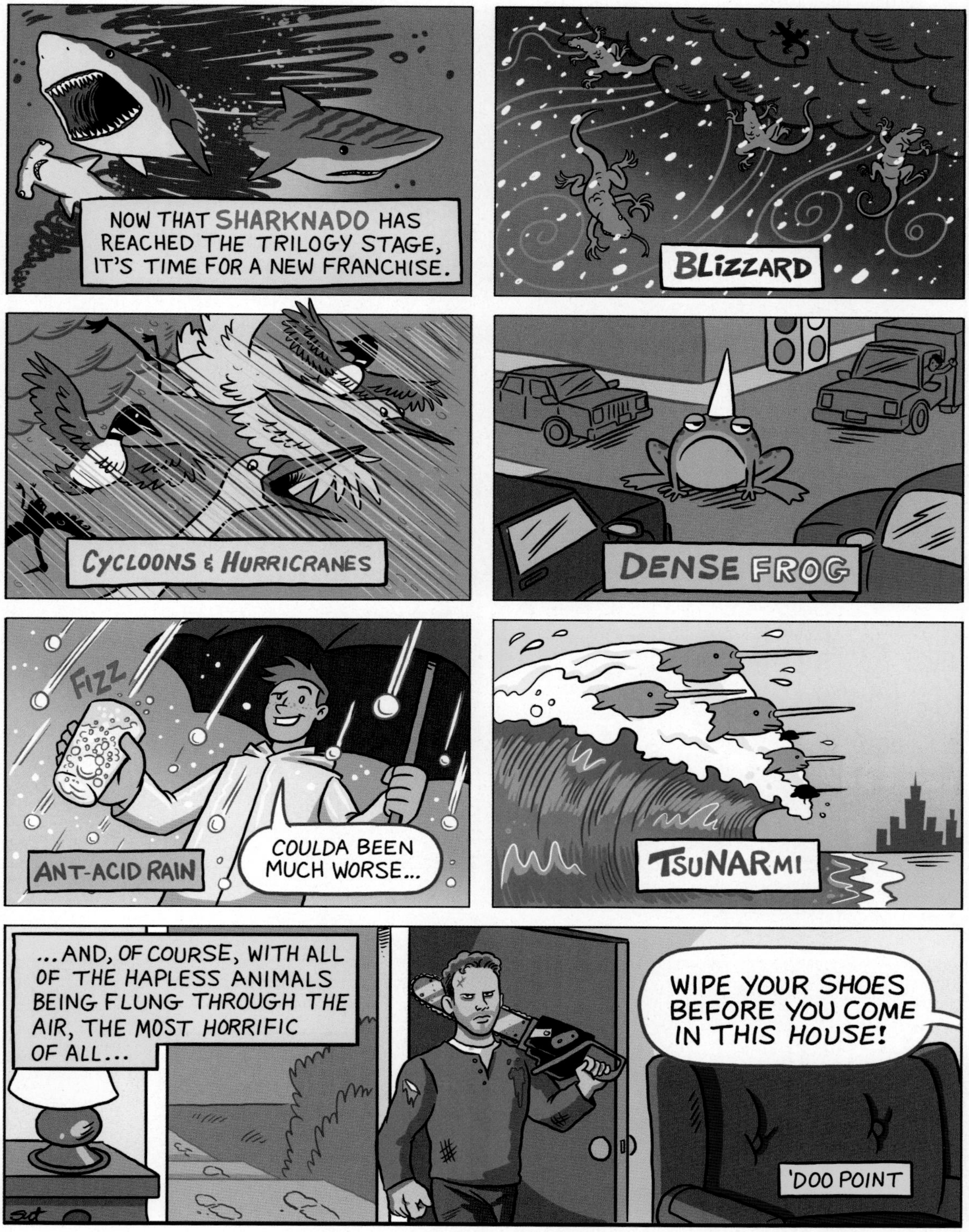
NOW THAT SHARKNADO HAS REACHED THE TRILOGY STAGE, IT'S TIME FOR A NEW FRANCHISE.
BLIZZARD
CYCLOONS & HURRICRANES
DENSE FROG
FIZZ
ANT-ACID RAIN
COULDA BEEN MUCH WORSE...
TSUNARMI
...AND, OF COURSE, WITH ALL OF THE HAPLESS ANIMALS BEING FLUNG THROUGH THE AIR, THE MOST HORRIFIC OF ALL...
WIPE YOUR SHOES BEFORE YOU COME IN THIS HOUSE!
'DOO POINT

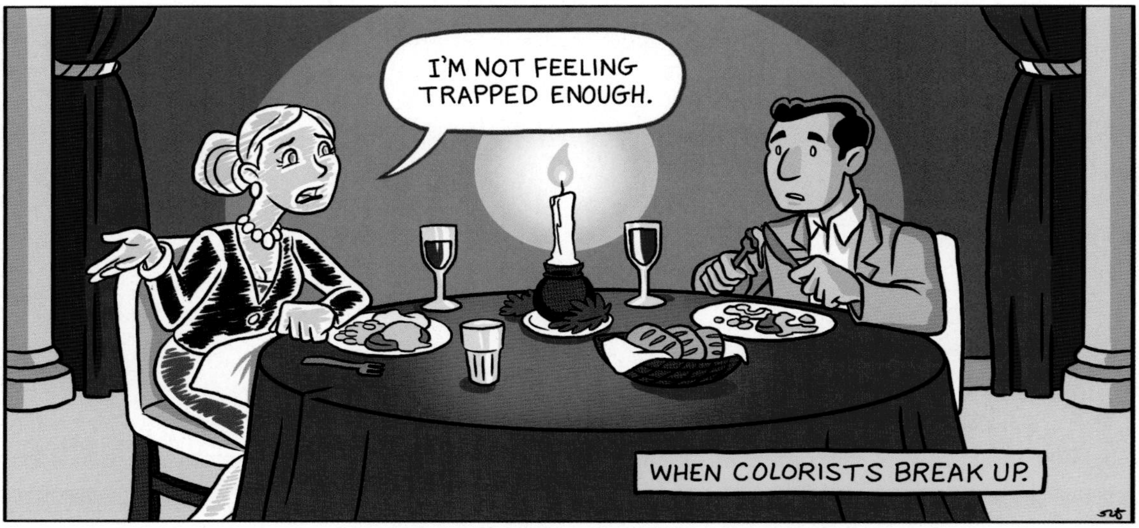
I'M NOT FEELING TRAPPED ENOUGH.
WHEN COLORISTS BREAK UP.

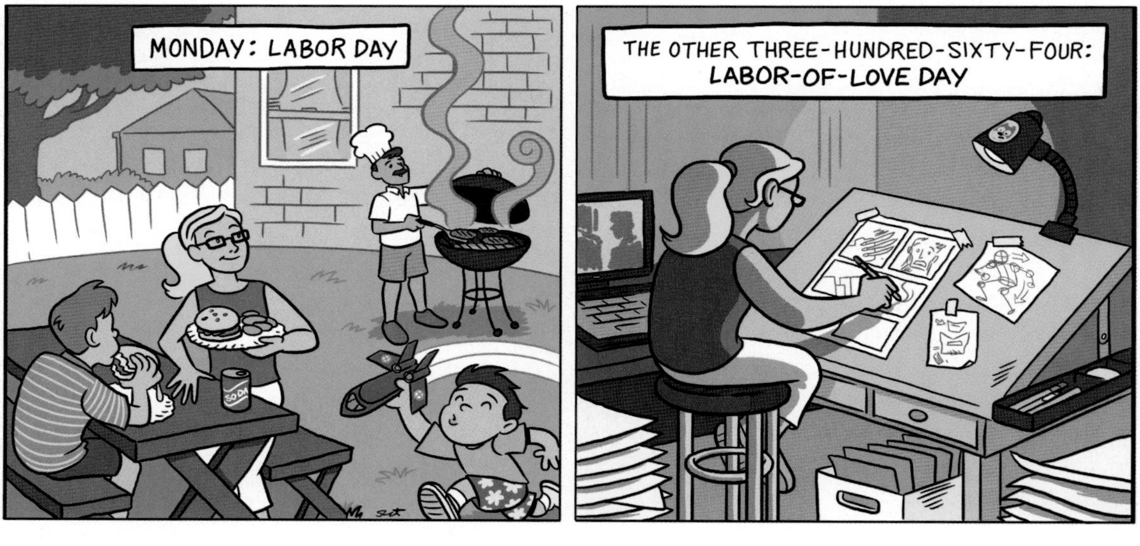
MONDAY: LABOR DAY
SODA
THE OTHER THREE-HUNDRED-SIXTY-FOUR: LABOR-OF-LOVE DAY

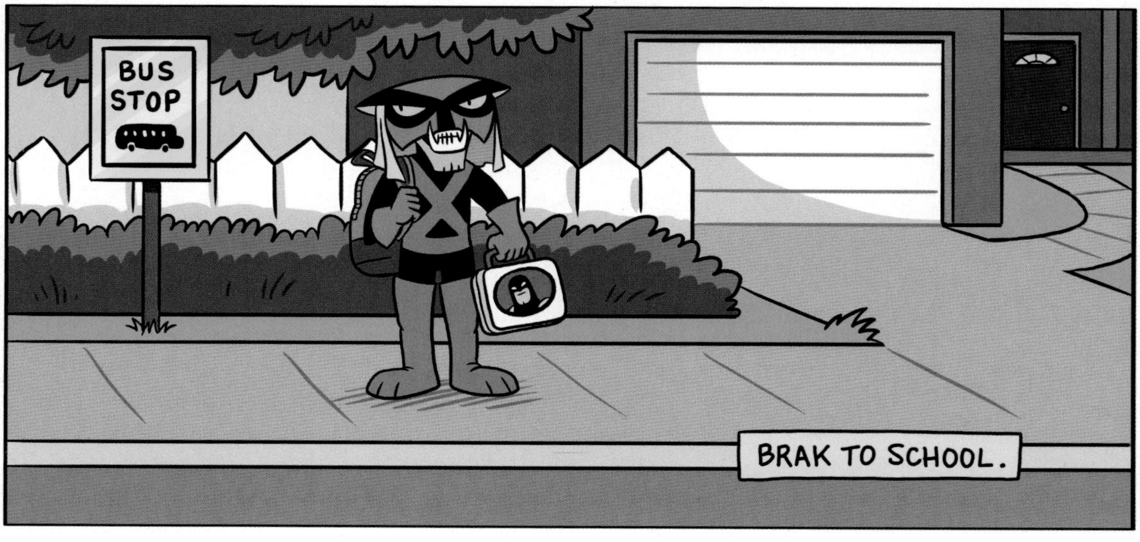
BUS STOP
BRAK TO SCHOOL.

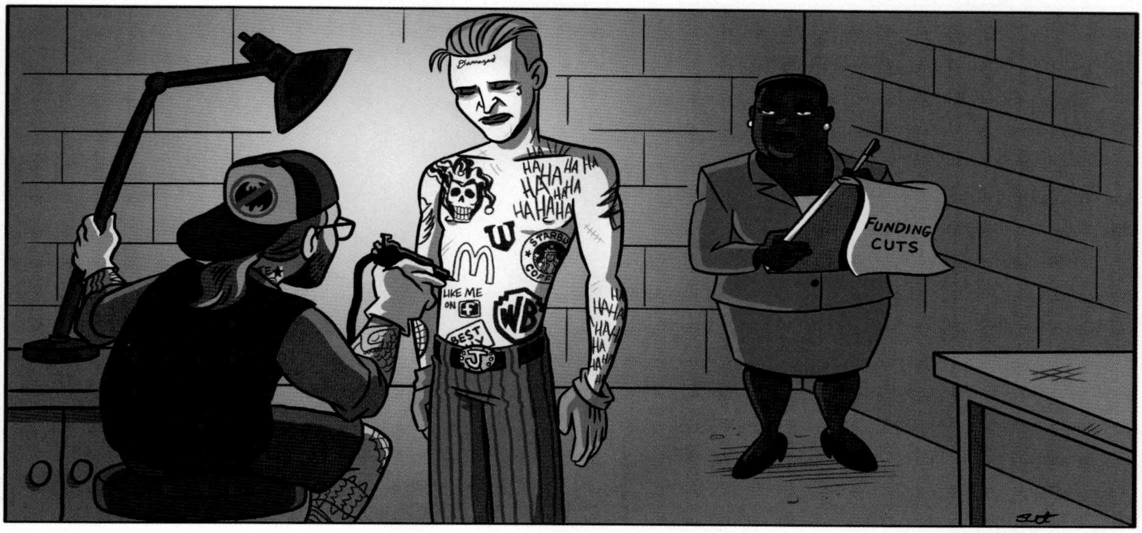
FUNDING CUTS

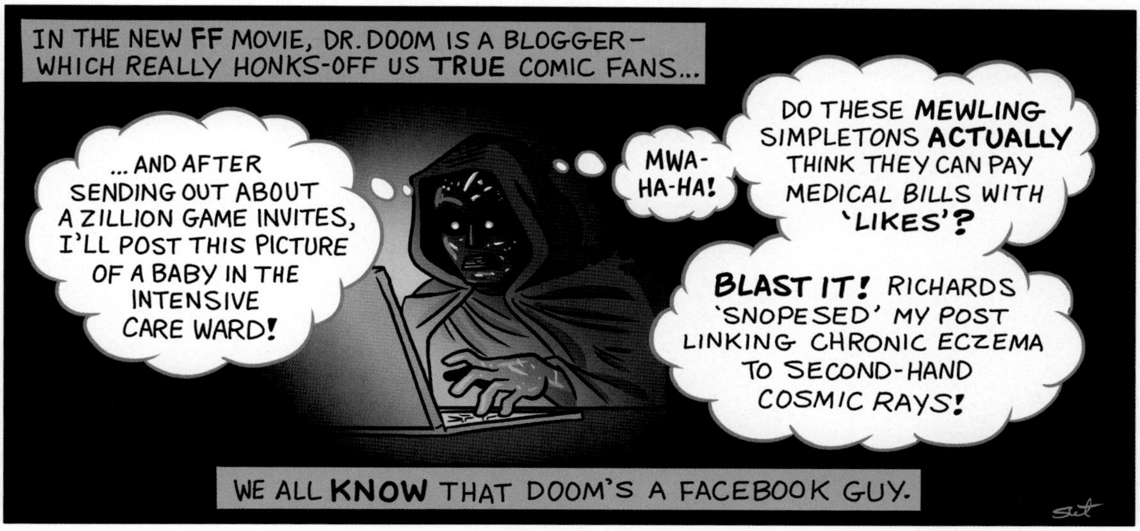
IN THE NEW FF MOVIE, DR. DOOM IS A BLOGGER– WHICH REALLY HONKS-OFF US TRUE COMIC FANS...
... AND AFTER SENDING OUT ABOUT A ZILLION GAME INVITES, I'LL POST THIS PICTURE OF A BABY IN THE INTENSIVE CARE WARD!
MWA-HA-HA!
DO THESE MEWLING SIMPLETONS ACTUALLY THINK THEY CAN PAY MEDICAL BILLS WITH 'LIKES'?
BLAST IT! RICHARDS 'SNOPESED' MY POST LINKING CHRONIC ECZEMA TO SECOND-HAND COSMIC RAYS!
WE ALL KNOW THAT DOOM'S A FACEBOOK GUY.

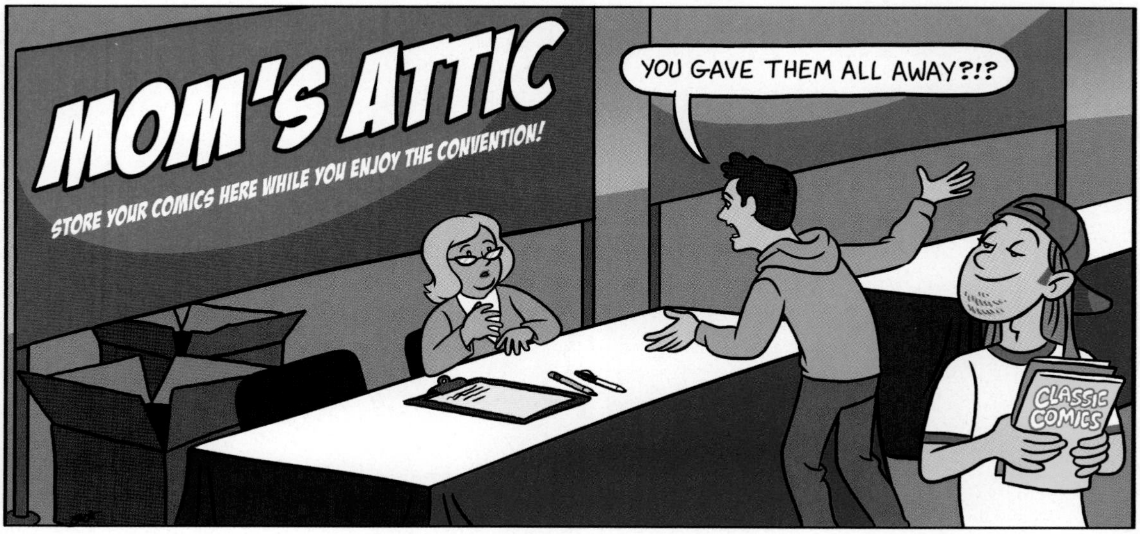
MOM'S ATTIC
STORE YOUR COMICS HERE WHILE YOU ENJOY THE CONVENTION!
YOU GAVE THEM ALL AWAY?!?
CLASSIC COMICS

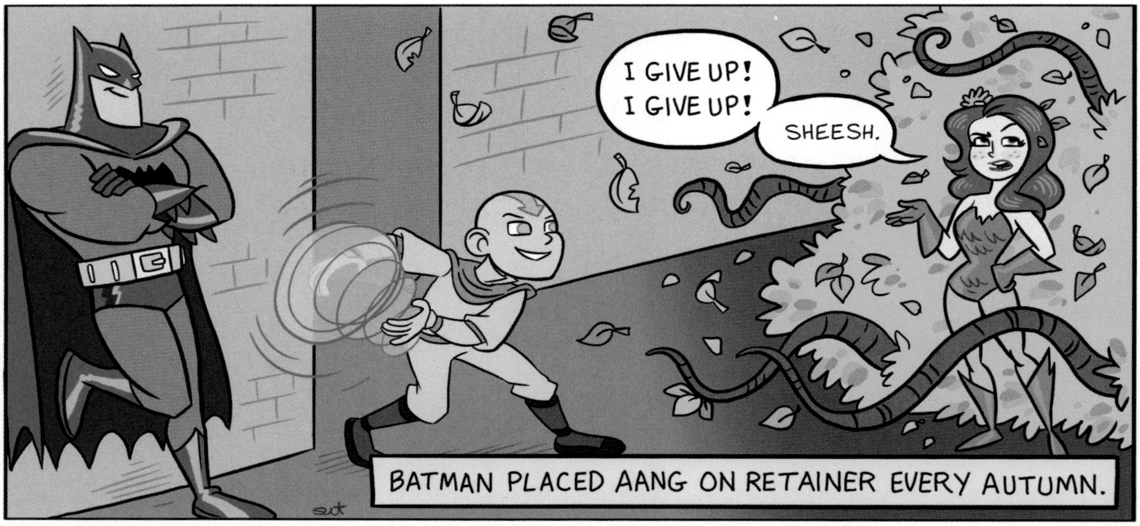
I GIVE UP!
I GIVE UP!
SHEESH.
BATMAN PLACED AANG ON RETAINER EVERY AUTUMN.

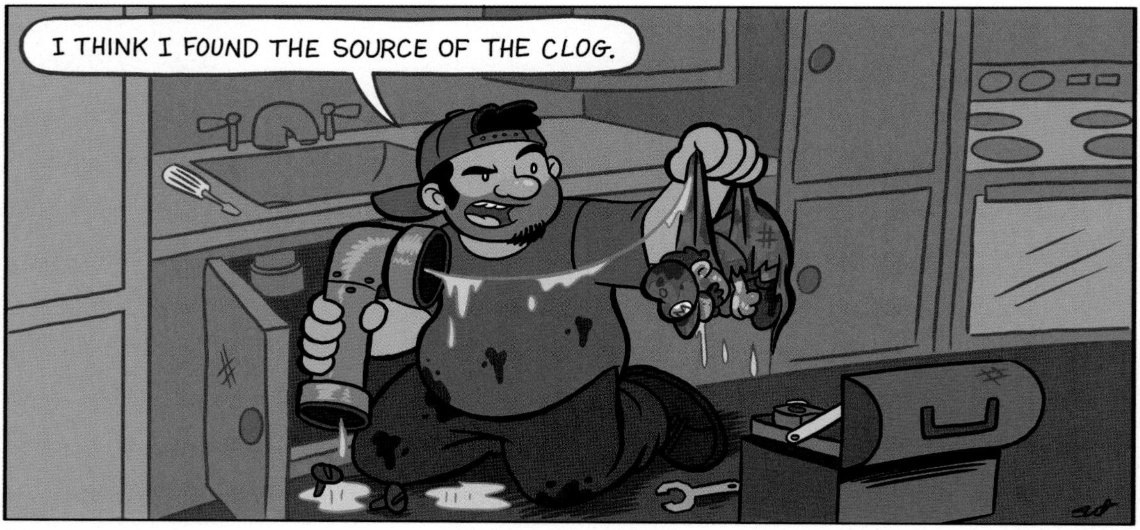
I THINK I FOUND THE SOURCE OF THE CLOG.

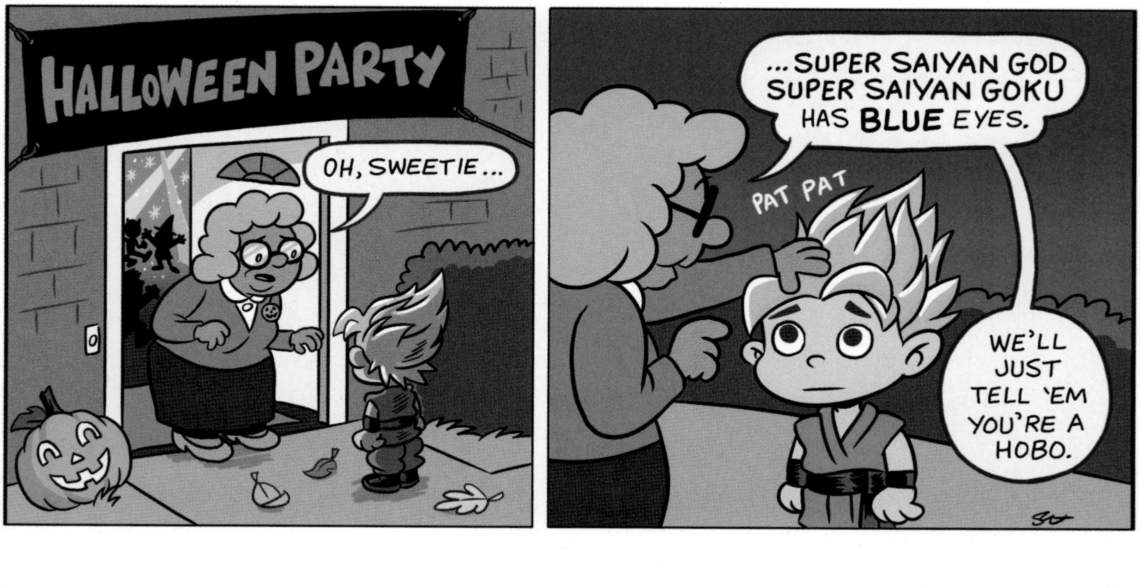
HALLOWEEN PARTY
OH, SWEETIE...
...SUPER SAIYAN GOD SUPER SAIYAN GOKU HAS **BLUE** EYES.
PAT PAT
WE'LL JUST TELL 'EM YOU'RE A HOBO.

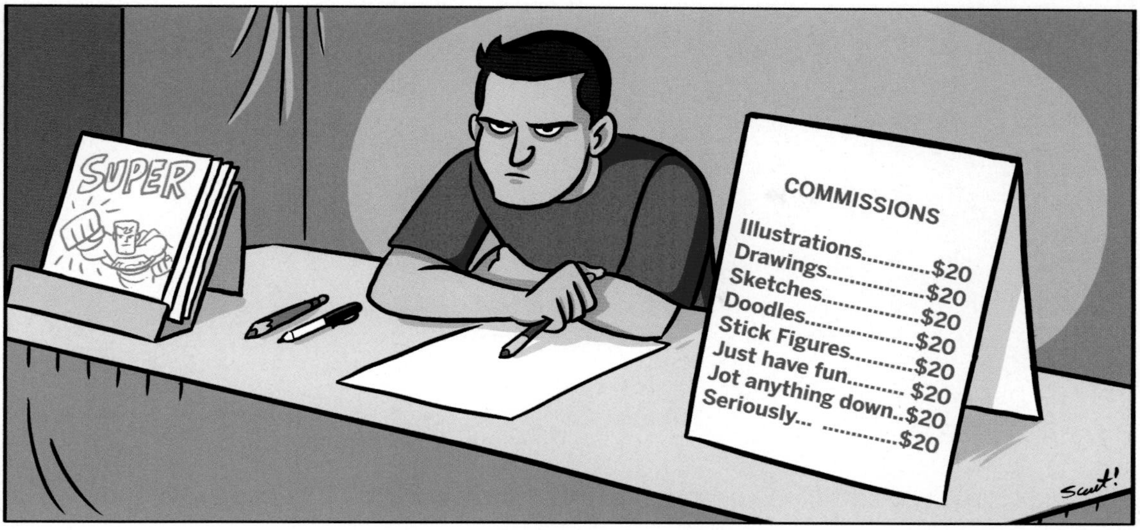
SUPER
COMMISSIONS
Illustrations............$20
Drawings..................$20
Sketches..................$20
Doodles....................$20
Stick Figures...........$20
Just have fun.......... $20
Jot anything down..$20
Seriously... ............$20

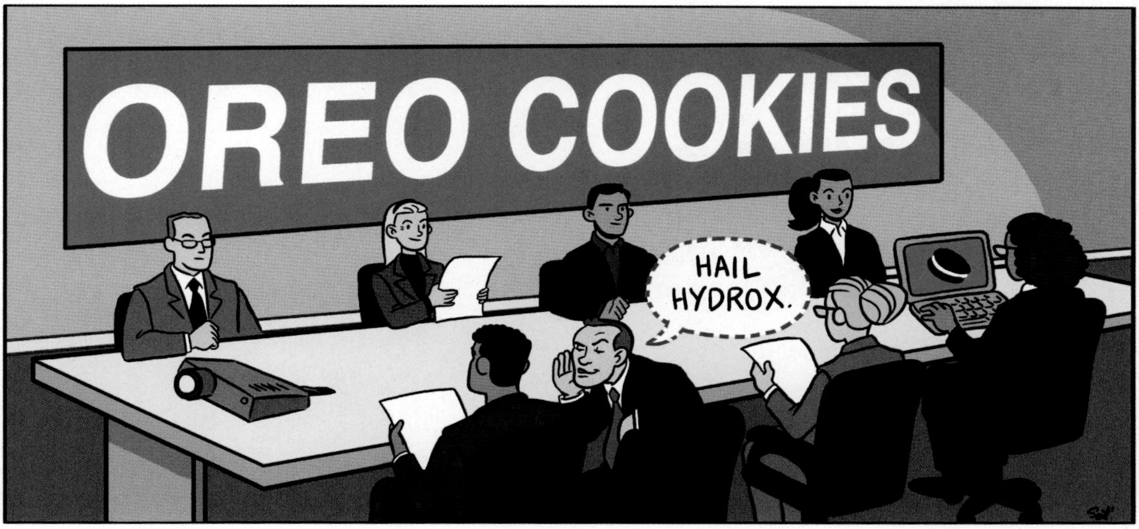
OREO COOKIES
HAIL HYDROX.

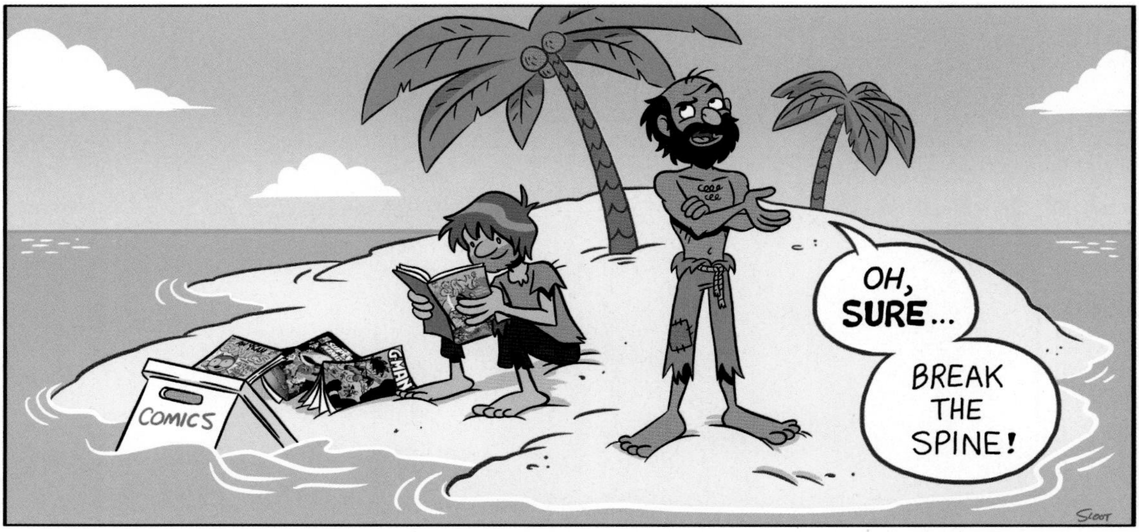
COMICS
GMAN
OH, SURE...
BREAK THE SPINE!

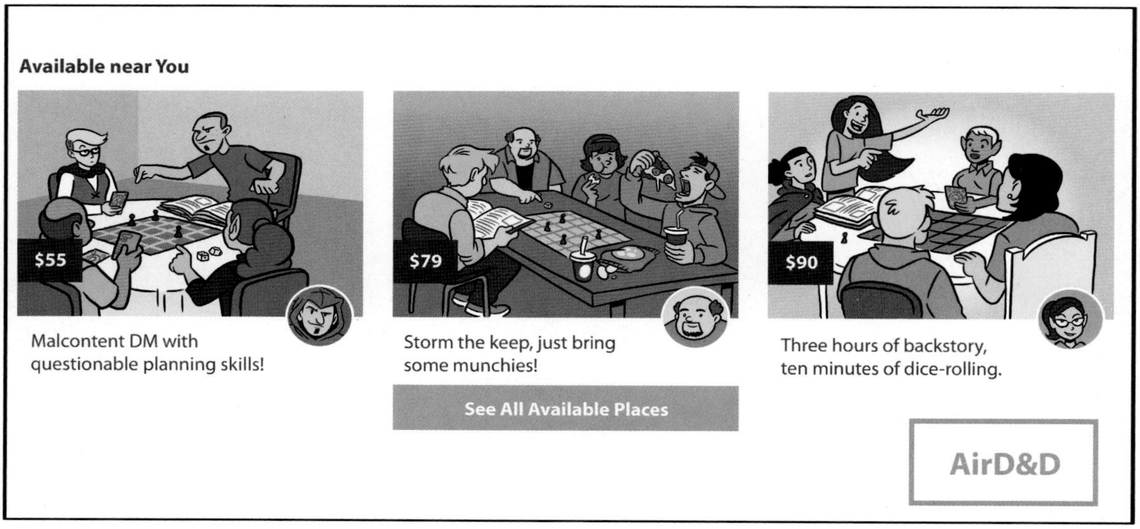
Available near You
$55
Malcontent DM with questionable planning skills!
$79
Storm the keep, just bring some munchies!
$90
Three hours of backstory, ten minutes of dice-rolling.
See All Available Places
AirD&D

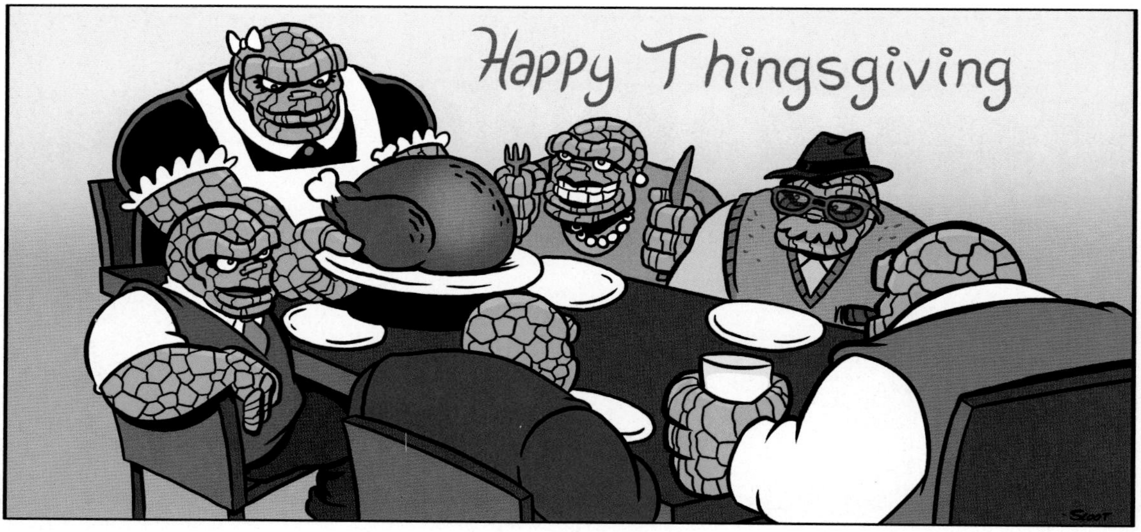
Happy Thingsgiving

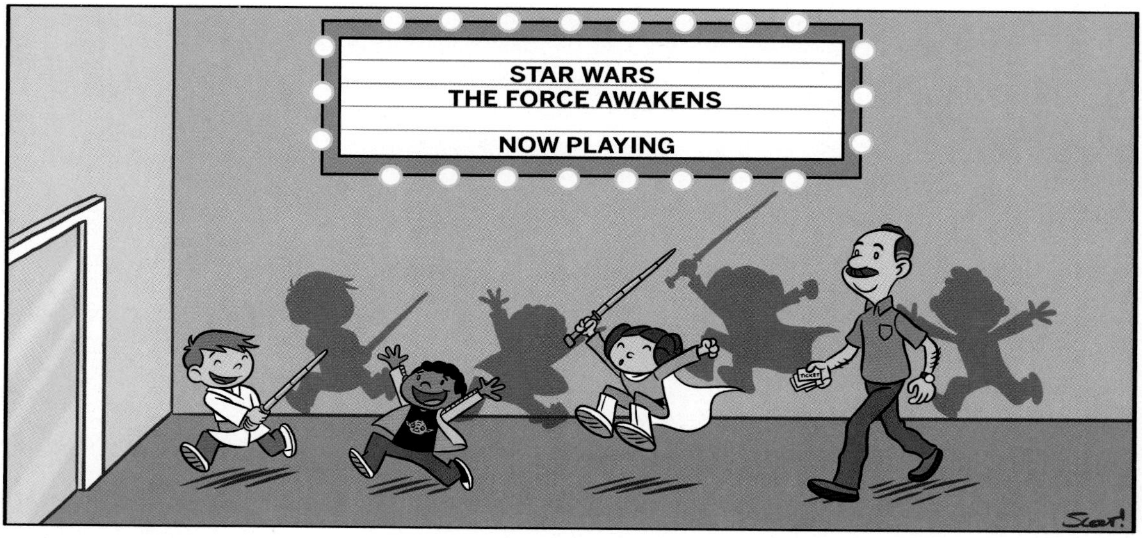
STAR WARS
THE FORCE AWAKENS
NOW PLAYING

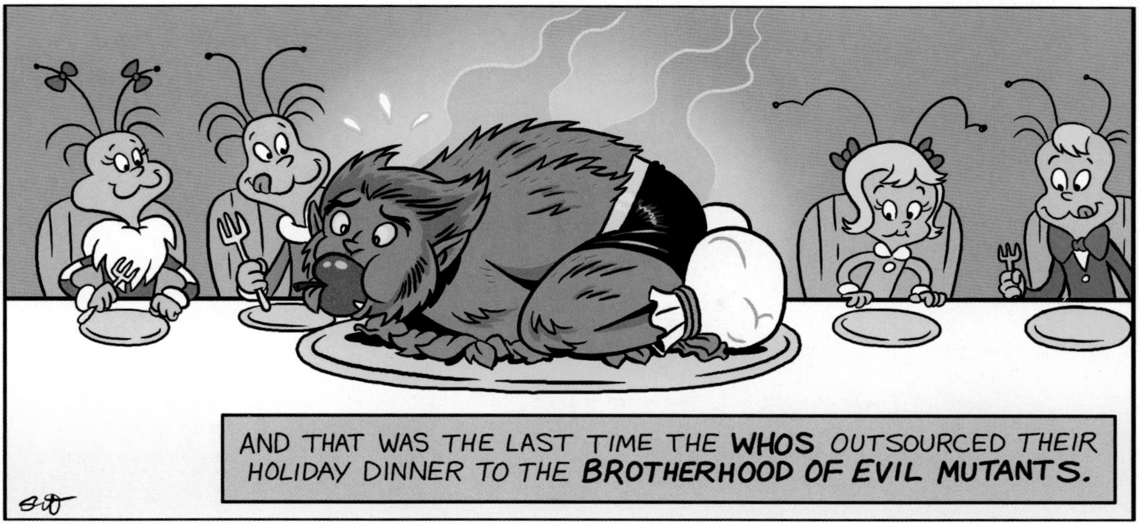
AND THAT WAS THE LAST TIME THE **WHOS** OUTSOURCED THEIR HOLIDAY DINNER TO THE **BROTHERHOOD OF EVIL MUTANTS.**

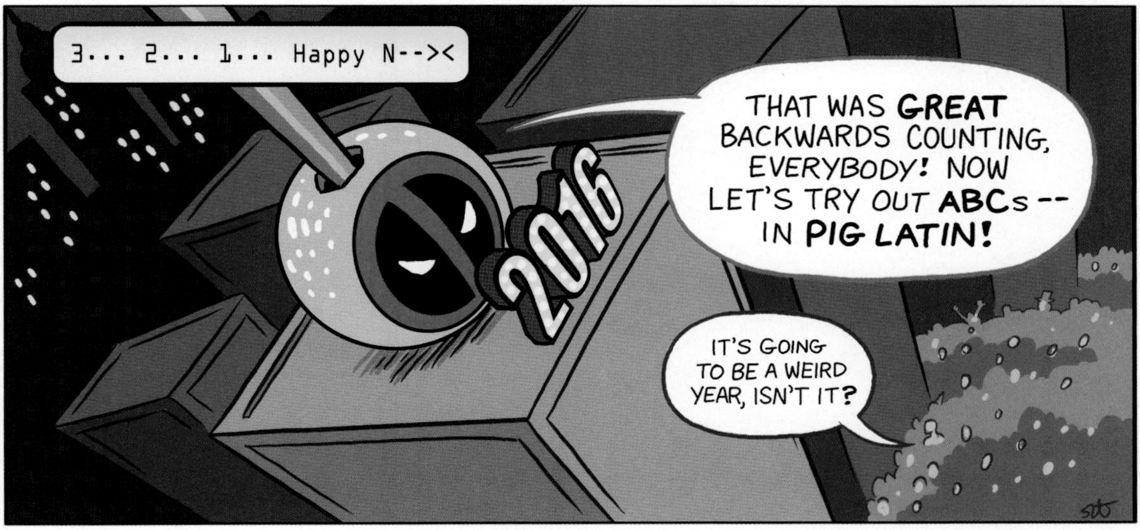
3... 2... 1... Happy N--><
2016
THAT WAS **GREAT** BACKWARDS COUNTING, EVERYBODY! NOW LET'S TRY OUT **ABCs** -- IN **PIG LATIN!**
IT'S GOING TO BE A WEIRD YEAR, ISN'T IT?

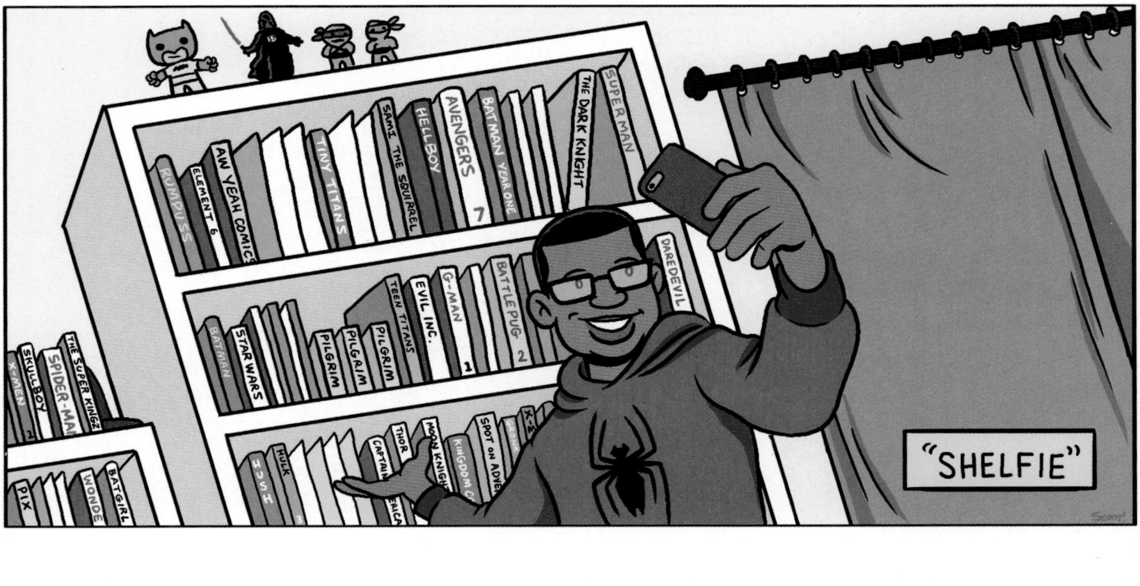
"SHELFIE"

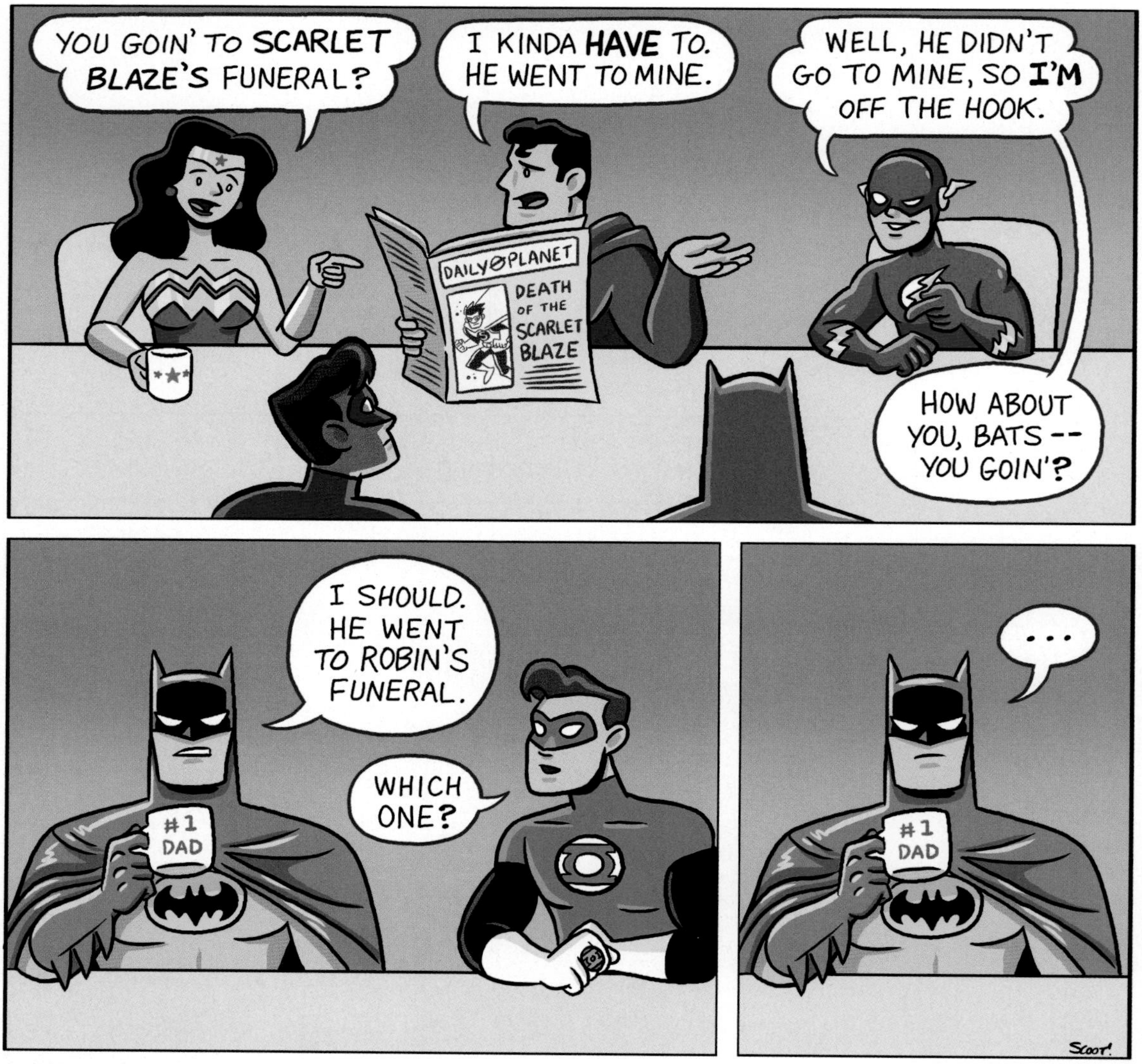
YOU GOIN' TO SCARLET BLAZE'S FUNERAL?
I KINDA HAVE TO. HE WENT TO MINE.
WELL, HE DIDN'T GO TO MINE, SO I'M OFF THE HOOK.
DAILY PLANET
DEATH OF THE SCARLET BLAZE
HOW ABOUT YOU, BATS -- YOU GOIN'?
I SHOULD. HE WENT TO ROBIN'S FUNERAL.
#1 DAD
WHICH ONE?
...
#1 DAD
SCOOT!

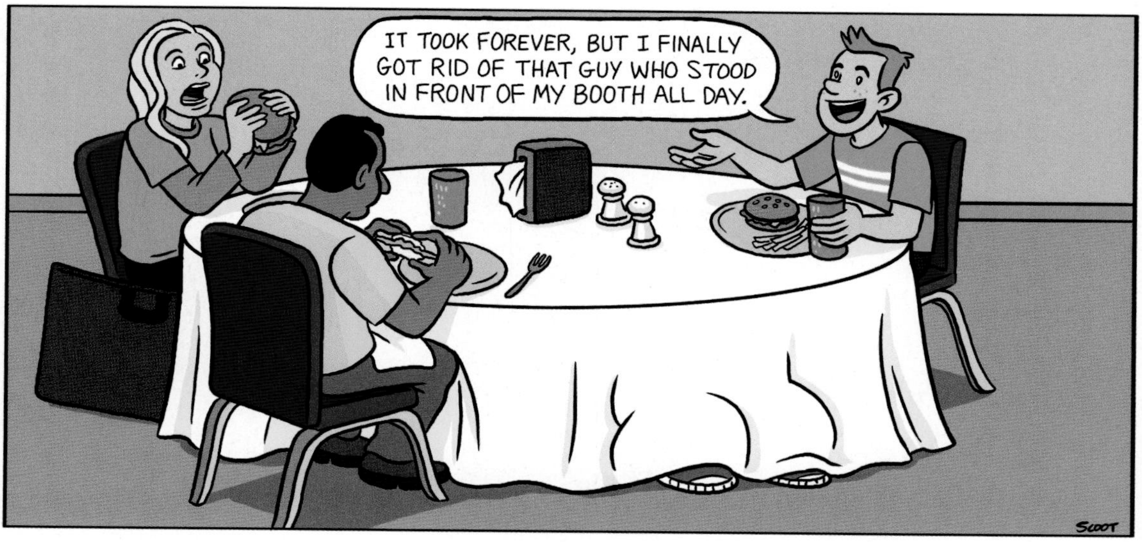
IT TOOK FOREVER, BUT I FINALLY GOT RID OF THAT GUY WHO STOOD IN FRONT OF MY BOOTH ALL DAY.
SCOOT

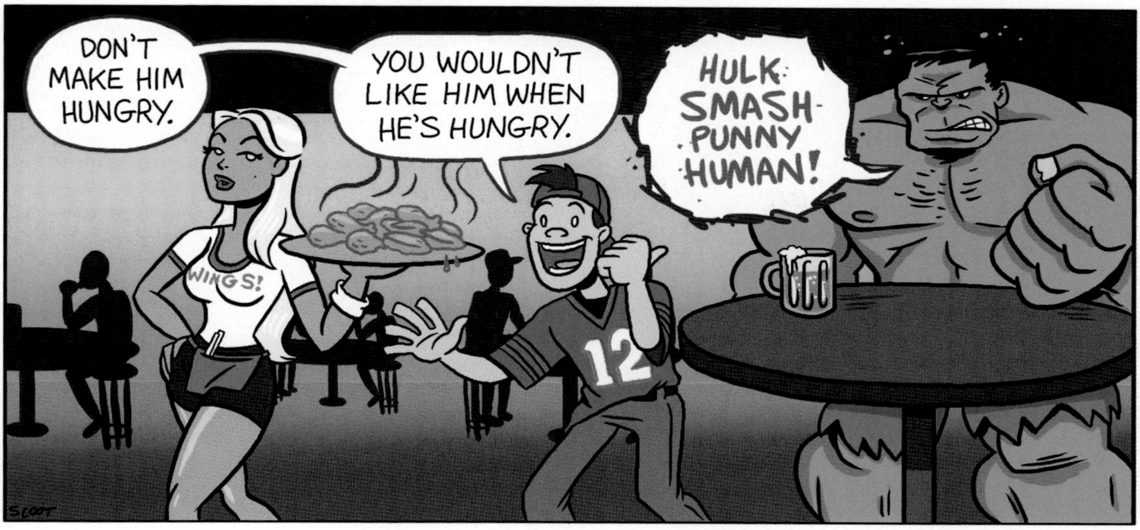
DON'T MAKE HIM HUNGRY.
YOU WOULDN'T LIKE HIM WHEN HE'S HUNGRY.
HULK SMASH PUNNY HUMAN!
WINGS!
12
SCOOT

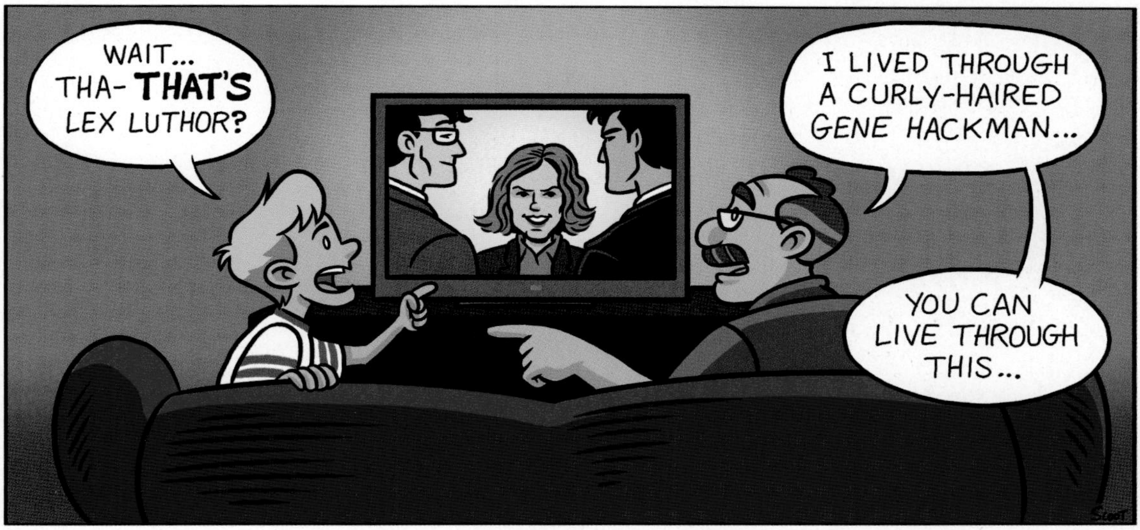
WAIT... THA- THAT'S LEX LUTHOR?
I LIVED THROUGH A CURLY-HAIRED GENE HACKMAN...
YOU CAN LIVE THROUGH THIS...
SCOOT

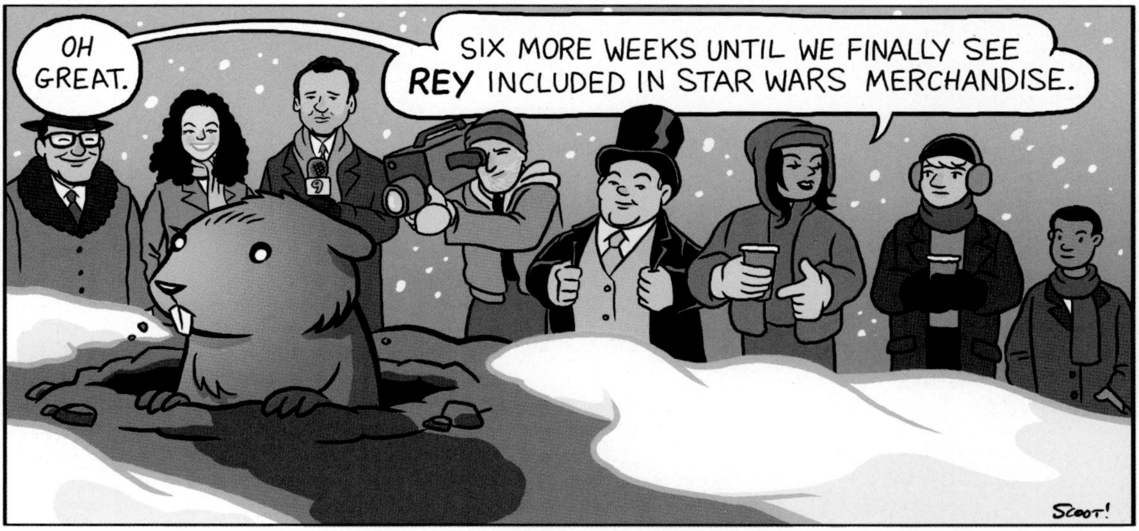
OH GREAT.
SIX MORE WEEKS UNTIL WE FINALLY SEE REY INCLUDED IN STAR WARS MERCHANDISE.
SCOOT!

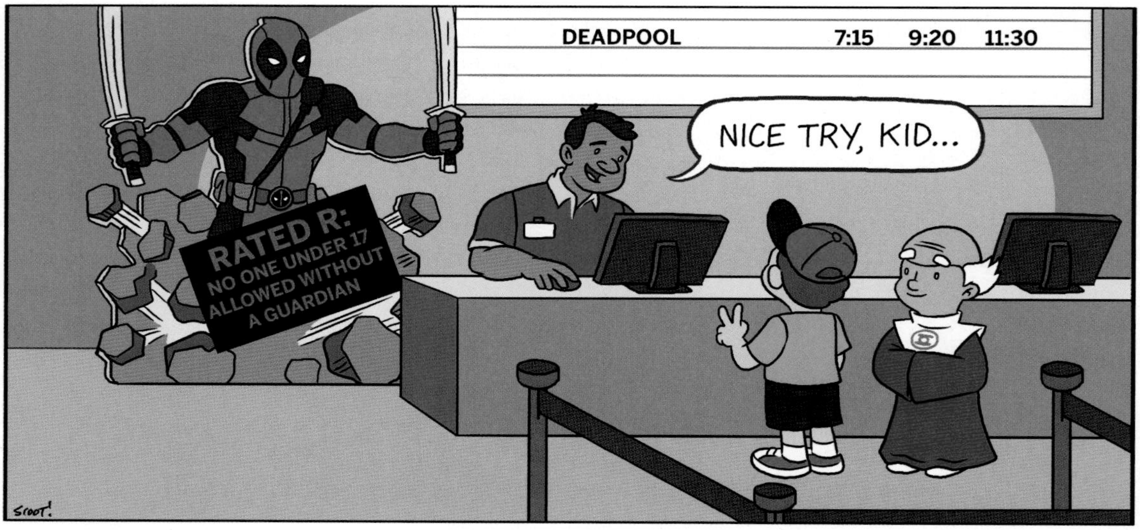
DEADPOOL 7:15 9:20 11:30
NICE TRY, KID...
RATED R:
NO ONE UNDER 17 ALLOWED WITHOUT A GUARDIAN
SCOOT!

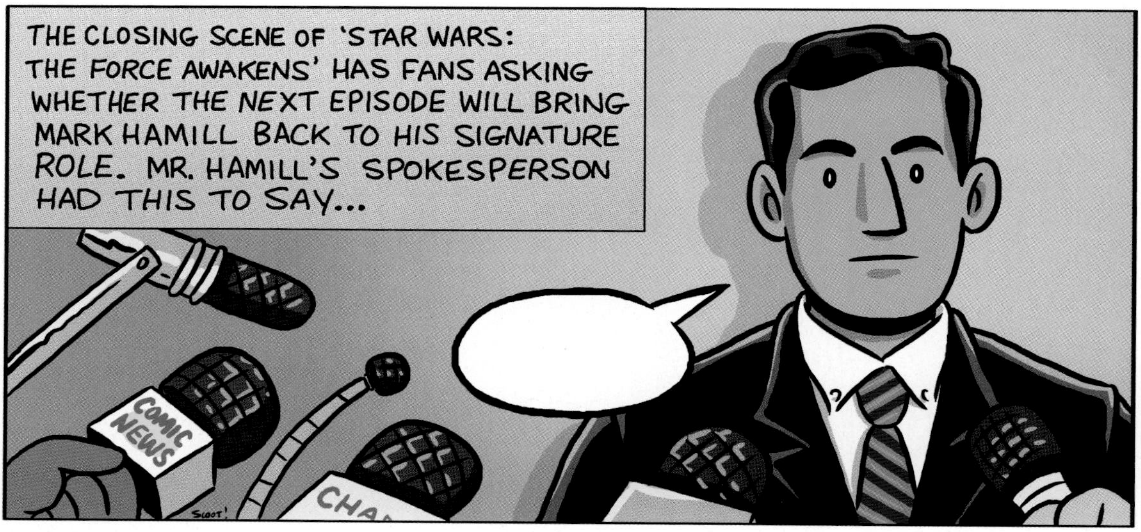
THE CLOSING SCENE OF 'STAR WARS: THE FORCE AWAKENS' HAS FANS ASKING WHETHER THE NEXT EPISODE WILL BRING MARK HAMILL BACK TO HIS SIGNATURE ROLE. MR. HAMILL'S SPOKESPERSON HAD THIS TO SAY...
COMIC NEWS
SCOOT!

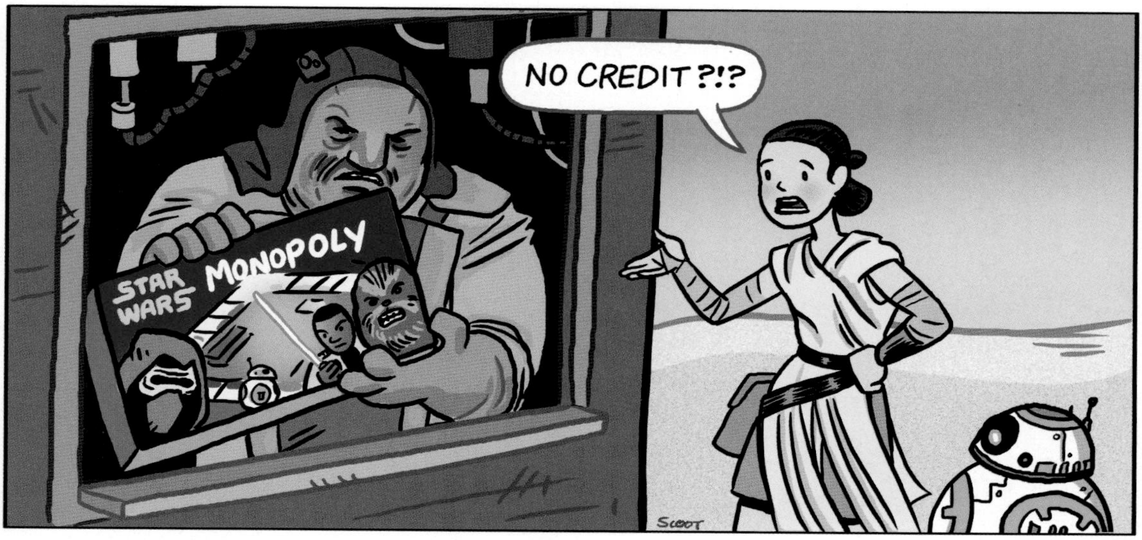
NO CREDIT ?!?
STAR WARS
MONOPOLY
SCOOT

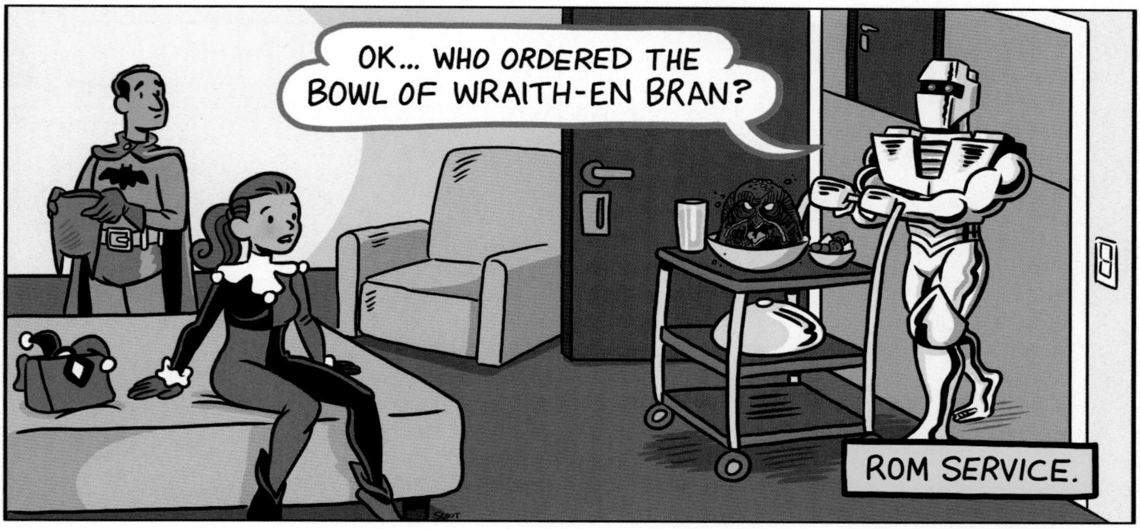
OK... WHO ORDERED THE BOWL OF WRAITH-EN BRAN?
ROM SERVICE.

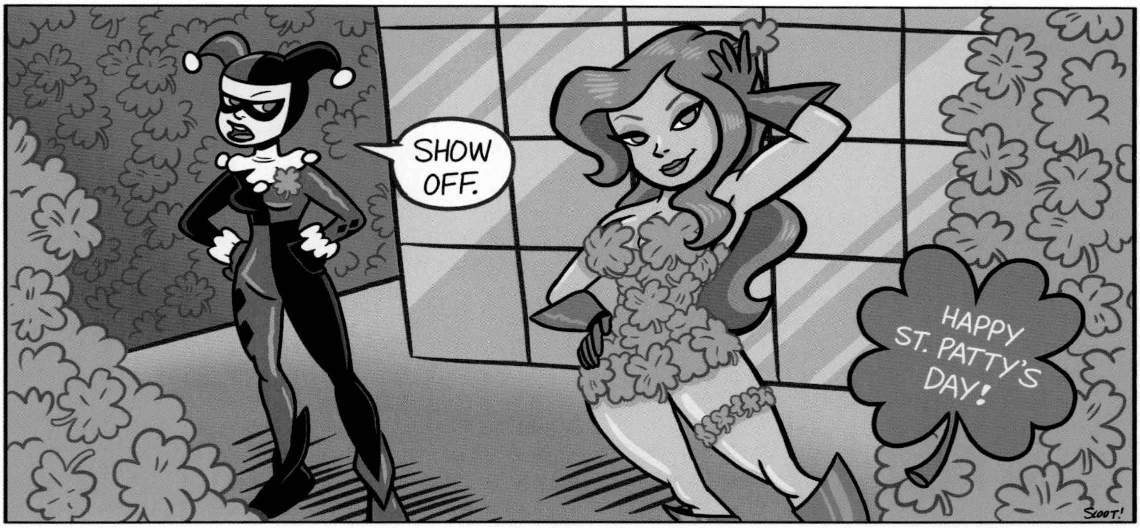
SHOW OFF.
HAPPY ST. PATTY'S DAY!
SCOOT!

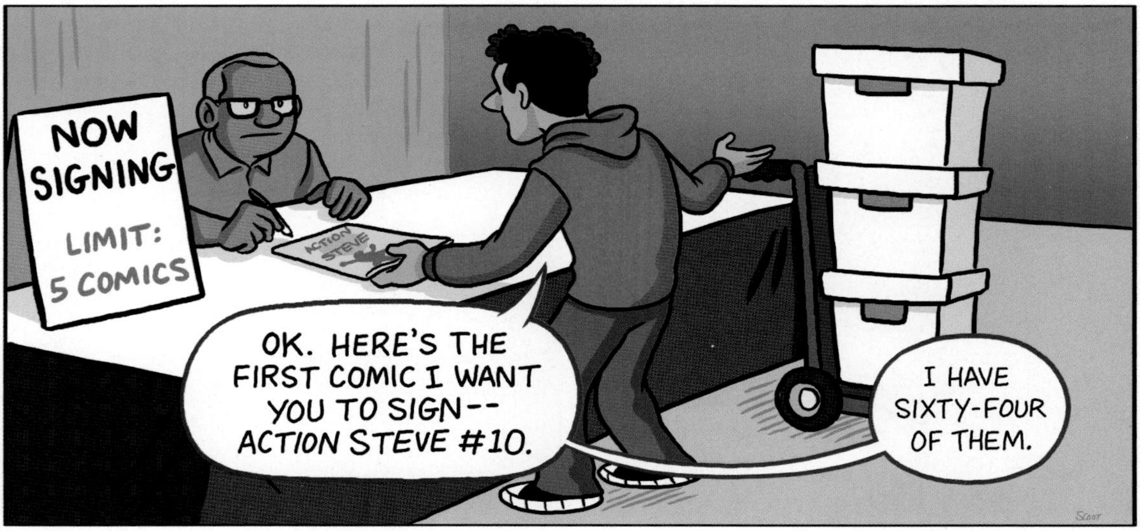
NOW SIGNING
LIMIT: 5 COMICS
ACTION STEVE
OK. HERE'S THE FIRST COMIC I WANT YOU TO SIGN-- ACTION STEVE #10.
I HAVE SIXTY-FOUR OF THEM.

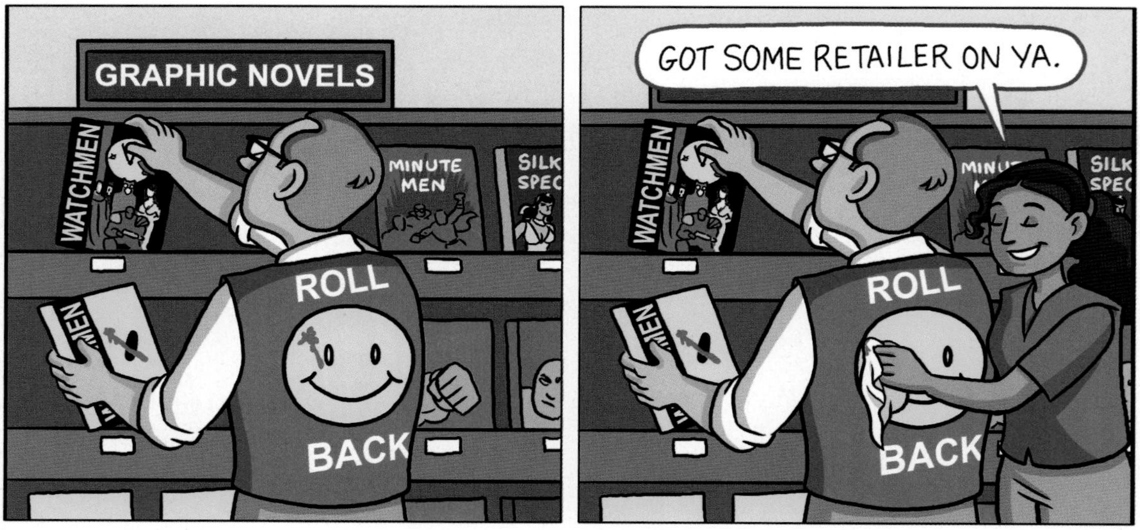
GRAPHIC NOVELS
WATCHMEN
MINUTE MEN
SILK SPEC
ROLL
BACK
GOT SOME RETAILER ON YA.

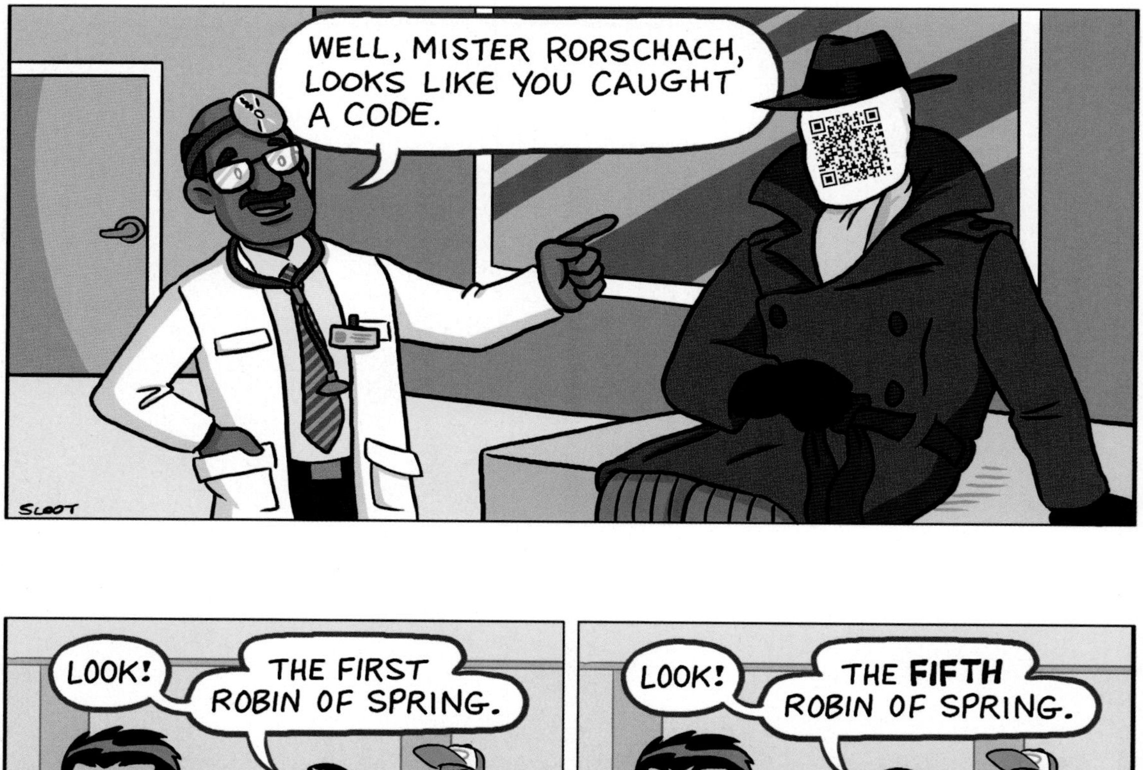
WELL, MISTER RORSCHACH, LOOKS LIKE YOU CAUGHT A CODE.
SLOOT

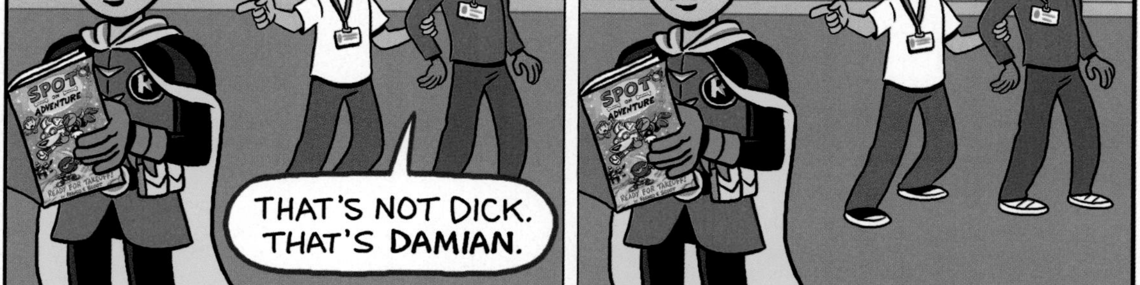
LOOK!
THE FIRST ROBIN OF SPRING.
THAT'S NOT DICK. THAT'S **DAMIAN**.
LOOK!
THE **FIFTH** ROBIN OF SPRING.
SLOOT

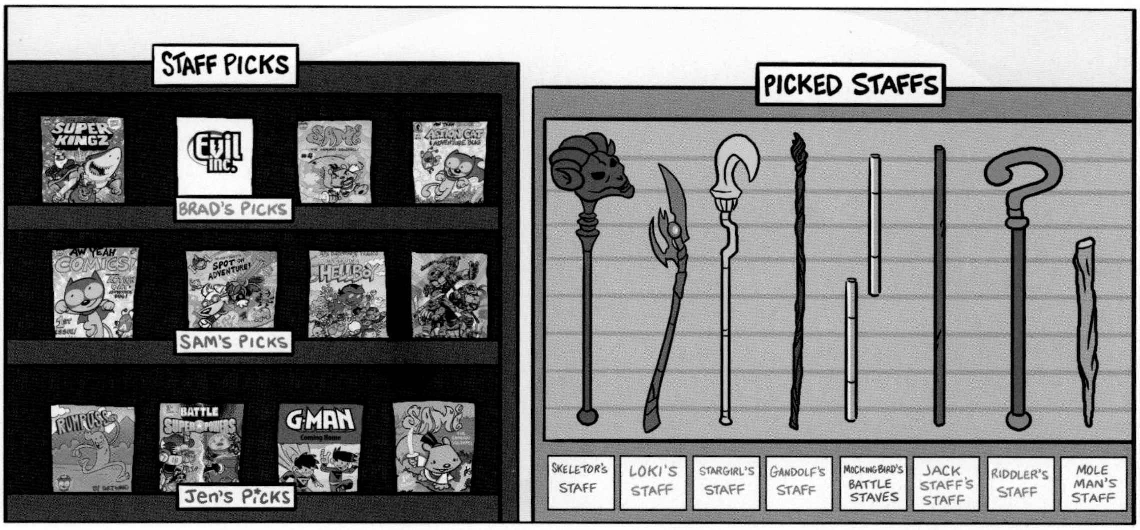
STAFF PICKS
BRAD'S PICKS
SAM'S PICKS
Jen's Picks
PICKED STAFFS
SKELETOR'S STAFF
LOKI'S STAFF
STARGIRL'S STAFF
GANDOLF'S STAFF
MOCKINGBIRD'S BATTLE STAVES
JACK STAFF'S STAFF
RIDDLER'S STAFF
MOLE MAN'S STAFF

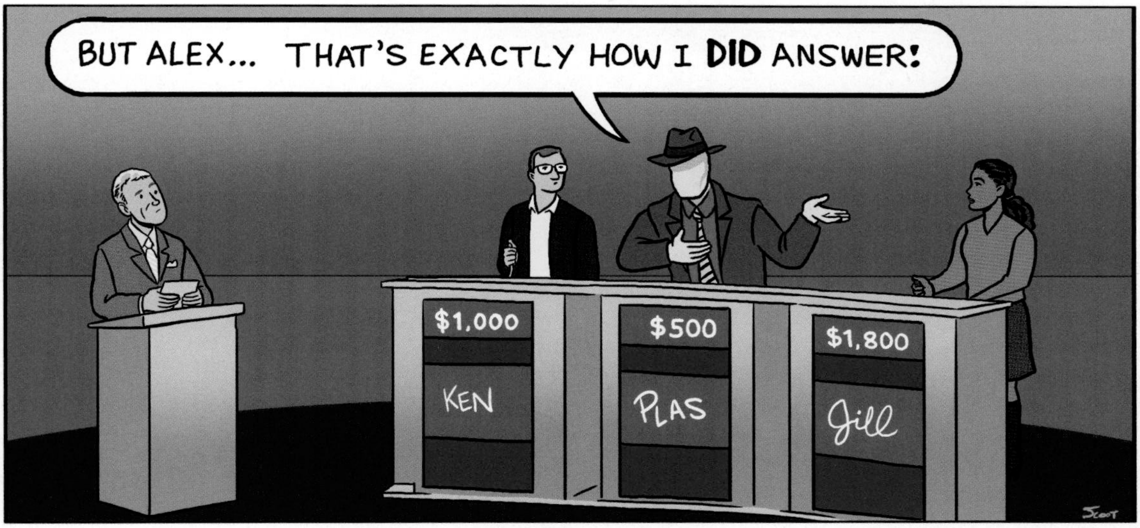
BUT ALEX... THAT'S EXACTLY HOW I **DID** ANSWER!
$1,000
KEN
$500
PLAS
$1,800
Jill

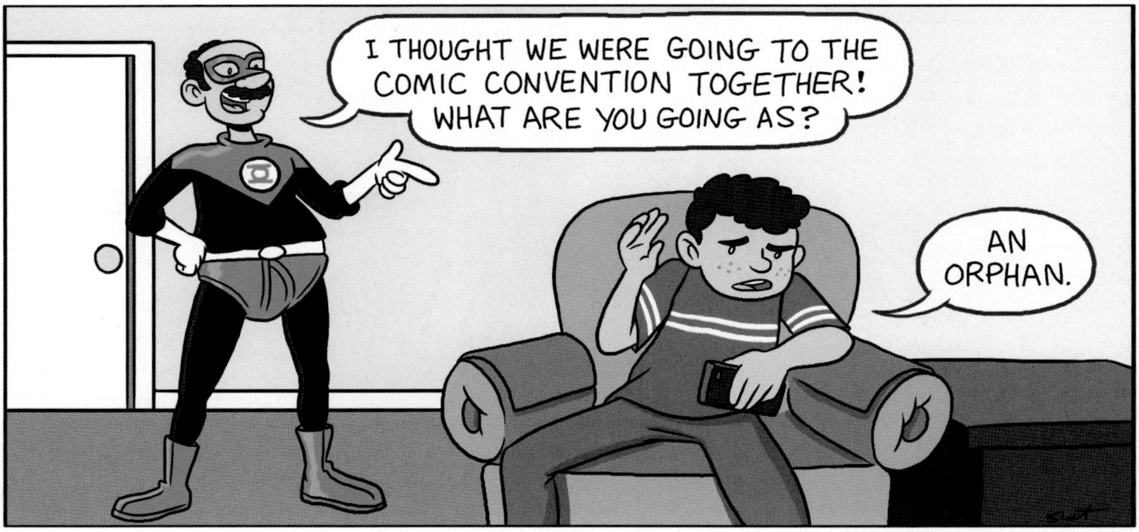
I THOUGHT WE WERE GOING TO THE COMIC CONVENTION TOGETHER! WHAT ARE YOU GOING AS?
AN ORPHAN.

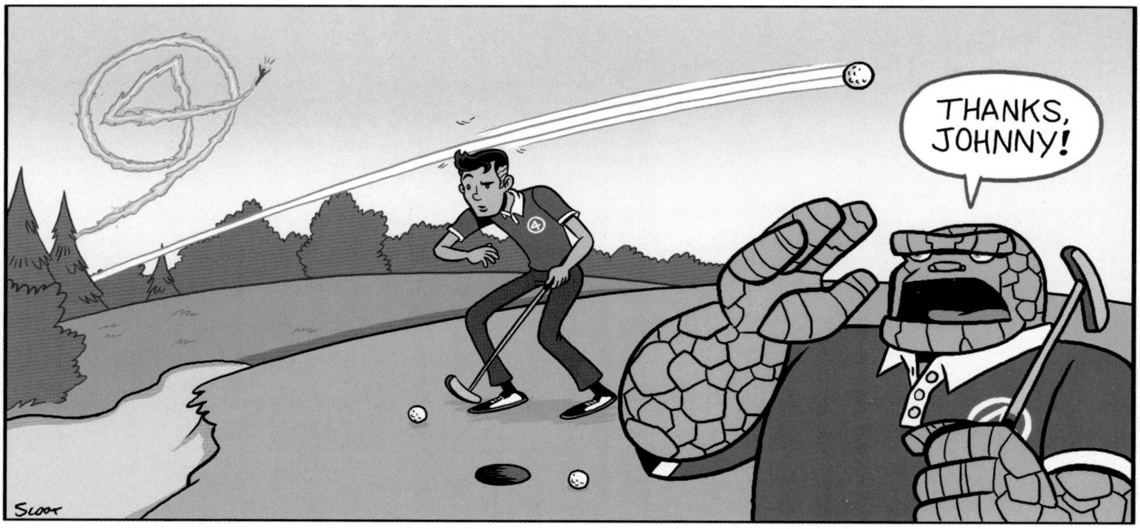
THANKS, JOHNNY!

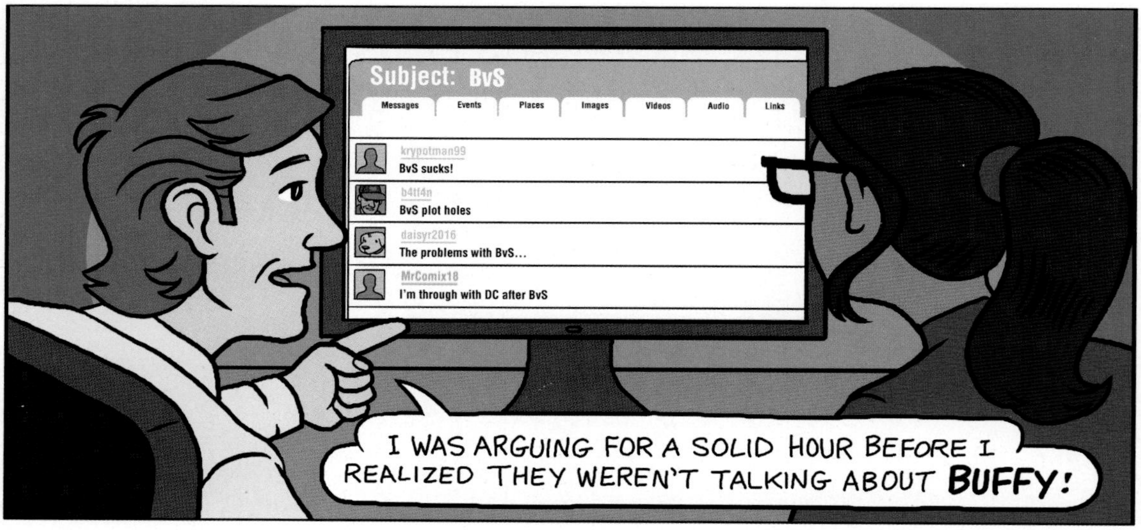
Subject: BvS
Messages Events Places Images Videos Audio Links
krypotman99
BvS sucks!
b4tf4n
BvS plot holes
daisyr2016
The problems with BvS...
MrComix18
I'm through with DC after BvS
I WAS ARGUING FOR A SOLID HOUR BEFORE I REALIZED THEY WEREN'T TALKING ABOUT BUFFY!

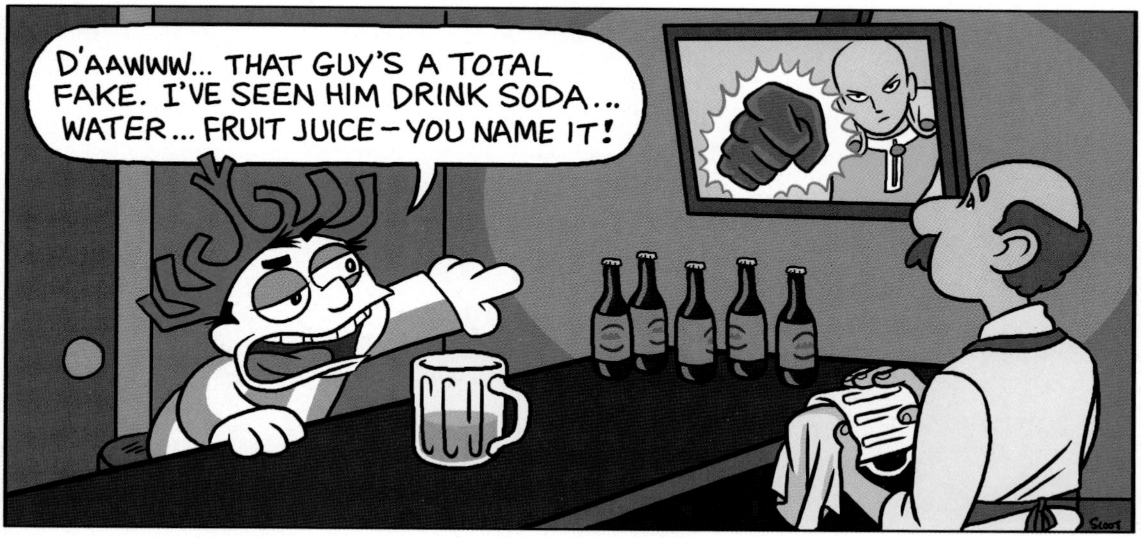
D'AAWWW... THAT GUY'S A TOTAL FAKE. I'VE SEEN HIM DRINK SODA... WATER... FRUIT JUICE—YOU NAME IT!

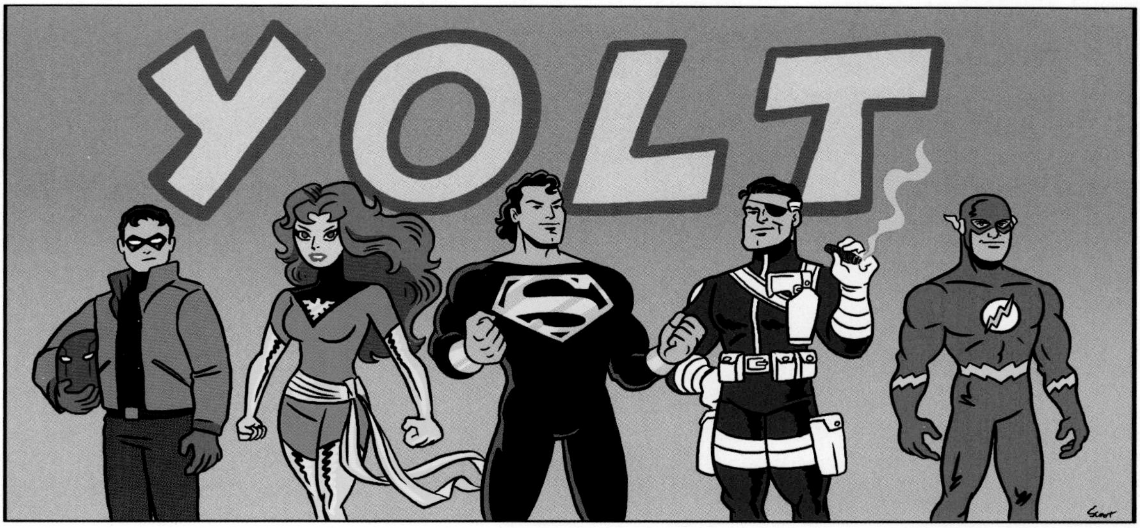
YOLT

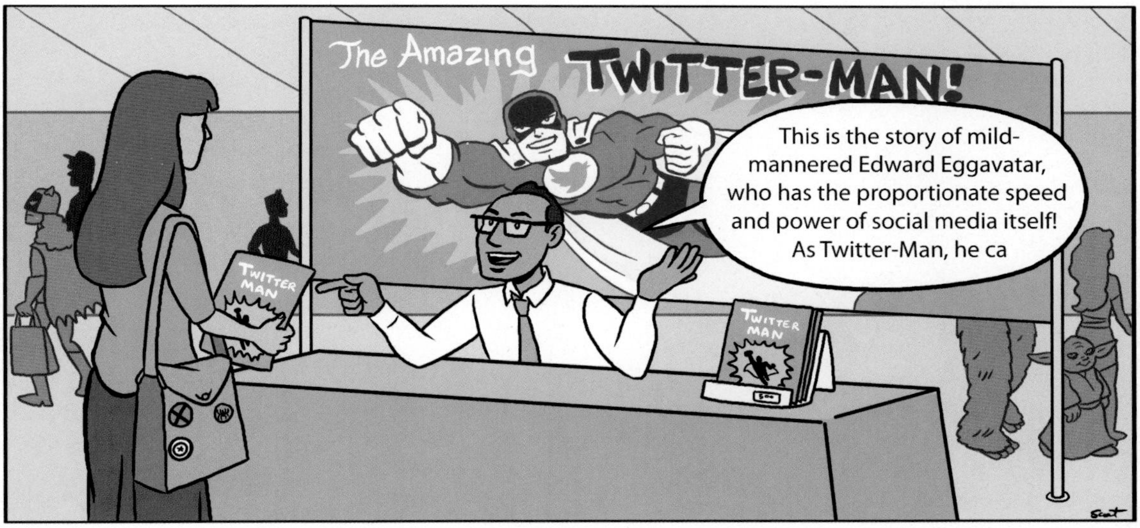
The Amazing TWITTER-MAN!
This is the story of mild-mannered Edward Eggavatar, who has the proportionate speed and power of social media itself! As Twitter-Man, he ca
TWITTER MAN
TWITTER MAN

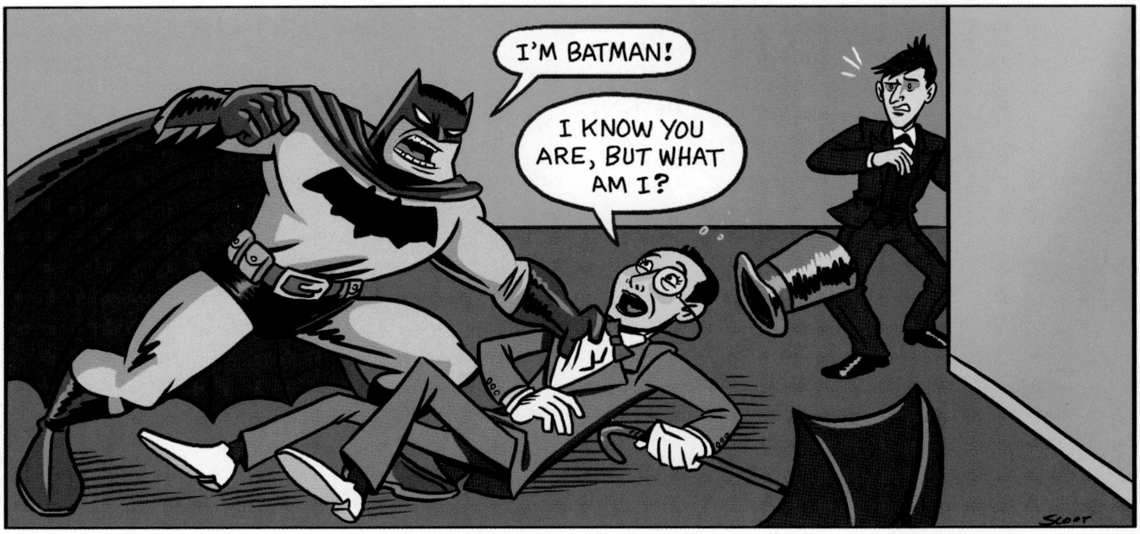
I'M BATMAN!
I KNOW YOU ARE, BUT WHAT AM I?

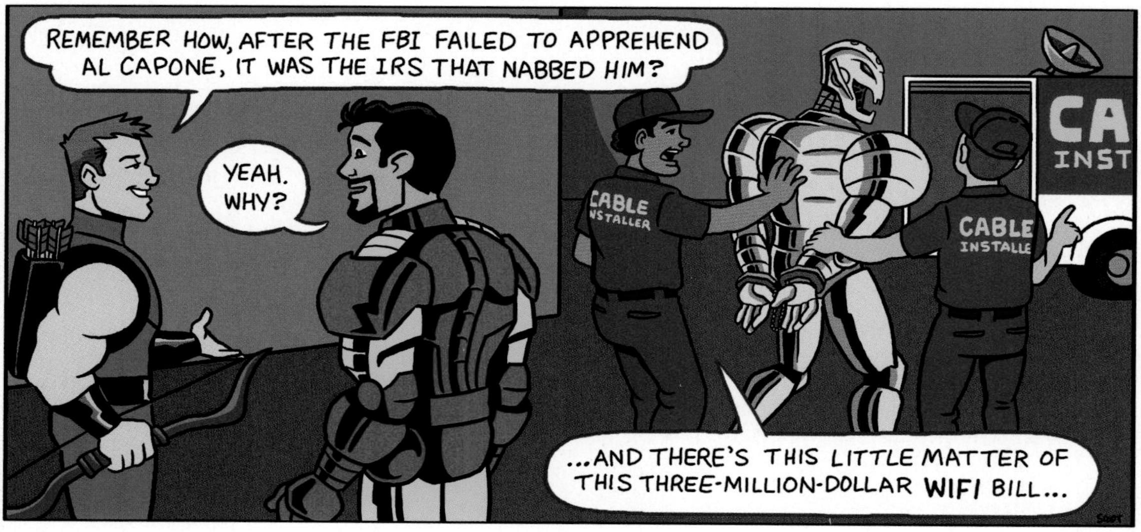
REMEMBER HOW, AFTER THE FBI FAILED TO APPREHEND AL CAPONE, IT WAS THE IRS THAT NABBED HIM?
YEAH. WHY?
CABLE
...AND THERE'S THIS LITTLE MATTER OF THIS THREE-MILLION-DOLLAR WIFI BILL...

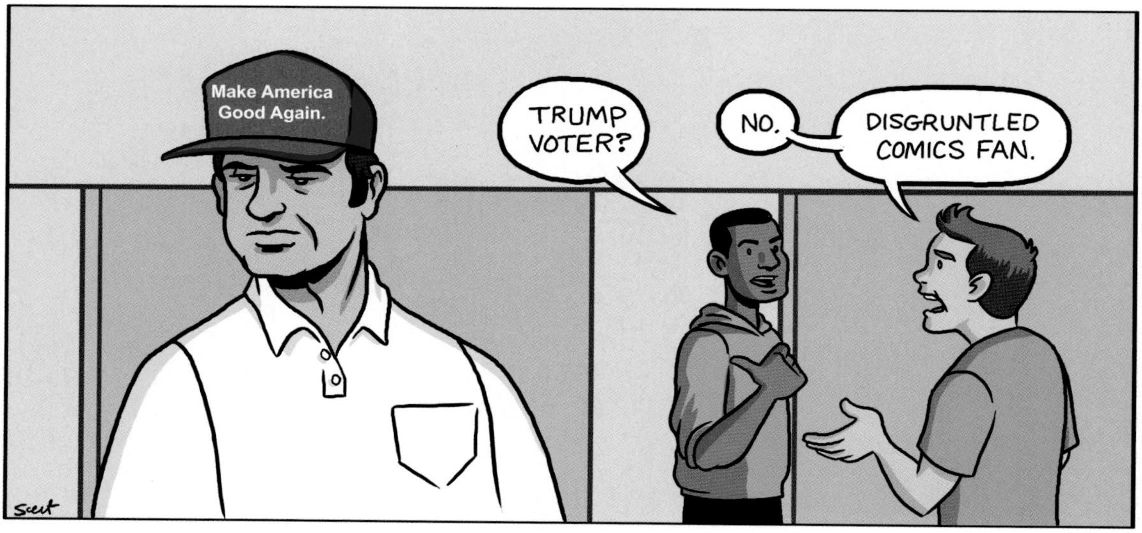
Make America Good Again.
TRUMP VOTER?
NO.
DISGRUNTLED COMICS FAN.

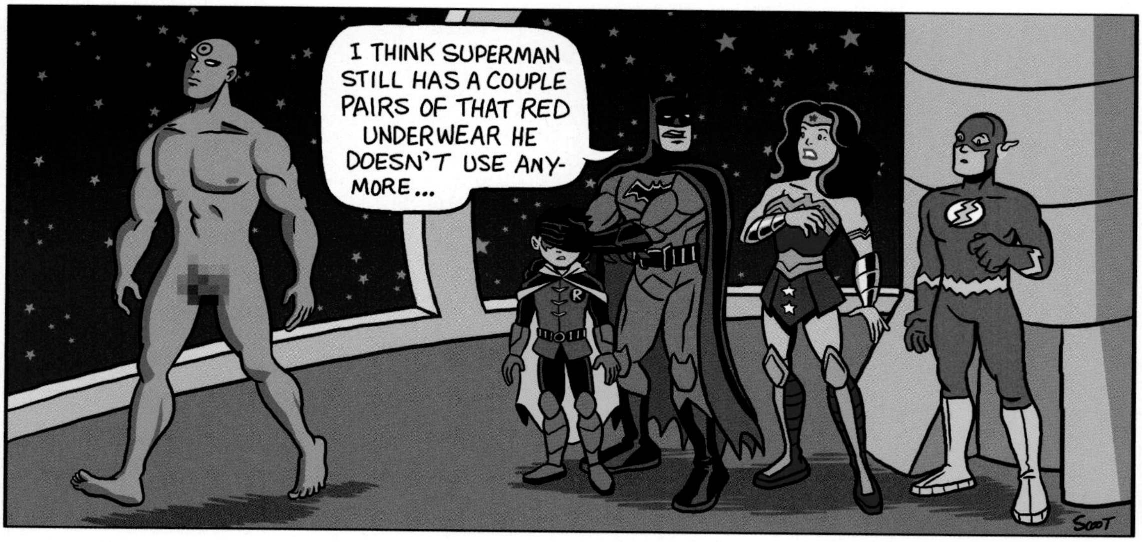
I THINK SUPERMAN STILL HAS A COUPLE PAIRS OF THAT RED UNDERWEAR HE DOESN'T USE ANY-MORE...

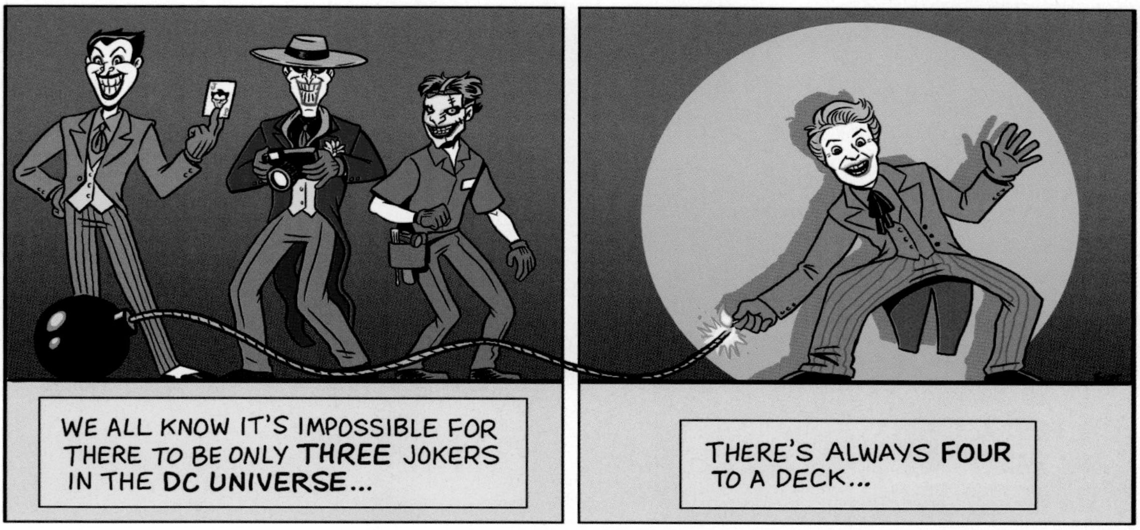
WE ALL KNOW IT'S IMPOSSIBLE FOR THERE TO BE ONLY THREE JOKERS IN THE DC UNIVERSE...
THERE'S ALWAYS FOUR TO A DECK...

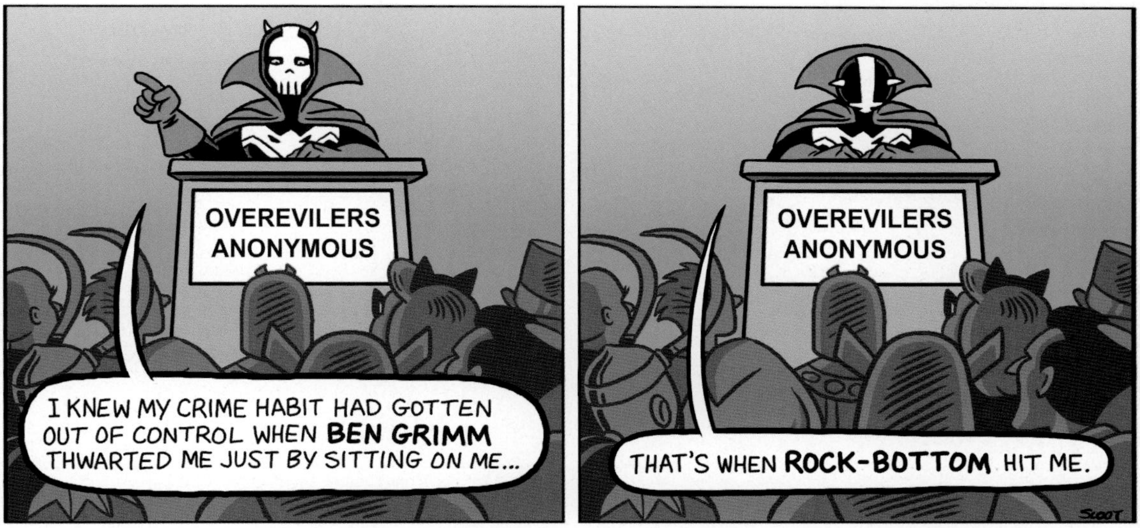
OVEREVILERS ANONYMOUS
I KNEW MY CRIME HABIT HAD GOTTEN OUT OF CONTROL WHEN BEN GRIMM THWARTED ME JUST BY SITTING ON ME...
OVEREVILERS ANONYMOUS
THAT'S WHEN ROCK-BOTTOM HIT ME.
SCOOT

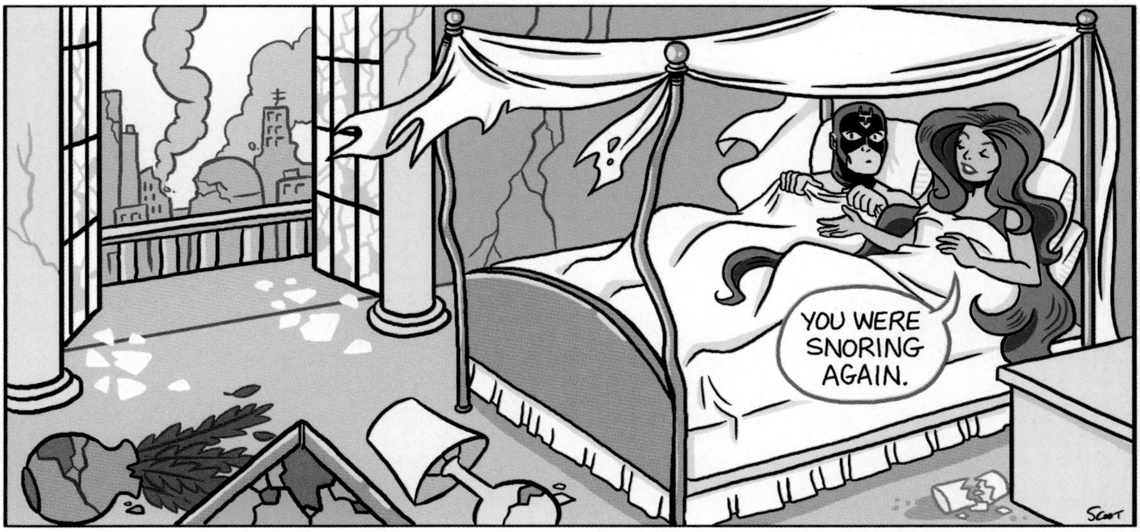
YOU WERE SNORING AGAIN.
SCOOT

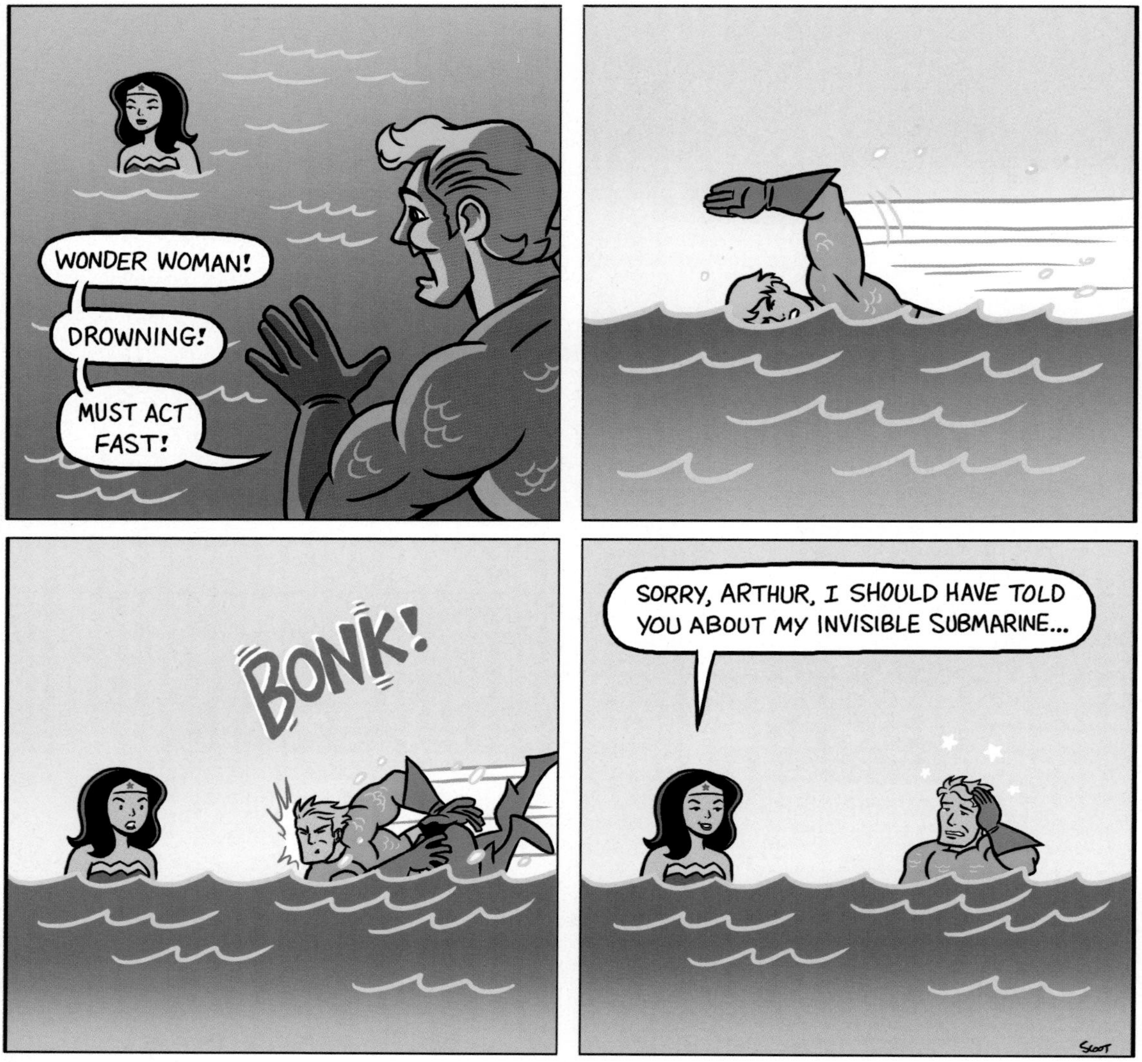
WONDER WOMAN!
DROWNING!
MUST ACT FAST!
BONK!
SORRY, ARTHUR, I SHOULD HAVE TOLD YOU ABOUT MY INVISIBLE SUBMARINE...

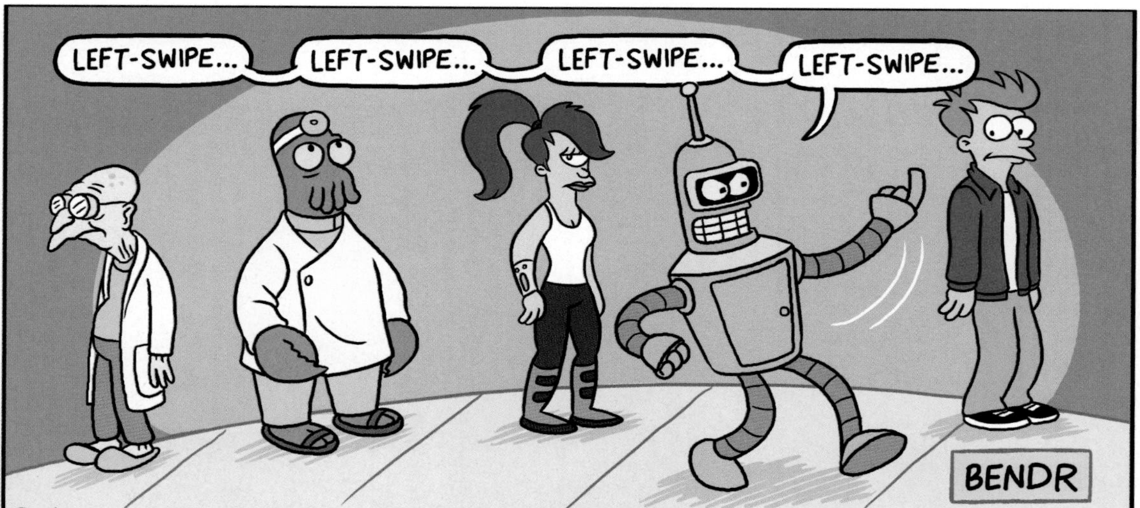
LEFT-SWIPE...
LEFT-SWIPE...
LEFT-SWIPE...
LEFT-SWIPE...
BENDR

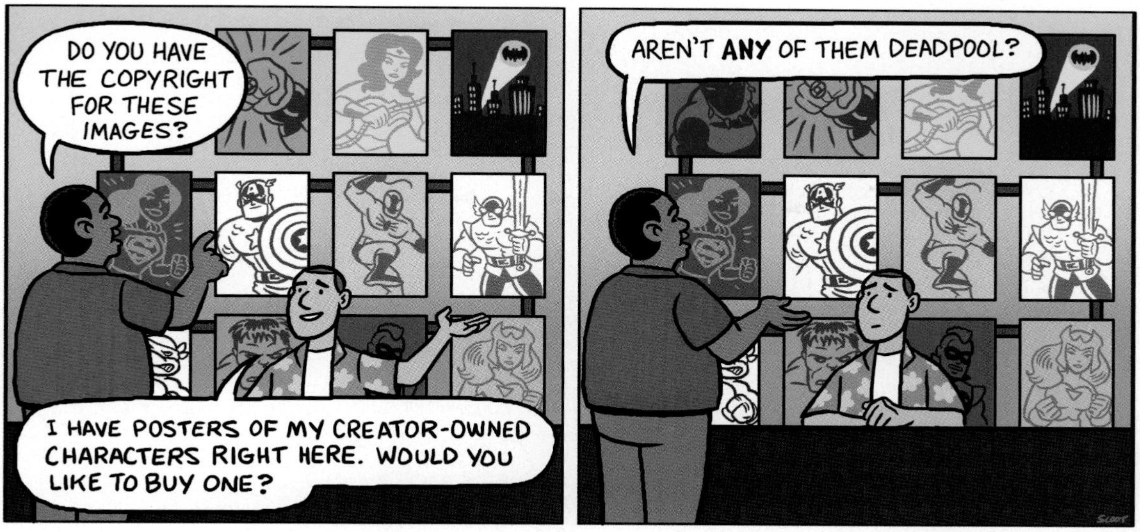
DO YOU HAVE THE COPYRIGHT FOR THESE IMAGES?
I HAVE POSTERS OF MY CREATOR-OWNED CHARACTERS RIGHT HERE. WOULD YOU LIKE TO BUY ONE?
AREN'T **ANY** OF THEM DEADPOOL?

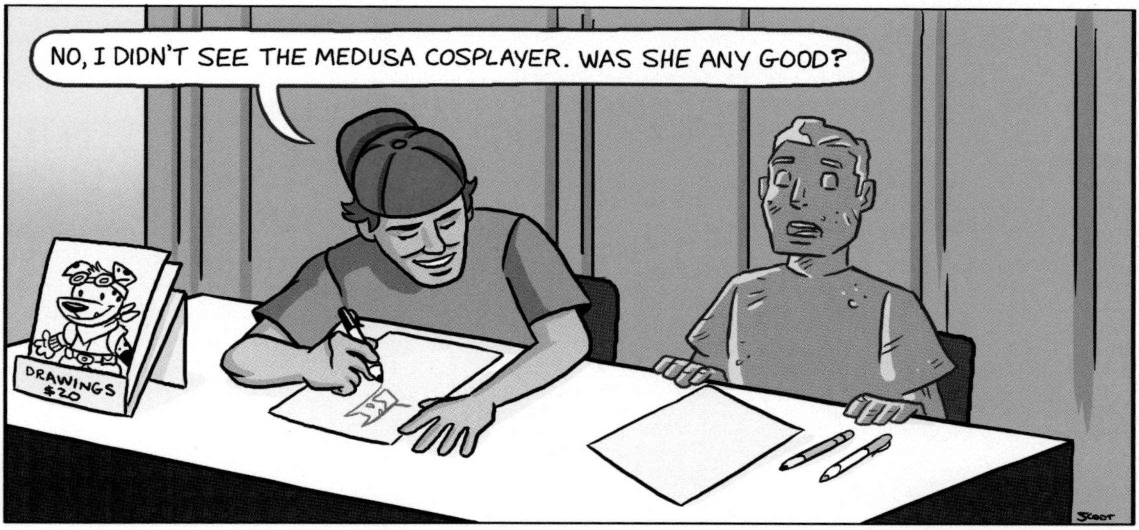
NO, I DIDN'T SEE THE MEDUSA COSPLAYER. WAS SHE ANY GOOD?
DRAWINGS $20

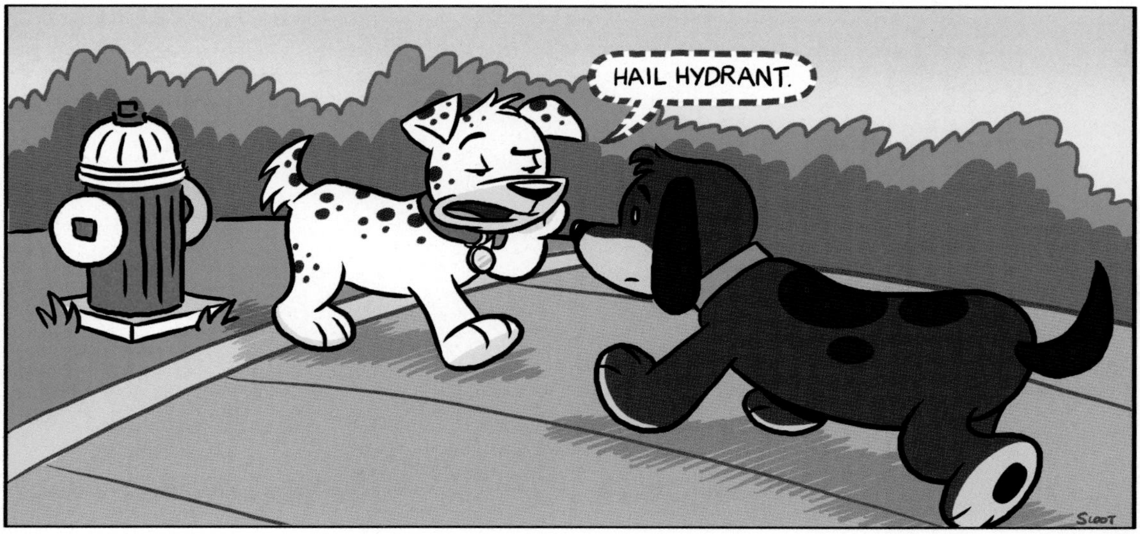
HAIL HYDRANT.

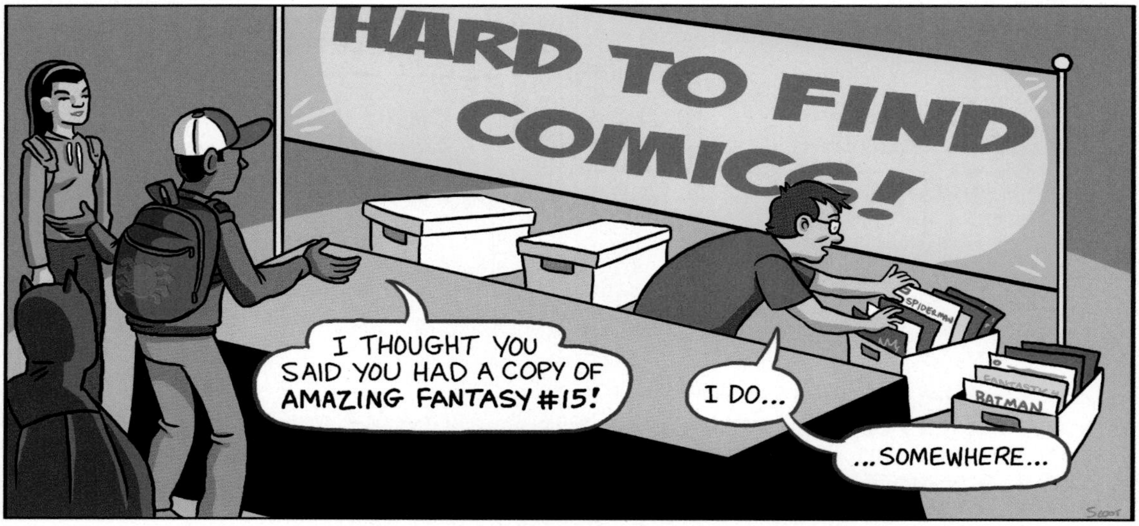
HARD TO FIND COMICS!
I THOUGHT YOU SAID YOU HAD A COPY OF AMAZING FANTASY #15!
I DO...
...SOMEWHERE...
SPIDERMAN
BATMAN

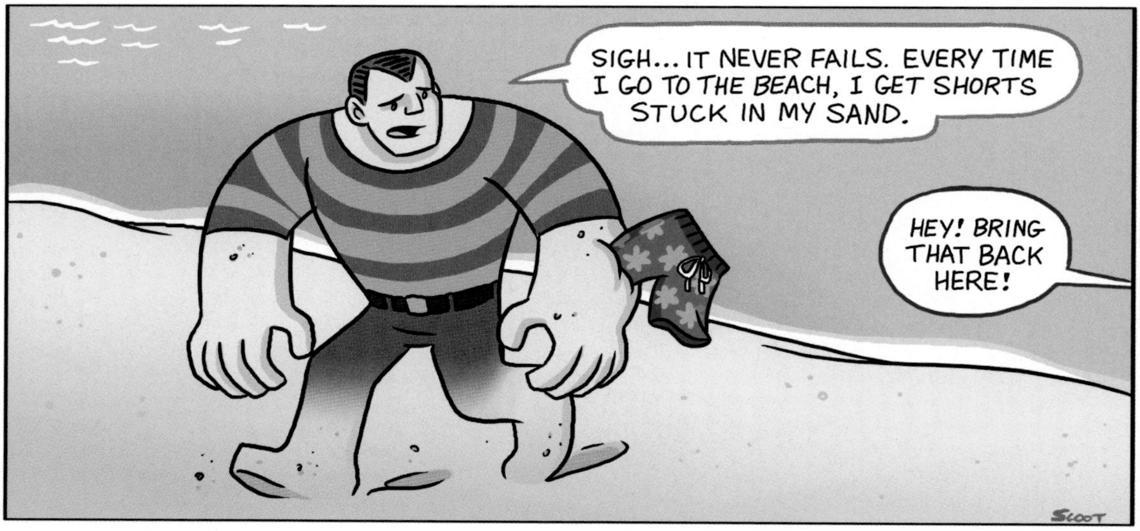
SIGH... IT NEVER FAILS. EVERY TIME I GO TO THE BEACH, I GET SHORTS STUCK IN MY SAND.
HEY! BRING THAT BACK HERE!

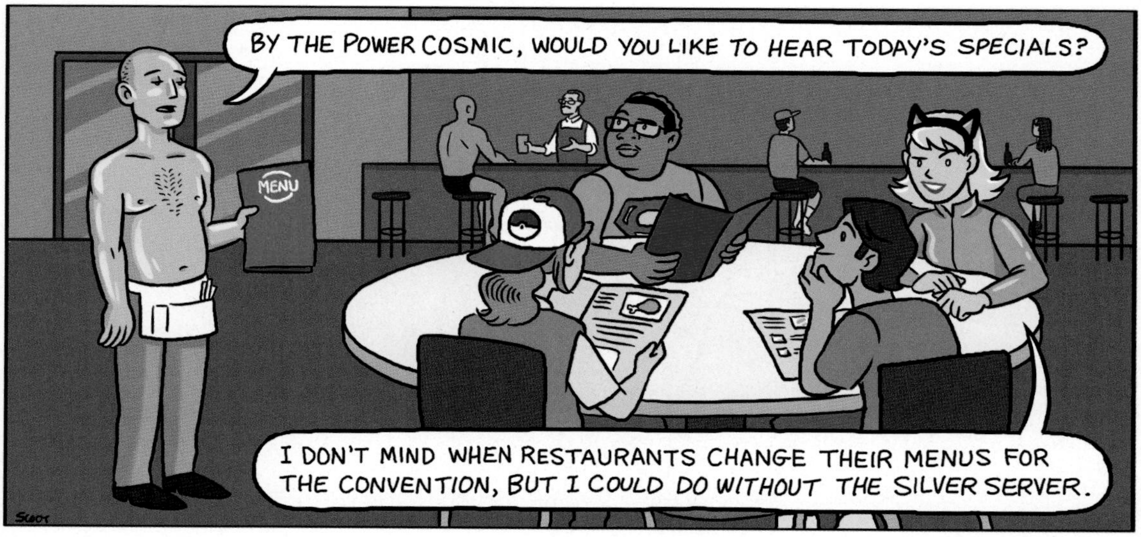
BY THE POWER COSMIC, WOULD YOU LIKE TO HEAR TODAY'S SPECIALS?
MENU
I DON'T MIND WHEN RESTAURANTS CHANGE THEIR MENUS FOR THE CONVENTION, BUT I COULD DO WITHOUT THE SILVER SERVER.

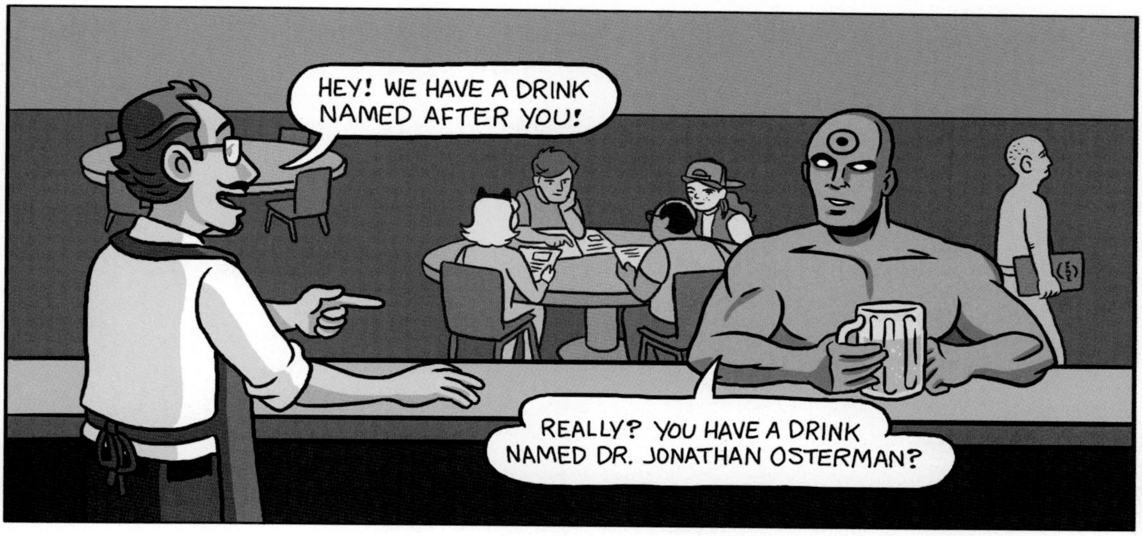
HEY! WE HAVE A DRINK NAMED AFTER YOU!
REALLY? YOU HAVE A DRINK NAMED DR. JONATHAN OSTERMAN?

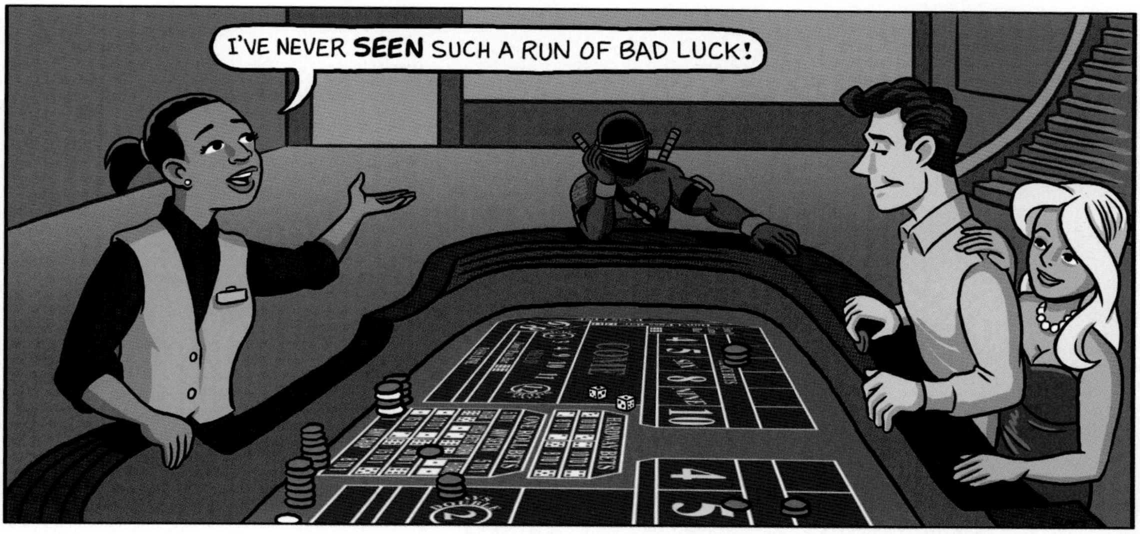
I'VE NEVER **SEEN** SUCH A RUN OF BAD LUCK!

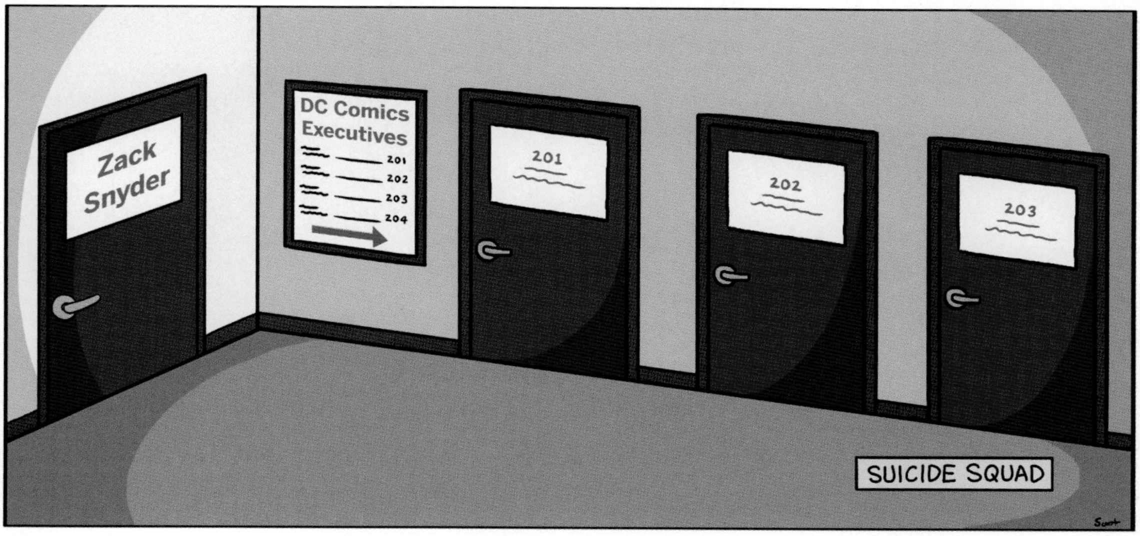
Zack Snyder
DC Comics Executives
201
202
203
204
201
202
203
SUICIDE SQUAD

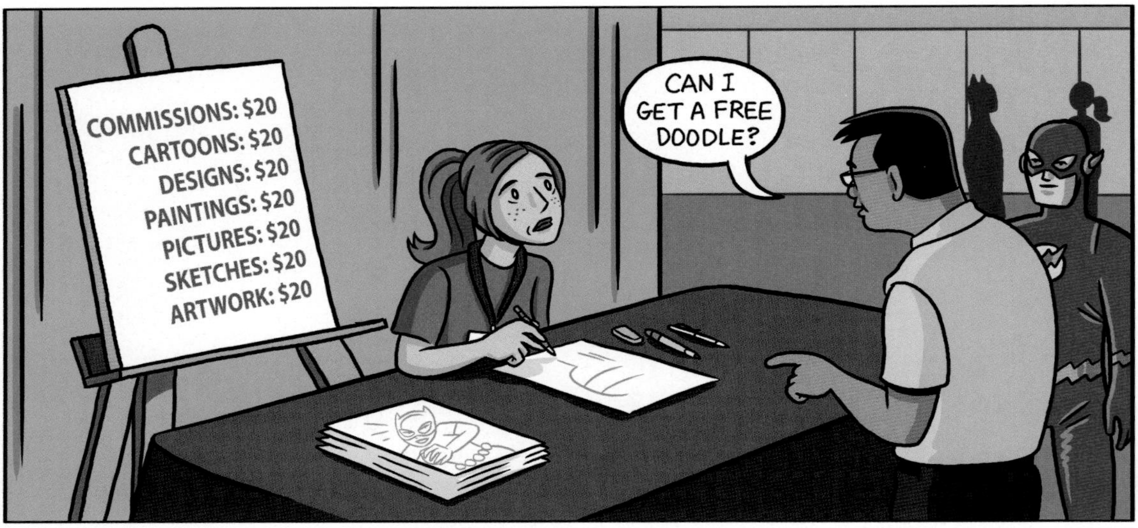
COMMISSIONS: $20
CARTOONS: $20
DESIGNS: $20
PAINTINGS: $20
PICTURES: $20
SKETCHES: $20
ARTWORK: $20
CAN I GET A FREE DOODLE?

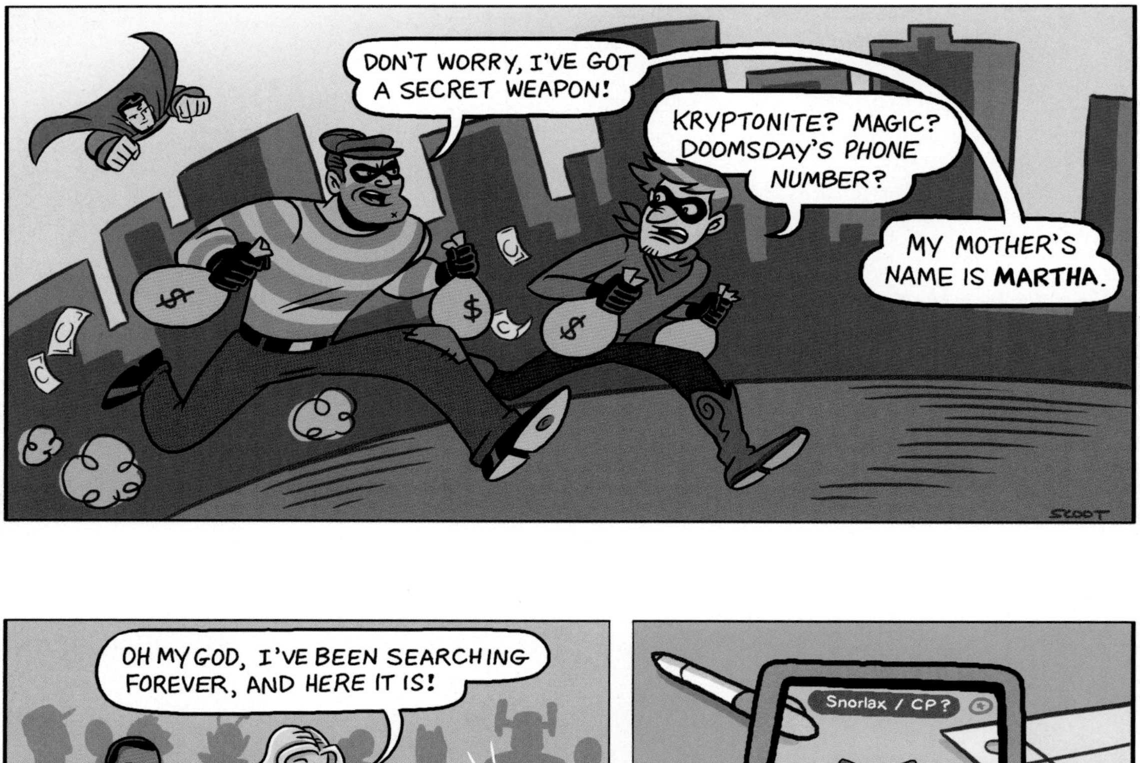
DON'T WORRY, I'VE GOT A SECRET WEAPON!
KRYPTONITE? MAGIC? DOOMSDAY'S PHONE NUMBER?
MY MOTHER'S NAME IS **MARTHA**.
SCOOT

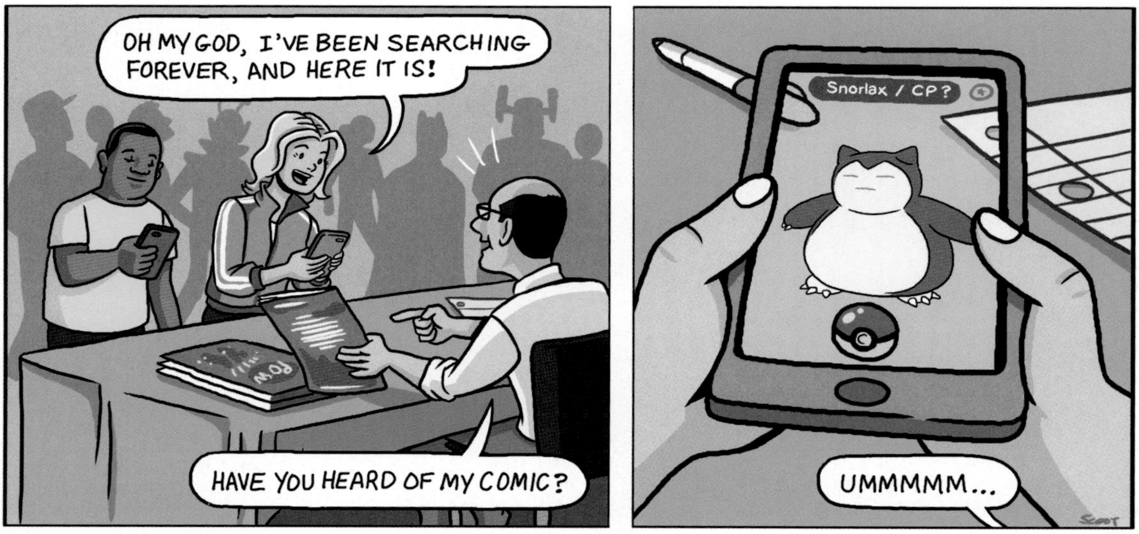
OH MY GOD, I'VE BEEN SEARCHING FOREVER, AND HERE IT IS!
HAVE YOU HEARD OF MY COMIC?
Snorlax / CP ?
UMMMMM...
SCOOT

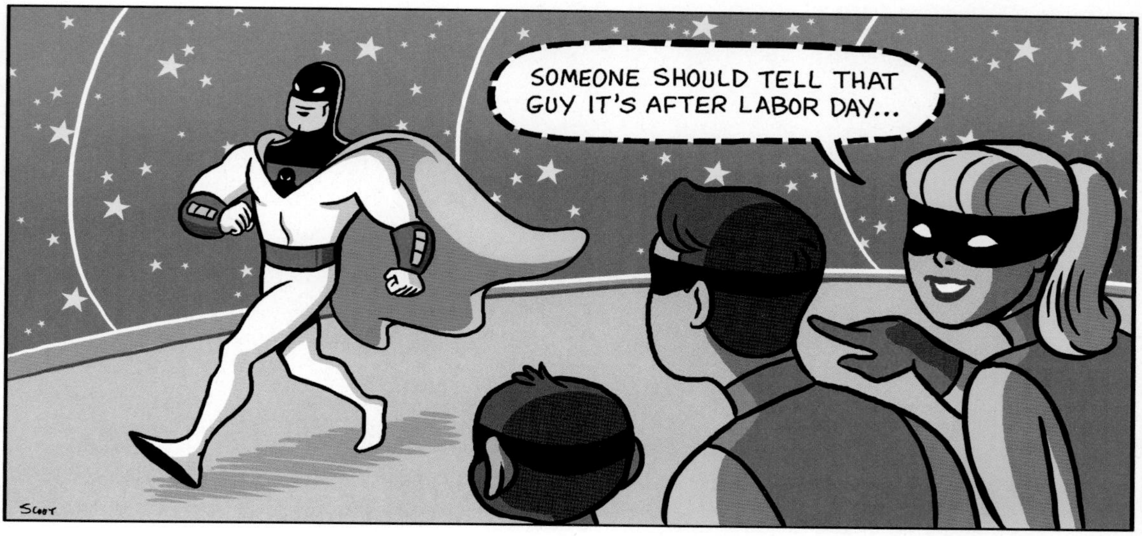
SOMEONE SHOULD TELL THAT GUY IT'S AFTER LABOR DAY...
SCOOT

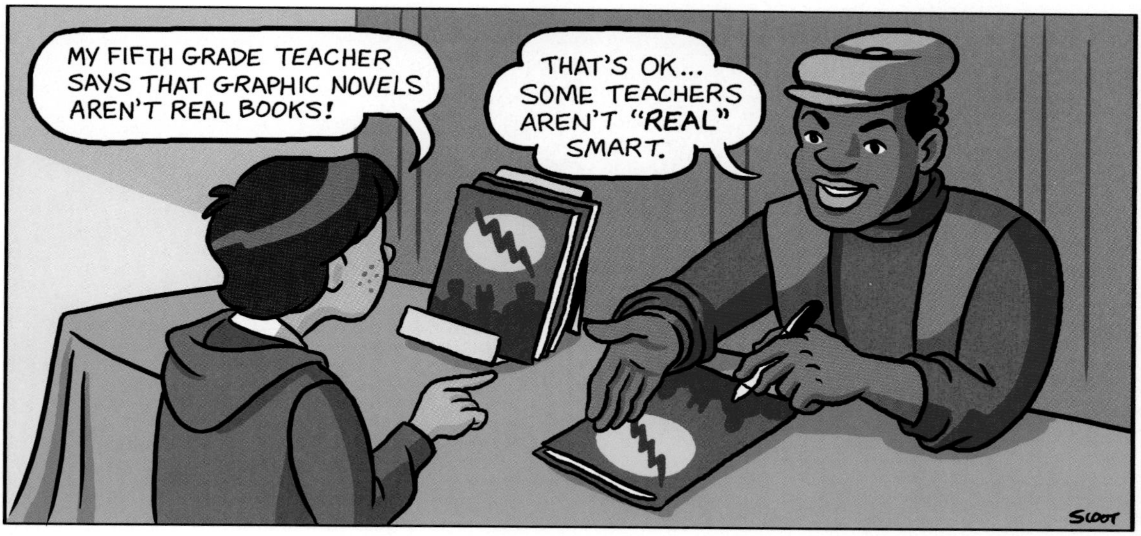
MY FIFTH GRADE TEACHER SAYS THAT GRAPHIC NOVELS AREN'T REAL BOOKS!
THAT'S OK... SOME TEACHERS AREN'T "REAL" SMART.
SCOOT

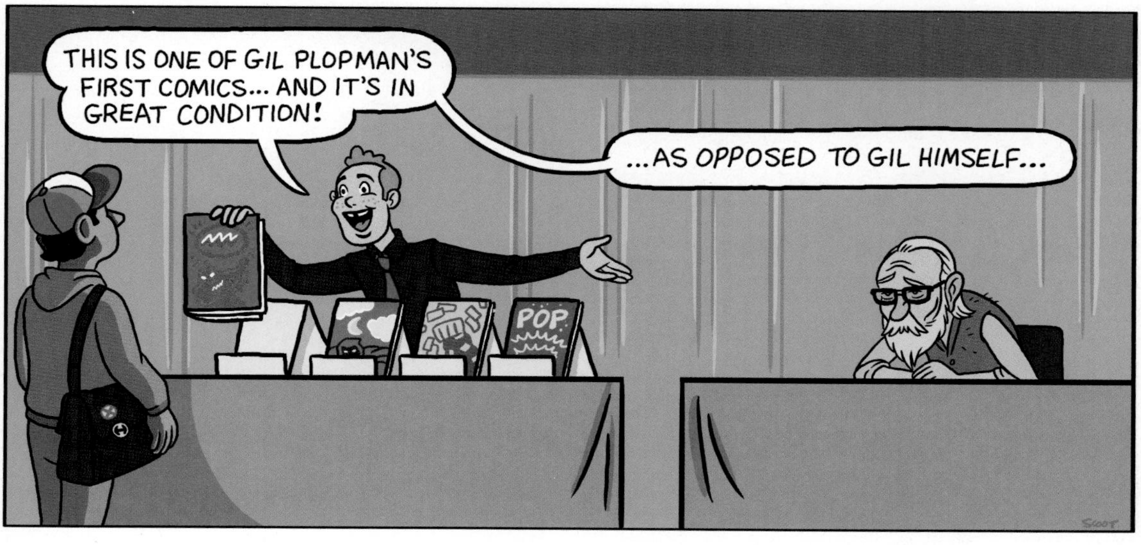
THIS IS ONE OF GIL PLOPMAN'S FIRST COMICS... AND IT'S IN GREAT CONDITION!
...AS OPPOSED TO GIL HIMSELF...
POP

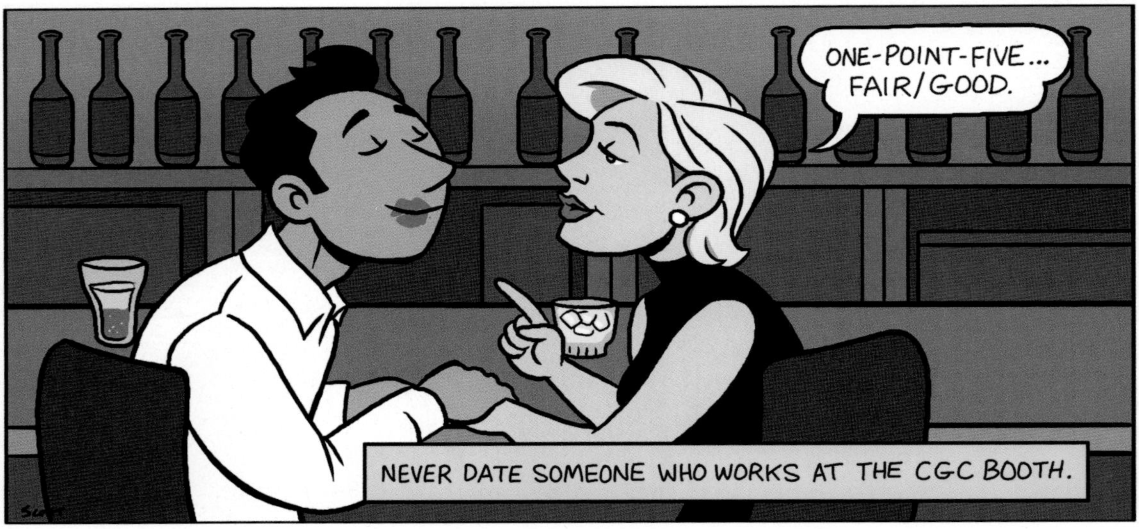
ONE-POINT-FIVE... FAIR/GOOD.
NEVER DATE SOMEONE WHO WORKS AT THE CGC BOOTH.

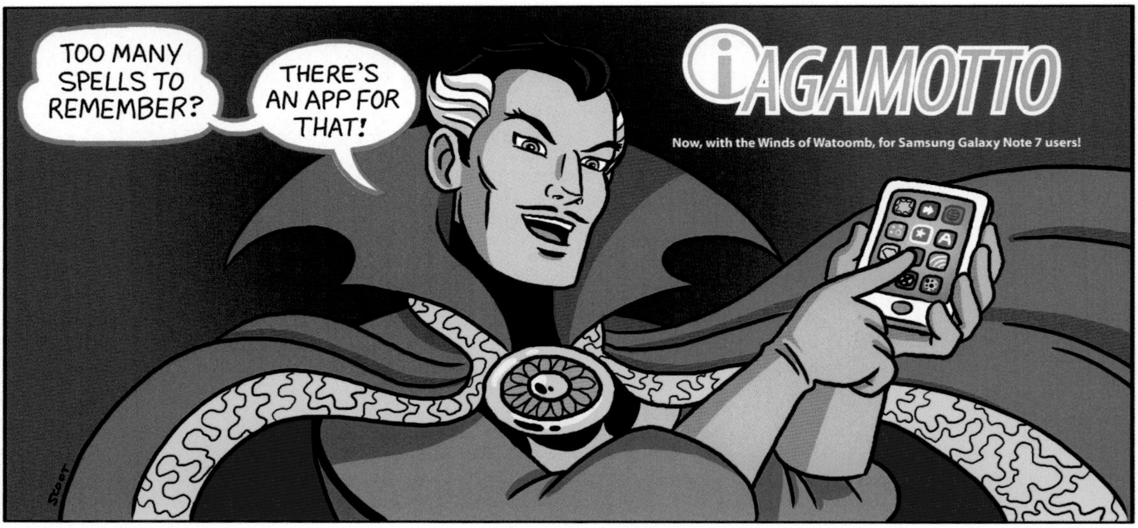
TOO MANY SPELLS TO REMEMBER?
THERE'S AN APP FOR THAT!
iAGAMOTTO
Now, with the Winds of Watoomb, for Samsung Galaxy Note 7 users!

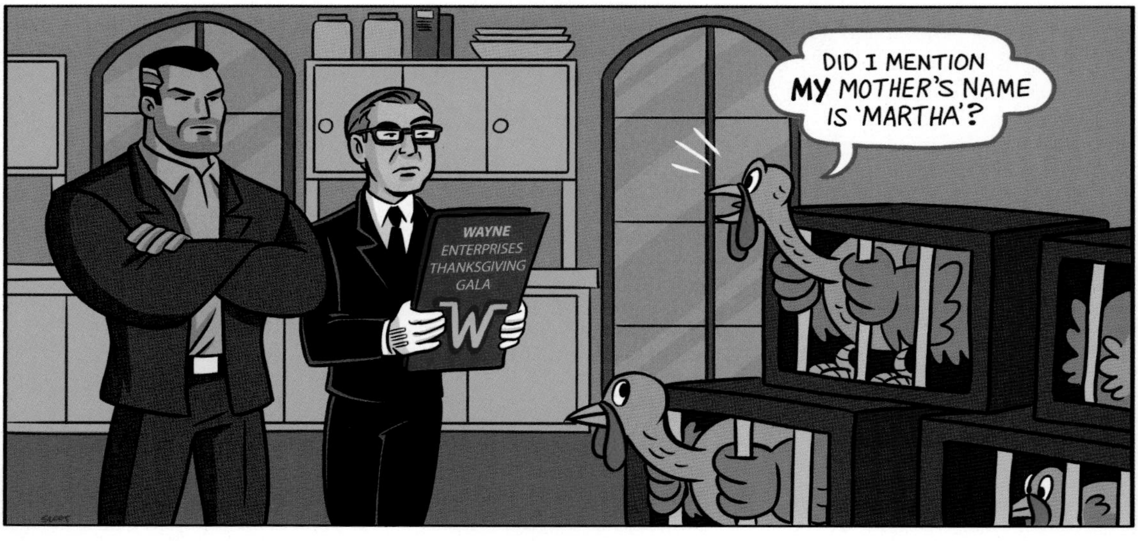
WAYNE ENTERPRISES THANKSGIVING GALA
W
DID I MENTION MY MOTHER'S NAME IS 'MARTHA'?

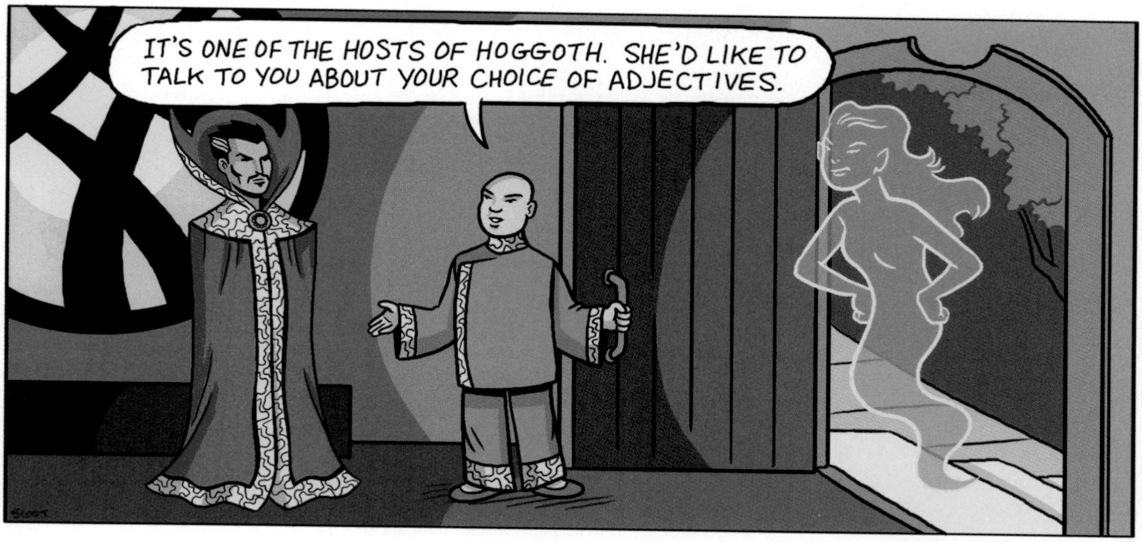
IT'S ONE OF THE HOSTS OF HOGGOTH. SHE'D LIKE TO TALK TO YOU ABOUT YOUR CHOICE OF ADJECTIVES.

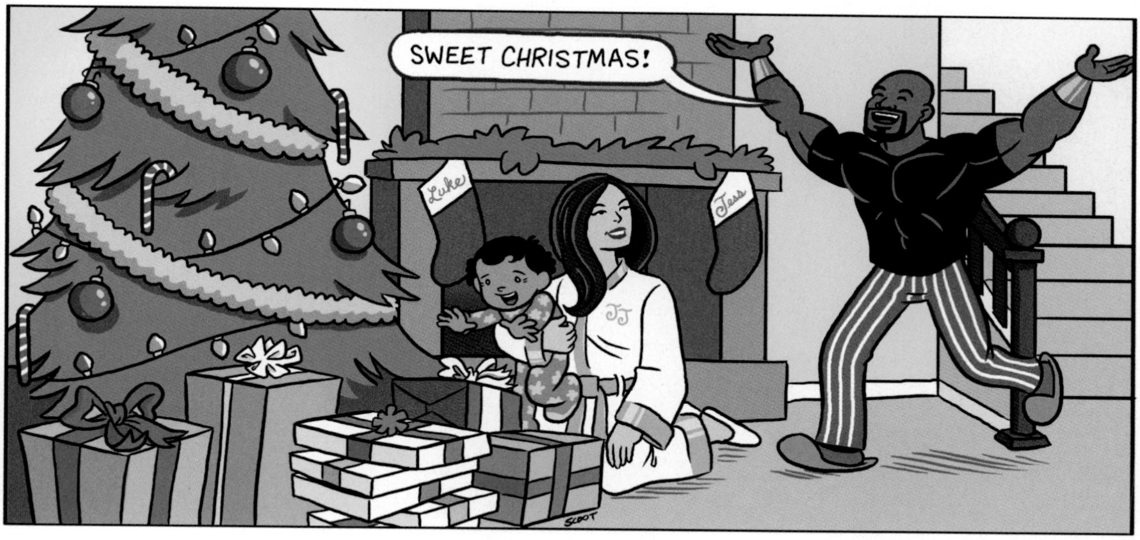
SWEET CHRISTMAS!
Luke
Jess

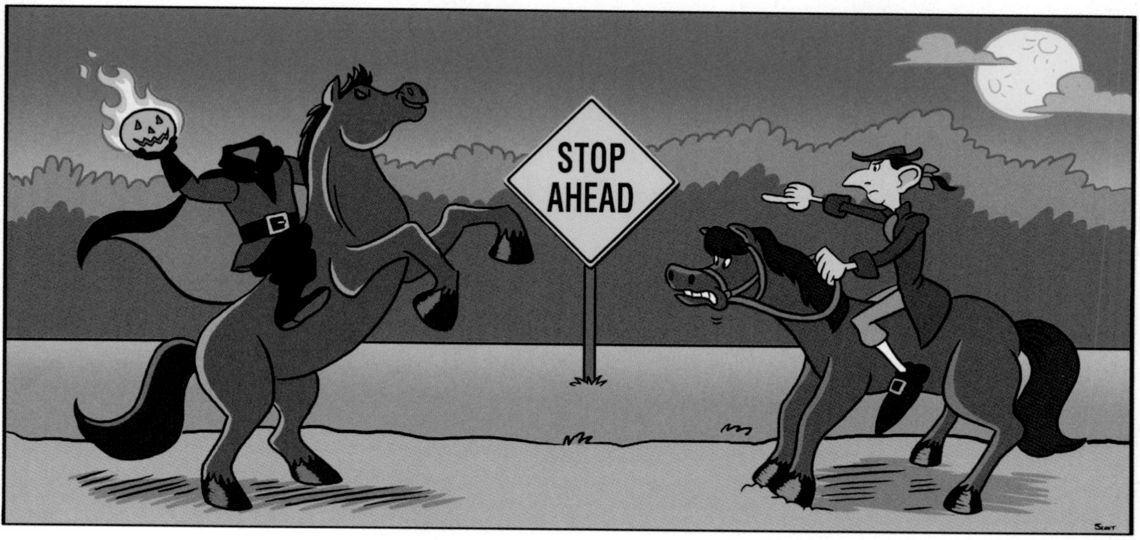
STOP AHEAD

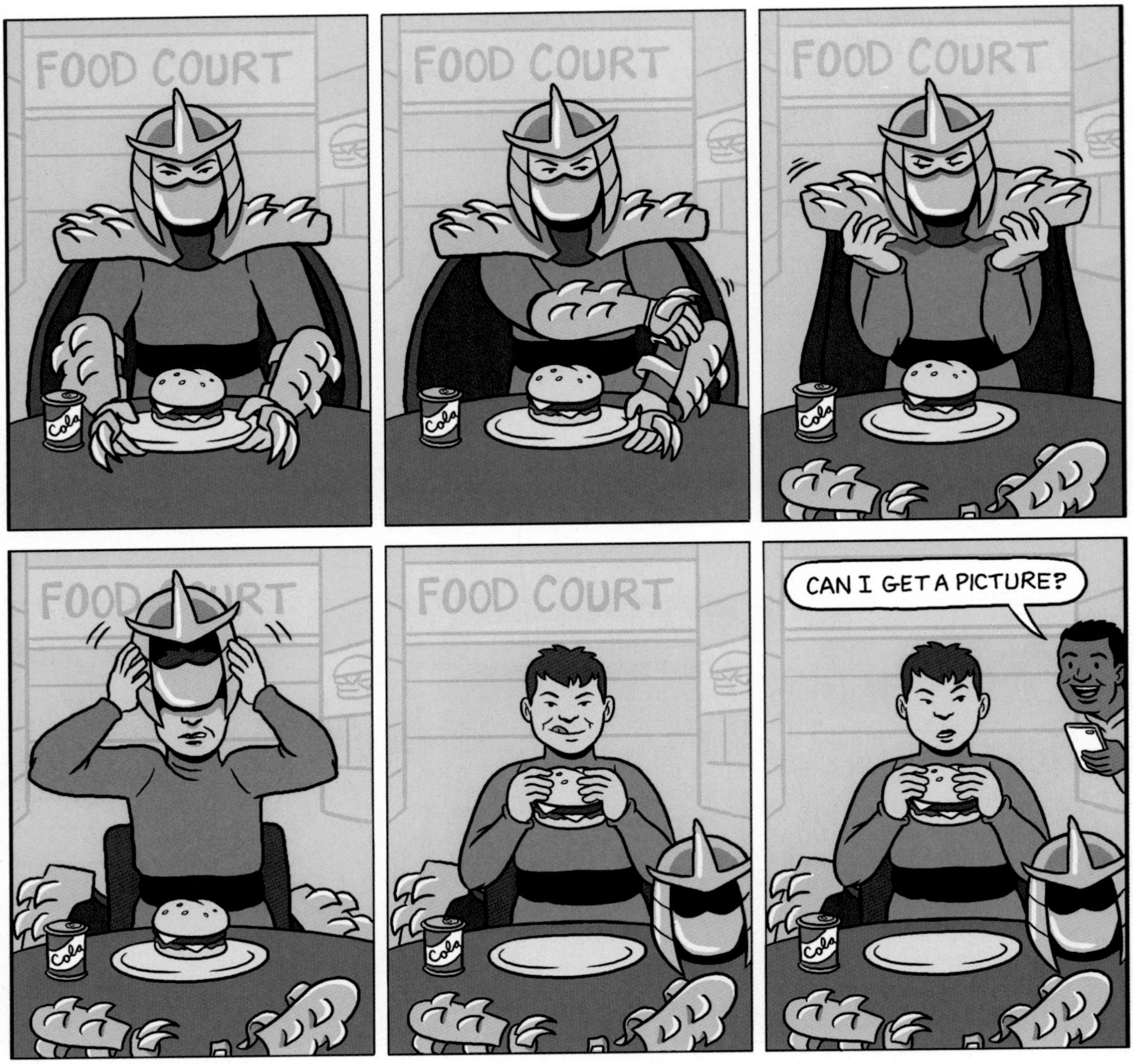
FOOD COURT
Cola
CAN I GET A PICTURE?

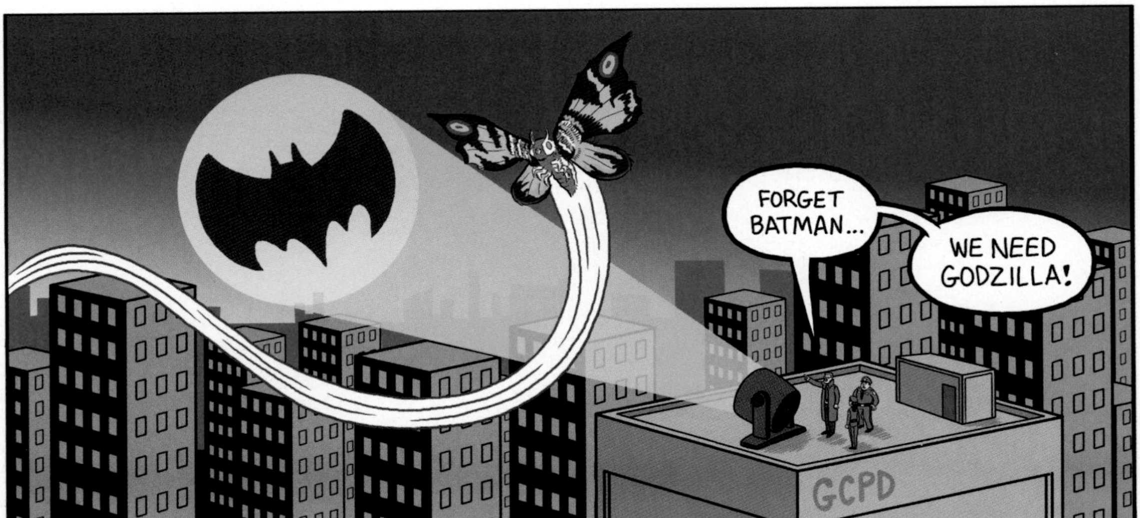
FORGET BATMAN...
WE NEED GODZILLA!
GCPD

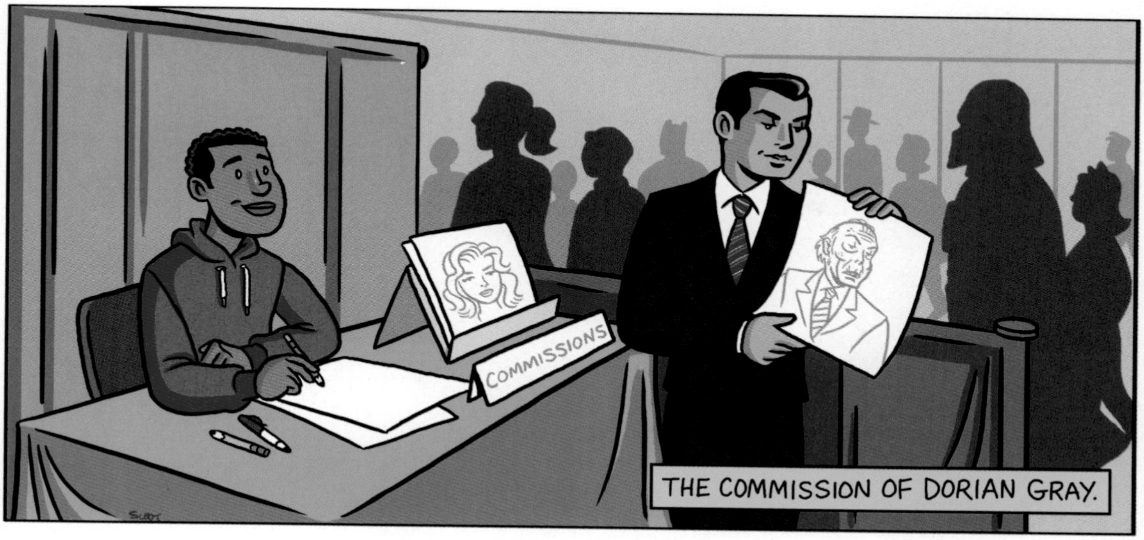
COMMISSIONS
THE COMMISSION OF DORIAN GRAY.

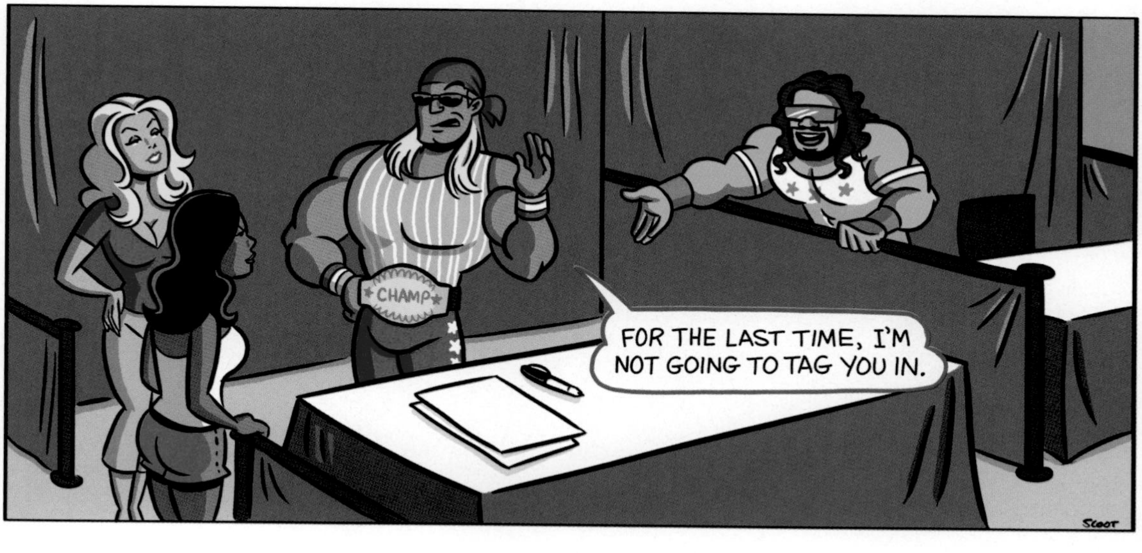
CHAMP
FOR THE LAST TIME, I'M NOT GOING TO TAG YOU IN.
SCOOT

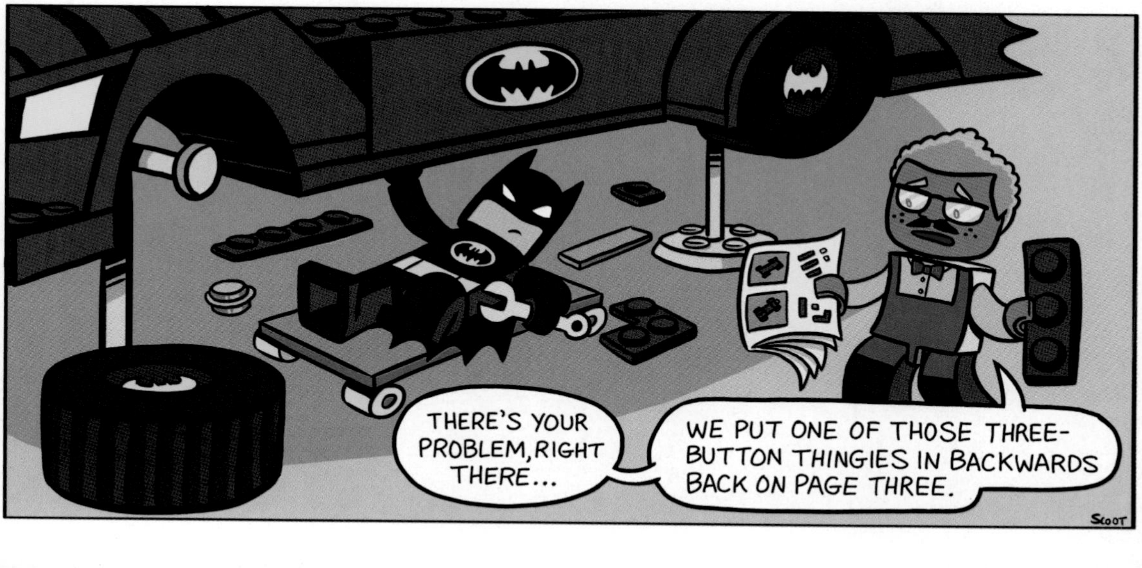
THERE'S YOUR PROBLEM, RIGHT THERE...
WE PUT ONE OF THOSE THREE-BUTTON THINGIES IN BACKWARDS BACK ON PAGE THREE.
SCOOT

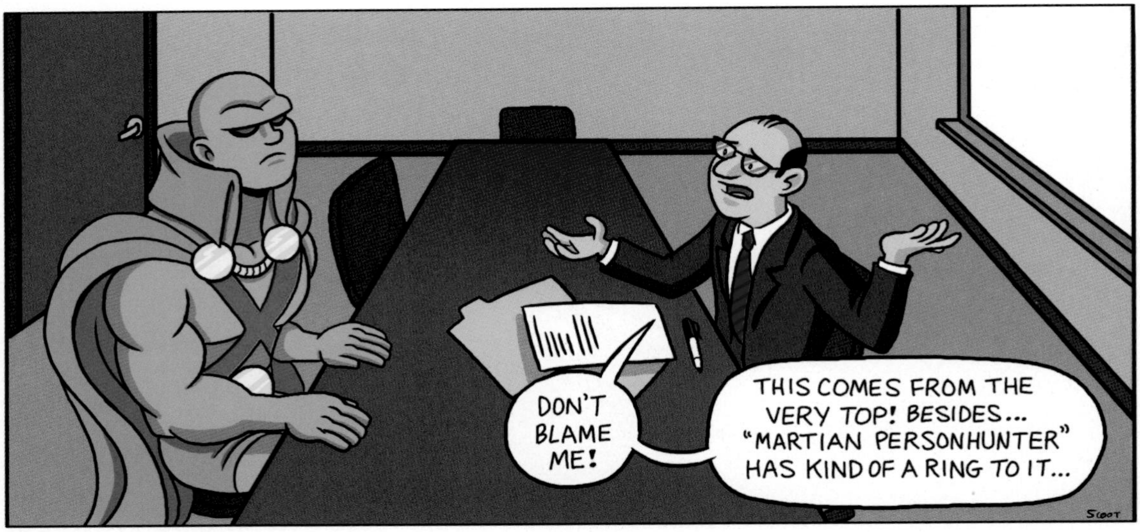
DON'T BLAME ME!
THIS COMES FROM THE VERY TOP! BESIDES... "MARTIAN PERSONHUNTER" HAS KIND OF A RING TO IT...
SCOOT

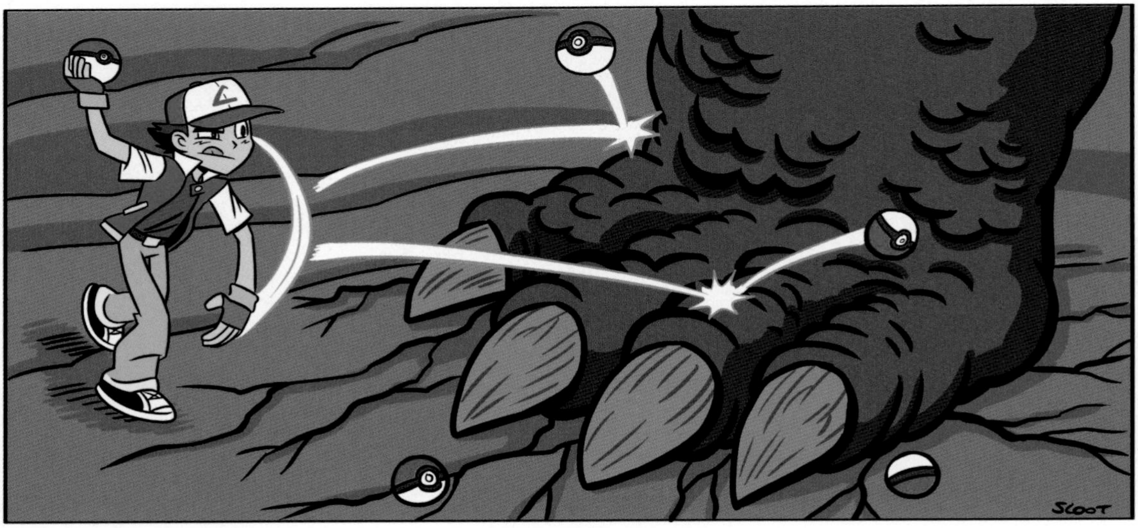
SCOOT

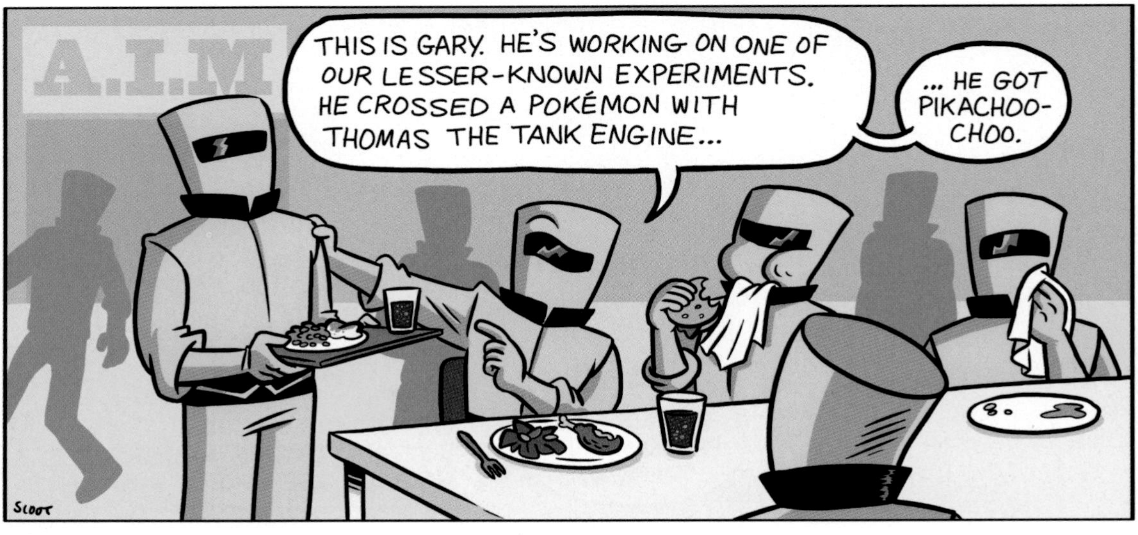
A.I.M
THIS IS GARY. HE'S WORKING ON ONE OF OUR LESSER-KNOWN EXPERIMENTS. HE CROSSED A POKÉMON WITH THOMAS THE TANK ENGINE...
... HE GOT PIKACHOO-CHOO.
SCOOT

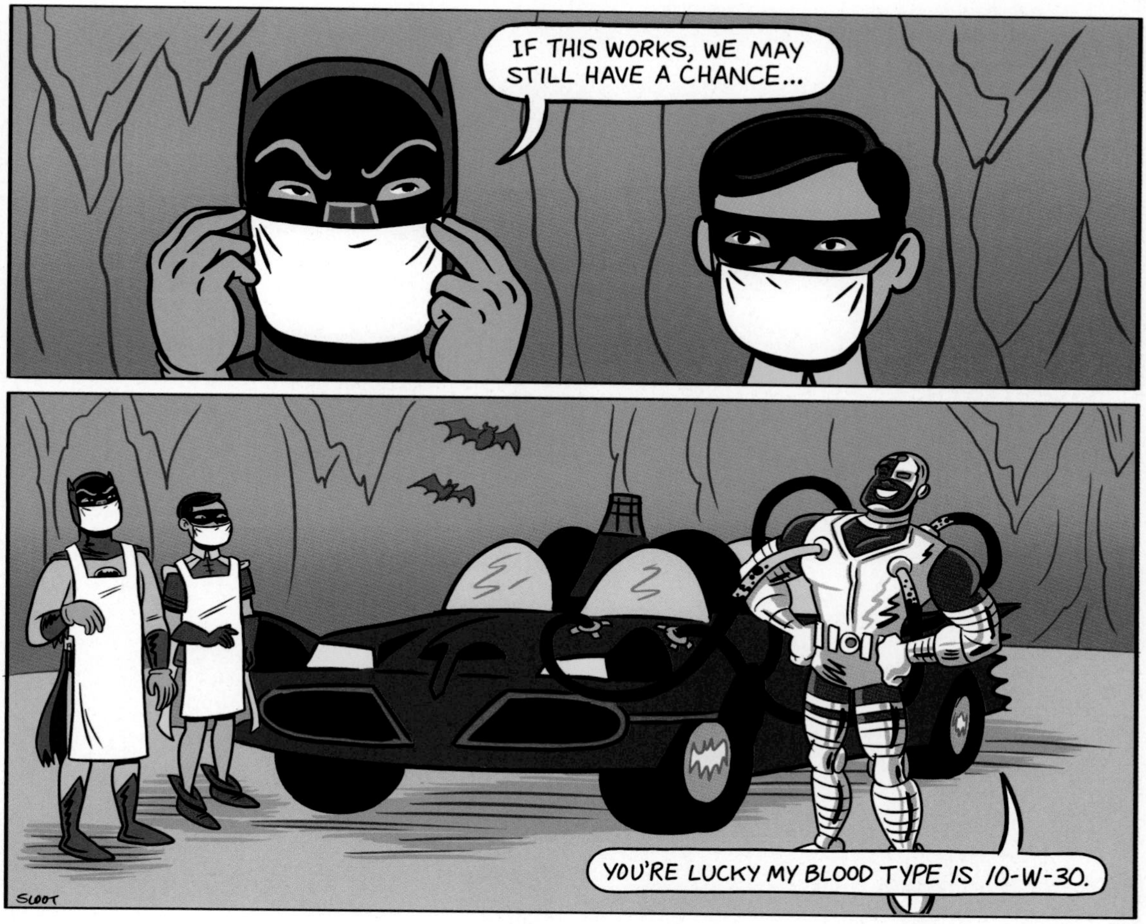
IF THIS WORKS, WE MAY STILL HAVE A CHANCE...
YOU'RE LUCKY MY BLOOD TYPE IS 10-W-30.
SLOOT

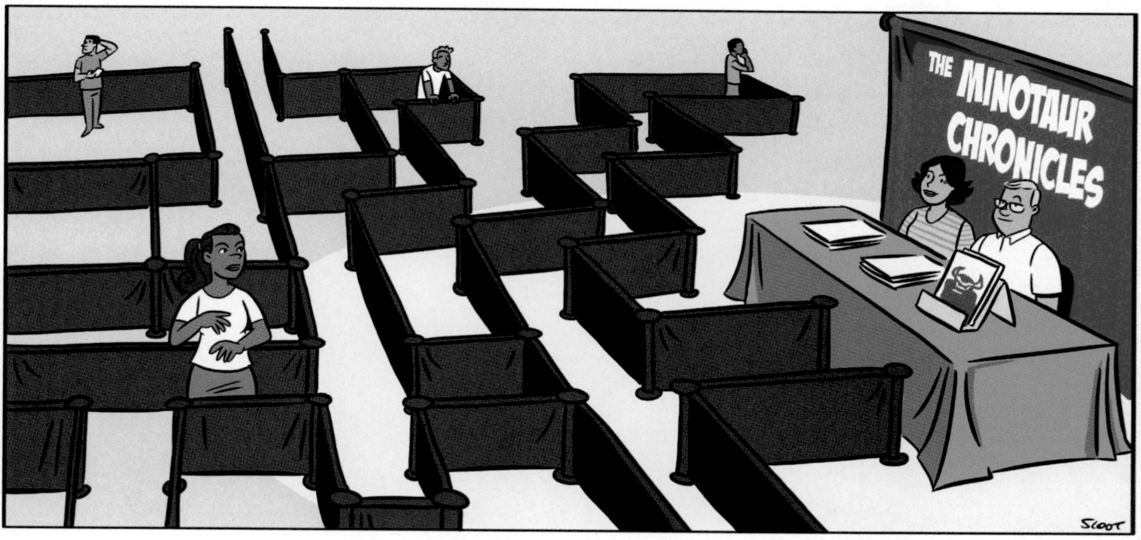
THE MINOTAUR CHRONICLES
SLOOT

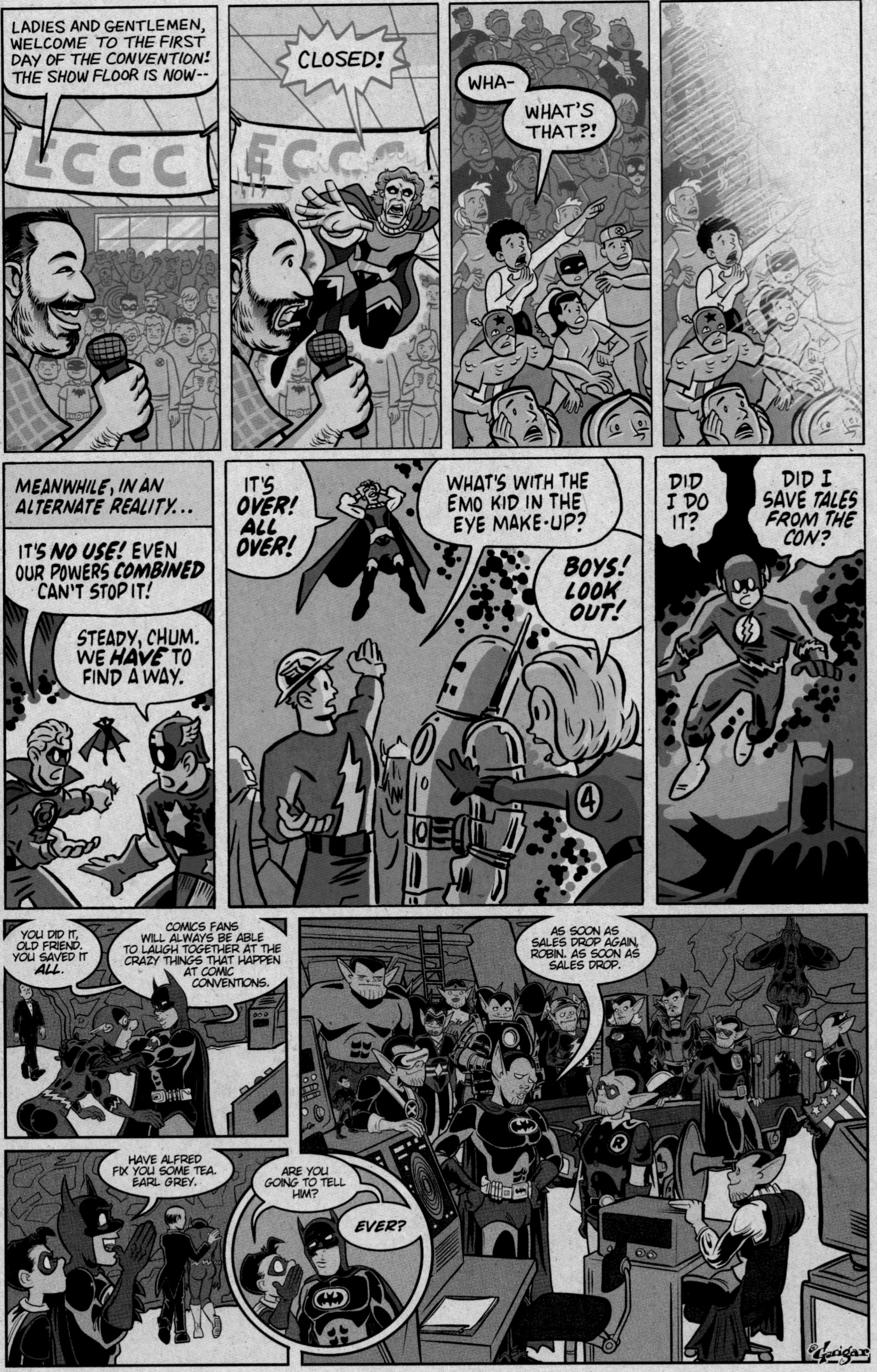
LADIES AND GENTLEMEN, WELCOME TO THE FIRST DAY OF THE CONVENTION! THE SHOW FLOOR IS NOW--
ECCC
CLOSED!
ECCC
WHA-
WHAT'S THAT?!
MEANWHILE, IN AN ALTERNATE REALITY...
IT'S NO USE! EVEN OUR POWERS COMBINED CAN'T STOP IT!
STEADY, CHUM. WE HAVE TO FIND A WAY.
IT'S OVER! ALL OVER!
WHAT'S WITH THE EMO KID IN THE EYE MAKE-UP?
BOYS! LOOK OUT!
DID I DO IT?
DID I SAVE TALES FROM THE CON?
YOU DID IT, OLD FRIEND. YOU SAVED IT ALL.
COMICS FANS WILL ALWAYS BE ABLE TO LAUGH TOGETHER AT THE CRAZY THINGS THAT HAPPEN AT COMIC CONVENTIONS.
AS SOON AS SALES DROP AGAIN, ROBIN. AS SOON AS SALES DROP.
HAVE ALFRED FIX YOU SOME TEA. EARL GREY.
ARE YOU GOING TO TELL HIM?
EVER?